Other Books Written Under the Name of John C. Payne

Three and Out: The Saga of a San Francisco Apartment Manager

This is the initial book in the exciting new Three and Out trilogy featuring Rod Richards as the main character.

The novel features life, fun and games at The Seville which is located near downtown San Francisco. The building is owned by a cheapskate Frenchman who is only interested in maximizing profits from his investment, even at the expense of the occupants.

The book highlights the interpersonal relationships of the diverse and interesting characters who reside there as they interface with the manager, the owner and each other. Rod Richards and his wife Janice are torn apart from every direction trying to balance their managerial responsibilities with their own safety and sanity.

Did the Zodiac killer of the late 1960's really live there?

Three and Out: Murder in a San Antonio Psych Hospital
Note: Title change from Running a Mental Health Hospital in San Antonio

Three years was long enough in the apartment management gig so Rod and Janice head to San Antonio, Texas. Janice unexpectedly dies catapulting Rod into depression and despair.

He ultimately crawls out of his self-imposed quagmire and grasps the opportunity to become the administrator of a downtown psychiatric hospital. He didn't know that an embedded CIA agent was viciously murdered in the upstairs dayroom. A new al-Qaeda cell was thought to be operating in the area. Several patients and two nurses were identified as persons of interest by the feds.

An investigation was conducted by CIA Agent Marie Martini, whose promiscuous background attracted her to Boyd Bounder, the chief nurse and a former Texas Longhorn football player. Meanwhile, Rod engages in several interesting love interests which take quirky turns and challenge his resolve. The chain of events that follow the investigative process will leave the reader in a constant state of suspense.

EDITOR NOTE: This book is now a Regional Best Seller!

A Few Excerpts of Reviews on Three and Out: Running a Mental Health Hospital in San Antonio by John C Payne. (Old book cover)

Just finished reading "Three and Out". I greatly admire your ability to make a character jump off the page with just a few words -- the person immediately has features AND a personality. What a skill! The plot was complex and riveting. I enjoyed reading it much and my husband is reading it now. (Posted from a personal letter to the author).

From Amazon.com, 2011
Excellent read!!!, December 14, 2011
By**Timbear** - See all my reviews
Amazon Verified Purchase
This review is from: Three and Out: Running a Mental Health Hospital in San Antonio (Kindle Edition) (Old book cover title)
Great book by John Payne! Very in-depth character study, interesting plots, and Payne displays a tremendous knowledge of the current state of healthcare in the U.S.
You will get a tour of all the finer points of the beautiful city of San Antonio, Texas, while trying to guess who the murderer is.
We see a fuller development of the main character, Rod Richards in this book, and I look forward to book 3 in the trilogy to see what happens to Rod in his pursuit to find "eternal happiness"!!!
This book will not disappoint!!!

Lawrence - See all my reviews

Amazon Verified Purchase
This review is from: Three and Out: Running a Mental Health Hospital in San Antonio (Kindle Edition) (Old book cover title)
I just finished this novel by Payne. A must read if you live in San Antonio or work in a hospital setting. Interesting plot with a lot of "who dunnit's" to sort thru. Fast moving with a lot of interesting characters. I enjoyed the book; and look forward to his next novel.

THREE AND OUT

THE CHICAGO TERMINUS

A WORK OF FICTION

BY

JOHN C. PAYNE

ACKNOWLEDGEMENTS

The one special person in my life, my loving wife Carol encouraged me to finish this third book of my trilogy. We spent many hours wrestling with how best to portray Rod's last adventure.

My good friend Brenda Turner was critical in her editorial comments and I thank her for the valuable insight. My brother Larry Payne and wife Patricia helped me in the editing process for which I am thankful. Donna Taddeo designed the book cover once again. And finally, special thanks to Ken Riddell who conducted the last edit before publication.

I am grateful to all of these individuals for their time and consideration in making this 3rd book of the trilogy an exciting read.

AUTHOR'S NOTE

My book is dedicated to the conscientious professionals who work in the tumultuous business of private investigations. Without the support of these well-trained individuals, many families would have no person to turn to for assistance in finding their loved ones. The many tax-supported public agencies provide assistance to some degree but are usually burdened with mandated higher priority issues.

This is the third and final book in the exciting trilogy involving Rod Richards, the principal character in the three books. He is a restless man who gets bored easily and thrives on the dynamics of change. Always seeking personal fulfillment, he loves to relocate to exhilarating geographic locations and work in fields where he has little or no formal training or education. Rod flourishes on the challenge of the unknown, wanting to do something different all of the time. This boredom of job and location seems to run in three year cycles. The titles of the first two books, Three and Out have a subheading describing his newest adventure.

The primary setting of this book focuses on an independently owned private investigation business in Chicago. Rod meets up with an old Army buddy on a cruise out of Galveston, Texas. Bradley Simmons operates the agency. Rod conducts some initial surveillance work and then is hired by a rich socialite to find her son who was scheduled to be released from federal prison, having served time for an all too often occurrence. There are many twists and turns that will keep the reader in suspense, not to mention Rod's somewhat truncated personal life issues.

This story is a complete work of fiction. Names, characters, places and incidents are products of this writer's imagination. Any resemblance to any persons living or dead is purely coincidental. Agencies, company and restaurants names and locations are for the most part fictional.

Library of Congress Control Number: 2012937261

ISBN 9781935377801

Reprinted January 2013 with this new book title.

Enjoy!

Prologue

HIS strong hands gripped the weathered wooden guard railing of the gigantic cruise ship. It was dark outside. He made sure there wasn't anybody lingering in the rear of the ship. Beads of sweat formed along his receding blond hairline. He was drained of all emotion. Streams of salty spray slapped his face. The Caribbean was acting up, unusual for the normally smooth-sailing cruise season. Bolts of lightning streaked across the sky creating figures resembling racing chariots of old.

Rod raised his right leg and slid it up over the railing and paused for a second. He stared down into the choppy water and saw flaming red devils riding the backs of sleek dolphins. There were three of them. The lead devil was carrying the head of his mother, followed by the other two dolphins with the smaller devils waving triumphantly the heads of his father and kid sister. All three had been decapitated and their bloody skin flaps were jerking frantically in the breeze.

"Janice, oh Janice my dear deceased wife, why have you abandoned me?" he shouted as he lifted the entire weight of his body up on the railing, precariously balancing in a prone position on the six-inch wide structure. Just as he was getting ready to release his grip and flip overboard, a strong hand grabbed his upper left arm and yanked him from the guard railing.

"You bastard, leave me alone, mind your own business," he turned and shouted at the figure who released his grip but not until Rod was safely back on deck. Rod balled up his right hand into a tight fist and swung as hard as he could at the face staring back at him. The man behind the grim face easily deflected it.

"Rod Richards, it's me, Bradley Simmons you crazy idiot. I'm your old buddy from way back when we wore combat boots. What the hell's going on here?"

Chapter 1

Texas, April of 2007

SAN ANTONIO through the little Honda rear view mirror reminded Rod of the popular C&W tune about a cowboy leaving Lubbock as he motored down Interstate 10 toward Houston. He was on his way to Galveston to board a well-deserved cruise line vacation extravaganza.

He had never been on a cruise before so he cornered one of the psychiatrists at the hospital from his previous employment to prescribe some scopolamine patches to apply just in case he became seasick. Parachuting out of perfectly good airplanes when he was an airborne soldier in the Army never seemed to faze him. His endorphin level was off the chart whenever he packed his chute for a jump.

The traffic was horrendous in and around Houston. He almost got t-boned turning on to Interstate 45 heading south to Galveston. It didn't help matters that he was reliving the last few days of his San Antonio stay.

He stiff-armed his best friend who invited him to dinner his last night in town. He preferred to be alone but did end up at Teddy's Tavern for one last hurrah. He didn't get drunk but went home with a headache.

Boarding the Port Caller was easier than he had expected.

"Sir, don't touch a thing. We'll have your luggage stowed in your stateroom for you. Please go aboard and enjoy yourself."

The balcony cabin that he had reserved was acceptable but small. Instead of a queen-sized bed he would have to snuggle into a standard double. Two leaping dolphins were chasing each other on the brightly painted wall mural above the easy chair. At least there were five port holes that gave him a decent view to the outside. Rod missed his deceased wife. Janice would have complained about the cramped space. He was thankful that there were not many kids on board as he wanted nothing more than to relax and project ahead in hopes of firming up his plans for the future. He was feeling a little off balance.

Maybe it's that crazy scopolamine patch I'm wearing.

He settled in and read all of the marketing materials neatly placed on a small desk next to the bathroom door. The cruise itinerary highlighted each interesting stop along the way. He was starting to get hungry and regretted not stopping for lunch.

Finally and not too soon for Rod it was time for dinner. He took the elevator up to the deck where the dining room was located and was led to a table of four near the main entrance. An older couple and a younger single woman were already seated. The older man was in an animated conversation with his wife. She was slightly younger than her husband but had no problem lashing back at him periodically with a few choice words.

The younger woman was pleasantly surprised to have a good-looking gentleman seated with her. She had a soft spot in her heart for blond-headed men, especially one who was six feet tall and in obvious good shape. She initially ignored him but after another glass of wine while waiting for dinner she decided to take the initiative and introduced herself.

"Would you mind pouring me another glass of red wine, kind sir? My name is Angie Ward. It appears that our waiter has something more important to deal with right now than our own particular needs."

Rod obligingly refilled her wine glass, and his.

Angie Ward was all arms and legs and adorned with every conceivable jewelry device known to man. Rod guessed her age to be one or two years either side of forty. She was tall and thin with curly ebony hair. Rod concluded that a chunk of West Virginia black coal was ten shades lighter than her hair. She wore it in an asymmetric cut; one longer swath swept to the right side of her head, the other short and tight on the opposite side. When she turned her head slightly to the right, Rod barely noticed a five inch scar running diagonally along the side of her temple wiggling down to the back of the ear lobe. The long hair and serpentine pendant hanging graciously from that ear lobe failed to hide the jagged scar.

"So what are you staring at?" she asked Rod as he was giving her the visual make-over.

"Oh, I'm sorry, nothing in particular, ma'am. Is that a scorpion trying to slither into your ear?" he asked humorously as he pointed at the pendant.

She gave him a…"what the hell do you care" kind of stare.

He was quick to change the subject.

"Where are you from, Angie?"

"Libertyville, Illinois, a small town northwest of downtown Chicago. You probably never heard of the place. I'm a history teacher at a neighboring school district; been there for fifteen years. It's a nice quiet village but I get bored…need to get away as often as I can. This cruise and other adventurous trips help."

The server brought their salads and everyone at the table of four began to eat. He quickly finished, snatched a wheat roll from the sterling silver basket and while buttering it, stared at some of the other tables in the huge dining room. There must have been a hundred different conversations taking place at once; some were loud and penetrating.

"What part of this wonderful world do you live in, Rod?" Angie asked him, breaking his prolonged stare at the other table.

"I'm on my way from San Antonio, Texas to somewhere exciting and adventurous, somewhat like you. I need change."

"And where might that be?" she asked with a quizzical look.

"Don't know yet. That's one of the reasons for the cruise. I'm waiting for a stroke of heavenly enlightenment to strike me while I try to sort out my future plans."

The elderly lady sitting next to him gave him a quick look and chuckled to herself. Her silver-haired mate, probably her husband, couldn't contain himself and laughed out loud.

"Sometimes a man has to do what he has to do," said the lady trying to repair the breach in etiquette.

Rod wasn't at all taken aback and appreciated Angie's insight for not probing the issue any further. He stabbed a piece of sliced turkey off a silvery plate that was being served and sliced a bite-size portion for quick consumption. He wasn't in the mood for a discussion about his future with total strangers. He finished eating and excused himself deciding to go to bed early…still feeling a little "strange".

As he walked away from his table he heard a loud voice coming from the table immediately in front of and to the right of his own. A distinguished gray-haired gentleman was standing and spouting off in great oratorical form about some subject. All but one of his tablemates were looking at him and listening intently. The disinterested person had been staring intently over at Rod's table.

Rod turned and headed in the other direction leading out of the dining room. He loved the stately ship paintings hung along the foyer way. There were pictures of the USS Enterprise, the Duke of Lancaster, SS Independence, the Queen Mary and the SS America all vividly displayed with eight-inch overhead lights.

The way I feel right now there ought to be a picture of the Titanic hung among the others for added inspiration! I'd gladly join the unsuspecting 'goners'. What the hell's wrong with me?

As he opened his stateroom door and stepped in he made a mental note to determine the origin of the ugly scar gracing the side of Angie's head. There had to be an intriguing story waiting to come out of that flawless mouth. She intrigued him.

When he undressed and crawled into the small bed he began to reminisce about the wonderful years he spent with his deceased Janice. He felt guilty thinking about her and at the same time wondering how he would pursue the lady from Libertyville. He was confused, got up and took another anti-depressant pill.

He was restless, couldn't get to sleep and once he did, had a series of horrific dreams. He broke out in a deep sweat and started to shake. Janice was calling out to him again and again to help her. She was falling off a steep cliff into the treacherous Atlantic Ocean. He couldn't reach her in time before she plummeted to the jagged rocks below. He kept tossing and turning in his narrow bed screaming incoherent phrases. The wrinkled sheets and top half of his blanket were soaked with his perspiration.

Something hit him hard on the side of his head. He blacked out. Several minutes later he finally came to and shot out of bed, turning on the overhead light. His head hurt. There was blood smeared on his pillow and another smattering of the sticky red substance was beginning to dry on the steel wall next to his bed. He must have thrust himself into the wall trying to escape the dreams. He started to retch and then heaved a stream of vomit on the chair next to the bed.

What's going on here? Am I getting seasick? What are the side effects of that scopolamine patch? I got to get out of here! Maybe I spent too much time back there at the funny farm hospital I managed assimilating some of those twisted personalities. I don't care; I can't take this any longer! I quit!

He pulled on his Bermuda shorts and yanked a polo shirt over his still throbbing head and then shoeless, left his stateroom in a hurry. He took the elevator to the top deck and swiftly walked to the aft of the ship. Fortunately, he didn't see any passengers; he had a mission to accomplish and didn't want to be interrupted. He stared over at the dark, threatening horizon and then headed to the guard railing. Tonight was the night he would finally end all of his pent up misery and jump overboard to join his loving wife Janice.

Chapter 2

ROD was still shaking from his near miss at trying to end it all in the darkened waters below. He was trying hard to regain his composure and stared at the other man in deep thought. Several long seconds passed by before either of them spoke.

"Bradley Simmons, is it really you? Please come closer, I can hardly make you out. I'm so sorry, I've been having hallucinations. I lost it big time, my friend. I wanted to end it all right here and now. Perhaps I mixed too many gin martinis with my medications."

"You're forgiven, Rod. But you are okay now. I sure would appreciate some sort of explanation to help me put my arms around the reasons for this suicide attempt."

"I'll try to explain; let me catch my breath. It's been years since we've seen each other. Believe me, I hardly recognized you. If I had a gun on me I would've shot you between the eyes for interfering with my death wish. Why haven't we kept up with each other over these past years; we were such good friends?"

"Yeah, everyone knows that. Every time I sent mail your way it was returned undelivered. Either you fell off the deep end of mother earth or moved so many times without leaving a forwarding address with Uncle Sam's untimely delivery service."

"Let's meander over to those lounge chairs underneath the canopies," suggested Bradley. "It's starting to get cold and I think you need to decompress a little. The sea breezes can be challenging at this time of night."

Just then a strong, swirling wind approached from nowhere and buckled up their faces. An unwelcomed eerie purple mist hung over the entire Port Caller.

When they were settled on the soft loungers Rod elaborated, "Janice and I liked to move around and jump into different things. We needed new challenges to keep boredom from dominating our lives."

"Speaking of Janice; where is she, Rod? I haven't seen her aboard."

Rod told him the entire story about them managing an apartment in San Francisco and then deciding to move to Texas. He shared with him every detail of her sudden death and the emotional suffering he went through for several years. For some reason, he was now able to talk freely about her demise without getting choked up. Maybe he was past the several difficult stages of mourning he would have to negotiate.

"So…that might explain why I caught you trying to springboard off the side of this ship."

"I can't explain it. There's more to it than that. I've been a complete and utter failure with the opposite sex ever since she passed away."

"Whoa, that's something new for you."

"Well, sort of," Rod said dejectedly.

"Naturally, it took a while for me to adjust to Janice's death. I missed her so much, even suffered a bout of severe depression. One of my shrinks pinned a bipolar tag on my lapel but as time passed, I was able to move on with my life. Other women started to interest me but every relationship I got into went south quickly. I guess I'm just unlucky with love."

"Look, Rod, it's getting late and I think we should call it a night. I'll walk you down to your cabin and you can get a decent night's sleep. We can reconvene tomorrow night in the lounge. I hear their martinis can't be beat."

Bradley put his arm around his friend's shoulder and led him over to the elevator where they went down several decks and then walked to Rod's cabin. He left him at the door.

"I'll meet you at the bar tomorrow evening, nine o'clock sharp," Rod advised. "We'll renew old times."

[14]

Bradley had one last comment, "Before I leave you for the night I'd recommend you lay off the medications."

Rod nodded in the affirmative and disappeared into his cabin. He yanked off the scopolamine patch and tossed it in the waste basket. He was anxious to finally get a good night of rest.

Chapter 3

ROD slept so soundly that he missed breakfast and lunch, a rare feat for him. He decided to catch a sandwich in the ship's deli later in the afternoon and try once again to finish the novel he started reading a week ago.

Nine o'clock in the evening finally arrived and he headed up to the lounge. He immediately picked Bradley out of the crowd. His friend was wearing pink Bermuda shorts with an oversized teal green t-shirt depicting a brightly colored picture of Captain Kangaroo. Rod noticed his Army buddy was beginning to bald on the front part of his head but conveniently found a way to flip some longer strands of hair back over the top to disguise it.

"Hey there, you beat me up here," Rod yelled. They slapped hands in a friendly greeting, slid up to an opening at the bar and then straddled two stools.

Crowd noise and the penetrating sound of music threatened the top ranges of the proverbial decibel meter. Several older couples were dancing to a hyped-up version of the Tea for Two Cha Cha. It looked more like they were engaged in the popular Zumba exercise. One couple was drunk and nearly fell over on every exaggerated dip. The youthful band members were getting a big kick out of the blue hair crowd trying to be young again.

"What'll it be, gents?" asked the willowy blonde tending bar.

Rod ordered a Bombay Sapphire gin on the rocks with a twist of lemon. Bradley asked for two shots of the house cognac.

"I'll never forget that time we were stationed together in North Carolina at Ft. Bragg when we took downtown Fayetteville by storm on our first weekend pass," Bradley said a little too proudly.

"Tell me about it."

"Remember Shorty's Bar and Clover Grill on the main drag? There was a group of bikers raising all kinds of hell at the pool table. Shorty went over there several times and politely asked them to cease and desist, but to no avail."

"Yeah, I vaguely remember that," replied Rod. "I got this little souvenir that night"...as he pointed to the side of his head. "We had no business jumping into their shit. Shorty should have called the cops. What the hell, everyone likes a good fight, right?"

"If you say so, Mr. Richards, and I recall vividly that back in those days you were a damn sledge hammer looking frantically for a nail!"

Bradley continued, "There were two off-duty cops that tried to break it up but you decked both of them for meddling into what you famously called...our affair!"

They both laughed and ordered another round.

"Do you remember that big red-headed broad who broke the cue stick over your thick head, Rod? She was tougher than the other leather jackets that jumped into the fray."

"Somehow I don't remember that small part," Rod snickered.

"Weird, it took six stitches to close the gap in your thick head."

The band played their last piece and people slowly started to exit and head for their staterooms. Two couples helped the drunken oldsters out of the lounge. They were totally danced out.

"Hey, my long lost friend, Rodney Richards, it's getting late and I think they want to close up the joint. You sure you're feeling okay now? How about getting together tomorrow after breakfast? There are a still a ton of things I'd like to talk about."

"Please don't call me Rodney, I hate the name."

"Well, for Lucifer's sake, please don't call me Brad like you did when we were wearing the uniform. I'm now Bradley, okay? It's more fitting with my present image."

"Sure Bradley, whatever. How about we meet at the big pool on the main deck?"

"Roger that. See you in the morning."

They shook hands firmly and then wrapped their arms around each other's shoulders. The two of them marched in step out of the lounge.

On the way back to his stateroom Rod sensed that a new day was dawning. His renewed friendship with Bradley could not have come at a better time.

Bradley's changed from his easy-go-lucky earlier days when we overcame the rigors of demanding and overzealous drill sergeants. Too bad we didn't keep in touch. He's a lot more formal now but who cares, he's probably a rich man. The son-of-a-bitch...I'm happy for him!

Chapter 4

THEY met each other at the pool mid-morning. Bradley was already doing some speed laps in the pool before Rod arrived. He saw Rod pull one of the lounge chairs over to the edge of the pool and sit down.

"Good late morning to you," Bradley said as he swam to the edge of the pool and pulled himself out of the water. "For awhile I thought that you forgot about meeting me here this morning."

"No, I didn't. I got one of the best nights of sleep I've had in ages; even missed breakfast and I don't skip the first meal of the day often."

"I don't either, Rod."

Bradley wore his dark brown hair much longer than he remembered, probably due to impending baldness. He even dressed better, resembling an Ivy-leaguer. They were much more the opposites now than when they were in the Army together. Their common friends often referred to them as "the twins".

Funny how he's changed so dramatically and I remained the same, Rod chuckled. He used to go by the name Brad back then but now insists on being called Bradley. And what's with the wacky clothes he's wearing on the cruise? I can't imagine what prompted the radical change.

Bradley grabbed a beach towel and started to wipe his body dry. He was a few years older than Rod but his muscular six foot-three frame would belie that fact. He worked out every morning, primarily on weights and a punching bag. He earned a black belt in karate several years ago and traveled around to the various tournaments offered by the American Shotokan Karate Federation. His ripped abs was the envy of much younger men who trained with him.

"Here, pull up one of these loungers and relax," Rod ordered. "I did my daily dozen exercise routine in my room this morning, believe it or not."

Bradley did as suggested and slid the chair over next to him.

"Hi guys," shouted Angie Ward as she flew past them toward the deep end of the pool. She stood for a few minutes and surveyed the water as she pulled on a swim cap that covered most of her black hair. She then dove in and separated the water like a sharp knife slicing through a stick of hot butter. They both stared at her in awe.

"There goes my tablemate, showing off," Rod laughed. "We had a really neat discussion at dinner the other night…feel like I've known her forever in such a short space of time."

He liked the skimpy yellow bathing attire she wore as it revealed a sleek, evenly tanned body. Bradley caught his exuberance.

"She seems like a neat lady, maybe worth getting to know better."

"Rest assured I'll work on it, my friend."

Two young couples sauntered over to the pool area. The ladies spread beach towels out on the rubber-matted decking and sat on them. The guys raced to the pool edge and did cannonballs off the side. Water from the pool spewed everywhere.

"Hey, knock it off you goons," Bradley shouted angrily. "Can't you read the signs?" Water was dripping off the side of his head. The guys splashing in the pool either didn't hear Bradley or simply ignored him. Angie was on the far end of the pool and waited for a reaction from Rod who snickered aloud, surprised at Bradley's outburst.

The two men quickly climbed out of the pool and headed over to their women. Bradley stood up as though he was about to go over and have a meaningful chat with them about pool rules and regulations.

"Hey," shouted one of young men to his associate before Bradley reached them. "It's Bloody Mary time, let's open up the bar."

Their female companions initially objected but acquiesced and soon followed their men out of the pool area. Bradley came back and plopped in his lounge chair.

"Oh to be young and frivolous again," Rod smirked.

"Yeah, and finding ways to impress the finer sex while irritating the shit out of the rest of us."

Angie did a few more speed laps in the now empty pool, and then nudged herself out. She ambled over to them and took off the tight bathing cap. Her black hair popped out like it was shot from a canon, desperately in need of immediate resuscitation.

"Mind if I join you two?"

"That'd be nice. I haven't formally met you yet. My name is Bradley Simmons," he said and offered her his hand.

She introduced herself.

Rod again noticed the long scar on the left side of her head. He threw her an extra beach towel he had tucked under his head. She sat down next to him and started to get dry. He was mesmerized by the slow, deliberate strokes she used toweling off.

She noticed his interest.

"How about meeting me for lunch in the ship's deli, Rod? I hear they have great sandwiches and I don't like to eat the large noon meals in the dining room; too formal. Your friend is invited to join us if he'd like."

"Sounds like a winner to me."

"Great idea; and how about you, Bradley?"

"Nope, I brought along some work for the cruise and I'm way behind on catching up. I'll see you guys later tonight, maybe in the bar after dinner for a nightcap."

"Speaking of work, where are you employed and what kind of activities are you involved with?" Rod asked his friend. "I'm sorry for not inquiring earlier."

"No problem. I own a private investigation agency in Chicago."

"Wow! Did you get into that when you got out of the Army?"

Bradley laughed. "Nope, fell into it after I got married. The wife's brother was in the business so I thought it would be neat if I could parlay the many skills Uncle Sam taught me into a meaningful career."

"Is your wife also on this cruise?" Angie was curious.

"No, she gets seasick. I won the cruise in a fundraiser back home and instead of them offering it to someone else the wife insisted that I go…so here I am."

"I'll tell you more of the gory details later because I know you'll ask a ton of questions. I need to head back and take a shower and I normally skip lunch so hope to see you two tonight."

Bradley left the pool area which was now starting to get crowded. The dancing crowd from the lounge last night was in evidence. None of the oldsters went into the pool, preferring to lie on the deck and bombard their lily white bodies with the now burning hot sun. Every one of them would become a dermatologist's dream in a short period of time.

Angie and Rod hung around a little longer.

"Bradley seems like a real nice guy."

"He sure is Angie."

"Have you known him long?"

"Yep, we were in the Army together training to become Airborne Rangers. We both went to fight the war in Vietnam but were assigned to different units. After his stint was done in 'Nam he was reassigned to an Army base in El Paso. I went back to the Presidio of San Francisco in California, a neat Army installation at the edge of the Golden Gate Bridge."

"My, that had to be a nice assignment."

"It was great. We communicated with each other periodically but then our lives went separate ways. I left the service and got married to a wonderful lady. I'm not sure what he did immediately after he got out of the Army. He appears to be doing fine now."

"How very interesting; you two fellows seem to be alike in so many ways."

"We used to be, once."

"By the way," she continued, "Out of curiosity, were you at the Presidio when all those babies were brought over from Saigon by the adoption agencies? The fall of Saigon impacted so many innocent human beings that many will never recover from the horrors of war. I was young at the time but followed it closely on the news."

"Yes, I was there. In fact I was with the MPs at the time and assigned as one of the project coordinators for the installation. We worked day and night processing those little kids. I often wonder how they all are doing. Most of them should be in their mid-thirties by now."

"Some of those kids turned out to become pretty successful in life," she added. "I even go to a Vietnamese dentist."

"Getting back to your questions about Bradley for a minute," he switched subjects. "By some stroke of good fortune he recognized me in a stupor on the upper deck of the Port Caller last night."

"What do you mean by that?"

"Someday I'll tell you the whole story. I'm sure you'll find it interesting."

"I can't wait; see you later in the Deli."

Chapter 5

REUBEN sandwiches were one of his favorites. "Go ahead and order one if you want to," she encouraged him. "I absolutely love the corned beef and sauerkraut combination but sometimes it comes back to haunt me and everyone around me. The tuna on rye will do fine."

She was dressed in a golden sarong wearing a pair of fashionable and trendy sandals. They were seated comfortably in a booth near the far corner of the ship's deli when the two young couples from the pool came in and sat behind them. They were loud and asked the waitress if the music could be turned up.

"Hey guys, settle down a little, okay?" Rod said sternly as he turned around to address one of the guys. "We're having a nice quiet conversation here."

"Pops, cool it, okay?" the young guy replied. "Don't be so serious, we're all here to have a good time; you don't want to spoil it for us."

Angie put her hand on Rod's arm to steady him down. She knew he was becoming irritated and she didn't want a confrontation. They finished their sandwiches as the music got louder and louder, turning from a smooth jazz to Reggae.

"Let's get the hell out of here before I do something I'd regret later on."

"How about coming up to my stateroom and have a glass of wine. I got some great Omar Khayyam cabernet that I picked up on my last trip to Egypt. I smuggled it aboard. They want you to buy their wines here but I don't like to be told what I can and cannot do on this ship. You'll love it if you enjoy fine wines."

"Sounds like a winner to me."

As they passed the booth behind them the young couples were wrapped around their partners in a passionate embrace. One of the young men winked at Rod and flipped a "V" for victory sign with his one uncommitted hand. Rod angrily flipped him the "bird" as he and Angie passed through the wide deli door. She didn't see it and he was glad for that; no need to get her agitated when he had his sights on something else more pleasing that afternoon.

"Neat pad you have here," he commented when they entered her stateroom. It was twice the size of his cabin and had a large opened balcony overlooking the water. A medium-sized guard railing circled the perimeter of the balcony but was not tall enough to prevent someone from catapulting off the top, even some little kid. He immediately thought about his own attempt to go overboard.

Angie went to the bottom dresser drawer and retrieved the bottle of wine, opened it and poured them a glass.

"Cheers, Rod, I'm glad to share some private time with you. We need to get to know each other better, right?"

"Yes, of course we do. I think we have an awful lot in common."

They chatted for an hour or so, sharing stories and various life experiences. He found her charming and sexually attractive. She experienced shivers racing up and down her spine and the hair on her arms curled up. The Omar Khayyam was long gone and Angie replaced the empty container with a bottle of Butler's Gin which she hid in a carryon coming aboard. She was saving it for special occasions and this certainly qualified.

"What do you think, Rod? Are you ready to go and explore the Nile?"

"Um...yeah, this is some good stuff. You took a chance bringing it on the ship. They expect you to drink their booze."

They were sitting on the edge of her king-sized bed when Angie bent down and slowly started to take off her Cleopatra sandals. The jagged scar behind her ear was exposed and looked mean to him. It seemed to wiggle back and forth like a snake. Maybe it was his heightened imagination or the liquor playing games with him.

[25]

He stared in awe at the high-backed sandals with the scaled, thin gold laces circling her ankles and ending at the front of her shin bone. The end of the straps had a miniature head of an Egyptian cobra with glaring red eyes. Rod quickly glanced at her ankles and saw two miniature gargoyles breathing fire from their mouths on the inner sides of each ankle as if they were trying to destroy the tight-fitting sandals. He hadn't noticed the little dragons with bat-like wings at the pool and wondered if he was having some kind of mental setback. Her long toe nails were painted in a green sheen which matched her fingernails.

She startled him. "Please excuse me while I change into something a little more appropriate."

He quickly snapped out of it.

"I'll just be a minute. Go ahead and pour us some more Mr. Butler. I kinda like him too," she laughed.

He was stunned when she came out of the bathroom totally naked. She motioned for him to undress. Hesitantly, and urgently he stripped off his clothes and embraced her. Mr. Butler was totally ignored as they came together like seasoned lovers.

She was surprised how caring and sensitive he was to her needs. They lay exhausted in each other's arms, not saying a word, just reliving the last sequence of wonderful events. She finally got up and ambled over to the walk-in closet door, opened it and then went in. He didn't have a closet like hers in his miniature cabin. After several minutes she came out with a pink silk robe loosely slung around her body without a belt.

"I want to completely relax now and a good smoke always does it for me."

She opened the drawer on her night stand and took out a joint roller and set it on top of the stand. Reaching in her robe pocket she took out a brown zip-lock bag, removed some of the leafy contents and put them in the roller which was preloaded with black, slow burning cigarette papers.

"Want one?"

"That's marijuana, Angie. I gave it up for Lent a long time ago."

[26]

"To each his own," she laughed as she lit up.

He couldn't stand the sweet smell of pot. He remembered his days long ago in Vietnam where almost everybody in their barracks smoked the weed. He was on it for a while but slowly weaned himself before rotating back to the States. He recalled that girl he dated back in San Antonio who smoked pot; even used a ridiculous looking bong at times.

"How come you're smoking pot? I'm sure you know it's illegal and maybe even harmful for you?"

"C'mon, get real. Did you forget where we're docking tomorrow? Jamaica, home of Bob Marley and that God-awful Reggae music he allegedly created. He mentions the use of cannabis in most of his songs. So Rodney, here's my tribute to Jamaica and everything it represents. When I go shopping I might even buy you one of those neat Rasta-stripped beanie caps."

She's really riding high in the saddle, he concluded. I better high tail it out of here and let her fanaticize to her own delight. I'm not ready for whatever might be scheduled in the next act!

He skipped dinner and decided to hook up with Bradley for that nightcap he mentioned at the pool. He knew his buddy enjoyed a few drinks before retiring for the evening. He spotted him sitting on a bar stool chatting with the same female bartender they had the night before.

"What's going on, Bradley?"

"Not much; Missy here and I were trying to figure out how to balance the national budget and get rid of the humongous debt our government is burdened with."

"So what did you two economists conclude?"

"Her solution is to eliminate the Department of Defense."

"And yours is to…"

"Eliminate Congress, let each state secede from the Union, determine their own destiny and then we'd have fifty reliable countries to help fight our ridiculous wars abroad."

[27]

"Missy, give him another one of whatever he's tossing down the hatch and I'll have one also," Rod ordered her.

The two of them bantered back and forth on many issues. They rehashed the events of the previous night but Rod was quick to move on to other topics. Bradley had filled him in on more of the details of his private investigation business which he found interesting. He decided it was time to go up and check in on Angie. He wondered if there'd be an encore of this afternoon's surprise event.

He took the elevator up to her deck, swung around the corner to head down the short hallway to her suite and stopped in his tracks. A young man was coming out of her stateroom and heading his way. He was dressed informally with jogging shorts, a worn polo shirt and flip flops. They bumped each other slightly when they passed in the hallway.

"Sorry about that, sir, I think I had one too many."

Rod didn't say a word back to him, just stared at the back of the man's head when the handsome guy rounded the corner to the elevator.

She better have a damned good explanation for this stud's visit to her stateroom! I think I'm being taken for some big time fool!

He rapped excessively hard on the metal door and she finally opened it. The knuckles on his right hand were oozing small droplets of blood. He walked right past her without saying a word and glanced around the entire suite. He saw an empty bottle of wine sitting on her bedside stand.

"Do you mind telling me what the fuck is going on here? I just bumped into your young friend in the hallway."

"I think I sense an element of jealousy in my new boyfriend," she responded with a slight smirk on her face. "Are you snooping on me now, or is this just a coincidence that you happened by when Paul Keller was leaving?"

"I'm slightly confused, Angie. You partied it up big time with me this afternoon and gave me high hopes that we had something special going on. Tonight I caught you entertaining another man the same day you seduced me."

[28]

He took out his handkerchief and wrapped it tightly around his fist. The blood hadn't coagulated yet. She came over to him and kissed him hard on his lips. He reeled back and fell into the chair by her bed.

"Listen up here, Romeo. That young man is Paul Keller. He was one of my first history students when I started teaching. He graduated with honors from Yale Law School and is now a well-known defense attorney in Chicago. We bumped into each other when leaving the dining hall after dinner tonight, shocked that we were both on the Port Caller enjoying this pleasant cruise. If you were sitting with me at the table like a good soldier boy you would have met him earlier."

He was at a loss for words and regretted making a fool of himself when he was trying to cement a relationship with her. Yet, he was still confused.

"What's with the wine, Angie? And did you both smoke some pot or was he just high on something else?"

"Paul doesn't normally drink and we didn't share a joint. He told me his pregnant wife down on deck five was experiencing some discomfort and told him to take a walk so she could deal with her problem alone. That's when he decided to come up here and chat for awhile."

There was a long pause while they stared at each other.

"Sorry about all this. I guess I simply overreacted like a love-struck, pimply-faced teenager."

"Paul is a wonderful father and they have a little one back home being tended to by her parents. They elected to take this cruise to celebrate both their fifth year of wedded bliss and a big law suit he successfully defended. The notorious mayor of one of our suburban cities was hauled into court on a libel charge. You may have read about it in your San Antonio paper."

"No, I was too busy with other important matters than following someone else's trials and tribulations; but that's all well and good. Do you have any more of that fine wine left?"

"I sure don't but I have some more of Mr. Butler that we were too busy to finish off this afternoon."

Around midnight he made his way back to his own stateroom. They didn't make love again but talked about their situation and speculated where it might be headed.

Why do I always hook up with a lady that has such an unusual and questionable past? Can't I simply find a woman like Janice who is reasonably attractive, level-headed, gracious, loyal and yet, absolutely normal?

Chapter 6

JAMAICA was the next stop on the cruise itinerary. Angie was anxious to go ashore and do some shopping. There wasn't a jewelry store in the world that she didn't like. She also had a lead from one of the card dealers in the casino where she could get some good cannabis. Rod planned to stay behind and finish his Vince Flynn book.

The Islamic terrorists had captured a nuclear power plant near Pittsburgh and planned to blow it up!

Bradley had a specific mission planned for the day.

Angie was so excited at breakfast she couldn't finish her meal. Rod had no problem "wolfing" his down. The old geezer sitting across the table from her was dressed in a colorful Hawaiian shirt, khaki shorts and white deck shoes. He was bald and overweight compared to his sleeker-looking wife who wore a tight perm for the cruise. He hadn't missed many meals.

They both watched their tablemate as he stabbed the remaining slice of bacon on his plate and quickly shoved it in his fat mouth. His wife shot an elbow to his ribs and he spit out the half-chewed piece of meat on his napkin. Rod looked over at Angie and they grinned.

"Have you signed up for any of those exciting tours to explore the island, Angie?"

"Of course not, I hate those pre-packaged boring tours," she laughed. "I plan to shop 'til I drop. I have a list of things I need to pick up. There are some good buys on the island and you should come with me and take advantage of the sales."

"No thanks. I plan to hit the pool, go to the ship casino, play some craps, and then finish my readings. I carried three books with me and I've only finished one of them."

"I wish you'd come with me."

"Not here in Jamaica. It's not my cup of tea. Maybe you can join us on our next stop when we dock in the Cayman Islands. Bradley and I plan to snorkel. I'm sure you'd like that. You swim like a tripled-finned fish, Angie. Maybe you could protect us from those little sea monsters that look like giants through our swimming goggles."

The Port Caller dropped anchor about 1000 yards from the main shore pier site. The captain announced that the waters were rougher than usual this morning so he planned to split the tourists into two groups. The shore boat would then make two separate trips because of the large number of tourists going ashore. Bradley joined them on the deck level where the tourists would transfer over to the shore boat. Angie climbed aboard with the first group.

"Have fun, guys, doing your silly things today," she shouted back at them as the shore boat slowly separated itself from the cruise liner.

"I thought you signed up to go ashore, Bradley; at least that's what you told me last night."

"Yes, but with the second excursion. I didn't want Angie to see me waiting here for the water craft."

"Why not let her see you? Is there something I should know about?"

"I started to tell you last night in the lounge but you were too anxious to head to her place for whatever reason."

"Get on with it, Bradley!"

"Angie's cousin hired me to follow her around on this cruise and keep her out of trouble."

"What the hell are you talking about?"

"Did Angie tell you how she got that ugly scar on the side of her head?"

"Yeah, she told me that she and her husband were in a terrible accident one night on the way home from their summer cottage in Wisconsin. They were hit head-on by a drunk driver. Hubby died in the crash and she was thrown through the windshield but somehow survived the accident."

"Well, that's only part of the story," Bradley continued. "Angie still has nightmares about the horrible scene. She has severe emotional problems and at times acts the Doctor Jekyll and Mr. Hyde scene. Nobody knows when the big switch in personalities is programmed to take place."

"Are you aware that she is a pot smoker?"

"Yes, I am. Her cousin told me that Angie has a physician friend in California who believes strongly in the medicinal value of marijuana and somehow gets her a stash on a regular basis. She claims to have severe migraine headaches from the accident and smokes joints to relieve the pain."

"I think I witnessed an example of her personality changes on the cruise earlier," Rod responded, "But it's no big thing and probably a transient act. It's certainly not harmful and she came out of it right away."

"What else is there about her, perhaps another version of the story?" Rod continued trying to flush out more background information on this unusual woman he was becoming deeply involved with.

"She was awarded over five million dollars from a court directed settlement. Some hotshot lawyer by the name of Paul Keller found so many loopholes that three insurance companies were begging to settle for a collective five-mil."

"Wow, that's something I wasn't aware of."

"Her husband was an active duty Commander in the U.S Navy stationed at the Great Lakes Naval Training Center in Illinois. Angie picked up all of his death benefits and will receive free medical care for the rest of her life."

He was still wrestling with Bradley's lengthy explanation.

"The only thing she shared with me was that she was a single female having some fun in her middle-aged life. I didn't challenge her any further figuring if there was any baggage in her life she had the option of remaining silent or sharing the goods with yours truly. Anyway, why is this cousin sticking her nose in Angie's business? You told me earlier when we talked about your business that your agency takes only cases that involve missing persons."

"Her cousin is a big-time cop in Chicago who has referred several missing person cases to our agency. I could almost retire on her business alone. She's calling in a favor."

"So you are tailing her to keep her out of trouble?"

"Well, I mean yes and no. Her cousin told me that Angie has a tendency to latch on to men like a drowning rat grabs for any piece of floating debris he can climb on. She has already gone through a million bucks in just two years. Your new friend is extremely gullible."

"How in the hell does cousin cop know all this?"

"I told you she is one of Chicago's top investigators. Need I say anything more?"

The shore boat was returning to pick up the remaining tourists. Rod's dinner mates came back with the boat. When they got off he asked them what happened.

"The old fart forgot to bring his wallet with him," his angry wife spewed. "He told me to leave my purse behind because of all the criminals ashore that steal from us dumb tourists. I ought to feed him to the frickin sharks!"

Bradley hopped on and when the last tourist was seated, the boat headed for the shoreline. Angie had a fifteen minute head start but he had an idea where she might be shopping. He was told there were a series of nice jewelry stores five blocks inland from the main pier. He quickly took off in that direction. Two blocks away he saw her come out of a coffee shop with another female tourist. They headed toward the shops.

"Need some company, nice man?" asked a young girl probably no older than sixteen. She'd come up from behind him and startled him when she tapped him on the shoulder.

"No thanks, I'm trying to catch up with my wife over there."

"You have no idea what you're missing," she laughed haughtily at him. "I show you special new things, very cheap."

He closed in on Angie. Her tourist companion spun off and went into the first big jewelry store they came to. She went further on ahead. All of a sudden two shabbily-dressed men appeared from nowhere and jumped in front of her. The taller dark black man with an attitude seemed threatening to Bradley. She was startled but listened to what they were telling her. They were frantically waving their arms and talking in loud voices.

Bradley sped up his pace to intercept them. He knew from the international crime courses he took in college that there was a lot of crime on this island. He suddenly jumped behind a building when he heard her laughing.

My God, he thought, was she propositioning them just like I was confronted by the young whore moments ago? What's going on here?

As he peeked around the corner he saw them lead her into a large store. The entrance way had an obnoxious replica of a huge hand clasping a golden nugget between the fingers. He walked over to the store and peeked in. The two men were with her at the Rolex watch counter. All of a sudden she swung around and slapped the taller one in the face. Both of the men then hustled out of the store.

"Goddamn bitch if I ever met one," screamed the shorter man.

They brushed past Bradley and hurriedly crossed the street. Two cars blasted their horns as the lead car, an old broken-down cab, almost smashed into them. The driver gave them a tongue lashing as they disappeared into a small building.

Bradley waited a full hour outside in the hot sun. He was perplexed and felt useless. He had no clue what was happening inside with her...shoplifting maybe?

Angie finally came out of the jewelry store carrying a small gift-wrapped box. She was smiling as she headed back in the general direction of the pier. She then entered a dilapidated building with no signage, just an address handwritten on a slab of wood. Bradley was all set to rush into the building for fear of something awful about to happen.

"Hey, Bradley, what's up?" she asked him on the front porch when she came out. She wondered if he was also coming in to get some weed.

"Nothing's going down, really. I was on my way back to the pier and saw you go in there. The place intrigued me so I thought I'd join you. What's in the package?"

She hesitated for a few moments and responded, "A gift for Rod and I want to surprise him so don't say anything, okay?"

"Roger that, young lady, I won't snitch on you. We'd better head back right away as I think the shuttle boat is ready to make its second run back to the Port Caller."

Rod will really love this gift, she thought. It's only a friendship ring but it could well lead to a more intimate and lasting relationship. I'm going to press on harder, I'm sure he'll be receptive. I won't push weed on him though. I think he had some trouble with it in the past so I better not open up a can of worms at this stage of our friendship. I can't wait to be with him again...he intrigues me...I got to...!

Chapter 7

THE CAYMAN ISLANDS was the final stop on the cruise before returning to Galveston. Rod and Bradley went ashore and enjoyed snorkeling in the warm waters. Angie decided to remain behind. She was "shopped out" and wanted to rewrite the syllabus she used to teach a summer history course at a junior college near Grayslake. She also preferred to swim in a pool that was free of little creatures and the sticky salt. She hated the way it stuck to her skin and was sure that it would bleach her ankle tattoos.

"Hey, everybody, can you believe that it's our last night on this cruise ship," Angie exclaimed at the dinner table.

"Yes indeed," said Rod. "I have an announcement to make. Bradley asked me to join his private investigations firm earlier today while we were snorkeling...and I accepted."

"Great and then you'll be closer to where I live," Angie smiled.

"As an additional bonus, I'll be near my oldest son, John, who works in Wisconsin with the Green Bay Packers."

"Oh, forget the stupid Packers, I'm more than ready to get home and do some exciting things," reported the older lady sitting next to Rod at the dinner table. "This old coot that I married decades ago didn't want to do anything or go offshore with me except one time...then sat and drank margaritas at a watering hole near the dock the entire time I shopped. All he wanted to do on this wonderful ship was to read stupid mysteries. I should've left him home for all he's worth."

Her husband belched out loud, gave everyone a faint smile and then totally turned a deaf ear to his wife during the remainder of the meal. He played with a wet napkin trying to get a grease spot off of his stripped tie.

Rod glanced over at Bradley's table but didn't see him sitting in his usual chair. He thought that something might have happened to his friend. Meanwhile, Angie was into another animated discussion with the old lady. They seemed to love talking trash back and forth!

"Please excuse me," Rod interrupted. "I have something to tend to before the wonderful desert is served. Angie, if it's alright with you I'll come up to your suite later this evening while you are getting packed up."

He went to Bradley's stateroom, knocked several times but there wasn't any response. He headed to the lounge thinking he'd find him there. When he walked past Miss Willow Blond draped behind the bar like a wet towel she pointed to a booth in the corner. He saw Bradley sitting with Paul Keller. They were deep in conversation and didn't notice him approaching the booth.

"Bradley, what's going on? I didn't see you at dinner. You had me worried. I was afraid you got sick on those raw oysters we gobbled down after our snorkel run."

"I'm fine, meet my friend Paul Keller."

"Good to meet you, Paul, you almost ran me down the other night when you left Angie's suite. She said that you two were old acquaintances."

"That's right, Angie told me all about you and she's so thrilled that you two are getting engaged."

Bradley stared at his good friend whose jaw slung wide open.

"What...what are you talking about?"

"Don't be so coy, Rod, she filled me in on all the details. I couldn't be happier for her after the emotional trauma she'd experienced the past few years. I love her dearly."

"Come on friend, front and center; render a report," Bradley said coyly.

Rod squirmed in next to Paul. He signaled over to Blondie to bring him a double Bombay Sapphire gin martini, straight up. His two associates were sharing a pitcher of beer. They both had a buzz on and he wondered how long they'd been drinking in the lounge.

"First things first; you guys are nearing the proverbial drunken stage and are imagining colossal inaccuracies about yours truly.

"Bring it on, baby," Bradley smiled. He was having a ball.

"Secondly," continued Rod, "Angie and I are good friends and I am fond of her. We are not on a crash course to the marriage altar!"

"Jesus H. Christ," Paul responded with a serious look on his face, "Can't you take a joke, Richards?"

"Yeah, loosen up," laughed Bradley. "We're just having a little fun with you. Consider this the first stage of the initiation process for coming to work for me."

"I'm not so sure I want to work for you anymore, you overgrown kid!"

All three of them then started to laugh heartily as Rod climbed down off of his high horse. He had been a little edgy lately. The developing relationship with the pretty school teacher had smitten him.

"Paul and I have done some business together in the past. We were discussing a case where we could use your considerable talents while you are going to school and studying for your P.I. examination. I told him you were the ideal candidate to get to the bottom of a big-time infidelity issue. Paul has been contacted by the wife of a successful Chicago trucking executive to represent her in a potential divorce case."

"We need an outsider; someone who isn't known in the area to do some heavy duty surveillance," Paul offered on a serious note. "Bradley fingered you since his other two associates have strong Chicago ties and reputations throughout the community."

"Sounds interesting and I'm up for it; can't wait until I put my arms around it...so to say. I think you two should get back to your staterooms while you can still walk there. In case you forgot, we're docking in Galveston in the morning. I've got a date with a neat woman so I've got to run off now. I'll see you tomorrow, Bradley, and maybe catch up with you in Chicago, Paul."

[39]

He slid out of the booth and left the lounge. He was anxious to see Angie and discuss what to expect in the future once the ship docked and everybody went their separate ways.

"Come on in, Rod, I just finished packing. Want to help me finish the last bottle of wine I brought aboard? I'd hate to sterilize the sink drain with it."

They talked and sipped wine for several hours and then she presented her gift. He was dumbfounded, not knowing for sure what to say. He hadn't bought anything for her. They made love throughout the night. Rod was appreciative of the expensive gold piece she gave him from the shop in Jamaica. She told him it was a symbol of their new-found friendship. They awoke when the porter knocked on the door to secure her luggage because they would be docking in Galveston in several hours.

"So...where do we go from here, Angie? If it's acceptable to you I'd like to stop up in Libertyville for a few days on my way to Chicago to start my new career. Are you comfortable with having this ole boy around for a few days? Would any of your friends or neighbors be curious about me staying with you?"

"Yes, I absolutely want you there for as long as I can have you. I couldn't care less what anybody thinks; we're adults and it's our business how we spend our time together. I have to get back to the classroom right away but you can find something to do while I'm at school. There's a wonderful mall in nearby Gurnee that you could spend hours roaming around to kill time; even has one of those Bass Pro Shops. That'd be a real hoot for you outdoorsmen types!"

The Port Caller came to a complete stop at the pier and everybody was anxious to disembark, pick up their luggage and head to their final destinations. Rod bid his farewells to Bradley and Paul Keller as they were walking down the long gangplank. He assured Bradley that he'd be joining him in Chicago by the first of the month. He caught up with Angie inside the terminal.

"Hurry up and get your things done in San Antonio. I'll be counting the days until we see each other again, Rod."

After a big kiss and a long hug they secured their suitcases and went their separate ways. He wondered if he would ever see her again. Strange things happen in the pursuit of a love interest.

I for one am an expert at that; could even write a book on the subject. Not sure, though, if anybody would take the time to read it.

His little Honda started with ease which surprised him. The battery was old and sitting in the parking lot for so many days without being driven had worried him. He was excited about hooking up again with Bradley and accepting his offer of what should certainly be an adventurous job in one of the most exciting cities in the country.

He didn't see the flashing lights until the last moment and got pulled over by an unmarked police car just south of the Houston city limits.

"Sir, do you know how fast you were driving?"

"I'm sure I was within the speed limits, officer," Rod smiled. "This car barely hits sixty unless running downhill and only with a strong wind behind it."

"Don't be cute to me. You were doing seventy-five on a level stretch of the highway and...against a head wind."

Rod stared at the cop. He was an Asian, either of Vietnamese or Cambodian descent. There were so many immigrants in South Texas, many of them coming over after the Vietnam War. Flashing through his mind were images of the helpless orphans coming through the Presidio of San Francisco when he was stationed there.

What's your big hurry?" the cop asked breaking Rod's prolonged train of thought. "Tell me you're heading for a funeral and they're about to lower the casket into the hole."

Rod fingered the gold friendship ring that Angie gave him.

"No sir, officer, more than likely a wedding!"

Chapter 8

Vietnam, Spring of 1975

SAIGON was surrounded by the ferocious North Vietnamese Army. Loud, thunderous blasts of artillery were accompanied by billowing black clouds dancing over the city. Fires were breaking out everywhere. Residents were lumbering around like Zombies through open graveyards in dazed confusion, trying to locate their tombs. There was no longer a government in place to direct or guide the citizenry. Rumors were rampant that the city would soon be overrun and taken over by the hated Hanoi soldiers. All hope for any other outcome of a positive nature would soon be lost. They were doomed!

Sixteen year-old Sno Tran waited tables at an upscale French restaurant in downtown Saigon. She was pretty and customers would ask for her by name to wait on them. Most of the other eating establishments except the few outdoor ones near the U.S. Embassy were starting to lose clientele and a few of them were already out of business and boarded up.

The restaurant owner was a father figure to her as she never knew her own. When time permitted he taught her how to cook, be gracious to customers and how to purchase food items from a horde of scheming vendors. He was surprised how rapidly she was able to digest the business challenges of operating a busy restaurant.

"So Sno, which do you prefer; meeting and greeting our customers or preparing our famous spring rolls?"

"I prefer the people aspect of our business."

A year ago she had been attracted to a black military police officer assigned to provide security at the U.S. Embassy compound. Every weekend he came while in uniform to eat at the restaurant and soon they began seeing each other frequently. Her mother was wary about her daughter dating any man, especially a U.S. soldier because she was so young and vulnerable.

She remembered so vividly the discussions she had with her mother when she began dating the handsome man.

"Oh mother, he's always so nice to me and he brings me wonderful gifts to brighten my dreary days. Don't be so concerned."

"Yes, I know dear. I think you need to slow down with him; you are getting way too serious. Just be courteous to him and his companions whenever they come in to have a meal."

Sno disregarded her mother's advice and began seeing him at night away from work and far from their modest home. The serviceman impregnated her on a steamy night down by the lower secluded banks of the Saigon River. When he found out she was pregnant he accused her of being a dirty street whore claiming the baby couldn't possibly be his. The military policeman disappeared the next day, never to be seen by her again.

Now, over a year later the terrible war was on their doorstep. The enchanting country had enjoyed centuries of independence until the French colonial period began in the late 1800's. French Indochina collapsed at the end of WWII but still exerted a major influence in the country until defeated by Ho Chi Minh in 1954. The country was later divided in two and a new chapter of history was beginning to unfold. The U.S. government was pressured by its citizenry to abandon the war and bring the troops home. The North was too strong and too committed to abandon its goal of unification.

"You need to give up your little son so that he might grow up and live a normal life in a peaceful nation."

Mama had heard about orphanages all around the country being emptied out before the final siege of Saigon would take place. It was inevitable; they were a defeated country and everybody knew it. The citizenry were now scrambling like red ants racing out of their disturbed

[43]

nest to save their own lives. The few belongings they owned were strapped haphazardly on their backs as they fled the city in droves.

"Mama, I just can't do it. He is my flesh and blood. He needs me now more than ever."

"Look my dear Sno, it's for your own good and his too. I can make the arrangements through my uncle. He is highly placed in our collapsing government, at least for today. Tomorrow is another story. We need to move fast."

Sno grappled for several days with her mother's suggestion to give up her tiny baby. She finally relented after news of the rapidly imploding city alarmed her. Frightened residents on the far outskirts of Saigon toward Bien Hoa were witnessing the threatening explosions and nightly kaleidoscope skies far off in the distance. She urged her mother to contact the uncle and give her child over to the nearest orphanage that would accept her little baby boy.

It was over in four days…little Chien Tran was gone. Sno was beside herself, crying and then reassuring herself that it was best for both of them to go their separate ways in search of a new life.

The uncle then convinced Sno and her mother to collect their belongings and get out of Saigon right away. There was a group of trusted friends leaving that night and they should join them on their trek out of the country. Twelve men and women, young and old, boys and girls were scheduled to leave. A Vietnamese Army Captain by the name of Quan, his son and a gray-bearded bald man agreed to act as guides. Mama learned that the old man was both a man of cloth and reputedly a medicine man.

What about your uncle?" Sno inquired with a soft and concerned voice. "Is he also coming with us?"

"No, don't you worry about him. He told me he planned to work with the new government that will be formed when our beloved city succumbs to the marauders. Nobody around here knows this but he served with Ho Chi Minh when the French stranglehold over our country was eliminated years before you were born. He is a career politician and has skillfully maneuvered his life to take advantage of the future. Somehow he envisioned that one day our entire country would be unified again."

"Where are they going?" Sno asked with a concerned voice.

"They're on their way to Thailand. We've got to accompany them right away if we want to live. We have to walk a long way through jungle, swollen rice paddies and mountainous terrain but we are young and healthy. We can do it. We must do it!"

"Mama, you know there are ferocious animals roaming around the jungle out there. I've heard stories told in my restaurant about man-eating lions and poisonous snakes. I don't know if I can make it."

"If we stay here any longer we'll all be rounded up, tortured and even raped by the conquering savages. All is lost here; we have to leave the city right away."

Sno had one last visit with the restaurant owner. She had grown fond of him and appreciated all the support he gave her during the difficult pregnancy.

"I will miss you so much," she said genuinely. "You have been so good to me and I really don't know how I will ever be able to repay you."

"No need to worry about that. You have a major challenge ahead of you. Because you are going to Thailand, I want to give you the name of the original owner of this restaurant. He was supportive of me over the years and even let my older brother purchase the restaurant from him for almost nothing."

"I'll give it to mother and ask her to guard it with her life."

"His name is Henri Louie Moreau and he owns a French restaurant in downtown Bangkok. He also had a restaurant up in Da Nang but I think he abandoned it when the North Vietnamese Army took control of the city. Make sure you find him and give him my regards. I think he's also aware of your well-known and respected uncle. I'm sure he will help you any way he can and I'll write to him about you."

They hugged each other for several minutes in a final farewell.

Chapter 9

Somewhere in the Vietnam Jungle

DARKNESS enveloped them when the travelers finally slipped through the outer defenses which had begun to fall like dominos. Some were carrying straw baskets propped up and balanced on their heads while others were lugging worn-out cloth suitcases. Five dogs and two small pot-bellied pigs rounded out the caravan.

Flash fires broke out everywhere and the cries of the injured could be heard intermittently between the deafening artillery barrages. Rickshaws and other wheeled transport could be seen heading in every direction with confused and delirious passengers. Around midnight the leader theorized that it was safe enough for them to camp for the remainder of the night.

On the second day out of Saigon two Montagnard tribesmen who had been trailing the refugees came up to the leader and Captain Quan offering their help. They reported that they had worked for the U.S. Army Special Forces and knew the terrain like the back of their hands. They assured the high priest that they would get them through the treacherous jungle and snake-infested swamps. They would lead them to Chau Doc. The uncle had made arrangements there with a local official to provide a Mekong River boat to bring them to a location just south of Phnom Penh, Cambodia. The official had provided Captain Quan with appropriate paperwork if the boat was intercepted by enemy river patrols.

"Mama, who are those strange little people talking to the Captain?" Sno asked edging closer to her mother's side.

"They are known as 'Degers', a tribe that was driven to live in the sparsely populated mountainous areas of the Central Highlands. Many were converted to Christianity by the early missionaries. The Deger do not share our common language and culture."

"But why are they willing to help us?"

"It's complicated. Almost twenty years ago the Deger started a movement to unite their various tribes against us but they remained somewhat under control until the start of this war. Both our government and the United States government began to train minority groups to fight against the enemy."

Captain Quan and the leader huddled together off to the side.

"What do you think?" the bearded leader asked. He had no use for and was suspicious of the mountain people.

"What do we have to lose? I've worked with them in the past. They are vicious fighters and if you offer them money, they will help us. I'll keep a close eye on them."

The leader agreed and promised the two mercenaries a generous sum of money to lead them.

Screeching nighthawks and angry raptors punctuated the thick jungle every step of their route and frightened the younger travelers. Insects constantly pestered them in the stifling hot, humid and dense vegetation. On the third night out three of the older travelers disappeared. They were never seen nor heard from again. It was a draining physical and emotional challenge for both Sno and her mother to continue.

"We should have stayed back in the city."

"No, my dear, you are wrong. We both must sacrifice in order to gain the new life ahead of us. We are protected by our leaders and the tribesmen. My uncle told me that Captain Quan was the driver and former bodyguard to our President. He and the two tribesmen will lead us safely through."

The refugees all agreed to their leader's proposal of releasing the Montagnards when they reached Chau Doc. The jungle canopy was so thick that little light got through to the ground. They had to travel only at night in the suffocating humidity and black darkness. Everyone knew that this was necessary to avoid rampaging enemy patrols that might be operating in the area. It was still dangerous as wild animals and other fearful species owned the terrain both during the day and especially at night.

"Everybody quiet down, now!" ordered Captain Quan. "You boys muzzle those dogs. I'm going to backtrack with the Montagnards who spotted something suspicious alongside the trail. We're going back to check it out."

About ninety yards back they uncovered a small opening in the ground several feet from the trail. It had been covered by dead branches and the flora didn't look natural to the soldier. They pulled the branches off and to their shock discovered a number of small spider holes leading down deep into the ground.

"It's the Cong," whispered one of the tribesmen to Quan.

"I agree, be quiet."

They moved in a little closer to inspect the site.

"They have a complete underground network which they spring surprised attacks on the unsuspecting Americans," Quan whispered. "We need to hurry out of here because these underground hiding places are occupied. Can't you smell them?" The mercenaries concurred.

They quickly and quietly returned to the other refugees and the soldier advised them of the situation. They had to proceed with great caution. He directed them not to talk until the all clear signal was given.

Tragedy struck on the fourth day. One of the elderly women collapsed on the trail. The medicine man was unable to stem the high fever she had developed since her departure from Saigon. She never told anyone she was sick. They buried her after a brief ceremony. The medicine man had tossed a handful of nut-like objects into the shallow grave before it was sealed with dirt.

"Mama, tell me why he did that."

Her mother quickly silenced her for fear of being heard by the others. She pulled Sno close to her.

"The evil spirits that live in the jungle will not disturb her now," she said making up a story to appease her daughter. "The objects have been used in past ceremonies but only the medicine man understands how they prevent the foraging animals from digging up her grave and eating the bones. Do not question the actions of our high priest."

"Alright, I won't."

The refugees collected their belongings and resumed their convoy through the jungle.

"We are making good progress now," reported her mother after they had moved on for several more days.

"I agree with you but more people keep dropping out. At this rate, we might be the only two to make it to Thailand!"

The trip had been fairly uneventful for several more days until late one afternoon when they were almost clear of the wretched jungle. The sun was starting to drop over the thick green canopy. They were all exhausted from the day's travel. A scattering of monkeys was annoying with their penetrating communication with each other while swinging from the tree vines. There was constant movement in the brushy areas but nothing was seen. The medicine man attributed the activity to the good spirits guiding them along their journey.

Sno's mother yelled out in shock when something struck her in the lower left leg. She had stepped on a snake along a narrow pathway leading out of the jungle exit.

"Somebody, anybody please help us," screamed out the young Sno to nobody in particular. She reached out for her mother.

"What's wrong here? Be silent, young girl," an older lady traveling next to Sno whispered harshly. "We mustn't be heard." She didn't see the snake strike her mother.

"A snake bit my mama and she's going to die!"

"Settle down, Sno, be quiet. It really doesn't hurt that badly. I'll be okay in a few minutes."

The medicine man moved judiciously down the trail to inspect her mother's bite. One of the younger men raced over and grabbed the slithering serpent by the neck as it wiggled toward a clump of underbrush.

"I got it, I got it!" he said proudly and loudly to the shocked assemblage, holding the undulating snake in the air by its slippery neck.

"It's a Krait," another man whispered.

"How do you know?" asked the lady next to him.

"They're normally only active at night. Look at the yellow and black bands. They're twenty times more poisonous than the king cobra! My brother died from one of their bites."

"Shut up you fool," the medicine man ordered. "I know what it is. Cut the head off and toss it into the trees. Bring me two of our young men right away."

Two boys appeared out of nowhere and stood next to the medicine man.

"Strip off your clothes and go over there and jump into the middle of that muddy ditch that we just went around. It looks deep but don't go in over your chest. Stay there until I tell you to come out of the water."

The boys ran off without objecting to the medicine man's strange order and worked their way immediately to the middle of the fetid water.

Captain Quan had seen this type of bite before and the victim's bodily reaction to it. He experienced several of his soldiers dying in agony from the bite. Strangely, Sno's mother wasn't in any type of immediate pain. The medicine man took the soldier aside.

"She's going to feel the pain within six to twelve hours later, accompanied by severe respiratory failure and ultimate suffocation if not treated. I have to act right away to prevent the inevitable."

The soldier nodded his agreement; he knew what was coming.

"Bring those boys back right now," the medicine man finally ordered.

When they returned each had several huge brownish-black leeches sucking blood out of their lower legs. Sno gasped loudly when she saw them.

The medicine man opened up the snake strike wound carving a two inch "X" incision at the bite site with a sharp knife that was sheathed at his waist. He wanted it to bleed out some.

"Rip three or four of those leeches off your legs and give them to me," he ordered the young men. They tore off a half dozen of the wormlike parasites and tossed them on the ground next to Sno who was soothing her mother.

The medicine man shoved her aside and sponged off the slowly oozing reddish fluids from her mother's leg and attached the semi-bloated leeches to the site. Before long they could see the leeches begin to puff up like party balloons. When he was satisfied that they had sucked out a large amount of the pinkish fluid at the site, he lit a match to their bottoms and the bloodsuckers dropped to the ground.

"That ought to do it for now; she'll be alright," he said confidently. Quan knew otherwise.

One of the other young boys and the captain's son came over and stomped on the bloated parasites before they could wriggle away to safety in the brush. Blood squirted like water from a charged-up fire hose and sprayed Sno on both of her legs.

"Stop it, stop, you monsters," she cried out.

One of the elders tossed her a cloth to wipe the hot blood off. The boys sheepishly walked away.

"Mama, does it hurt much?" Sno asked when she had recovered from the bloody assault on her little legs.

"No, not really but I hate those blood-sucking parasites. I hated them when I worked in the rice paddies as a young girl. I was terrified that they were going to drain me of my entire body fluids or infect me with an incurable disease."

The medicine man mixed some of her mother's spit with a handful of crumbled powdered herbal leaves he carried for just this occasion. He then vigorously worked the saliva mixture into the wound and then applied a splint to help her ambulate. In his own mind he knew she didn't have a chance for recovery but he couldn't stop the convoy here and rest for a day or two. They had to keep moving for at least a few more hours.

Nobody said a word during the time he ministered to Sno's mother. The monkey's screeching was now replaced by a myriad of birds announcing the end of another sweltering day. The monsoon-like rain had lifted and the incessant humidity would drop in tomorrow morning like a heavy blanket enveloping each traveler.

"Can you walk okay with that stick tied to your leg?"

"I'll do the best I can, Sno. I don't want to hold up the convoy."

After several more miles of trudging along they found an adequate location to pitch camp for the night. Toward midnight Sno's mother started to experience severe abdominal pains and began to tug at her stomach. Observing her through the light of the smoldering camp fire Sno thought that one of her mother's eyes started to droop considerably.

"Please, can somebody help her?" Sno begged loudly. "She's getting faint and has difficulty breathing. She can't catch her breath!"

Nobody moved in to help. They had nothing to offer. The medicine man had wandered away from the camp site to pray and never returned. Someone saw him disappearing into the jungle followed quickly by the two Montagnards who reportedly hadn't received their compensation from him. None of the three ever rejoined the convoy.

Sno hugged her mother tightly and started to sing a series of chants she learned as a child. Four hours later Sno's mother died quietly in her arms.

"What am I going to do now?" Sno pleaded with another elder who offered to assist Captain Quan in leading the few remaining survivors.

"Don't you worry; Quan and I will get all of us to Chau Doc safely. We need to bury your mother right away."

Hurriedly, Captain Quan's son dug out a narrow grave in the jungle floor with his bare hands. He felt sorry for Sno and the leech incident and wanted to make amends any way that he could. The burial ceremony was short and simple. She wouldn't allow anything to be thrown into her mother's grave other than a small picture of Buddha she carried in her belongings. She placed it next to her mother's snake-bitten leg over the objection of the new leader.

She became assertive and argued vehemently with him. He had to be restrained by Quan when he took three quick steps toward her. The old man insisted that the picture of Buddha should never be buried in the ground.

"Get this monster away from me," Sno yelled out. "He's crazy!"

Quan stepped in and had a few choice words with the leader who began to sulk and then sat down with his arms crossed staring wildly at Sno. She ignored him. Finally Quan got the column moving again.

Several hours later they heard a rustling noise in a clearing which opened up ahead of them. Quan moved cautiously ahead to check it out. When he stepped through the clearing he saw a water buffalo tangled up in two trees. There was a wide clay road which ran diagonally to their narrow pathway. No other refugees were in sight.

"What's going on?" Sno asked Quan's son.

"I don't know...please be quiet!"

The water buffalo was still tethered to a large cart; breathing heavily and completely spent. The front and rear axles were completely snapped off the mainframe. Behind the cart was a deep furrow as far back as Quan could see; the water buffalo dragged the cart until overcome with exhaustion. He cautiously moved up to the animal, cut the tethered straps and unbuckled the heavy yoke around his thick neck. The beast heaved forward and took off.

After this incident they rested for a short while, moved out and made good headway through the jungle for the rest of the day and into the early evening. At dusk they found a sheltered site and struck camp for the night.

Chapter 10

In the Jungle nearing Cambodia
Several days later

CAPTAIN QUAN took total control of the column. The former leader continued to be moody but very verbal. Sno hated the wicked old bald man and his yellow cone-shaped beard. He constantly flashed a set of brilliant red rotten teeth. He knew Sno had a bastard child outside of wedlock. The old man was also aware that she was still in agony over the death of her mother.

"You will go on no matter how you feel about the many demons that possess you. Don't let your mother die in vain; we all loved her! You will survive; you are the youngest of us. You will live the remainder of your life in gratitude for your mother. She sacrificed herself to be bitten by that snake which the spirits arranged to strike you instead of her."

The lecherous old man followed her whenever she went off to bathe in the few streams they encountered. He had visions of raping the young girl if he could maneuver her far enough away from the other travelers. Sno thought he was paying too much attention to her. Even Quan suspected that something was going on and took her aside.

"Don't let that old man bother you," he said in a comforting manner. "He chews 'boo-eye' day and night and doesn't have control of his tongue. I'll talk to him and keep a closer eye on him the rest of the way."

"Thank you, sir, he's scary. Does the boo-eye make his teeth red?"

"Yes, many of the old men and women from the villages chew green Betel nuts which give them a certain type of euphoria and a false sense of freedom. It's part of their custom."

Sno Tran was so vulnerable. She ached from the loss of her dear mother. The dying woman never complained about her condition. She constantly reassured her daughter that whatever happened to her, Sno would have the strength and courage to move on and live out her own life.

Captain Quan finally had enough of the old man and physically forced his departure from the traveling group. Sno thanked him repeatedly.

Now there were only five refugees remaining from the original group: Sno, the captain and his young son, and an older couple whom Sno knew from her days growing up in Saigon. Three of the dogs were eaten during the first two weeks of travel and the last pig would be gone tonight.

They were now making noticeable progress with fewer rest stops and in one full day of travel they would reach Chau Doc and the Mekong River. Soon they would be out of Vietnam. The countryside had opened up and stands of trees were strategically located to give them some element of cover.

Suddenly, a loud boom was heard and seconds later the back side of a large rubber tree next to Sno was blown to pieces.

"Duck, everyone hit the ground," Quan ordered. "Someone is firing at us. Cover yourself with some of those fallen branches and stay put. I'll try to outflank whoever's trying to pick us off."

While on his knees, he removed the rifle from his shoulder harness, checked the breech and loaded several .30 caliber rounds into a magazine. He jammed the magazine home and then chambered a round. Crouching as low as possible he then started to circle back and find the shooter.

Another crack was heard and immediately another round whizzed over their heads. They were frightened and began sobbing, hoping their sounds wouldn't be heard.

"He's going to get killed," Sno whispered to the elderly couple hunched beside her. "The enemy outnumbers him. What will we do then? We will be slaughtered like pigs!"

"Don't worry about him, Sno; he's a seasoned veteran who has fought many battles in the jungle. He'll find and kill whoever is trying to harm us."

Three shots followed by a loud scream were heard off to the left from where they were lying. Nobody moved; everybody held their breaths. Several minutes later Quan reappeared carrying a bloody scalp, another rifle and some more food rations. There was a gasp from the travelers and a big sigh of relief could be heard.

"This Viet Cong fought his last fight," Quan bragged with special emphasis on the word "last". "He'll rot in the very jungle that he chose to launch his ill-timed attack on us."

"Did you find any more of them out there?"

"No, Sno, but there have to be more of them nearby."

The young boy snapped the scalp away from his father and held it high. He then went over to a nearby tree and strung it up on one of the low-lying branches. He wiped the blood off his hands with a checkered cloth that he had worn around his neck.

Sno screamed at him and then got in his face. "Did you have to do that, you fool? If he's discovered the rest of the enemy will hunt us down like dogs!"

"Okay you two," Quan bellowed. "Let's not fight among us. We're almost out of danger so let's get going and be quiet!"

The river boat trip up the Mekong went without incident. They decided to dock just short of Phnom Penh. The arduous trip through the jungle, followed by traveling through miles of open land, her mother's death and the affair with the enemy sniper had taken its toll on everyone. Captain Quan warned them about Phnom Penh, the capital of Cambodia.

"Listen to me everybody. There are still North Vietnamese Regulars and some Viet Cong soldiers still active in the area. We also have to be concerned with millions of refugees from both Vietnam and Cambodia flooding the area in and around Phnom Penh."

"I've seen evidence of that," the captain's son offered proudly. "Multiple footprints and knocked down brush gave it away."

"Do we have to worry about Khmer Rouge troop's operating in the countryside?" The older man who had served with Ho Chi Minh years ago and fought against the French was concerned about their continued safety.

"For sure," Quan responded.

The older man continued, "I'd heard that a new communist regime was formed here with an army of murderous thugs who take no prisoners."

"Yes, that's a major concern; it's a hornets' nest here. That's why we're not going anywhere near the city. Everyone has to be careful the next few days. I don't want any loud conversations taking place. In fact, we'll move in silence until I feel it's safe to resume talking to each other."

They swung far wide of the city and miraculously didn't run into any enemy soldiers. Captain Quan was careful in his planning and methodical in his execution of the plan. He had on his person the newest maps of the region and relied heavily on them and the sun's position in the sky. Being in Cambodia presented only one problem. They had eaten one of the last dogs as the pigs were all consumed earlier. The refugees were short of rations although enough rice was still available to hold them for several more days. They would have to continue to forage off the land for anything more to supplement their diet.

"See if you can find any of those long-horned tree beetles," he ordered his son on a brief mission. "Beetles and any cockroaches we might collect can be dried and eaten. If you see any snakes, kill them…they're good eating."

They reached the city of Kampong Chhnang where their leader felt it was safe enough to board a bus to Battambang. There they would skirt around a mountain range and walk the rest of the way to Thailand. When they were just a few days away from the Thailand border, an older woman fell from exhaustion. Her skin was hot and dry without any evidence of perspiration. Her husband applied wet packs to her head and neck in an attempt to control a raging fever.

"What more can I do?" he asked the soldier leader.

"Keep her in the shade and continue applying the wet packs. I can't offer any more help. We can camp here for a day and hope that she regains her strength."

The next morning the older man confronted Captain Quan. "She's not going to recover here. I'm bringing her back to Phnom Penh. It's the largest and most advanced city in Cambodia. The French helped established a network of medical clinics when they had influence in the area. I will find some needed medicine for her there."

"She'll never make it back," Quan said with a sad voice.

"We're going anyway."

The three remaining travelers: Sno, Quan and his son helped them pack up and leave. They gave them what they could spare of their rations to help sustain them for their journey back and bade them farewell. Quan knew full well that the wife would probably be dead in a day.

They finally reached the Thailand border and traveled through the town of Bo Rai. The scenery presented a noticeable change from the thick jungle and the stifling hot and humid weather they experienced. The trio replenished their provisions and followed directions to Makham, a nearby community where they could find a bus heading to Bangkok.

"We're here everyone, we're finally here," Sno shouted when they reached the outer perimeter of Bangkok.

Captain Quan and his son closed their fists and shot their arms high in the air in triumph!

"I've been given directions to a small encampment where some of our countrymen are living," Quan said to an excited Sno Tran. "There are several other refugees from Cambodia, Laos and Burma living there. When we get to that location I will leave you in the hands of someone who will help you get settled."

"What will you and your son do?"

"From there we are going to explore Bangkok and find some place to live and work. I'd be happy to send for you when that occurs. You can then join us or stay wherever you find comfort and security."

Captain Quan located an elder couple from Saigon who had settled in the outskirts of the city near the Chao Phraya River estuary. They and the others lived in tents and make-shift structures that protected them from the elements. The old man agreed to take Sno in but his wife was hesitant. She envisioned nothing but trouble having a pretty young lady living with them in their makeshift home. The aggressive young men in the encampment would be after her the next day. After several harsh words from his wife, he welcomed Sno into his abode.

Quan had given her some of the local currency to live on for a short period of time, and then she was on her own.

"I really don't know how to thank you. You have saved my life on several occasions. I will never forget you. I hope you and your son find a wonderful life here and new-found happiness with many rewards."

Sno bowed to Quan, gave him a warm hug and politely shook his young son's hand. He trailed behind his soldier father, occasionally glancing back at her wondering if they'd ever meet again. Soon they were out of sight.

She was anxious to get on with her new life but waited to make contact with Henri Moreau until she was totally recovered from the arduous trip out of Saigon. Sno wondered how her "adopted" parents would integrate her into the new community. It wouldn't take her long to find out!

Several long weeks passed by. She felt that she was being ignored by everyone in the encampment for some unknown reason. She sat down and cried while cleaning up after an evening meal. The elders were off talking to some neighbors.

What's wrong with me? Nobody likes me. I'm trying my best to get along but it's just not enough! I don't like the way the young men stare at me; I'm frightened of them. They seem to be out of control!

One sunny hot afternoon several younger men cornered her at the river where she was alone washing her clothes. They tried to gang-rape her. She suffered a few bruises when she fought them off but they would heal; her mind would never forget!

Sno decided it was time to leave this wretched and wicked environment. She searched frantically through the few belongings she owned for Henri Moreau's address. She thought she might have lost it on the long and danger-filled trek to Thailand.

Mama, where did you hide it? Please show up, I need your information so badly to get me out of this horrible mess! Oh, now I remember where you put it.

She found the address sewn into the lining of the one dress she still had. Her mother made her protect the address at all costs. That afternoon she headed into downtown Bangkok determined to befriend Monsieur Moreau.

Chapter 11

San Francisco, 1975

CHIEN TRAN arrived in the United States on a cold, windy April morning literally cuddled up in a small wooden basket which served as his make-shift bassinet. A white ID band on one arm had his Vietnamese name and case number; the band on the other arm contained the adopting parent's name, matching case number and a color-coded destination. Tran was headed for a family in Chicago.

He was one of the over 2,000 infants and children hustled out of Vietnam just before the fall of Saigon. Most of the orphanages were emptied out in South Vietnam when President Gerald Ford approved the massive humanitarian effort known as "Operation Baby Lift". A host of international service organizations such as the Pearl S. Buck Foundation, Catholic Relief Services and several governmental agencies took the lead.

Chien was eleven months old when his young mother tearfully and reluctantly gave him up to a Catholic Relief Service representative for a new life in a foreign land. A World Airways commercial carrier landed in Oakland and Chien and his fellow planeload of young war refugees and orphans were transported to the Presidio of San Francisco, an Army Post located at the base of the Golden Gate Bridge. The staff of Letterman Army Medical Center and other post support personnel and city-wide organizations worked around the clock processing the infants and children for the final step of their long journey.

"Excuse me," said a young Sergeant Rod Richards interrupting a nurse while she was talking to an attendant.

"Yes, Sergeant, what's up?"

"I'm part of the team assembled by the installation commander to support the orphan transition. I understand we have a problem with one of the little ones."

"Yes we do and we'd better get him checked out," she said with a stethoscope slung around her neck. "I think I detected an irregular heart beat but to be sure, we'll send him to a pediatrician at the hospital and have him thoroughly evaluated."

"What's his name?" asked the male attendant.

"Chien Tran," responded the nurse after carefully inspecting his wrist band.

Rod smiled; he had just completed a tour in Vietnam and thought he'd take few minutes to orient the workers on several Vietnamese customs. He liked to demonstrate his knowledge to those who might be interested in learning how the Vietnam names are derived and used.

"In Vietnam, the family name always comes first," he told them. "So this little guy is officially Tran Chien. The Chien stands for warrior, or one that does battle. However, in our country he will probably be referred to as Chien Tran. As you know, it is our custom to list the family name last."

"I thought there were more kids brought out of Vietnam than we have coming through here," commented another volunteer worker while holding Chien. She rubbed his soft forehead with her little finger circling the miniature strawberry birthmark.

"Yes indeed, many of the children were airlifted to Canada, Europe and even as far away from here as Australia," Rod answered.

"Hey folks, we best get moving on this little guy and get him up to the hospital. Another bus loaded with orphans is on the way over from the airport and I've got to head out."

The pediatrician at Letterman Army Medical Center evaluated little Chien and concluded that a minor heart murmur was indeed present. It wasn't life-threatening and any surgical intervention could be delayed for several years if closely monitored.

When the situation was reported to the Babylift supervisor it was determined that Chien was medically stable enough to be transported to his ultimate destination in Chicago. The congenital heart condition was duly recorded in his medical record and Chien was returned to the staging area.

& & & & &

Meanwhile, a man and a woman back in Illinois were anxiously awaiting word of the status of the orphans' arrival in the United States. They had been waiting patiently for this day to arrive.

Charlie Duke served as the president of a large and prosperous bank in downtown Chicago. He had worked his way up from a teller position in the same bank years ago. Fortunately, and with wife Gwyn's encouragement, he went to night school and was finally awarded a degree in finance from DePaul University.

Gwyn Duke was a forty-eight year old social worker employed by the City of Evanston, Illinois where they lived. She was active in her Catholic church and one night while doing some voluntary work heard about the plight of the orphanages in the war torn country. She and Charlie discussed the possibility of adopting one of the orphans. They applied to the regional Catholic Relief Service Organization for one of the children, preferably a boy. They deemed this was another golden opportunity to make it happen. The Duke's always wanted a boy.

"So, you want a young boy from a country that many people hate because of the long war," commented her contact at the adoption agency.

"Yes, both Charlie and I would be honored and thrilled to raise another child."

Gwyn was told by her obstetrician after delivering the twin girls twenty-six years ago that she shouldn't get pregnant again and was disappointed, as was Charlie.

"In our opinion, Gwyn, you and Charlie are really too old to be raising children again." The interviewer from the relief organization was adamant. "You both work full time and that factor alone is a major negative for us in awarding custody of a child, especially a baby. You certainly qualify from a financial perspective but we still have to deny your request. I'm so sorry."

Gwyn was heartbroken but she was not to be denied. As a social worker she had worked with every adoption agency in the tri-state area in one capacity or another so it was time to call in some favors. Charlie thought that he could pull some strings because he was a well-known businessman in the community. He was also chairman of the local Chamber of Commerce.

Shortly after the first of the year they were notified by the Catholic Relief Service that their appeal had been approved but with one stipulation. All of the allocations had already been filled but they would be placed on the "standby" list if another family backed out for any reason.

"I'm having a hard time with this," Gwyn moaned to her husband. "They're trying to stiff us, thinking we're too old to start raising a child again. I'm ready to cancel the whole thing…let someone else take the kid!"

"Whoa, hold on, don't get so excited. You know how complicated this is. You're a seasoned social worker. We've just got to be more positive that things will work out for us."

The call they had been waiting for came at the end of March. An opening just occurred and with their concurrence, they would be receiving an eleven month old baby boy. They were told to be patient as final arrangements had not been made yet for getting the orphans out of Vietnam.

"I can't believe it," Gwyn yelled after she hung up the phone. "I almost lost hope. We're in, Charlie, we're in; they're giving us the baby boy we always wanted but never could have. I'm so happy I'm going to cry for a week!"

Operation Baby Lift had begun. Charlie and Gwyn Duke were anticipating the arrival of their newly pre-adoptee child. They were alarmed when they'd heard through the media that the C-5A carrying the first plane load of orphans crashed just after takeoff from Tan Son Nhut

Airport outside of Saigon. The plane landed in a rice paddy and killed almost everyone aboard. They were fearful that their young son was one of the unfortunate ones. Charlie immediately called their contact and was informed that their son was scheduled out later that day on the next aircraft to take off.

"Do you think he will like Evanston, Charlie?"

"Good gracious, woman of mine, he's not a year old yet. He'll like anything and anyone who will give him warmth, love and a stable environment after all he's experienced in his short life."

The Dukes had two grown twin girls who were married; one lived in upstate New York, the other in Florida. Both of the girls encouraged their parents to adopt when they learned of the possibility that existed for them to finally get a son.

One of the daughter's spouses was a career soldier and knew of the many plights and sacrifices that were being made by the Vietnamese both during and at the close of hostilities. He had served with the First Cavalry Division in Vietnam and kept abreast of the progress of the unpopular conflict. The war plug was being pulled by Washington and the fall of Saigon was inevitable.

"How is it possible that there are so many orphans?" asked the soldier's wife. "I can't believe it!"

"That's war, honey. A large proportion of the babies in the airlift were fathered by American soldiers who had no intention of marrying their Vietnamese lovers. Most of the poor and destitute young mothers couldn't care for their babies and the little ones got hustled off to orphanages throughout the country."

Meanwhile, back in Evanston, Gwyn Duke was in the study knitting some baby booties. Charlie was working in his home office trying to reconcile their bank account when the telephone rang.

"Honey, I just got an update from Catholic Relief that our son has arrived in Oakland and is being processed at an Army base out there for further transport to Chicago. I've got several bank examiners coming in

[65]

next week to do a mandatory audit. They could be at the bank for a full week. I definitely want to be here when the little tyke gets in."

"I wish they would hurry up and get him here," he said emphatically. "The flight has been delayed three times. What could be the problem?"

Charlie sat back in his chair and rubbed his double chin. He loved working at the bank and other than being slightly overweight enjoyed great health in his fiftieth year of birth. This weight issue didn't bother him so long as his tailored suits still fit properly. They both belonged to the local YMCA and tried to work out three times a week.

"They would have notified us if there was a major problem. You're just so anxious to get the little guy in our home. Believe me, so am I."

"No kidding, Charlie, I'm on pins and needles too. The last word I got from the agency was to expect an arrival at O'Hare within three or four days. We just have to be patient. I know you are eager for your son to arrive; I think more upbeat than when we learned that our twins were girls."

"That's nonsense, my love. How about fixing a pot of tea and we'll cool our heels for awhile."

They got the welcomed telephone call three days later. The little orphaned boy with the strawberry birthmark on his forehead would finally reach his new home in Illinois.

& & & & &

One month after Operation Baby Lift was completed at the Presidio of California, Rod Richard's term of service came to an end. He declined to extend his enlistment. Six years in the Army was enough. He'd performed his civic duty to the country in both peacetime and war. It was time to make arrangements to return to St. Louis and begin a new chapter in his young life.

Chapter 12

Bangkok circa late 1975

HENRI LOUIE MOREAU was eating lunch when the front doorbell rang. It startled him. He wasn't expecting anyone until later in the afternoon when three food vendors were scheduled to call on him. His housekeeper was shopping at the street market for fresh vegetables he needed to prepare the evening meal.

"Who's there, please?" he shouted into the announcer microphone resting on a table in the foyer. He never opened the door when the bell rang having been mugged several years ago when he was more "trusting".

"It's Sno Tran out here to see you."

"Who? Speak louder, I can't hear well." He really could but needed a moment to recollect whether or not he knew her. The voice was soft.

"Sir, it's Sno Tran from Vietnam," she yelled out.

He immediately opened the door and asked her to step in out of the rain which had been slapping at her and they felt like miniature steel pellets. It was that time of the year when the rains were a daily nuisance in Bangkok. Henri was pleasantly surprised to finally meet her. He expected a moon-faced taller girl with short hair. Her beauty paralyzed him for several long seconds before he spoke.

"My restaurant owner friend back in Saigon wrote me that you and your mother would be coming to see me. It was the last communication I got from him. I sure hope that he's not in any sort of trouble with the new regime there. They can be ruthless."

"Yes sir, I know all about that. They're raping and killing and plundering everywhere. I'm so glad we got out."

"Where's your mother? I thought that she would be traveling with you and the group fleeing the city."

"She died from a poisonous snake bite in that awful jungle we had to travel through day and night for so many days." She began to cry.

"I'm so sorry, Sno, it must have been difficult for you. Please come in and rest. I'll fix you some tea and we'll share some of the croissants I baked this morning. I think you'll like them."

"Thank you very much, I would like that. I haven't eaten today and I'm hungry."

"We'll take care of that right now, young lady. Relax on the couch and I'll be back in a few minutes."

This is going much better than I ever hoped for, she thought. He is older than I expected but much nicer than most of the French men I've met in my old restaurant and he seems to be a considerate man.

"Here's your tea. The croissants are warm and there is some honey in that small bowl. Please eat."

They had a pleasant exchange and she answered most of his questions. She didn't want to go into all of the details about life in the encampment where she lived. She didn't want to relive the attempted rape ordeal, especially with this well-dressed and successful restaurant owner even though she felt comfortable talking with him.

"How would you like to come and work for me? I own a very busy restaurant and need to break in a trustworthy person to take some of the load off my shoulders. Your friend was complimentary about your work experience at his French restaurant in Saigon."

"I would love to, Mr. Moreau, but the encampment is so far away and I have no means of transportation. It was difficult coming over here today with the mobs in the street and the terrible weather."

"Maybe this will be enough to convince you. I have an upstairs sitting room with an adjacent bedroom in the Cordon Bleu restaurant. When I get tired or need a rest during the day I go up there and stretch out. Once in awhile I stay overnight when there's a problem at work. Occasionally I have to stay late for other reasons."

"Thank you so much. Whatever wage you determine to be fair is fine with me, Mr. Moreau. I trust your judgment and thank you for your generosity."

Uncle told me that Henri was fifty years old and never married, or as uncle clarified, he's married to his work. He is handsome and kind-hearted and I know we'll get along real well. I just have that feeling.

The housekeeper returned with three bundles of groceries and went directly into the kitchen without hesitating or stopping to acknowledge Henri and his young visitor.

"She's a crusty old lady; don't pay any attention to her. She is a hard worker and sometimes helps me in one of the restaurants not too far from here. I'll have that upstairs unit ready for you in three days so bring all of your belongings and say goodbye to the encampment. I'm sure that you have many friends there who will miss you when you're gone."

Friends he says. I really don't know anybody in that hell hole. He probably thinks I'm pretty and assumes I have many acquaintances; no need to tell him the truth.

The rain had subsided when she left Moreau's house. She was so happy with her good fortune that she failed to notice the speeding motor scooter heading in her direction. At the last moment she hurled herself back to safety but got clipped on the foot by the fender as it sped past her. The pain was intense but she was sure that her foot or ankle wasn't broken.

Sno made it back to the encampment as the sun was about to disappear from the earth. A new day had dawned and a new life was about to begin.

Chapter 13

Chicago, 1996

GRADUATION with high honors from Loyola University and a degree in financial management with a minor in psychology was a breeze for twenty-one year old Chien Tran. He never took any books home nor studied for exams. One of his psychology professors convinced him to take a standardized intelligence test to see if he would qualify for membership in Mensa International. He scored in the 99th percentile and gained entry into the esteemed organization.

Charlie Duke was happy for his son and wanted him to enter the banking field from which he had retired many years ago. Gwyn wanted him to become a doctor but that was before she developed Alzheimers several years ago. She was in an institution that specialized in the care and treatment of that debilitating disorder and only referred to "little" Chien when prompted by Charlie. She never remembered any of his activities growing up but seemed to recall that he found happiness in the arms of one of his married female professors.

"So what's next on the agenda, son? I'm sure you'll hear something soon from those interviews you had recently."

"Father, you forgot about my big medical appointment over at the University Hospital. My new cardiologist wants to evaluate me for possible enrollment in an experimental protocol developed in Canada. The researchers think they've found a way to circumvent heart transplantation for patients with a wide range of heart disorders.

"That's certainly good news," his father said.

"Yes and no, however, I'm not ready to have another person's heart put into this body. Who knows…it could be a relative of one of those hated Viet Cong. Anyway, the doctors advised me I might have a problem genetically finding a donor fit for a transplant. I'm looking forward to the evaluation though."

"I'm getting more and more forgetful, Chien; I'm sorry. Soon I might have to join your mother over at that 'house of wonderment' she's living in."

"Relax, my job interview process was a complete success. I've been offered a position at Howzer Securities in The Loop. Michael Howzer was a guest lecturer in one of my entreprenerial courses. We got to know each other pretty well because he had a hard time answering some of my pointed questions. He took me to one of the Northwestern football games last Fall. You'd like him. He's brilliant but at the same time…down to earth."

"Never heard of the company. Who do they bank with?"

"I have no clue but will find out soon enough. Obviously they don't bank at your old institution or you'd surely know him; he's a dynamic personality."

Charlie Duke often wondered about his son. Chien had the opportunity to change his family name to Duke when he was in high school but refused. He told Charlie and Gwyn that he was proud of his heritage even though he never knew his mother or father. Some day Southeast Asia and in particular, Vietnam would become respectable world trading partners and he wanted to leave that door open if a great financial opportunity presented itself. The Vietnamese name plus his language courses at the university would surely help.

Chien Tran was a handsome young lad. Because of his genetic skin composition, he had a perpetrual tan. He had the body of an athlete without putting in the required effort. Young girls were mesmerized by his aloofness and disinterest in them. They giggled behind his back about the cute little strawberry mole on his forehead. Chien was tall for an Asian and displayed perfect white teeth on the rare occasions he smiled.

"What are you going to do with your professor girlfriend now that you've graduated? I heard through the grapevine that she is divorcing her husband."

"Frankly, I used her. She opened some doors for me that I'd never been able to get through on my own. She's really not my type so I'll move on and wish her well."

There was a pause in their conversation. Charlie began to reminiscence about Chien's earlier formative years.

He had some doubts about whether his son could achieve true success. Chien Tran had been a taker all his life. He never gave back anything to anyone. During his high school years he couldn't participate in sports like the other boys because of his heart condition but found other challenging and exciting outlets. Chien was the captain of the debate team and reigning champion of the chess club. He organized an investment club which attracted several of his teachers but no students. Tran got a girl pregnant when she was a freshman in high school. She ultimately aborted, much to the relief of both sets of parents. The young girl moved to a new city the following year.

"Dad, wake up. I think I need a more professional wardrobe. What do you think?"

Charlie was in full agreement and steered him over to his favorite men's store with a blank check. His son came home with five packages of assorted shirts, ties, belts and socks, two blazers, three suits and six pair of pants. He handed the credit card receipt from the store clerk to Charlie who looked at it, smiled and shoved it his desk drawer.

Good Lord, thought Charlie, I worked for twenty years before I accumulated that size wardrobe! How times have changed!

Tran then drove over to the clinic for his appointment with the cardiologist which turned out to be a no-brainer. He didn't qualify for the new protocol based upon his age and the fact that his medical problem was considered congenital. Because of that they excluded him from the study.

"How'd it go, son?"

"They cut me loose, said they couldn't help me. I don't care, I feel great and have lived with the heart problem since birth…I'll survive."

The next day he flagged down a taxi and headed over to Howzer Securities. It was sunny outside which matched his disposition. The strong Chicago winds could not blow away his excitement.

"Hi, I'm Veronica Brown, glad to meet you Mr. Tran."

"Likewise, I'm sure," he said shaking her small hand.

Chien liked the plush office setting with its wall to wall expensive carpeting, mural wall scenes of ancient Rome and highly glossed Italian furniture everywhere he could see.

Veronica was a tall blond with a tight perm and sparkling green eyes. Chien guessed she was pushing thirty. Her well-proportioned build reminded him of the young high school girl he knocked up. He thought this lady might be a little too tall for him though.

"I have been assigned the duty of training you to become a stock broker. My first mission is to get you ready to take the Series 7 exam."

"Sounds good to me," said an excited Chien.

"If you successfully pass the exams you will be qualified to make different kinds of trades with all types of corporate securities excluding commodities and futures."

"Yes, I'm aware of that," he assured her with a smile.

From what Michael Howzer shared with her, Chien Tran would be a quick study.

"How long have you been working for Mr. Howzer?"

"It seems like forever. Michael took me in as a personal favor to one of his hunting friends after I moved down here from Wisconsin. I worked in a credit union in Sturgeon Bay but always had the desire to spread my so-called 'wings' into the world of investments."

"Well, you obviously are doing well as you're the only female in the firm and I'm told the only non-college graduate that Howzer ever hired. You must be damn good at what you do!"

"Michael thinks so but maybe that's because Michael likes me and I more than hold my own around here. All these wanna-be male money gurus are jealous of me," she laughed.

Tran liked her immediately and wondered if she was dating anyone. He didn't want to probe too deeply into her personal life after just making her acquaintance; that would come later. She wasn't wearing a wedding ring but that was no assurance anymore that a person was single.

His office was located next to the supply room at the end of the long hallway. He didn't have any windows but didn't complain; he was the newbee and would make his success with the firm known soon enough.

The broker next to him had a fantastic view of the 50-story Hancock Tower and Lake Michigan behind it. Veronica shared a huge office with Michael which to Chien seemed longer than a football field. He surmised that something interesting was going on between her and Howzer.

On his third day in the office, Veronica invited him to go down to Starbucks for a cup of coffee. It was shortly before noon so was not crowded when they walked in.

"You're soaking up everything I'm throwing at you like a sponge, Chien. I think by next week we can get you ready to take your Series 7 tests."

He was enjoying a slice of a frosted lemon pound cake, his favorite. He did have a sweet tooth but never seemed to put on any weight, much to the chagrin of the few friends that he had.

He eyed her steadily. "Are you and Howzer an 'item', Veronica?"

"What the hell do you mean by that?"

He smiled back at her. She softened.

"In terms of are we seeing other, the answer is yes. In terms of are we serious, the answer is no. Michael has season tickets to the Chicago Bulls

[74]

games and periodically invites me to their basketball games. Does that meet your classification as an item?"

"No, not yet. I'd like to invite you to go see Mary Poppins with me at the theatre next weekend. I have two tickets for a matinee show. Are you game?"

"Chien, I'm surprised. I wouldn't have thought you were big on theatre, especially song and dance."

"I'm not really. One of my new clients gave me the tickets. Something came up in his schedule which precludes his attendance that evening. How about it, do you want to go?"

"I'd love to. Where's it playing?"

"The Cadillac Palace Theatre; why don't we meet for an early dinner somewhere before the show. You pick the place."

Her choice was the highly popular *Nine* on West Randolph, not too far from the theatre. They enjoyed a delicious seafood dinner. After the show they grabbed a taxi and went to her apartment. She offered Chien a glass of wine but he turned it down.

You have any tea here?"

"Certainly," she responded. "I totally forgot most Asians prefer tea."

They talked for several hours. Tran thought he sensed an opportunity to be a little more aggressive with her but rationalized that his time would come soon enough and on her own initiative.

The days, nights and weeks moved quickly for him. He dove into every aspect of his work with unbridled enthusiasm. He took work home every night and surprised Veronica with his fantastic ability to learn. Mike Howzer made a point to introduce Chien to his inner circle of friends whenever they attended a social event together. Veronica was always with them and he enjoyed her company.

Six months after he began his employment with the company, Chien Tran became Michael Howzer's golden boy. He was aggressive to the point of being considered obnoxious by the other brokers in the office,

[75]

accept Veronica. His clients loved his audacity; "a breath of fresh air" they would tell Michael.

He was able to sell stocks or bonds to most of Howzer's personal friends, who in turn, recommended other friends and family members to invest with him. Howzer was not aware that Chien went behind his back and brought in some investors who did not meet Howzer's strict criteria for investing with his firm. Tran's portfolio was the envy of the entire brokerage house.

Chien was seeing Veronica regularly on weekends. She confided in him that Howzer was more of a father image to her than any kind of boyfriend. Michael enjoyed her company ever since his wife of thirty years passed away. He wasn't looking to hook up and get serious with any woman but periodically enjoyed Veronica's humor and social graces.

"So he keeps you for himself?"

"Not really. He made it abundantly clear to me from the beginning that our relationship was strictly one of convenience and nothing more. He encouraged me to date around and have fun."

"So, did you?"

"I certainly did. It was fun for awhile but I get bored easily with men. You might prove to be that one exception."

Chapter 14

Bangkok, 2000

MILLINEUM craziness was taking place worldwide; an era of new beginnings for some societies and a period of doom and gloom for others. In Bangkok and all over Thailand, the majority of Thai's were anxious to enter the new century and what it would mean for them.

"How are you holding up, Henri?" Sno Moreau asked him.

"I'm getting tired," he said as they walked through the maze of their many friends and loyal customers.

"You should probably take me home now."

They were celebrating their twenty-fifth wedding anniversary with the loud and rambunctious crowd. They had planned the grand opening of their second restaurant in Bangkok several years ago to coincide with this once in a lifetime occurrence.

The House of Saigon was located near the Grand Palace complex in the central downtown area. Tourists visiting Wat Phra Kaeo, the first permanent structure in the city, would wander over to the Moreau's restaurant for an exceptional meal. Henri's neighbor worked for the local tourist bureau and had a unique way of steering customers to his friend's popular eating establishment.

Sno had a difficult time managing the two restaurants while tending to Henri. He suffered a stroke last year and his seventy-seven year old body was failing rapidly. He still carried around a bullet embedded in his upper thigh as a result of service with the French Foreign Legion years ago.

"I'll have you home by ten, my dear. We still need to greet a few more guests. The outpouring of warmth and fellowship we're experiencing tonight is a real tribute to you, Henri. You have developed a wonderful clientele over the years. You've satisfied one of their basic needs; well-prepared, wholesome food that everybody could afford."

"Thank you for the kind words, Sno. Unfortunately, I was not able to satisfy all your needs. I couldn't give you the child that you so desperately wanted. God only knows we tried but it just wasn't meant to be. Perhaps I was being punished for some of my early indiscretions which I certainly am not proud of."

"Please don't be too hard on yourself. We have been rewarded with a good life. We've made an outstanding team from the day you brought me in from that wretched encampment. Thank goodness the authorities burned down those miserable structures years ago."

They bid their farewells and left The House of Saigon at ten o'clock. Henri didn't feel well on the way home and asked their driver to pull off to the side of the road. He climbed out of the car.

"Henri, Henri, what's wrong with you?" she cried out. He didn't answer her and started walking ahead of and to the right of the vehicle. He began to stumble.

"Please get out of the car and go help him," she pleaded to their personal valet. He jumped from the driver's seat and raced after Henri who was disappearing out of sight. It was so dark and foggy that the headlights were useless. She lost both of them in the dark. Sno jumped from the car and caught up with the valet who was kneeling on the side of the ditch cradling Henri in his arms.

"What's wrong with him?" she cried.

"I don't know, he's hardly breathing."

"Do something, anything; you've got to help him."

The last few words Henri Louie Moreau ever spoke was indelibly etched in her mind. "I will always love you my sweet, dearest Sno."

Chapter 15

Chicago, 2007

ROD LIVED in two different apartments on the South Side during his first year in Chicago before leasing a one bedroom apartment on Division Street. He told Bradley Simmons that he wanted to become fully acclimated to Chicago before he started his full-time job as a private investigator. In reality he wanted to be closer to Angie to continue their relationship and see where it was headed.

He was lucky to find the unit conveniently located near a Jewel grocery store and the Red Line Transit. Bradley had recommended the area because it was relatively close to Simmons & Simmons Investigations.

Goethe Street near Churchill Corner in the fashionable Gold Coast quadrant was Rod's favorite neighborhood. Rich and famous urbanites populated this desirable neighborhood. Young professionals mixed readily with older retirees. On a sunny day one could witness an assortment of dogs traversing the sidewalks either leading or being lead by their owners. Cats were noticeably absent on most of the streets. Going to college and working part time doing menial odd jobs had kept him busy.

Rod was out stretching his legs, speed walking and slow jogging after a marathon night of studying for his P.I. exam. He was in a daze.

"Oops, I'm so sorry sir," pleaded the young lady knocking Rod almost to his feet as she raced around the corner. He spilled a half cup of Starbucks' finest on his sweaty t-shirt.

"Rambo is so hard to control at times. He doesn't have a slow gear in that little body. Bad boy, Rambo, where are your manners?"

"Does he bite?" Rod asked, duly concerned.

"He does, but only if you try to take his milk bone away from him," she laughed heartedly.

Rod liked the way she curled her lower lip when she smiled. She was likewise impressed in the way he showed his pearly white teeth. There was an immediate feeling of energy and electricity between them. He wasn't sure about the fat, squat dog; he hated dogs.

"My name is Torrie Strait. What's yours?"

"Rod Richards; did I hear you call the pooch, Rambo?"

"Yes you did. He's my one and only true love."

There was a pause while she attended to her four-legged guy.

Rod's mind began to wander back to his relationship with Angie Ward that had first developed during the cruise but had turned sour after they spent more time together in Chicago.

"I insist that we get married and we need to do it soon." The ultimatum soon followed. "Don't come around me anymore unless you're ready for the church."

He certainly enjoyed her company and the passion she so unselfishly bestowed on him. There was never a dull minute when he was around her but he wasn't committed enough to take that gigantic step. They decided to part ways.

Rambo's persistent yapping startled him back to reality.

"What kind of dog is he? I mean, what's his breed? I don't think I've ever seen this kind of dog before."

"He's part Sheltie and part Pomeranian and don't ask me how that mix of breeds ever came about. I found him wandering up and down my street for several days. He didn't have an ID tag so I brought him home with me."

Rambo was tugging hard on his leash, sniffing at the hind end of a cute poodle twice his size that just happened to stroll by. The poodle must have enjoyed the contact because she let Rambo's long nose do its thing.

[80]

"Bad dog!" shouted the old lady on the other end of the leash. "Can't you control that beast, young lady? It's people like you and that mutt who give our neighborhood a bad reputation."

Rod stared at her in disbelief.

She should talk, he thought. Hair in curlers, dentures missing and wearing a tattered stripped bathrobe to match her worn-out bathroom slippers...what a beauty!

"I apologize, ma'am," Torrie said, "He's going to obedience school right now and I promise he won't be a pest in the future."

All of a sudden the poodle became aggressive, turned around and snapped at the unsuspecting Rambo. Not to be outdone, Rambo let out a vicious growl and the poodle took off dragging the old lady down the wide sidewalk. The dog then ambled over to the corner and lifted his leg under the Churchill plaque. A yellow splotch appeared on the wall, snaked its way down the sidewalk and pooled in the street. Either the scent of the poodle was out of this world or Rambo hadn't been let out all day.

Torrie was embarrassed, at a loss for words and gave Rod a...what the hell look.

"I like him," he said. "He's definitely my kind of dog, won't take any crap from a thoroughbred. I'm in agreement with you that the obedience class will round him out a little, make him more of a social animal."

Rambo came over to him and started to lick his hand.

"Where do you live, Rod and what kind of work do you do?"

"I'm just a few blocks from here over on Division. Soon I will be a licensed private investigator. I'm knee deep in studies to take the qualifying exam."

"Oh my God, have you been following me around?"

"No way, I love to walk-jog in this area because I meet neat people like you."

She laughed in appreciation.

"So you're going to become a P.I., one of those guys who snoop on other people. My suspicious mother hired one of them to follow dad around and try to catch him with another woman. I'm not so sure I like these kinds of people prying on unsuspected human beings."

Rod laughed and continued to pet Rambo who seemed comfortable lying down on one of his smelly tennis shoes.

"No, Torrie, the company I work for specializes in finding missing persons. The owner determined long ago that this category of investigations was more meaningful and frankly, a lot more challenging than trailing some loser. You should see the look on the faces of the parents, husbands or wives and even relatives when we bring home one of their loved ones. It's gratifying to us who have experienced family tragedies."

"Oh, that's different, Rod. I think I would like 'People Finder' as the job description. Are you married?"

He wasn't sure about this young and attractive lady. She was a prober and he normally held personal information close to his vest. However, there was something special about her that attracted him besides her good looks and slim build. He decided to take the offensive.

"Nope, I'm not hitched. How about you? Where are your digs and do you work or go to school?"

"I have an efficiency apartment further down Goethe. It's really cute and Rambo has his own niche in the little kitchen because I don't cook much. He slobbers whenever he laps up his water so nothing gets on my carpets. Well, not much anyway. If I decide to hit the library after night school I have a problem with Rambo. He can't hold it until I get home."

"Tell me about yourself, Torrie."

"I'm sorry. Sometimes I get carried away about my buddy here. I go to college downtown and will get my associate degree in business administration in three more months. I want to become a full-time stock broker. Wall Street and the stock markets enthrall me. I believe that capitalism is where it's all at, wouldn't you agree?"

[82]

"I do, sort of, unless you want to live in Cuba or Russia. Do you also have a job to support your ambitions?"

"Certainly, I've been working for two years at a small brokerage house run by a Vietnamese guy who is doing well. I'll be taking my required security exams about the same time you take your qualifying exams to become a P.I. There, I have spoken; we both have something in common now."

This lady is interesting, talks a little too much but seems sincere. I think she's interested in me from what I can determine...worth pursuing.

Rambo was now snoring at his feet, having taken over both of the dirty tennis shoes. Torrie put her hands on her hips and glanced at his spotted t-shirt noticing the coffee stains.

"I've got to run now. Give me a call some day and I'll spring for a Starbucks' latte to replace the one you're wearing on your t-shirt."

They exchanged business cards; their hands touched and he thought that hers lingered a little longer than normal. He agreed to call her Saturday night.

"We could catch a few drinks and have dinner down on Rush Street. I frequent a place I know you'd like. I'll pick you up at six."

"You got a date, Rod Prichards."

"It's Richards."

"Sorry, I'm not that good with names."

He heard some commotion down the street and saw the witch with the white poodle heading back their way. He quickly but softly edged Rambo off his shoes and bid her a warm farewell.

"I look forward to seeing you Saturday, Torrie Strait."

"Me too, I'm impressed that you remembered my name."

Rambo saw the French menace approaching. The animal started to show his teeth. Rod slipped away, not wanting to get into the middle of another confrontation, especially one involving two stupid dogs and one old maniac owner.

He needed to return to the garage where he rented a slot for his Honda, a parking space he was lucky to find so close to his apartment. The car needed an oil change and tire rotation. It also needed a new battery; it died last week in the middle of busy Michigan Avenue in heavy traffic.

Oh for the joys of big city living, I love it! It'll take some more adjustment for me as I'm not used to living in mega-cities like Chicago. The city has a different and more exciting ambience than the relatively sleepy city of San Antonio. I like this neighborhood and who knows, maybe developing a relationship with one of the residents!

Chapter 16

SIMMONS & SIMMONS INVESTIGATIONS was situated on the top floor of an office building on Halsted Street with an outstanding view of the Belmont Harbor and the Chicago Yacht Club. The twelfth floor where Bradley Simmons had his suite of offices was formerly an open-spaced storage warehouse for a department store that occupied the first five stories of the old building.

"Wow, what a fantastic view," Rod said on his first full day of work. He had stopped by periodically to visit with Bradley during the past year either at his home or at a restaurant convenient to them both. The sun was bathing the roof tops of neighboring buildings with a bright golden hue. Bradley was dressed in a checkered pair of outlandish knickers. He led Rod to the back library where they stood in front of a bay window with a panoramic view of Lake Michigan and a sweeping stretch from Lincoln Park all the way down to Navy Pier.

"You get what you pay for, Rod."

"Tell me something I don't know."

"It cost me a mint to renovate this old warehouse and convert it into decent office space. You will notice my office is on the same side of the building as the library so I have the great view. Your office and those of our other two investigators are on the opposite side facing that ugly brown brick monstrosity with boarded up windows."

"Is there some callous reason for that?"

"Nope," Bradley chuckled, "But it might serve as an incentive to get off one's butt and get out there, hit the streets and bring in some caes."

"I get the message loud and clear. I didn't see the secretary's office when I came in. Where's she located?"

"There is no 'she' person around here, we don't have a secretary. We all do our own clerical work; cuts down on the overhead."

"But I'm not proficient in the word processing arena," Rod chimed in. "Going back to school did bring me up to date somewhat with all the fancy bells and whistles students use now-a-days. I guess I can bone up more at home on my new laptop."

"Sure you can, and you will. We don't want anybody on our work force that could jeopardize our confidential dealings. The typical secretary is unskilled in matters of security. We had one when I first opened up and it was a disaster. The other guys don't complain so get comfortable with it."

"I saw a bunk bed in the back room where you store some supplies. What's that all about?"

"We work odd hours around here. I live in Lake Forest and sometimes just sleep here instead of heading home late at night. It works well when I'm locked into an early morning meeting down in The Loop. Your little apartment over there on Division is convenient for you so I don't expect you sacking out here."

Rod was staring out the window and glad he didn't have to drive to work every day. There was a six car pileup on Lake Shore Drive which stalled traffic as far back as he could see.

Bradley observed him and laughed, "Get used to it, some days it looks like a demolition derby out there."

The telephone rang in Bradley's office and he went back to answer it.

"Well screw you, mate," a shrill voice sang out from his office.

Rod didn't recall seeing anyone in the chief's office when he walked by it earlier. Perhaps somebody just walked in.

He plunked down in one of the four comfortable chairs in the library which took up almost one half of the entire office space on the east side of the building. An oak conference table was located in the center of the room. He noticed that the overstuffed chair he sat in and the other three had rollers which enabled them to be placed at the conference table thus serving a dual purpose. A fax machine, printer and four computers were located at the far wall of the library.

"Son of a bitch," moaned Bradley ten minutes later when he returned from the phone call.

"What's up, boss? Who the hell was that screaming in your office?"

"I forgot to tell you about Graybeard. When I was in Panama for jungle training back in my Army days the Panamanian scout leader carried around a big blue parrot on his shoulder. We were all enthralled by the bird. He sang, cursed up a storm and chewed out all of us whenever he saw us each morning. He was amazing! I swore I'd get one of my own when I had the chance. Years later when I opened my office I wired back to Panama and had the old scout send me one; cost me a damn fortune."

"Was it worth it?"

"No."

"Is the bird a male or female?"

"Funny you ask that question."

"Why's that?"

"According to my contact back in Panama, Graybeard belonged to one of those old time pilots who guided the big ships through the locks of the canal. He got it from a retired sea-faring captain and was told that Graybeard was a male bird. The pilot put another male in the cage for companionship and to keep Graybeard from squawking all the time. Before too long there was a baby bird that hatched in the cage."

"What the...?"

"Right, either Graybeard is a female and that other bird a male or visa-versa. Nobody knew for sure or cared to have it checked out. Bottom line, I don't know the sex of that crazy bird back there in the cage nor do I really care."

"Suit yourself. Who was that on the phone?"

"It was Irene Finerty, the big time Chicago cop who hired me to keep an eye on her cousin, Angie Ward. She called to thank me for the report; said the check was in the mail."

"Sounds like good news to me," Rod laughed. "Whoever complains about getting paid?"

"Well, she dropped a big time bomb on me that I can't defuse."

"What the hell does that mean?"

"It means that we have to move in a little different direction for the time being. She confirmed what Paul Keller told us that night in the Port Caller lounge."

"Refresh my memory. We discussed many things in the lounge. You and Paul had tipped a few too many! Is this the infidelity issue we talked about?"

"Yes, Irene is officially hiring me to tail her brother for a month or so. She's convinced now more than ever that Shamus Fenerty is cheating on his wife. A male friend of hers who works for the Transportation Security Administration at O'Hare spilled the beans. He told Irene that Shamus periodically hooks up with a gorgeous blond arriving Chicago on one of the flights from the West Coast. It's easy to recognize Shamus; his face is plastered in the Trib almost monthly."

Rod recalled seeing an article about Shamus and the fact that some local big wigs were pushing him to run for governor.

"Who's the chick?"

Bradley whistled. "The TSA guy told Irene that the blond is to die for! Her screen name in Hollywood is Candi. She doesn't go by any last name; another Cher type."

"So what, that sounds pretty routine to me, the tailing part that is. You performed admirably on the cruise for Finerty by shadowing Angie wherever she wandered."

"That's another story, different set of circumstances and fairly easy to accomplish. This request could be explosive and possibly dangerous. We're not dealing with the average Joe Citizen here."

Rod sat back with interest, enjoying Bradley's enthusiasm about the assignment. Bradley went on to explain in great detail the nature of the case.

"Irene's older brother, the Shamus Fenerty that I mentioned is the CEO and majority owner of All-State Trucking Enterprises located in one of the western suburbs near O'Hare. The company is extremely successful and made Shamus a multi-millionaire. He lives in a colonial style mansion in Highland Park with his wife Lois and two teenage sons."

"He sure is a biggie!" Rod commented.

"Shamus is politically wired and known throughout the Chicago area as a big philanthropist. He contributes heavily to the Democratic Party. The cancer wing of a local medical center is named after him. Rumor has it he could be the next governor of the state."

"I have two questions," Rod interrupted before his boss could paint the entire picture. "Why is he a *Fenerty* and his sister a *Finerty*? Secondly, why is she even involved in his personal life and dropping this rat's nest on your door step?"

"Good questions, I'll break it down for you. He was born in Chicago and the Cook County Clerk processing his legal birth certificate failed to correct the last name discrepancy from the records sent over by the hospital. His parents didn't look twice at the birth certificate when they stashed it away. He went with the Finerty name all through his adolescence."

"I'm with you so far."

"His mother became a combative drunk over time and his father resorted to beating her whenever she tipped the bottle too much. Shamus tried to protect her but he too suffered from the indignity and sting of the leather belt. He ran away from home during his sophomore year of high school and lived for a few years in old freight train boxcars and under just about every freeway bridge in the Midwest. He wanted nothing more to do with his biological parents."

"This is an interesting story, sounds like he could've been my best friend back in St. Louis who suffered through the same rough and tumble upbringing. Shamus is unique in several ways."

"Please go on, Bradley, this sounds like a chapter from one of Vince Flynn's novels."

"The perfect opportunity presented itself when Shamus befriended an old veteran living on the streets who encouraged him to join the military. Through some miracle his sister Irene was able to find his original birth certificate with the Fenerty name and sent it to him. He took it to the County Court House wanting to register for the draft. The Vietnam War was long over and the draft had ended. The clerk suggested he visit an Army recruiting office to talk to them about enlisting in the service."

"Well, what more could a mouth-watering recruiter ask for, right?" Rod mocked. He remembered how he was "lured" into service.

"Correct; the recruiting sergeant saw a chance to pad his enlistment quota for the month and convinced Shamus to find two friends to join him in the 'buddy system' program. Supposedly in those days you and your buddies got your choice of assignments and the assurance your friends would stay with you throughout the entire enlistment. After two nights of steady drinking, Shamus strong-armed not only two but three others to go in to the Army with him and they all served a three year hitch. Shamus came out a three-striper."

"Wow, and look at him now…a big wheel and well-respected citizen," Rod commented. "How did Irene Finerty handle the disjointed family situation?"

"She was much younger than her brother and was shipped off to be raised by an aunt in another state. She kept the Finerty name. Irene was a superb student and earned a scholarship to Northwestern University, after which she joined the Chicago PD and became one-of-a-kind in solving complicated crimes."

Rod was in awe at the story, reflected for a few minutes and then said, "Now I know where I heard her name. It just popped into my head. She was called in by the San Antonio Metro Police Department to assist them in solving a complex murder case. An embedded C.I.A. agent was viciously slain in the hospital that I took over after the incident."

"Irene also thought she'd remembered your name from that investigation. She was a sorority sister of Lois at Northwestern and double-dated with her many times both during college and afterwards. They remained close friends. One Christmas she brought Lois to her aunt's home in Iowa. It was shortly after Shamus got out of the Army and was living at the time with the aunt. He and Lois hit it off big time and the rest is history."

"Thank you for filling me in on the interesting background but I ask you one more time; why did Irene contact you in particular? There are many other investigative agencies in the greater Chicago area that could do the job."

"Irene has referred many cases over to us in the past that the Police Department felt was beyond their prerogative to handle. She knows we are the best P.I. agency in town and fully able to handle high profile cases without any adverse publicity."

"When are you going to start on it, Bradley?"

"I'm not, you are."

"Hold on here, Lone Ranger! Why me? I'm not even licensed yet. I can't legally carry a gun."

Bradley laughed at his uneasiness.

"This isn't a 'Dirty Harry' shoot-em-up like in the movies, for Christ's sake, partner. You've done a lot of surveillance work while in the service. I know it; you know it so this should be a breeze for you."

"But why can't you or one of the other guys in the office with more experience handle it? I'm almost ready to take my P.I. licensure exams and am afraid this might complicate or even delay it."

Bradley was getting a slow burn. He knew Rod well enough but didn't understand why he was so hesitant to jump-start his career on such an interesting case.

Has he lost some of his get up and go? I don't believe this guy.

"Here's why I'm assigning the case to you. Shamus knows me and the other two investigators because we've also done some work for him and his company in the past, primarily checking out character references. Irene knows this and was initially concerned with me putting you on the case. I convinced her that you were a seasoned professional and would wrap it up in record time."

There were several moments of silence. Rod was in deep thought. Bradley had him over a barrel. He hadn't done much challenging work before he began his full-time employment with Simmons & Simmons.

Well, this is what I bought into. It seems far-fetched, not like managing an apartment complex or running a mental health hospital. Oh, what the hell, go for it!

"Thanks for the confidence in me. When do I start?"

"There is a confidential folder sitting on your desk. Here's the key to your office and another one that opens our surveillance equipment closet. When you have time, inventory every item in there. The equipment and gear is top-shelf, believe me."

Rod suppressed a grin. "I wouldn't expect anything less."

"I locked the office last night for fear the other guys might go in there and see the dossier. I don't want them to know what you are doing. If they ask, tell them you have more class work and additional study before you're ready for the big P.I. test. They'll understand; both of them flunked it the first time."

"What the hell! Why are they still here?"

"I'm just kidding you! They're both lawyer types and passed their bar exams with ease. Neither of them studied a day for the P.I. exam."

"Why aren't they out there lawyering?"

"One of these days I'll fill you in on that but for the time being, let's just say it's my infectious personality that drew them to me and the art of 'P.I.ing' around this great city."

They both laughed. Rod was more relaxed. He liked Bradley's sense of humor but certainly not the ridiculous outfit he was wearing.

Bradley got off his chair and came around to the door. "Let me introduce you to the other brain trusts around here."

After the introductions and small talk, they all went out to lunch at an Italian restaurant down the street. Rod liked the other two investigators. The tall dark Hispanic guy named Jorge played basketball at Northern Illinois. He wore a do-rag on the top of his head to semi-control the deadlocks. He stood six-eight and because of his easy going demeanor, nobody suspected him of being an investigator.

"I remember going down there to see your old college team play a game shortly after I got here," Rod said. "A nephew of mine from St. Louis is currently enrolled at your school."

The stubby Jewish gent who preferred to be called Saul, wrestled his way through Notre Dame, allegedly both on the mat and academically. Not to be outmatched by his tall cohort, he wore a multi-colored yarmulke.

"What do we call these guys...Mutt and Jeff?" Rod chided.

"How about...Curley and Moe?" Jorge said with a deep laugh. He took the comment in good humor. Saul nodded in agreement with a big grin.

They were at least twenty years younger than both Rod and Bradley. The two associates didn't hesitate giving both of them a hard time on every issue that came up for discussion over the ample serving of spaghetti and meatballs.

Rod decided to leave work early and grabbed the Red Line over at Belmont. He took the confidential file home with him. He planned to finish his review after an early light dinner with Torrie. He was still full from lunch. She would be excited about his first assignment although she would never know the real mission. He would keep her guessing.

Chapter 17

Bangkok

SNO MOREAU was advised that she needed to visit the Citizenship and Immigration Services in the U.S. Homeland Security Office located next to the Embassy in Bangkok. The world had changed drastically in the past five years with the horrendous assault on the United States of America by the Muslim radicals. The entire world was put on notice and new security measures were implemented everywhere, even in far flung Bangkok. Sno hoped to receive the necessary clearance to apply for an immigrant visa. She hated to fight the heavy traffic to get to the Sindhorn Building, especially during the rainy season.

"But I don't want to wait for the outcome of a green card diversity lottery, sir. I realize the chances of getting that quickly are low. I want a visa as soon as possible so I can travel to Chicago, Illinois and see my son. I've waited long enough."

"Please be a little more patient, Mrs. Moreau, it shouldn't take that long," said the Consulate representative. "I feel this is the best course of action for you."

"I'm so frustrated, sir, it's taken so long to process my request to go to America."

"Yes, I fully understand but you have to bear with us. I do see that all of your paperwork is in order. Hopefully in several short months you'll be on your way."

She left the building dispirited and alone but she was not about to give up. It was time for her to begin planning for the relocation. Sno spoke fluent English and was a confident, worldly-educated woman which would ease her transition to another foreign country. She spent hours at night studying U.S. customs, laws and regulations and sometimes slept with a map of Chicago.

The following week one of her close childhood friends from Saigon was in Bangkok on business and looked her up. She was able to locate Sno after much difficulty. They had a happy reunion and the friend elected to stay the night with her. They talked for hours on end.

"We should have gone with you and your mother when you traveled out of Saigon back in 1975. It was pure hell living under the new regime. They took everything we owned away from us."

"Yes, I heard all about that. The sad part of our escape from Saigon was mother dying in that jungle. Her horrible death was a real shock to me. I had to dig deep down to find the inner strength and resolve to go on in life without her!"

Sno told her friend about a hand-written letter she received several months ago from her aged uncle in Ho Chih Minh City. She was sure that her friend knew of his reputation.

"I'll bet that made you happy. No doubt you thought he was certainly dead by now."

"Yes I did. I was excited when I received it. He had to pull some strings but found out through unnamed sources that my son Chien Tran was finally airlifted out of Saigon in 1975 at the last possible moment. An earlier flight of the poor orphans crashed shortly after takeoff but my Chien was destined for greatness. He said that Chien ended up in one of three cities in the United States but couldn't pinpoint the exact city."

"And what cities were the orphans evacuated to?"

"He told me in the letter that Chicago was one for sure and possibly Seattle but nobody could find out the name of the third city. Some said New York, others told him Philadelphia. I finally went on the internet and found several Tran names in Illinois and only one Tran family in Seattle. After exhausting my last bit of patience I was able to locate a Chien Tran in the greater Chicago area."

[95]

"Why didn't you try and make direct contact with him?"

"Oh no, I couldn't do that. He doesn't know me and I wouldn't want to embarrass him. I want to be able to explain everything to him in person. I'll figure it out when I get over there."

"What do you intend to do to while you're searching for your son in Chicago?"

"I'm going to open another restaurant. Henri left me with considerable financial resources. I just can't get over my love for preparing delicious food for thankful customers. If I've learned anything in the years that Henri and I have operated our restaurants it's how to satisfy the basic needs of people. In my opinion, food ranks near the top of that list."

The day after her friend left the city, she put both The House of Saigon and the Cordon Bleu up for sale. She knew their worth in the competitive restaurant marketplace. The sales agent specialized in retail eating establishments and they soon came to an agreement on the selling price. Two small restaurant companies were interested in buying her out. In addition, several other friends who operated restaurants in the city asked her to contact them first before she sold out.

The Bangkok economy was on an upward spiral and Sno was sure that she would be out from under the properties in no time. She read and reread copies of the Chicago Tribune she had subscribed to. They usually arrived in a week or two. Of particular interest to her were the business and real estate sections of the paper.

"What are you going to do if we sell the properties before you get your green card?" the agent asked one day while they were having tea.

"That would be wonderful; the sooner the better."

"No, I mean where would you stay?"

"Why, with you of course. I love your home, it reminds of the sacred temple in the middle of Bangkok!" They both laughed and clicked their tea cups together.

Two months later Sno got a call from the U.S. Consulate Office. "Are you ready to go to America, Mrs. Moreau?"

"Yes sir," she cried out.

Later that same day her realtor came into her restaurant with a full price offer. Sno could not believe her good fortune.

"Don't get your hopes up too soon. We need to run this through the system and make sure that we can finalize the transaction. We've already checked them out and they certainly qualify financially. In fact, they could probably buy yours and two others in Bangkok without blinking an eye."

That evening Sno sat in the Cordon Bleu remembering her years in the restaurant.

"Are you going to bring me to America when you get settled?" asked Petri who was busy washing and slicing vegetables.

Petri and Sno had developed an unusual relationship over the years. When Henri Moreau died she lingered with his casket at the funeral after the private memorial service. Petri hung around also. He offered his assistance in whatever matter she needed help.

Her dear Henri Louie taught him everything about how to run a successful business and the many social skills that Petri lacked from years working in the fields. The man had kept his distance from her throughout the years.

"Am I going to whisk you over there when I'm settled? What an interesting question. You are married with family. How could I ever do such a thing to your loved ones without carrying a ton of guilt in my heart the rest of my life?"

"You too are a part of my family, Sno. I couldn't have succeeded without your and Henri's help. Promise me that you'll send for me and my family when you become rich and famous like you've become here."

"I won't promise you a thing. My goal the remaining years of my life is to find my son and reunite with him and whatever family he may have. You know you love your life here and furthermore, your English is awful."

Petri soberly nodded in agreement.

"You need to remember one important thing, Sno, he may totally reject you. You abandoned a tiny defenseless baby years ago in Saigon. If you find him he may well hold that against you."

"You're not the first to tell me that. I'm prepared for any eventuality. I'm stubborn beyond all doubt. You of all people should have learned that!"

She almost fell in love with Petri after Henri passed away. He came around often to see how she was doing. They would hold hands and talk for hours. She yearned for the physical contact that only a man could provide. Henri had lost all desire and the capability of having sex early on in their marriage. He tried his best to give her what she so desperately required back then but to no avail. She remained faithful to him to the day they lowered him in the ground.

"I promise I'll always keep in touch with you," Sno said sincerely.

"Please do that." He was remorseful and hated to see her leave Bangkok and the wonderful closeness they held for each other.

Maybe, just maybe one day we will reunite again. My family is no longer an issue ever since my wife left me some time ago. Sno Moreau was never aware of this fact. I will never forget her!

Chapter 18

"THANK YOU so much for the referral," Sno Moreau said after attending her last church ceremony in Bangkok. The high priest was knowledgeable about former Vietnamese citizens residing in Thailand who immigrated to Chicago and had furnished Sno with much information. He had traveled to Illinois himself on several occasions in the past. Three weeks later she would be on a Thai Airways International flight to Los Angeles. She would overnight there and catch a United Airline non-stop flight to Chicago.

Sno finally deplaned in Chicago, cleared customs and was happy she had pre-booked a stay at the O'Hare Airport Hilton Hotel before venturing off to the big city. There was a major difference between Central Standard Time and that of Bangkok and she needed to catch up on some sleep and also to get grounded. She had envisioned the Chicago area as being busy but had no idea of the speed within which everything around here moved. She had major jet lag and needed to adjust to the new reality.

She had been advised to contact the ministry at the New Age Buddhist Church of Mahayana for assistance when she arrived in Chicago. They would recommend several realtor agents to assist her in finding the best place to live in the city. She found the church on the internet and confirmed with the hotel which western suburb of Chicago it was located in. She hailed a cab from the Hilton and headed over there without an appointment.

"Good morning, please come into the foyer," said the receptionist at the church office. "Here in America our lamas are addressed as 'priests' in case you were wondering what to call him. It's a slight accommodation that was made to our being here in the Western World. Our minister is tied up right now but I know he would absolutely love to visit with you. May I offer you a cup of tea while you wait?"

"Thank you; I would love a cup of hot tea. It's pretty chilly outside. I guess I'll have to get used to the weather here."

After an hour of waiting the church leader came into the reception room to greet Sno in Vietnamese. It was great to talk in her native tongue after so long. She was also pleasantly surprised; the priest was dressed informally and wearing sneakers. She was quick to note that he was so tall and handsome.

"I am so sorry to keep you waiting. I was with an architect reviewing the plans for our expansion. You wouldn't believe the number of Vietnamese people relocating to our area. My associate back in Bangkok wired me that you might be stopping by."

They reconvened to a small library behind the reception area. He signaled for her to sit in one of the overstuffed chairs while he sat in a chair behind a small desk. There were three colorful paintings depicting life in Saigon at the turn of the century. They both glanced over at the paintings at the same time.

"Gone are the simple days of living one's life in a beautiful country," he remarked. "There are days that I wish I was a young child again, living comfortably in my parent's home, even though my soldier father was gone most of the time."

They talked on and on for over an hour, rehashing their childhoods. The receptionist came in with a plate of cookies and more hot tea.

"Sir, are you aware that you have another appointment in ten minutes?"

"Thanks for reminding me and thanks for the cookies. You are so thoughtful. We shouldn't be too much longer."

Sno felt comfortable enough to share her early history including having a baby out of wedlock and that she relinquished the boy to the nuns at a local orphanage. She also related the story about the big baby-lift that took place when Saigon was being captured by the North Vietnamese. When she began to describe their escape from Saigon and the dangerously long jungle trek to Thailand he quickly interrupted her.

"Hold on here. I have a burning question to ask you. By any chance were you and your mother in that small group that was led out of Saigon by a high priest who was also a medicine man and an older soldier who acted as guide?"

"Yes, we were. Why do you ask?"

"You won't believe this. I was also in that group. My father was Captain Quan who acted as the guide. He served our former government with distinction and protected our courageous leader before he abdicated his presidency. My father was his driver and personal bodyguard."

"I'm shocked. Your receptionist never mentioned your name. Even if she had, I'm not sure that I would've picked up the connection. So you were one of those young boys who were always getting in trouble along the wretched way through the jungle, right?"

He sat back in his chair, folded his arms, clasped his hands together and then looked her straight in the eyes.

"I was one of the idiots who crushed those big leeches that squirted your mother's blood on your legs. I hope you'll forgive me for admitting to such a gross injustice."

She gasped; vividly remembering the scene that took place that day. She hated both of those boys. Before she had a chance to respond the receptionist came back to the library.

"The realtor is here, sir. Shall I bring her into the library?"

"Yes, go ahead and send her in here."

"Sno, I want you to meet Li Chong," the priest said as the realtor came in. "She is a Chicago realtor who is familiar with the housing needs of our immigrant friends. From time to time we ask Li to help us assist them in their transition to Chicago. I trust she will be helpful for you."

Sno and Li clasped hands and sat down on the couch across from the small desk. She noted that Li was overdressed and much too old to be wearing a tight skirt that showed more hip than she probably realized.

Priest Quan excused himself to allow the two of them to discuss their plans. He was embarrassed to have told Sno about his actions in the jungle. He'd hope she forgave him long ago, especially after his father safely escorted her to Bangkok.

"Thank you so much for your hospitality and help in my case," Sno said to him when he stepped back into the room. "I trust we'll meet again now that we share so much in common."

He acknowledged her kind words and then excused himself. Li Chong and Sno finished their meeting and left the ministry. She dropped her client off back at the Hilton. They arranged to meet again the next day after Sno had a chance to relax and get organized for the task ahead.

The following morning Sno boarded the Blue Line at the airport and rode it downtown into Union Station. Juggling all of her luggage was a real burden but she found a way to handle it. By prearrangement, she met Li Chong at the McDonald's inside the train station.

"I have dedicated the entire day to show you around. We'll find you a nice place to live."

They flagged a taxi to take them back to the parking garage where Li had left her car. They then headed over to Michigan Avenue where the realtor proudly announced all the neat shops and restaurants along the way. Sno wasn't interested in a geography lesson and was anxious to start looking for an apartment.

"Are we almost there yet?" Sno asked in a frustrated manner.

"Yes, be patient. Let me tell you about Little Saigon."

"I already like it."

"It's located in the Uptown Community area of Chicago and mostly populated by people with Vietnamese and Cambodian heritage, many of whom became refugees during the Sino-Vietnamese war of the late 1970s. New Chinatown is actually the next neighborhood over from Little Saigon. That's where I live."

She had already targeted the Little Saigon location to begin her search for Chien Tran. She was so excited to start but had to remind herself that it could take a long time and there's always the possibility that he wouldn't be living in the Chicago area. Her initial internet search didn't specifically reveal a Chien Tran in Little Saigon. For all she knew he could even be dead. Regardless of the situation she was determined to leave no stone unturned until she found the answer.

"When we get to Little Saigon I'll show you some apartments off of Broadway that should suit your purpose. The 'L' is nearby on Argyle and you can easily take the Red Line into the city proper whenever you want to."

"Are there many 'Bui Doi' living around here?" Sno asked her as they toured around the small community.

"Yes, but we commonly refer to them as Amerasians here in the United States," Chong said biting her tongue. "The American soldiers fighting in that unpopular war found plenty of time off to impregnate your young ladies! Why do you ask? Is there a problem?"

"No, there is not! I know there were many of them cared for in orphanages back in my old country. Hundreds of them were airlifted to the U.S. before the fall of Saigon."

I'm not ready to tell this Chinese lady that I had a son with a handsome proud black soldier when I was a young girl and who now is classified as a so-called Amerasian.

"I think the greater Broadway area is a good idea," Sno said. "I heard that there are a lot of restaurants along Broadway and the several streets that intersect with it. I'm anxious to try every one of the eating places."

"Your referral sheet says that you owned two restaurants in Bangkok. Did they both offer Vietnamese food?"

"No, the Cordon Bleu was primarily French with a little twist of Vietnamese. The House of Saigon consisted mainly of food from my home country with a sprinkling of Thai choices on the menu. We had to appease the locals you know."

"I bet you're a wonderful chef," Li commented. "We have some fine culinary schools in the Chicago area that you may want to visit or even

[103]

attend. The Washburne Culinary Institute is one of them. You may have read about the school."

"No, I've only heard of the Culinary Institute in New York."

The realtor was really interested in her client's background. Her contact at the ministry had told her in an earlier conversation that this lady coming from Bangkok was not your typical green card person. She was radiant, classy and had lots of money.

Maybe I should be showing her around in Streeterville or the Near North neighborhoods, Li surmised but the lady insisted on Little Saigon so here we are. I could make much more in commissions if she settled on one of the more expensive estates.

"There is one skill that I'm lacking which could benefit from such a school. The baking and pastry component of the culinary arts is where I might fall a little short. I spent most of my later years in the operational aspects of running two big food establishments and it took me further and further away from the kitchen. If I have the time I'll check them out," she said trying to be polite.

She really had no intention of going back to school but played along with the discussion. She also concluded that this lady was asking way too many personal questions.

Li Chong took her over to Argyle Street, then down Broadway to Lawrence Avenue. They stopped and looked at several apartment units in the vicinity until Sno found one that she liked. It was a small rental unit with one-bedroom but large enough to accommodate the furniture and other goods she shipped from Bangkok. She knew she should have sold everything over there but couldn't part with the pieces her husband had originally brought from France. She didn't want a total disconnect.

"So, this will work for you?" They were parked outside the building.

"Yes, let's go back inside and make it happen."

The management completed all of the paperwork which turned out to be simple enough in Sno's mind. Back in Bangkok it would've taken a week to accomplish everything even with a lot of back-handedness. It didn't hurt that she was carrying one thousand U.S. dollars in her purse. She learned long ago how to get things moving!

"I'm going to drop you off at a nearby hotel where I made reservations for you. That apartment you selected was a good choice. I know you'll be comfortable there; I know the manager. It's actually only two miles or so away from the hotel. I'll let you know when you can move in. You may have to rent a few pieces of furniture from 'Rooms to Go' until you get your shipment in. Just contact the apartment manager tomorrow and he can get it done for you."

Chong dropped her off in front of the hotel and sped away. Sno checked in and soon crashed. The time change coming from Asia was still a challenge to her.

She went back to Broadway the next afternoon and found a small, intimate restaurant which was just what she needed. It was crowded with early lunch patrons. She was starved but would wait for a seat to open up. It was worth the wait. She loved the meal.

"Well, how do you like our food, Mrs. Moreau?" asked the chef at Bo Tan's restaurant. She had given one of her old business cards to the hostess who subsequently passed it on to the chef after she was seated.

"It's absolutely wonderful. Please give my regards to the chef."

"I am the chef, chief bottle washer and happen to be the owner of this fine establishment. I thank you for the complement. The shrimp is flown in live every morning and we don't let the little wigglers live another day," he laughed.

She enjoyed talking to the courteous owner. He was also handsome.

"I'm sure you saw our live crab over there. Next time you come in to my place I'll fix you the best tasting Crab Louie you've ever had."

Sno shot up in her chair. She turned white. The mere mention of the word "Louie" hit her square in the face. She hadn't completely forgotten about her dear departed husband, Louie Henri Moreau, who always went by the middle name in honor of his father.

[105]

"Is anything wrong; something I said?" the chef asked with great sincerity. "If so, Mrs. Moreau, I apologize for my poor choice of words."

"No sir, nothing is wrong, I was just reminded of something near and dear to my heart that I left behind in Thailand."

She settled up with the cashier and left Bo Tan's. She wanted to walk the entire neighborhood and check out restaurants. Someday she planned to get back into the food business, knowing it would be difficult, if not impossible to own and operate a business outright.

Well let them stop me! I'll not let anything or anyone throw up a wall that I can't tear down. My entire life has been one of great challenges. Yes, I'm in a foreign country but it will be my country soon and I won't stop until I find my son. From my research I'm certain he's somewhere in the area. On top of everything else I will own the most popular Vietnamese restaurant in Chicago!

Chapter 19

SHAMUS FENERTY was a two-time all-Big Ten linebacker for the fighting Illini and known for his hard-hitting tackles and equally feisty disposition. Initially he walked on at Illinois with no scholarship in hand but fortunate to have the G.I. Bill as the result of his military service. Eventually he earned a free ride because of his outstanding play.

He was older and probably more worldly-wise than his teammates because of his Army hitch. The cute co-eds who normally coveted popular athletes steered clear of Shamus. His "on-the-gridiron" personality carried over to most of his social activities. Standing six-four and carrying around two hundred forty-five pounds of muscle he became an enforcer for one of the area labor unions in his early working career before building his trucking empire. He really didn't care for unions but they paid him well.

"That's him getting into the black stretch Lincoln," Bradley said. "That's their maid behind them hauling out the trash."

"Nice digs."

They were positioned down the street from Fenerty's mansion in a Buick Regal from Hertz. Bradley never used the same vehicle twice when performing a reconnaissance. He told Rod he would accompany him on the initial familiarization run, then it was all his.

"He has his own limo and driver who sometimes takes his sons to sporting events and the movies. As you can tell from his physical appearance, Shamus should be able to take care of himself. He still plays touch football with some of his old teammates on weekends and I use the word 'touch' rather lightly."

Rod pulled down his binoculars. "I've never seen such flaming red hair before in my life. Does this guy dye it or what?"

"Not on your life."

I dare not tell Rod that I have my own hair dyed and tinted on a regular basis. He'd be the last person I'd tell about going to a beauty salon for my weekly haircuts!

"He wore his long hair in a ponytail when I first met him at a local fund drive luncheon but Lois finally got through to him that it wasn't consistent with their so-called 'social stratum' for him to wear it that way."

"Where do you think he's heading out this late in the afternoon? Shouldn't he still be at work?"

"Not necessarily. Lois sent Irene a copy of his work schedule for the next two weeks. She left yesterday to attend a week-long conference in D.C. Lois is a well-known psychiatrist in private practice here and active with the American Psychiatric Association. Irene told me she is heading up one of the panels discussing the alarming trend of marital infidelity among senior partners. I'd say that's a subject pretty close to her heart."

"Let's follow him and see where he's going," Rod suggested.

"No, I just wanted you to see his mansion, maybe some of his help and get a feel for the neighborhood. I suggest you begin your surveillance here, it's far enough away from his home so shouldn't be a problem."

Rod thought it would be better served to tail him from work. He wondered why a person would be promiscuous in his own home with the hired help and two sons running around the place. The neighbors could pick up on a juicy story if they noticed a gorgeous woman coming and going with Fenerty.

Bradley broke the silence. "Irene is convinced that Max Schnel, the limo driver brings him to wherever he does his thing. The guy is loyal to Shamus."

"What's the history between the two?"

"He once drove for All-State Trucking Enterprises. One winter night Max's rig jack-knifed on an ice slick causing it to careen off the Tri-State. He was seriously injured in the accident, breaking both arms and snapping his femur in half. He lay in the ditch for a long time before the medics

[108]

arrived and stopped the bleeding. They were concerned that he'd almost bled out. Max let his health insurance lapse months before the accident but Shamus jumped in and paid over a half million to help him out."

"I'd damn well be pretty loyal to Fenerty for forking over so much dough for coming to the aid of an employee."

They headed back to the office circling the block several more times. Rod decided to return the following evening and begin surveillance. He wanted to find the best location to set up his listening post and map out alternative escape routes if caught in a bind. He didn't like the location his boss suggested.

Bradley had just taken a call from Irene Finerty. She forgot to tell him that the Fenerty boys were away at an Eagle Scout camp in Wisconsin. They were on Spring break from their prep school. Rod was convinced that this situation presented a unique opportunity for the big redhead to engage in a little extra-curricular activity.

They got back to Simmons & Simmons and Bradley told him to hang on to the rental. He would park it over at Torrie's place for the night after they ate dinner. She had a little cut-out space on the side driveway of her apartment. It was easy to maneuver the little car into the slot whenever he drove over to see her.

"Why are you so fidgety tonight, Rod?"

Torrie had prepared a special dinner for both of them. She didn't like to cook but wanted to impress him with the few culinary skills she possessed. He didn't like chop suey or whatever she called it. He remembered his mother learning how to prepare Chinese food and he disliked every dish she tried. Both he and his father were meat and potato guys.

"I had to play hooky from class today. Bradley had a special event he wanted me to attend. I hope we didn't have that quiz the instructor has been threatening us with." He wasn't about to clue her in on the surveillance mission.

"By the way, how was your day?"

"It was terrible! I had to take Rambo to the vet this morning for his shots and he bit another dog. I was so embarrassed."

"Don't tell me, let me guess; it was that big white poodle we ran into on Churchill Corner when we first met."

"No such luck," she laughed.

He was in a romantic mood. The bottle of Hess Select merlot wasn't doing the trick. She loved red wine and claimed the grape melanin made her horny. It wasn't working tonight though.

They both had been extremely busy the past several days. Torrie was looking for new work because she hadn't been too comfortable with the Asian guy she was working for at the time. Recently, he seemed to be "hitting" on her every chance he could. She had started the interview process again and thought she locked in a position with the Fidelity Branch Office downtown. The manager told her after the interview that she was the best qualified applicant he'd seen thus far.

Yeah, he thought to himself, the young male manager probably liked the way she wiggled-waddled in her mini skirt which showed off those wonderful legs.

"Damn it, Rambo, stop it," she admonished her pet. "I'll take you outside in a minute."

The mutt had been passing a string of foul-smelling gas all evening. He had parked himself comfortably at Rod's feet throughout the entire meal. He didn't comment on the odor, thinking that the specially prepared meal got to Torrie. It was time to leave.

"Be sure to call me tomorrow, honey. I've got a neat idea for this weekend but want it to be a complete surprise." Rod had some big ideas before but he'd been entirely wrong.

He headed back to his apartment with all kinds of wonderful and wicked thoughts banging around in his thick skull about this coming weekend. He wasn't aware of anything exciting going on around town. He figured he'd find something soon enough.

Chapter 20

HIGHLAND PARK was busy today with sleek Lexus SUVs and boxy Mercedes vans traversing the neighborhoods with loads of kids heading to their soccer games. It was a Saturday morning ritual for many youngsters all over the state, as soccer had rapidly gained in popularity. The wind was whipping across from the lake kicking the sea gulls around like miniature ping pong balls.

Rod parked his rental about two hundred-fifty feet down the street from the Fenerty home across from a city park. Several older couples were walking the paved trails and chatting vigorously with each other. He was prepared to stay all day and into the evening if necessary. He brought along his high resolution car camera recorder with flip down screen and a parabolic sound amplification dish with a built-in recorder. Parked at his side was a thermos of Starbucks' coffee along with a chicken salad sandwich.

He wondered what the average cost of a home was in the area and how many Fortune 500 executives lived here. One thing was for sure; even the smallest castle on the block was way out of his price range.

"Move on, buddy, you been parking here too long," came a high-pitched voice from outside the opened back window. "You don't got no business around here, I been keeping my eye on you."

Rod quickly put a sweater over his equipment on the front seat and hopped out of the car. He did a quick assessment before approaching the tall, slim albino man with short white hair. There was a noticeable gap between the canines and the incisors. He was certifiably ugly and scary looking. Rod detected a slight bulge at the side of the guy's waist; he was packing.

"Are you an officer of the law?" Rod asked intently. The giant cop was not in uniform.

"Yeah, we're doing some undercover duty in the neighborhood. Some rich old bitch called in a complaint about a hobo stalking the streets. It was reported that some dude knocked off a convenience store over near Green Bay Road last night and the natives are restless. They don't see bums around here often."

Rod became suspicious.

If this jerk's a cop of some sort, I'm the Chicago Police Commissioner!

"I'm sorry officer. I'll drive around the block and see if my wife and daughter ended up over by the swing sets. The wife reads novels galore and probably didn't notice the time."

He drove around the block and headed back to the office. He decided he'd dump the Buick off at the rental car agency and pick up a Honda CR-7. His plan was to return to Highland Park in the early evening and see if Shamus was on the prowl. Maybe he'd be lucky and document something worthwhile.

"Hey," Rod said when he met Bradley in the hallway neatly dressed in a gray pin-striped suit. "How come you're in the office on Saturday? I thought you told me your wife had some important plans for you today."

"She did."

"Well...?"

"Do you call cleaning out the basement and the attic as a reason to hang around the home front?" Bradley replied sarcastically. "I told her we were in the middle of a big case and that you needed some backup. It usually works when I want to get away. By the way, what's with the bandage on the hand?"

"I told you about Torrie, right? I didn't tell you about Rambo."

"Rambo who?"

"R-A-M-B-O, her little furry protector, stands about a foot high, weighs about twenty pounds and is afraid of nothing. I was playing with

[112]

him the other night; he sort of likes me. Torrie told me to knock it off and she tossed him a big milk bone. It bounced off my shoes and I tried to pick it up and flip it to him. He nailed my hand like a piranha ripping off a chunk of flesh from an animal crossing the fucking Amazon."

"Did you get stitches?"

"Nah, I just flushed it out, dumped some anti-bacterial powder in and sewed it shut with some eight pound nylon fishing line I had at home."

"Jesus. Who's the Rambo here?"

"Screw you...you big ape," a loud voice came from the corner of Bradley's office. It was that obnoxious Graybeard again. Bradley informed his partner that he left the television set on in the office because Graybeard liked animated comics and cussed whenever a commercial came across the screen.

"I thought those birds were both near-sighted and color blind." Rod thought he read that somewhere.

"Who knows for sure if they have eyesight problems but they're not color blind," Bradley laughed. "I'm going back in there and I'm covering his cage. He'll squawk like mad for awhile, and then go to sleep."

Rod went back to the library and started to write some notes when Bradley joined him.

"How's the surveillance going?"

Rod explained how he got run off by some freak posing as a cop. He assumed something was going on and would find out tonight.

"I'm heading back at dusk and continue my recon. Maybe Shamus will be on the run tonight. Strange things happen after dark. I'll have my trusty night vision goggles handy and we'll go from there."

"Did you get an invitation to Angie Ward's wedding?"

Rod was caught off guard on this one.

"What the hell are you talking about? I haven't seen nor heard from her for some time. We'd agree to cool it for several months and see what

[113]

happens. Frankly, I got a little tired of running out to Libertyville every time she beckoned for me, and no, I didn't get an invitation. What's going on?"

"I know you mentioned that you two were going to lay low for awhile so I was shocked when it popped up in the mail at home a few days ago and forgot to mention it to you."

"Well…yeah!"

"I called Irene Finerty to flush out more facts. She's marrying a retired two star Navy admiral. Irene said that Angie met him at her husband's funeral and he started calling her up. She kept putting him off because she thought that you were still interested in her. I guess the Navy man was so unrelenting in his pursuit of her that she finally caved."

"Son of a bitch," Rod cried. "The lady was two-timing me all along. Screw her, let her marry the big Navy brass hero, see what I care."

"I hate to be a bastard here but haven't you hooked up with that Torrie person? Huh? That should certainly soothe your ego."

"Go to hell Simmons," he shouted storming out of the office.

He killed a few hours over at Lincoln Park feeding the sea gulls and cooling off from his confrontation with Bradley and then proceeded to Highland Park. He saw the sun slipping away and figured he had about an hour of light to set up his watch.

Rod decided on a different location for his recon instead of across from the park. After circling the block several times he pulled the CR-7 to the curb about two hundred feet from the mansion's cobbled driveway guarded by an opened wrought-iron gate. He noticed some activity inside when he drove by on the first run; hopefully Shamus was still at home.

It was dark when he decided to get out of the car and stroll over toward the property to get a closer look. Thick bushes lined both sides of the driveway intermingled with tall evergreens spaced approximately thirty feet from each other.

The driveway stretched in about a hundred feet. At that point a branch swung off and circled around to the front of the mansion and then veered back to join the main passageway. The driveway then continued deeper back into the property for another hundred feet and ended at a four car garage. The black limo was parked on an asphalt pad adjacent to the huge gated entranceway. Security lights were strategically placed around the entire perimeter of the property but for some unknown reason they were not turned on.

Rod wore a tan overcoat and flipped a black tam on his head. He walked slowly along the sidewalk supported with a cane. He wore a gray wig of medium length. He stopped in front of the gates for several moments and surveyed the entire area. Small accent lights shone on every evergreen tree. He perceived it was safe enough to stroll in a few yards to see if anything of interest was happening inside.

Ten yards into the property he didn't hear the footsteps coming up from behind him. He suffered a sharp blow to his ribs followed up by a vicious chop to the back of his neck knocking him to the hard driveway. He heard the metallic click of the hammer being pulled back on a hand gun. The ambient light of a full moon allowed a quick peek at the position of his attacker.

"Get to your feet you old-son-of a bitch before I pull the trigger."

"Oh, please excuse me sir," Rod muttered softly as he rubbed his neck. "I…I think I'm lost."

"I said get up!" the attacker demanded wiggling the pistol at Rod's head. He tried to focus on the man's face but couldn't see him clearly enough in the dark. Judging from his profile though, Rod knew he was tall and thin.

"Sorry, sir, I got a little confused on my nightly walk and thought this was my daughter's house. I think I've come down with a little dementia here lately."

"Shut up you old fool before I blow you away!"

As Rod started to edge up slowly, he took both ends of the cane and brought it up as rapidly and as viciously as he could smashing the large wrist bone of the thug's gun hand. The pistol fell to the ground. In a second flash he hooked the cane around the back of the man's right knee

[115]

and yanked him forward. As the man started to lean into him Rod released the cane from the leg and then took the lower end and then sent a crushing jab into the guy's windpipe.

"Ugh, oh…, shit!" the goon cried in agony.

Rod heard a low-pitched gurgling sound when the albino grabbed at his throat, groaned louder and then tried to curse at him. Nothing came out but a string of incoherent mutterings and spittle. Rod finished him off with a forceful upward snap of his right palm into the man's nose and heard the painful crunch. The victim slumped to the ground, now wordless, both hands clutching at his face.

Satisfied that his attacker was temporally put out of commission, he spun around, picked up the fallen weapon and then took off running back to his car.

He sped out of Highland Park vowing that he was finished with the home surveillance gig; too damn dangerous. He needed to get home and slap a bag of ice on his swollen neck. His rib cage was not hurting too badly.

I was lucky out there tonight. The security lighting was apparently out of commission allowing me to get into the property to check it out until that thug closed in on me. If I had my gun with me I'd have shot and maybe killed him. I'm thankful for the cane-chi lessons I took in that self-defense course back in San Antonio.

The next watch would take place the following morning in the parking lot at Fenerty's place of employment, the All-State Trucking Enterprises.

[116]

Chapter 21

A STIFF NECK, swollen left ankle and bruised right hand were still bothering Rod when he picked up another Hertz rental. Fortunately he remembered to remove the hood's gun from the trunk of the car and leave it in his apartment before he turned the other rental back in. This time he selected a Toyota Avalon. He thought that some day he would trade his vintage Honda in for one if these sleek vehicles so he liked the idea of "trying before buying".

Rod reasoned that Shamus Fenerty had too much security around his mansion so he decided to set up surveillance at his work site. His wife was still out of town so maybe Shamus would make a move today.

His brief encounter with one of Fenerty's henchmen last evening was a shocking revelation: he wasn't the young and athletic studsman he thought he was, even though he enjoyed a strenuous workout every other day. He vowed he would increase his minutes pounding the heavy bag and double his repetitions on the skip jump rope. One of the guys at the fitness center teaches Tai Chi so he'll ask him for some refresher training.

Rod jumped on the Kennedy Expressway and motored for O'Hare. He was comfortable with the short blond ponytail wig he was wearing. It matched the denim slacks and the red and white checkered shirt he had on…shades of Bradley's attire. A tight-fitting Chicago Cub baseball hat helped anchor the wig in place.

It was mid-morning and traffic out of the Loop was light. Whenever possible he learned to travel anti-commute in and out of the city. The weatherman predicted a light snowfall sometime later in the day. In some respects he hoped it would happen because trailing Shamus would give him more cover in adverse weather conditions.

All-State Trucking Enterprises was tucked in neatly behind O'Hare Field near Bensenville with easy access to three major Interstates: 90, 290 and 294. Shamus ruled his empire from a second story office adjacent to one of the truck motor pools. An eight foot fenced circled both the office complex and the motor pool. The dispatcher shack and football-sized parking lot were to the rear of the fenced complex. While neither was fenced, a guard booth controlled the entranceway to the entire truck park.

"How're you doing his morning?" It was Bradley checking in on his cell phone. He agreed with his partner to move the surveillance site to the office complex knowing Shamus would be there.

"I'll live to fight another day, boss."

"Did you have enough ice cubes in your little freezer to resolve the sore neck?" Bradley kidded. "And, how are your 'spare' ribs?"

"Screw you, Simmons!"

"Before I forget," Bradley continued, "Shamus has two other locations where his trucking fleet is located. One site is down the Tri-State near Hinsdale and the other is off I-55 in Darien. Irene told me he spends the majority of his time at his main office location where you are at now."

"I'll make a note of that. By the way, I got my binoculars trained on the black limo as we speak. Max Schnel just dropped him off and Fenerty went immediately into his office building."

"Maybe something good might happen today, at least for you. I'm home sweeping the snowflakes off the driveway. I'll be in the office after lunch. Give me a call if anything exciting happens."

"Roger that."

Rod was temporarily parked on the street across from the guard shed and down a block. He had an unimpeded line of vision to most of the trucking property. He observed Max maneuver the big limo over by the larger motor pool, get out and then go into the little maintenance building next to the huge open bay structure. He was the only one in the vehicle.

It must be their coffee shop. I'm glad he's alone. I'm not in the mood to take on any of Fenerty's gorillas today. I wonder where they're all lurking this morning.

Shortly after noon Shamus hustled out of his building as the limo circled over to pick him up. They left in a hurry. Rod tailed them at a safe distance and was surprised that Shamus was heading for O'Hare. The limo swerved into the roadway leading to Terminal Two and stopped abruptly at the U.S. Airways curbside. Shamus got out and ran through the front door.

What the hell is his hurry? Who's he rushing to meet?

Rod decided to take the risk of being spotted and parked the Avalon in the parking garage. He ran as fast as possible to the adjacent terminal. He went down to the U.S. Airways baggage pickup area hoping that whomever Shamus was meeting had to secure suitcases. He was in luck. Shamus was coming out of the men's room near one of the conveyors which was spitting out all shapes and colors of travel bags. Fenerty walked over to the entranceway leading into the baggage area and waited for his passenger.

Rod took a waiting position against one of the adjacent walls that gave him enough cover but yet a good line of sight to Shamus and the mystery person he was about to meet. He adjusted his thick black glasses with the built-in specially designed high frequency microphone embedded in the earpieces. He didn't like the stereo effect but learned to adapt.

"It's about time you got in, Candi," Shamus shouted when he spotted the short blond approaching him. "I've been waiting an hour for you," he lied.

"I'm sorry about that; the flight from Los Angeles was delayed. I'm fortunate to be here because I had a screening that lasted longer than the director promised me and almost missed the plane."

"I'm just glad you made it."

Fenerty threw his huge arms around the actress, almost choking her to death. They embraced for several minutes. Rod bemoaned the fact that in the rush to catch up with Shamus he'd left his high-speed camera back in the rental car.

Candi was dressed impeccably and expensively from head to toe in Prada's latest attire. The three inch thin spikes she wore elevated her up to Fenerty's red bearded chin. Rod tried his best to recall which movies he had seen her in but drew a blank.

Shamus really knew how to pick 'em!

"Let's get going, we have a big day and a bigger night ahead of us," Shamus said softly to her as they strolled past Rod. He had his trusty Rolling Stones magazine propped up to his face.

Fenerty secured her bright pink suitcase and arm-in-arm they walked to the exit. The black limo was waiting. Rod hustled to the next exit over and hailed a cab. He'd lose them if he tried to go back to the garage and get the parked Toyota.

"Follow that car, buddy, but not too closely...there's an extra twenty bills if you don't lose him."

The limo took the ten minute drive out to I-190, over to Des Plaines River Road and then parked in front of the DoubleTree Hotel.

So this is where the party begins, he thought. I'm screwed without my camera!

Shamus got out of the limo and walked over to hotel entrance, turning around and giving the seated Candi a "thumbs up" gesture.

Rod was totally confused because he couldn't figure out why both of them didn't go inside. The limo pulled away from the unloading area and parked further down the property. Candi got out, leaned against the stretch vehicle and lit up a cigarette.

He directed his cab driver to drive over to an area where they'd be out of sight from the limo. He got out and hid behind a dumpster but yet had his eyes riveted to the limo. Max was smoking a thick cigar. Rod decided to wait there until something happened.

"We're going to take a short break now," Rod told the driver. Fifteen minutes later Fenerty emerged from the entrance with a well-dressed young man in a herring-bone suit carrying a thick briefcase. He had long flowing golden-rod hair. They were chatting with each other but Rod was too far away to pick up the conversation. They both jumped into the limo and Max sped away, the cigar sailing out of the driver side window bouncing like shattered Fourth of July sparklers along the pavement.

"Follow them but please stay behind far enough so they don't suspect anything," he ordered the taxi driver.

"Look mister, I can't afford to get mixed up in any suspicious activity; know what I mean? Something bad is coming down. I smell it and I don't need to be a part of it. I'm going to drop you off back at the airport where I picked you up."

Rod took out a hundred dollar bill and waved it under the driver's nose.

"Will this buy a few more minutes of your time? They're heading back to O'Hare and when the three of them get out and the limo takes off, you can dump me."

"I'll think on it."

The driver decided to grab the bill and then shoved it in his coat pocket. They saw the limo proceeding to the O'Hare Hilton Hotel on the airport property. Shamus, Candi and Mr. Ivy League all got out at the hotel entrance and went inside. Max carried in the pink suitcase and came out ten minutes later, got back in his limo and took off.

"Pull the cab back about a hundred yards and we'll wait there and see what happens."

When he felt comfortable that his threesome was checking in or going to a meeting there, he told the cabbie to take him back to the airport parking garage. He planned to pick up the Avalon and then return to the Hilton Hotel property to continue his surveillance.

"I sure as hell better not read anything about this caper in the Trib tomorrow, buddy."

"You won't," Rod assured him.

He settled up with the worried driver and the cab sped off leaving a trail of burnt rubber on the road which had now dried up from the morning dusting of snow. He paid the parking attendant and went over to the Hilton and parked in a "guest only" slot.

It was rush hour on the roads, getting dark and had begun snowing again. He only brought a light jacket with him but had some other odds and ends of clothing to beef up his disguise. He placed the blond ponytail in a bag on the rear seat and took out another wig. This one was a slicked down head of black hair. He switched from the dark glasses to a pair of thinly wired bifocals. He pulled on a tweed sport coat and flipped a brimmed hat on his head. This time he didn't forget his camera.

"Can I help you?" asked the smiling registration clerk behind the front desk.

Rod checked out the lobby. It was empty except for an older couple plunked down in easy chairs near the large potted flower arrangement by the bank of elevators. Soft music was playing in the background.

"Yes, you certainly can. Do you have any conferences or meetings going on right now? I want to make sure I'm in the right Hilton. I'm supposed to meet some of my colleagues from Princeton University and they said that they'd be congregating at the Hilton by the airport. I've learned from my guide book that there are several of your hotels around here."

"We have a big conference beginning tomorrow but nothing is going on right now. The AARP is scheduled to meet here and we expect a lot of you elderly types checking in tonight."

He ignored the reference to him being one of the Medicare dudes here for the session.

"Would you please check and see if you have a Shamus Fenerty registered here. I've got to get some notes to him for his lecture to the assemblage tomorrow."

"Sir, I'm so sorry I can't release that kind of information. I can call his room to see if he would come down here to meet you in the lobby."

"What room is he in?" Rod asked soberly.

"Again, kind sir, I can't tell you."

"That's fine with me. I fully understand the need for privacy. We agreed to meet at the bar later tonight. I'll just hang around the lobby until happy hour starts, and then I'll mosey over to the bar and catch up with him."

While Rod was reading a Wall Street Journal, he noticed the man that hooked up with Shamus over at the DoubleTree walking by in front of him. The man was down in the front lobby apparently looking around for somebody. Rod couldn't figure it out but he leveled his camera at the guy and shot several pictures. He knew that this person was an intricate piece of the puzzle tied in with Shamus and the actress. He still was dressed up and his confident composure belied his apparent youth.

"How might I be of assistance?" the concierge asked him.

"I'm looking for a package which was supposed to be shipped overnight by Fed Ex yesterday and I need it immediately when it arrives. It will be addressed to Tom Scott, that's me. Please send it up to room 808 when it's delivered."

"I certainly will," said the young lady dressed in a sharply pressed dark suit wearing an indelibly printed smile on her cute face.

Rod studied the young professional.

This guy is a stud. What the hell's going on? Did Shamus arrange for a threesome tonight? What role does the irresistible Candi have to play in this mystery?

Tom Scott headed to the bank of elevators and went to the eighth floor. Rod was strategically situated where he could see the elevators and the floor level display lit up above the elevator doors. He swore that earlier Shamus went up to the tenth floor when he first checked in; looking at his notes, he confirmed it. He scribbled another note that the mystery man has a room on the eighth floor.

What floor is she on? I'm already confused.

"Shamus, you know I'd do anything for you," Candi said as she and Fenerty swiftly walked past him. They had just gotten off the elevator when he first spotted them. They didn't notice him.

Rod quickly pulled the Wall Street Journal up to his face and at the same time activated the audio switch on his eye glasses. When Shamus and the showstopper were ten yards past him and starting to turn into another corridor, he snapped a series of ten photos with his high speed camera. He now had secured pictures of all three of them. The question remained: why are they here and what are they up to?

Fenerty and Candi sat comfortably in the lounge and each ordered a dry Bombay Sapphire martini. They kept looking around as if they were waiting for someone to join them.

"I owe so much to you for getting me on the right track, Shamus. If it weren't for you demanding your Hollywood big shot friend to let me audition for a small part in one of his movies I wouldn't be the glamorous star that everyone loves and admires."

He took her hand softly and brought it up to rub his overgrown goatee. She then tugged it, pulling it back and forth like she was trying to yank it off his chin.

"When I see you next time you need to either get rid of this ugly growth anomaly or get it trimmed." She was playing with him and he enjoyed it.

"Why Candi, it's my pride and joy!"

"Getting back to my Hollywood buddy; we played football together at Illinois. I studied business but 'pretty face' studied drama. We used to kid him all the time not to get his handsome face messed up playing football. The ladies flocked to him but had no interest in me for some ungodly reason."

She laughed and took a long hit of her martini, tonguing the green stuffed olive and sucking it into her lovely mouth, then letting it roll back into the glass using her curved tongue as a chute. She knew how to turn him on but he had to control himself. This night was critical for the future of his company.

"I enjoyed being your secretary at All-State Trucking Enterprises," she exclaimed with a certain air of satisfaction. "It didn't matter to anyone that I was the only female in the company, right?"

"Certainly not to me; you were my best employee."

"Thanks Shamus. You and Lois were always so gracious to me. You treated me as though I were one of the directors of the company. In fact, you treated all of your hired help as though they each had ownership in your company. I guess that's why you are so successful. Now my special friend, let's talk about why you asked me to come to Chicago."

They clicked their empty martini glasses together and ordered another round.

"I introduced you earlier to Tom Scott when we picked him up over at the DoubleTree. He is an enforcer with The International Brotherhood of Truckers and Transporters, affectionately known to us in the trucking industry as the IBOTT. You wouldn't believe it the way he dresses and carries himself. Most people are of the impression he's a Wall Street financial wizard. Did you spot the Rolex he was wearing?"

"I always pick up those kinds of things, Shamus. I bet he is a 'hottie' with the women, too, with that face and physique they probably swoon all over him. So tell me, why is young Tom here?"

"Only a few select people know that I am negotiating with Goldman Sachs to make my company a public corporation. They are in the early stages of putting together the components of an initial public offering. Goldman is one of the best financial houses in the world to bring a company public through what they call an IPO."

"What's so unusual about this process?"

"Nothing at all, sweetie, it's a legitimate and commonly occurring business transaction."

"Then why act out this big charade with Mr. Goldilocks?"

"The IBOTT got wind of this somehow and sent him here to talk me out of it. My company is one of the largest trucking companies in the entire country that hasn't succumbed to the idiosyncrasies of an organized labor union. I treat my employees well and they are happy to be a part of my outfit. IBOTT leadership is trying to convince me that I should convert the company to an Employee Share Ownership Plan."

"What the hell does that mean?"

"It's called an ESOP. Under this plan, every single one of my employees would own stock in the company. Yes Candi, the company I created, grew and made highly successful with every ounce of my flesh and blood is now under attack."

"I don't think that's fair."

"Neither do I. That's why they sent Mr. Scott here to twist my arm. I can't believe any of my trusted lieutenants in the organization would leak such information to the big wigs in the labor union but somehow they found out about my plans."

"Are you going to convince Tom that it's in the best interests for you and your privately held company to go public but not as an ESOP?"

"No, Candi, you are going to do it."

"Good grief! How do you suggest I make that happen?"

"I want you to liquor him up and take him back to his room and do whatever it takes to persuade him and his fucking union honchos to back off. He should be down here in a few minutes."

"Does that mean you want me to…?"

"Yes, if that's what it takes. I've known you for a long time and I know that you are irresistible when it comes to getting what you want from a man. I wouldn't ask this of you if it wasn't important to me. I hope you understand and are willing to help me out without any regrets."

"Um…" she paused until he put a muscular arm around her.

"Will you do it for me?" he asked softly looking her square in the eyes."

"You know that I'd prefer to take you up to my room instead of some clown I know nothing of or care about. I'm sure you remember the good old days."

"Yes I do, and I don't regret a thing that we did back then."

"Well, let's dump Scott and...er...renew old times."

"I can't do that, times have changed."

"But Shamus!"

"Well, maybe the next time." He put her off and was starting to get irritated with her. "Remember, I have a wife who I believe still loves me and two adorable sons that I have to think about."

"Okay, that's it, I'll do it for you and only for you...you big good-looking Irish lug. I'm an actress and have played that part many times in some of my early B movies. Just get him good and drunk for me, okay?"

He smiled and said, "It's up to you to get him liquored up."

"Hello, people; happy hour time?" Tom Scott asked as he came bouncing into the lounge and pulled up a chair to join them.

"About time you got here Mr. Scott. Candi and I thought you deserted us."

"Sorry about the delay. I had to set up another meeting for the union. I'm coming back to Chicago next week to do some more business."

"Look kids, I got to go up and give Lois a call. You two get dinner, have fun and I'll see you at breakfast in the morning."

Shamus disappeared through the back entrance of the bar which led to the conference rooms and out the rear of the hotel. He needed to take an extended walk before heading back to his room but not one of his daily five mile jaunts.

Tom Scott ordered a Manhattan on the rocks and looked at Candi.

"You are a wonder to behold! You are so much prettier in person than on the big screen. Shamus said you wanted to talk to me. What's going on?"

Chapter 22

BROADWAY STREET in Little Saigon was busy this morning with shoppers scurrying around the open markets buying their fresh vegetables for the evening meal. Li Chong and Sno Moreau were having tea at Bo Tan's Restaurant, Sno's favorite hangout. She had moved into her apartment off Lawrence Street and was telling Chong about her furniture ordeal.

"So, the furniture finally arrived from Thailand and you had it delivered yesterday. How many pieces were broken?"

Sno frowned and replied, "Probably half of the big pieces were damaged to some degree. I had a claims adjuster in and hopefully the monies I receive from the insurance company will be enough to restore them to their original condition. I'd hate to lose those antique chairs Henri got from his mother in France."

"Are you happy living here?"

"I think it will serve its purpose until I find a home to buy later on. The tenants seem cordial enough and your manager friend can't do enough for me. I still need to find my son."

"Have you had any luck yet finding him?"

"I've done some preliminary investigation but frankly, have put the search on the back burner until I get more settled in. There is some culture shock I'm experiencing but that should resolve itself in due time. Also, the high cost of everything is a major adjustment for me."

"You told me when you called that you wanted to look for a location where you could either buy an existing restaurant or open a new one. Do you have a particular area in mind?"

"Your manager friend suggested that I research the Wrigleyville area in more detail. He's really a nice man and has driven me around several neighborhoods getting better oriented. By the way, is he married?"

Li laughed in a hoarse voice, almost like a donkey 'hee-hawing'.

"What's that all about, Chong?"

"I'm not sure of his status right now. He's been married three times and the last time we had a conversation he was dating a young Cambodian stripper over at Loo's Livery not too far from your apartment. Although I like the guy and he's given me at least a dozen housing referrals, I'd be careful. He does have a roving eye and he simply can't do enough for any of his pretty female tenants...got it girl?"

They drove around the Wrigleyville neighborhood for several hours. Central Lakeview, a common reference to the neighborhood was populated with low-rise brick buildings and rooftop bleachers. She did see lots of potential here. The enthusiastic Chicago Cub fans loved their team. Sno liked the "pulse beat" of the area even though she wasn't a baseball fan.

"Let's go back again to that area I commented on earlier. It's a good location for my kind of restaurant. What was that theatre called over near Waveland?"

"I think you mean the Music Box Theatre."

"That's it. I like some of the international flavor the venue reportedly offers from time to time. I think a Vietnamese restaurant would do well in the area. Let's see if you can bring up any commercial listings in that magic machine of yours. Maybe there is an existing property that would work for me."

Sno found an older run-down building that she imagined could be converted to her type of restaurant. After considerable research they put an offer in on the property and waited anxiously for the response. Two days later it was accepted without any counter offers or conditions. She found the exact location for her next restaurant.

"I'm so happy, Li."

"You should be; you got exactly what you wanted."

"Yes, but only with your outstanding realtor skills!"

& & & & &

Six months later she reflected back on the whirlwind of activity that happened since she bought the property.

I can't believe how lucky I am. Closing on the property was quicker than I thought it would be but the build-out took longer due to a temporary shortage of critical materials. I had to spend every waking minute personally directing and even coaxing the workers to speed it up. Planning for the grand opening events was no problem because I had experienced the excitement of starting a new restaurant in the past. Everyone congratulated me on the food I served at the soft opening. Thank goodness I had the foresight to invite some of the Chicago Cub baseball players…they brought in many customers on their own.

Within eight months of their grand opening, The House of Saigon was the most popular Vietnamese restaurant north of downtown Chicago. It was frequented by many players and executives from the Chicago Cub organization. Every employee of the restaurant was of Vietnamese origin and had to be proficient in discussing the geography and customs of their family origins back in the old country. She made no exceptions.

"Well, you have finally made an impact here, Sno Moreau. Are you ready to move out of the apartment in Little Saigon and into a more upscale home in a nearby area?"

"Yes I am, it's time to take the next big step."

"Would you consider buying a condo by Lake Michigan or would you prefer something out in the western suburbs?"

"I would prefer to be closer to my business. How about finding something for me over in Lincoln Park? I like that area."

After a relentless search of real estate in the area over several long days she closed on a two bedroom condo on the tenth floor with an incomparable view of Lake Michigan.

Chong came to visit her a week after she moved in.

Pointing out the bay window Li said, "There's the Lincoln Park Zoo over near the Chicago History Museum, Sno. You shared with me that you learned to love animals even after the bad experiences you had as a youth. Now you're close enough to visit the cute animals they have there."

"Yes, and I love to walk along the shoreline of any large body of water absorbing both the energy and peacefulness it gives me."

Up to this point in her stay in the United States Sno didn't own an automobile but found public transportation to be convenient. It was time to change her means of transportation. She consulted with the owner of a limousine company and contracted for full-time limo service.

"You won't regret it, Mrs. Moreau, every single client of mine loves the service, exclaiming they should have arranged for it years ago."

She was finally living the American immigrant's dream. She would now shift gears and begin a serious search for her son, Chien Tran, which had been postponed too long to suit her.

Chapter 23

RENO was wet and rainy and the Southwest Airlines flight they were flying on skidded to the end of the runway before coming to a halt. Everyone on board gave the female pilot a round of applause as they deplaned past her. They had waited twenty minutes before a taxi pulled up to the curb. She was freezing in the swirling wind, cursing that she hadn't dressed properly for the trip. In fact, neither of them had any warm clothing or even any luggage with them to speak of.

Chien Tran preferred the less congested Reno to the flashier Las Vegas for a "quickie" wedding. He started to flash back on the exhilarating events of the past forty-eight hours.

They had spent the previous day and entire night in Chien's loft condo across from Millennium Park in Chicago. They were almost inseparable from the day he started training as a stock broker. When they drained the second bottle of Louis Roederer Cristal Champagne they decided to get married.

"Are you really sure you want to go through with this, Chien?"

"Of course I do Veronica. I'm thirty-five now and not getting any younger. I wouldn't be freezing my rear end off in Chicago for any other person in the entire world. I love you so much."

"And I love you too" she mumbled softly in his ear, "But I always dreamed of a church wedding with all of the bells and whistles. My mother would be upset if she wasn't able to plan every detail of the ceremony. She was the real star at my sister's wedding last year."

They made love again and drifted off to sleep only to be awakened by a fire engine screaming down Michigan Avenue. They both shot up in bed and looked into each other's eyes.

"The hell with waiting any longer, my love; let's do it now! We can do a big church wedding reenactment in September. Mother will get her chance to shine again."

Chien was jolted back to reality when the cab driver slammed the trunk shut. He'd opened it assuming they had luggage. "Where to, sir?" he asked as he climbed back into the driver's seat.

"Find us that infamous drive through wedding chapel."

"Got it mister, was just there yesterday with an older couple. The gent slouched in the rear seat was in a drunken stupor. He proclaimed with a laugh that he was going on wife number four."

Veronica asked Tran, "Would you tell the driver to stop at a store on the way to the chapel so I can buy a warm sweater? I'm freezing." He did as instructed.

"No problem, ma'am, there are several department stores in a mall not too far from the chapel. I'll wait for you to get your sweater and then run you over to the county clerk's office to get your marriage license."

"Don't we need one of those quickie blood tests?"

"Lady, not in this town," the cabbie answered with a cheerful response. "Furthermore, there are no waiting periods so you'll be good to go; get you two lovebirds married off in no time."

They got their license and immediately headed to the drive through chapel. The entire ceremony took less than ten minutes.

"Where do we go now?" the cabbie asked after being delighted with his key role as a witness. "There's a comfortable hotel about two short blocks from here that I know you'd like. Shall I head over there now?"

"No, swing back to the airport, we've got a return flight to catch," Veronica ordered. Tran was in deep thought.

I really should go to one of the big casinos before leaving town. I feel lucky today and am riding a pretty good streak. I'll play with that grand I won at the off-track betting place on Cicero before Veronica slipped over to the condo yesterday. When you're hot, you're hot!

[133]

Chien looked over at her and gently placed his hand in hers. A radiant glow was emanating from her entire body. Streaks of sunlight refracted off the back window of the cab and enveloped her.

I am so fortunate this unrivaled beauty would marry me.

He couldn't believe in his good fortune. Twenty-four hours ago he was contemplating the purchase of an engagement ring. He was trying to decide what magical location would be the most appropriate setting to spring the proposal. She loved his loft condo so that would suffice. He was now a married man and anticipating the great future that Buddha laid out for them.

All of a sudden and without any warning he grabbed at his chest. He hit Veronica on the arm as he twisted and turned with pain on the back seat.

"Agh, ooh God, please, not now!" Chien gasped, quickly reaching into his jacket pocket and pulling out a small pill case. He then took out a nitroglycerine tablet and stuck it under his tongue.

"Honey, what's wrong with you?" she shouted out in shock.

The taxicab driver swerved to the curb, narrowly getting t-boned by an SUV that skidded in front of him on the wet street. The roads were slick from the earlier heavy rain that saturated Reno.

"Want me to head straight to the hospital?"

"Ah, no, just park here for a few minutes."

The pain in his chest was unbearable. It felt like a huge vise grip was squeezing him. Bolts of lightning shot out to every extremity of his twisting body. His arms dropped as though they were weighted down with cast iron sleeves. He vigorously massaged his sternum area hoping to push the pain away.

"Forget what he told you and go immediately to the nearest hospital emergency room, driver; can't you see my husband is dying?" she shouted in a hysterical voice.

"No, absolutely not," Chien groaned. "I'm sure it'll pass soon because it happened to me before. I'll be okay in a few minutes."

[134]

"I'm concerned about you, my dear. Please let the cabbie drive you to the hospital right away and get this checked out. You never mentioned to me before about having a heart problem. What's going on?"

The cabbie was also getting concerned. He never hauled a stiff around in his cab before and this wasn't about to be the first time. All of a sudden and without any warning he pulled out into traffic and headed to an emergency room cross-town that he'd been to last night.

"Airport, take us to the airport right this minute or I'll call the cops," Tran screamed at him. He jerked out his cell and flashed it in front of the cabbie's eyes.

"Alright, man; I'm warning you though. You better not die on me before we get there."

Veronica was still in a state of shock and sat there cupping her head in her hands not saying a word. She then composed herself and gripped his arm tightly. She slid over and hugged his shoulder.

"The pain is going away," he said convincingly. I'll be alright. Please, everyone relax, okay?"

"How long have you known about the heart problem and why haven't you shared this with me before?" she said now more composed.

"Hang on, we're almost there," shouted the taxi driver, "The airport, not the hospital!" He studied the rear view mirror to assure himself the guy would live for another ten minutes until he dumped them off at the Southwest Airlines departure curb.

"My dear concerned wife, I was born with a heart defect. It's been under control most of my life and I am being monitored by a cardiologist back home. I guess the excitement and utter thrill of marrying you prompted this reaction. I'll get it checked out when we get home."

She wasn't satisfied with his reply. "Just what exactly is the medical condition?"

"They call it a form of aortic stenosis which tends to restrict the arteries around the heart and even cause obstruction of the valves. Congestive

[135]

heart failure is often the end result but definitely treatable. I've lived with this a long time so you need not be alarmed."

"Will you ever need a heart transplant?"

"Probably not because I don't think it's severe enough to warrant such a dramatic course of treatment."

"Okay, Doctor Tran, but promise me that you'll live long enough to see our kids get married and give you many happy grandchildren."

"Whoa, hang on there. What are you trying to tell me? Aren't you on the pill?"

The cabbie sped around a long black limo and parked at the airport check-in curb with a sudden and dramatic stop.

"Everyone out, we're here." The cabbie raced around the vehicle to open their door. "That'll be fifty bucks and off you go."

They exited the vehicle and he handed the driver four twenty dollar bills. The cabbie quickly swiped the bills out of Tran's hands and shoved them in his back pocket, and then hopped back into the cab and sped away.

"The bastard never thanked me for the big tip," Tran moaned.

They talked non-stop on the flight back to Chicago. Both agreed they had a ton of things to work on when they got back home. He promised her that he'd see his cardiologist the next day. She'd told him that she wasn't with child…yet. Her plan since childhood was to have two boys and two girls.

They transferred planes in Las Vegas and both of them slept until they saw the welcomed skyline of Chicago.

"We're finally home, Mrs. Tran."

"I couldn't be happier, Mr. Tran."

Chapter 24

ROD was getting impatient. Candi and Scott had been in the lounge for what seemed to him like several hours. He decided to take up another position in the front lobby. He also stowed the thin-rimmed glasses and replaced the brimmed hat with a Chicago Cub baseball cap.

Shamus came in from his walk and briskly headed over to the elevators. Rod was in a position to see what floor the elevator stopped on. Again it was the tenth floor. He made another note verifying Fenerty's room location.

"Is there anything I can do for you, sir?" asked the concierge as she walked over to him. She had been watching him for some time and was getting a little suspicious. She couldn't figure out why he kept changing his appearance and contemplated calling security.

"Oh, no thank you," he responded with a smile. "I'm writing a novel and no doubt you've observed me making notes in my journal. I'll be heading back to my room pretty soon. Thanks for your concern though."

"Yes sir, glad to be of assistance."

No sooner had the concierge left him when a loud burst of laughter emanated from the lounge entrance. There they were, twenty yards from him, hand in hand, pecking at each other's lips. Candi gave him a slight tug to the side to avoid an overstuffed lobby chair but it was too late. Scott plopped down in it and couldn't pull himself out.

She admonished him loud enough for everybody in the lobby area to hear. "C'mon, lover boy, you promised me an evening of excitement so get your butt up and let's get going."

Rod chuckled to himself. This circus has more acts in it than Ringling Brothers and I didn't have to pay the price of admission.

Scott finally got right-sided and they meandered over to the elevators like two drunken sailors returning from a weekend pass. They were talking much louder and incoherently.

"You'd better deliver the goods, big blond man," Candi chided.

Scott snickered loudly.

Rod decided to wear the pair of glasses that had the electronic microphone implanted in the stems. He quickly grabbed his camera and hid it in the rolled up Wall Street Journal and snapped five quick shots.

"Now, tell me again what floor we're going to, Tommy?"

Scott had that alcoholic stupor glaze strewn all over his handsome face. "Let's listen to what my room key has to say," he blubbered and began to search all four pockets before he was able to retrieve it.

"Aha, I think I heard the key whisper the number 808 to me, darling. Maybe we should go up to your room instead, mine's all messed up. What'd ya think?"

"No, I'm on the fourth floor. You have a better view from your room so we'll go up there, okay?"

"Who gives a shit about the view, sweetie, all I want to do is shower some love on that power-packed body of yours."

He had a difficult time putting his finger on the elevator key pad. "Hey, somebody keeps moving these numbers up and down." He slammed his right fist into number pad hard enough to activate an alarm.

The concierge came running over with a key and turned off the alarm. "Please, let me help you with the elevator," she pleaded and shoved him aside. "What floor?"

"We're going to the eighth," Candi chimed in. The elevator door opened and she quickly shoved Tom inside. He looked like he was getting ready to barf.

Rod waited to make sure that the elevator light reported a stop on the eighth floor. It did. He was satisfied that Shamus and Candi weren't shacking up and decided to leave the hotel. He flipped open his notebook and made a few final notes, got up and left the lobby area. As he was heading out the front door he was almost knocked over by a tall thin man racing through the other set of revolving doors.

"Get the fuck outta my way you joker!"

Rod recognized him immediately. He was the albino cop who interrupted his surveillance of Fenerty's home in Highland Park. The bruiser had a wide bandage taped across the bridge of his nose and a cast on his lower right arm.

So Whitey here is one of Fenerty's strike team members. I did him in pretty good the other night but what the hell is he doing here? Are he and Shamus planning some strong-armed tactics on Tom Scott? I've had enough for one long day and night. I think we can reasonably conclude that Shamus is not cheating on his wife but he is involved in something much bigger and more explosive than a case of infidelity! I should stay around and find out but it's beyond my pay grade at this point in my young P.I. career. Maybe Investigators Jorge and Saul should jump in if Bradley feels the need for a more definitive and extensive follow-up.

Chapter 25

MARRIAGE for Chien and Veronica Tran may not have been the best course of action for either of them. Reno was all fun and fuzziness. But after the excitement wore off he found that the day-to-day living with her became a boring exercise of reaction and restraint. Veronica was much more demanding than he'd ever envisioned. She found Chien to be self-serving and stubborn to the core.

Co-workers were quick to pick up the constant bickering between the two of them that carried over to their working environment. In one such incident they almost came to blows.

"Lay you ten-to-one Las Vegas odds it won't last six months," the senior analyst at Howzer Securities chortled to his buddies.

"I'll take it for two hundred, no more, no less," responded the newest member of the team. He'd been on-site long enough to observe the situation between the two and draw his own conclusions.

Even Michael Howzer was quick to pick up the tension between them and felt sorry primarily for Veronica. He recalled the many past experiences he had with her; she was a "giver" and not a "taker" like him. Michael called them into his office one morning before the rest of the staff arrived for work. They had foregone their usual daily stop at Starbucks.

"I think you two should be aware that the guys are talking behind your backs and making fun of you. I've discounted the jealousy factor. They've known for some time that they can't hold a candle to you when it comes to bringing revenue in here, Chien."

"We are having some problems at home, Michael and I have tried not to bring them to the office," Veronica said. "Is it that obvious?"

"I'm afraid it is."

She stared at him in disbelief. He was serious.

"You are two of my most favorite people," Howzer continued. "I have rattled this thick grey head of mine time and time again to come up with some sort of encouragement but I'm too close to the problem. Have you two sought counseling? I have a friend in the business and not one of our clients. In fact, he invests elsewhere only in real estate and not stocks and bonds. Would you like his name?"

"You mean have we been to…or even in need of a shrink?" said an agitated Chien. He was hot under the collar.

The nerve of this old man!

"That's what I'm asking," Michael replied sternly.

"No, we haven't and I don't intend to seek any outside help. If Veronica and I can't work this out as rational adults then we should throw in the towel."

"Hold on a minute," Veronica exclaimed. "I've asked you repeatedly to go with me for counseling but you said mental health professionals need far more mind manipulation than we do."

"True," he responded sarcastically. "I don't trust them and nothing will change my mind." He got up and shot out of the office slamming the door shut behind him. Michael and Veronica looked at each other and sighed.

"Take a week off, get out of town and go somewhere you can come to grips with this, Veronica. Go up to Wisconsin and use my summer home. I was up there last week and it's well-stocked with everything you need; and it's clean! I had a maid service from Sheboygan come in to clean and, ah…sanitize it. My old buddies and I played some serious poker up there; smoked stinky cigars and I won't tell you the rest of the story."

"Oh, Michael, you are so considerate and kind. I'll talk to him tonight and get with you tomorrow. I'm sure he will agree."

It was late June. Summer had come in like Nazi storm troopers stomping the sunless and overcast dreary May skies to death. Everyone was in a festive mood. Young girls could be seen everywhere on the downtown Chicago streets in shorts and sandals soaking up as much sun as they could absorb. Veronica took a crowded city bus back to their condo on Michigan Avenue.

"Chien, I'm home. Where are you dear?"

When she entered the kitchen she saw a note on the counter: GONE TO THE FOOD FEST–DON'T WAIT UP FOR ME

"Damn it," she shouted out loud, "He knows I'll never find him in that mob down in Grant Park."

The "Taste of Chicago" is hyped by the local media as the world's largest outdoor food fest. Two to three million people enjoy the culinary treats and exciting entertainment offered there every year.

She decided to wait up for him. After she read several magazines and watched a late TV show she decided to go to bed. It was past midnight. He never came home. She was sure of it because she stayed awake all night and never heard the front door open or close. The cops were having a field day down below and were busier than usual judging on the numerous sirens heard through the opened bedroom window.

When she hauled herself into work the following morning he was sitting at his desk going over a prospectus. He didn't look up at her.

"Where in the hell were you all night?" she asked him loud enough for everyone to hear. "You bastard, you could have told me you didn't intend to come home last night!"

"Why, Veronica, I really didn't know you cared that much. I got caught up in some of the activities at the food fest last night and totally lost track of time."

Howzer walked by Chien's office and politely asked the two of them to tone it down. They both nodded at him and she scurried down the hall to her own office, ignoring the penetrating eyes of her co-workers.

That night she told him about Michael's offer of using the Wisconsin summer home for a quiet getaway and chance to work out their marriage issues. She was hoping for the best.

"I'm not interested. We don't need to take valuable time off and travel all the way up there to discuss our problems. You need to reassess your own negative attitude toward me and you can do that right here on Michigan Avenue."

"What, my attitude?" she shouted at him. "I can't live like this any longer. This marriage was a big mistake; I should have known better, me of all people."

He went over to her and slapped her hard in the face. She half expected that kind of reaction from him and shook it off. It did hurt though.

"I don't think you were ever really in love with me, Veronica. You never expected me to be the top producer in the office. I think that Michael Howzer envisioned you to be his successor one day until I came along. Your professional jealousy has caused irreparable damage to our marriage."

"That's a crock of bullshit. Michael and I gave you everything you needed to succeed and you know it. He was a little leery of you initially until I interceded on your behalf. Without a doubt your Northwestern degree brought you in the front door but your cocky self-adulation stupidness damn near sent you out the back door!"

"You know what I think? You and Howzer are still connected. I see it in his eyes and you are way too obvious. I overheard one of the staff cronies giggling these same thoughts to his office mate. Water cooler talk is admissible in court. They say if repeated enough it must be fact, not suspicion. Say it, Veronica; say it to me loud and clear and I'll happily give you your release."

She started to shake and cry. Then she balled her fist and took a swing at his chin. He took the defensive posture his martial arts background taught him and warded off her thrust with his left hand. He quickly seized her other hand and flipped her to the floor. While in the fall she struck her head on the corner of the end table. Blood began to ooze from her forehead. She almost blacked out but slowly regained her thoughts.

"Go to hell," she shouted wildly at him. "I knew you had a vicious streak in you just waiting to jump out at the right moment and this is it."

"Screw you, bitch!"

She raced into the kitchen, grabbed a towel and then jammed it at her bleeding head. A steak knife was sitting conveniently on the edge of the counter. She eyed it for a moment and then grabbed it. She hurried back to the living room.

They didn't teach me growing up to tuck my tail between the legs like a coward and take off running away from conflict. I'll show him!

When she reached the living room he was strewn sideways on the couch. His heart beat had accelerated into an irregular rhythm and was racing for the finish line. His chest caved in and that same pain he had before reached out at him and enveloped his entire body. He didn't have time to pop a nitro into his mouth. He lost consciousness.

"Get up coward," she yelled as she put the knife to his throat. When she saw that he was unconscious she withdrew the weapon and threw it at the bay window and raced out of the condo. She didn't stop running until she crossed the Chicago River at Wacker Drive. A cabbie narrowly hit her crossing Lake Street but she jumped out of his path just in the nick of time.

A cop walking his beat saw her stop running and peering down at the water. He hustled over to her and saw the blood coagulating on her face.

"What the hell happened here, young lady? I'm going to call in an EMS unit to check you out."

"No, please officer, I'm alright. I was going into my apartment scanning through my mail and didn't see this lady flying out the front door. It caught my forehead, almost knocked me out."

"Okay, ma'am, I get it but why the footrace to the bridge?"

"I can't explain that officer but when I was a kid I use to run as fast as I could whenever I got hurt. One way or another it seemed to make things alright for me. I wasn't going to jump."

He flashed his service light at her forehead and did one final assessment. "It looks to me like it's stopped bleeding. Promise me you'll go immediately back to your apartment and cleanse the wound. We certainly don't want an infection to hospitalize you."

"Thank you for your concern and help, officer, I'll do that."

She headed back down Michigan Avenue but had no intention to return to their apartment. Instead, she hailed a cab.

"Take me to Union Station and don't stop at 'Go' to collect the $200 dollars. I need to get out of town fast, and right away."

The driver took off in a hurry and checked her out through the rear view mirror

Another street tramp beat up by her john. I'm getting tired of being stiffed by these son-of-a-bitch cheap whores!

Chien finally came out of it after several minutes clutching his chest and then began to vigorously massage it. He finally gained a sense of mental normalcy but was still hurting all over. His body was limp. He saw the steak knife on the floor underneath the window and a trail of blood leading to the kitchen. He couldn't remember the sequence of events after he threw her to the floor.

Did I kill her? Oh my God! I can't afford this shit. My career is already in jeopardy.

He frantically searched the spacious condo but couldn't find her anywhere. He surmised that she was probably alright. He smoothed under his chin and came away with some dried blood on his fingers. Nothing surprised him anymore. Chien plopped back down on the couch and tried to think this through.

It's about time that we end this ridiculous charade. I'll see a lawyer tomorrow. Maybe he can get this big time mistake annulled. I'm sure a hotshot lawyer could find a way to invalidate a stupid five minute drive-through marriage. I don't even remember a witness being present. Maybe the cabbie sat in. In fact, I can't even remember if the so-called preacher was a man or a woman!

Chapter 26

"AWESOME, just plain awesome," said Bradley Simmons as Rod walked into Simmons & Simmons Investigations. Bradley was still wearing his felt fedora plopped sideways on his head. Rod always loved the way he dressed, never knew what outfit the boss would be in the next day. How his friend had changed over the years!

"What do you mean by awesome, Bradley, it's still snowing outside?"

"Not the weather, that's for sure but our benefactor Irene Finerty."

"Wasn't she satisfied with my report last week on the Shamus non-affair situation? I think we've put that to rest."

"Well...?"

"Well what, boss?"

"Finerty is super sensitive about her family's public image. Shamus just donated another million to the city fathers who are hoping to get eighty percent of the monies collected before starting construction on the new library. It was all over the papers."

Bradley sat back in his chair looking out his gigantic window at the snow fall. "Yes, she was happy with our report as was Lois. After the good wife returned from her psychiatric conference she and Shamus spent a cozy weekend skiing up at Iron Mountain, Michigan."

"Tell me boss, what did Finerty want?" Rod asked curiously.

Bradley got up and went over to the window. He flipped his fedora on a hat rack. The snowfall had subsided and a weak sun was pushing its way through the heavy clouds.

"Did you read about the murder that went down on Navy Pier last night?"

"No I didn't. Torrie and I went to the Bears' game and witnessed a rare defeat. The Lions pulled it out with a last second field goal. So tell me about the murder."

"They found the victim lying next to one of those docked sightseeing ships. A young couple discovered the body just before the park was closed for the night. The poor guy had his throat slit from ear to ear. A long braided strand of his blond hair had been sliced off. The cops ruled out robbery as a motive because the stiff still had a wad of one hundred dollar bills in his pocket."

"Has he been identified yet?"

Bradley returned from gazing out the bay window and sat down next to Rod, and then got up to pour a cup of coffee from the heated coffee pot next to his desk. He hesitated a long time before he spoke.

"The dead man was positively identified as Tom Scott. I believe you remember him from your surveillance of Shamus at O'Hare."

"Oh my God!" Rod uttered in disbelief.

"Irene Finerty gave me a heads up because she read your report in great detail and questioned why the labor union would be putting the heat on Shamus. Privately held companies go public all the time. It doesn't make any sense. She's afraid that Shamus might be involved some way in the murder."

"How did they tie Fenerty to Scott?"

"Besides the money, the cops also found a book of matches from the O'Hare Hilton and Fenerty's business card in Scott's back pocket."

There was a prolonged silence. Rod meandered over to the water cooler and tapped it. He then strolled over to the bay window peering out in deep thought.

Why Scott? Why Fenerty?

"I wonder if the albino working for Shamus had anything to do with the murder," Rod offered. "He's certainly programmed to running interference for Shamus. I know the zombie runs around with a pistol strapped to his

[147]

waist. He was in a gigantic hurry when he almost knocked me over rushing into the Hilton that night."

"That's interesting. Irene told me her brother also has two other loyal lieutenants on standby to support him. Have you seen anyone other than the albino hanging around?"

"I've only seen Whitey and of course the limo driver they call Max. He must be hiding some other muscle in that storage shed at his trucking terminal. Look boss, this is certainly a police issue and not within our realm of work. I'd like to stay clear of Shamus and all his people, okay?"

"Finerty was just giving us a heads up. She said that either the local cops or an FBI agent would be getting in touch with you for a formal statement."

"Why me?"

"The cops got the overhead security tapes from the registration desk at the O'Hare Hilton for the entire day and night in question. Besides Scott, Shamus and Candi being identified on the tapes, you were seen three separate times on film. Irene Finerty identified you."

"Am I considered a 'person of interest' by the investigators for Christ's sake?"

"No, Finerty cleared you," his partner responded with a slight chuckle. "She validated your reason for being there which satisfied the investigators, at least for the time being."

"So let it rest. I'm going over to the Hancock Building for lunch with Paul Keller. Care to join us?"

"I was not aware that they had a restaurant over there."

"You probably haven't been around long enough to visit the Signature Room on the 95th floor. It has a great 360 degree view of Chicago and the food is good. Paul offices out of the building and is even considering buying one of the plush condos in the Hancock Center."

"Thanks but no thanks; I'll take a rain check on it. Torrie wants me to run a few errands for her. I'm working on increasing my 'attaboys'. For some unknown reason she seems to pay more attention to the damn dog than to 'yours truly'. Say hello to Paul for me."

Rod completed his to-do list and swung by Torrie's apartment. He parked and grabbed the three shopping bags that took up most of the back seat of the Honda and rang the doorbell. She was already home and he heard Rambo at the front door.

"Hi, Rod, I didn't expect you back so soon. Put the bags on the kitchen table for me and don't try to pet Rambo. He ran back to the bedroom to grab a toy before you stepped in. He knows you love to play the 'toss and fetch' game with him."

He couldn't believe what he saw. Rambo was coming out of the bedroom with a huge cone enveloping his head.

"What the hell happened to him? Did he crash through the bedroom window or what?"

"I feel so sad for him. We went for our morning walk and a big black cat came up to him and stopped, sat and waited for Rambo to do something. I didn't like the scene as this cat looked mean to me, ready to pounce on poor Rambo. I pulled back on his leash but it didn't hold him back. He broke loose from me and went for the cat."

"What did the cat do?"

"The cat just sat there waiting for him and when Rambo lunged at him, the cat swiped him across the eyes with his gigantic clawed paw. It happened so fast. My poor dog lay in pain crying on the sidewalk. The cat spit at me and then took off down the street. I took him to the vet and the doctor thinks he might lose his right eye."

"Why the big cone on his head? He looks like a cloistered nun."

"That's not funny!"

"Sorry."

"The vet told me that it's a precautionary move to prevent him from scratching his eye and causing more damage. I have to bring him back in a week for an evaluation to see if we can save the eye."

"Well, it sure hasn't slowed him down. I better not play fetch with him; he might bang into something and cause further damage to the eye."

"I think you're right. So what's going on at work with you super sleuths?"

He wasn't ready to tell her about the murder at Navy Pier and that he might be questioned by the cops. She had enough on her plate with Rambo and her demanding job. She confided in him that it was getting worse every day.

"Not much activity at my work for the time being but Bradley is working on a big proposal that could keep all of us occupied for some time. I'd love to share the specifics with you but for the time being it's confidential,"

"Oh you sneaky Pete's; everything you boys do is secret to the rest of the world. Doesn't that bother you?"

Rod let out a deep sigh. "It's the nature of the beast, so to say. The security and investigations businesses are not for the feeble of mind and fragile of body. There are so many precautions and restrictions involved when you're dealing with people's lives."

"Let's eat, I'm hungry," he quickly changed the subject.

She heated up some leftovers and they shared a bottle of chardonnay with the tuna casserole. He needed to get back to his apartment and do some of his own chores so left earlier than usual, much to her chagrin. In reality, he couldn't keep his mind off the murder of Tom Scott. Something about the entire scenario didn't make sense to him.

"Why kill the guy for sticking his nose in your business, Shamus? You got way too much to lose being a public figure and favorite son of the local Democratic machine. Shame on you!

Chapter 27

CHIEN TRAN was eased out of Howzer Securities shortly after the final messy sequence of events with Veronica. He didn't care, he didn't need any of them; he knew he was destined for greatness. He opened his own firm, Windy City Partners. The small brokerage company was conveniently located on Clark Street near Washington Square.

Shortly after he left Mike Howzer his parents died within six months of each other. One slow business day he sat back comfortably in his overstuffed chair and reflected.

I regret not spending more time with them; they were extraordinary parents. I often think about my own birth mother and wonder if she ever survived the Vietnam War. What would it be like if for some miraculous situation happened where I would see her again?

Chien specialized in acquiring real estate assets, both in the U.S. and abroad. His holdings included several condominiums across from Millennium Park and colonials in Lincoln Park. He also invested heavily in some apartment projects on the far west side.

Over a relatively short period of time he was able to amass millions of dollars from willing investors anxious to buy into his enormously successful hedge fund. What they didn't know was that he was in the process of bilking them out of twenty-five million in an elaborate Ponzi scheme.

"Good morning Tran," his associate greeted him when he came in. "I can't fathom the crazy weather at this time of the year."

"One must accept Mother Nature and her right to make changes, a known and accepted female prerogative; otherwise it would be boring to live in this wonderful city, Torrie."

It had been raining heavily for days and a squall line had formed somewhere off Lake Michigan near Milwaukee and extended downward to Navy Pier. He shook off his umbrella and stacked it next to hers in the oversized empty flower pot shoved in the back corner.

"The coffee is brewing in the study and I stopped by to pick up a dozen glazed curlers from Forester's downstairs. I know you love their baked goods."

"Thanks," he said as he took a deep whiff of the Sumatra one-hundred percent Arabica coffee which he was addicted to. The curlers were just okay; he preferred plain cake donuts. He was gaining weight and ignored his doctor's scolding on his last visit.

Torrie sighed and grabbed one of the curlers and chomped it down.

Chien's congenital heart condition required continued monitoring even after he had given up smoking. The Marlboro man had become his best friend over the years and it was difficult saying goodbye to him.

Torrie Strait had been the third and final associate he'd hired. He preferred to jettison his office help before they really learned the intricacies of his business, in some cases just a few weeks after hiring them. Most of the ladies would quit anyway on their own after learning they were stuck in a dead end position. During their job interviews he would tell them he invested primarily in safe securities such as municipal bonds and longer term certificates of deposit.

He wanted to keep matters simple with them and the new help understood those relatively unsophisticated investment modalities. He personally handled all of the transactions, did the banking and relegated them to the simplest of administrative chores.

Torrie impressed him during the first of her three interviews before he pulled the trigger and hired her. He learned some interesting things from one of his workout buddies who knew her family history. He reflected back to the conversation they had in the steam room.

"She comes from an old line of Chicagoans who gained their wealth from real estate investments over a period of fifty years. The word on the street was that Torrie opted out of the traditional college routine that most

[152]

Strait women were forced to pursue and picked up an Associate Degree in Business.

"I can't imagine why," Chien Tran commented.

"She had disgraced her parents repeatedly while in high school by dating young men from the other side of the tracks. She sought more excitement in life than lugging text books around ivy-strewed campuses on the east coast and joining the so-called 'in' sororities that her cousins bragged about when they came home for summer vacations."

"How come you know so much?"

"Trust me Chien; I also came from the other side of the tracks."

Her career goal was to become a stock broker. He pushed her unmercifully to study and learn as much as she could about the business. She achieved her objective early on by securing her Series 7 license.

Torrie came in with some of his reports and set them on his desk. "Don't forget your ten o'clock appointment over at Northern Bank and Trust. You rescheduled it three times so it must be important."

Tran was anxious to obtain funding for his next big project. He also was overdue paying some of the earlier investors their quarterly stipend. Word of mouth had resulted in drawing in new investors anxious to fork over their mini-fortunes with few questions being asked as long as the results were *ker-ching...ker-ching...ker-ching*!

"Did you have a fun weekend, Torrie? I remember you telling me you were going up to Lake Geneva with some friends."

"Yes and no," she replied.

"Care to share the specifics with me?" he asked with a warm smile.

He really wanted to learn more about her personal life ever since he hired her but she held internal issues close to her breast. He was physically attracted to her and hadn't had sex with a woman since Veronica left him. He suffered from the illusion that Torrie might be a candidate for some after-duty activities. She accidentally brushed up to him on several occasions when they were searching the files for an investment report. He probably read way too much into it but couldn't totally put it to rest.

Her face turned red after digesting Chien's question. "Not a good idea to share secrets with the office staff," she laughed out at him.

He wondered if his associate had a steady boyfriend. She was reasonably good-looking and perky to the degree that challenged his imagination. Her past history intrigued him and came to the forefront of his mind on occasions.

Why would she give up the silver spoon fed to her by rich parents just to flaunt her independence? Something is grossly missing in this picture and I'd love to find out what.

He hopped a cab over to the bank and spent the remainder of the morning stating his case and presenting supporting documentation for the sub-prime loan request, his largest yet.

"You are asking for an awful lot here, Chien. Our board expects us to stay within the loan ceilings given to us and you are already nearing that limit with your other investments."

He sat back and smiled at the banker.

"I fully understand your position but my track record clearly supports my ability to retire this debt on the schedule I've given you for my other loans on your books."

"True, but we need more time to evaluate the documentation you supplied us. We'll get back to you within thirty days with a final decision."

He left the bank in a bad mood and headed over to Shorty's on LaSalle for a quick lunch. It was crowded with tourists and he forced his way in to claim an empty stool at the counter.

"What'll it be today, Senator Chien?" asked the fat black lady behind the counter. She remembered him from previous visits.

"How about the chicken stir fry?" he said with a special emphasis on the "stir" fry. "Last week I tried it for the first time and it wasn't fried well enough to suit me. By the way, I'm a governor and not a senator."

When he got back to his office Torrie told him that a neatly dressed young man came in asking for him by name.

"He had 'governmentese' written all over him," she exclaimed.

"What the hell did he want from me?"

"I have no clue. I stalled him and told him I'm not sure when you'd be back. I pressed the fact that you had several commitments outside the office today. He left his card and asked you to call him to set up an appointment."

Tran picked up the business card and scanned it. In huge embossed letters it read: William T. Hence, Jr., Regional Coordinator, Securities and Exchange Commission. A telephone number as well as an email address was listed on the bottom.

"Anything wrong?" she asked already having a good clue as to what was coming down.

"Not really; probably a routine visit required by the mandates of our over-zealous government to protect one and all."

Chapter 28

UNION STATION was crowded at noon. Passengers were in a festive mood. Commuters were coming into the city to shop and hit the popular restaurants. Halloween crazies in black vampire outfits were flying all over the place. She insisted they meet at the Buckingham Fountain in Grant Park. He didn't care: he just wanted to get it over with.

She hailed a cab on Van Buren which took her straight up to the park. It was another gloomy day in Chicago but her spirits were soaring. This was going to be her day of all days and she believed the same for him. She hadn't seen him for ages but that didn't matter; he would be thrilled to be with her again.

Rod was perched on a bench not too far from the world famous fountain. He saw her making her way over to the other side of the structure that was spewing water in a grandiose manner. Very soon it would be turned off for the season. She walked briskly and confidently with an obvious game plan. He guessed what it was. Bradley shocked him last week with the information. He reported that she aborted the big wedding three days before the event. Nobody knew why. Nobody asked…nobody cared.

He should have figured it out right away when she called last week and the week before leaving vague messages on his phone recorder. She didn't have his cell number. He no longer had an interest in her. Torrie captured his heart now and he harbored no intention to dismiss her in favor of an old flame.

"Angie, how in the world are you?" he ventured to ask when she strolled over to him.

"I'm great and you are looking chipper yourself," she said while biting her lower lip. "Life must be treating you well, Rod."

She was dressed in an expensive yellow tweed suit with three inch dark yellow heels. An expensive gold-linked belt was tightly wrapped around a thinner waist than he could remember. There was something about her hair. It was different; shorter. He observed there was no scarlet boa hiding the long scar that he caressed when they made love so long ago. The disfigurement had disappeared! He quickly checked her long slender legs. The ugly gargoyles on the inside of each ankle were missing! She was a pretty lady and still a desirable woman. It was time to get to the bottom of this evolving soap opera.

"You look captivating, Angie, your world has been mighty good to you. How are you and the admiral getting along?"

"I'm doing just fine." She ignored his reference to the "hubby" inference. "School is really my last bastion of normalcy these days. The kids are so smart and challenging that I have to keep three steps ahead of them."

"That shouldn't be a challenge, you could always dance and chew gum at the same time," he smiled and then laughed at his own far-fetched remark.

"You didn't say how the admiral was doing, Angie? I heard through the grapevine he's consulting with the Navy on special weapon systems." He didn't know that but threw it in for the sake of conversation.

She continued to sidestep his direct question. He was beginning to get frustrated.

Why is she being so elusive? Is she trying to hide something?

"I just love this fountain, Rod, and loved to come into the city and spend time here whenever I had a problem or pressing issue. It's one of the largest fountains in the entire universe. The ambiance seduced me, guided me and then propelled me to do the right thing."

[157]

I have absolutely no idea what she's trying to tell me. I think that it's best to let her continue. This was the typical Angie Ward that I knew before. Maybe she'd come in for a landing pretty soon!

"Too bad they have to turn the water feature off as the cold weather comes in. You may not know the fountain itself represents Lake Michigan and the sea horses stand for the states that surround our magnificent lake. This site used to be considered the eastern terminus for old Route 66."

"Hmm, no, I wasn't sure where Highway 66 either started or ended and I don't give a rat's ass about it, okay? You've addressed half of my pressing curiosity, now what's going on?"

Angie shifted from her history mode to one of a more serious nature. She had to tell him.

"When you abandoned me without any explanation whatsoever, I almost lost it. My days were horrendous. I was just going through the motions of living. The nights were long, dark and miserable. I couldn't sleep despite the medications I gulped down. I got tired of lying on a shrink's couch listening to all those false words of encouragement. The doctor told me in no uncertain terms to wipe my memories totally clean of you because they were leading to my self-destruction."

"Hold on one minute, Angie. I didn't want to be pressured into marriage and as I recollect, we both agreed to put things on hold. You were easing back into your teaching duties and I was off and running to start a new career as a private investigator. It was mutual."

"So you thought, Mr. Richards. I could never release myself from you no matter what we may have promised each other."

"I don't recall a promise, but it doesn't matter. We blew it off and we are both better off because of it."

Several screeching seagulls swooped from Lake Michigan over Lake Shore Drive and alit on an exposed portion of Mr. Charles Buckingham. She looked sharply up at them and then dropped the bomb on him.

"Three days before the scheduled wedding date I called everything off."

"What the…" he lamented in a muted voice. He already knew about the cancellation but didn't let on; he wanted to hear her version.

"I decided that the admiral was too old for me and didn't have the wonderful qualities that you have so I ended it. He preferred a three martini dinner to making love to me the way you and I always did it. I couldn't see myself waking up every morning next to the man. I'm so confused Rod, he was a good person but I want to go back to the excitement of being with you and sharing your love and interests. Is there any chance we can return to those wonderful times?"

"It's over, Angie. I've moved on; found another woman who I'm falling in love with. Suffice it to say that I enjoyed our times together but as we continue to live and thrive in this world, change is inevitable."

"You bastard, Richards, you dumped me for one of those young, sexy cutie pies seducing any man they come in contact with. I know all about your kind. My cop cousin keeps me informed about you."

What a line of crap, he reasoned. Finerty has no clue that I'm sleeping around. Bradley is closed-mouth about everything and that includes our personal lives. Angie is in serious need of psychotherapy. She's never recovered from that traumatic night when her husband was killed. I wonder if she's still on pot.

"I have to run now. I have a meeting at the Hancock Tower that I can't miss. We're negotiating a new contract and it's a big one. Bradley needs my input. Take care of yourself. Goodbye Angie."

He left her staring at the fountain. For some reason he knew that this wasn't the final act in Angie's convoluted pursuit of life, liberty and her strive for ultimate happiness.

I can't deal with all of this right now. Torrie's worried about her boss and work. Do I really want Angie back in my life? I need to put it all to rest for awhile.

Chapter 29

"**CHICAGO** weather is so unpredictable," Chien remarked. He and Torrie were having a coffee and several scones at Forester's. When they had come downstairs and walked outside on their way to the deli, the wind blew her skirt up to her waist. He was a step behind her and marveled at her slim but well-proportioned legs. He concluded that it was time to make a play for her. He'd held back for months but could no longer resist.

"I'm curious, Chien, what is all that official looking mail that I see unopened on your desk? Don't you think you should be opening it; could be important?"

He laughed and shoved the rest of his second scone into his mouth. He felt a slight twinge in his chest but wasn't too worried; he'd experienced that feeling many times before but it always seemed to go away in a few minutes.

"Oh, that stuff on my desk is nothing. I've been getting solicitations to bid on some government bonds but I'm not interested." He took her hand and squeezed it gently. "If it bothers that sweet mind of yours I'll trash them."

She frowned and slid her hand out of his.

This is starting to become a habit of his. I like him as a friend and co-worker but not in the "love-sense" way.

"I think we better get back to work. I'm expecting an important call." she really wasn't but had to get some distance away from him.

"Put it on my tab, Forest," he called over to the owner as they left the deli.

The wind had subsided and several thin clouds were chasing each other to see which one would be the first to get absorbed by the heavy passing rain cloud. When they got back to the office he told her to hold all calls. She thought that he had been acting odd lately and wondered what was wrong.

Chien sat in his office with his door closed. He didn't want to be bothered by anyone right now. He was reminiscing back to his rotten marriage and how it ended. Veronica beat him to the punch by filing for an uncontested divorce. She wanted out and wanted out quickly. All her lawyer petitioned for was the vehicle she drove and the savings account that was in her name only. He knew she had amassed a ton of money working for Howzer. He wasn't privy on how much was involved because the old man invested it for her. She'd never shared her personal finances with him. He didn't much care…good riddance.

At noon he came over to Torrie's office and asked her to join him for lunch. He was in a better mood; she was beyond hungry.

"You won't believe this, but I found a new Vietnamese restaurant over in Wrigleyville. I happened upon it several weeks ago when I was checking out a commercial property in the neighborhood."

"Wow…neat. My boyfriend loves that kind of food. He served in Vietnam during the war and got addicted to that *nuc mam* stuff or whatever you call it. I can't stand the fermented guts of dead fish!"

Chien ignored her reference to "boyfriend". He couldn't care less because he was confident that he could steal her away from any man.

From all I've heard the so-called boyfriend is surely old enough to be her fricking father. Why the hell is she playing around with this geezer; he must be loaded!

"Hey, c'mon, Torrie, it's a delicacy. I love to dip those warm spring rolls in the sauce. You stay by me and I'll make you a believer."

They climbed into his Mercedes and he drove at a high rate of speed passing Addison Street, Wrigley Field and on to the restaurant. Fortunately, baseball season was over, traffic was light and there weren't many cops around. He wondered if the Cubs were ever going to be in

[161]

another World Series. Chien liked baseball and came to the park once in awhile but only when they played the Cardinals, his favorite team. He parked in front of The House of Saigon, surprised that there was one parking space available. It was a handicap parking slot but he didn't care. He pulled into it.

"Good afternoon," said the hostess dressed in a bright orange *Ao Dai* with long panels worn loosely over white trousers. She couldn't be more than twenty and was pretty. She was Asian but Chien couldn't determine if she was born a local or had come over from one of the Asian countries.

"Do you have a seating preference?" she politely asked them.

Chien took a few minutes to appreciate the surroundings and took in the jaw-dropping Vietnam Asian calligraphy wall scrolls with embossed Kanji prints. He thought he noticed the Goddess of Mercy and Compassion hanging in the main entryway, one of his favorites.

"Hey, wake up. Where do you want to sit?" asked Torrie. "The lady is waiting patiently for your answer."

"Sorry, I was admiring the pieces on the wall. Would you seat us in a booth in the rear section; it doesn't look too crowded there and we want an intimate place to talk."

The hostess led them to an empty booth, placed two menus on the embroidered table cloth covering and excused herself.

Chien watched her as she walked away. "Not friendly, is she?"

"Oh but she's efficient. You didn't notice? There were three couples waiting behind us for a table while you gave the place the once over."

They ordered the house specialty of the day without even asking what it was; they wanted to be pleasantly surprised. Chien had assured her that every dish on the menu was prepared to perfection. He would enjoy the *nuc mam* and suggest a side dish of soy for her.

Midway through the fish plate an older woman came by their booth and asked them how they were enjoying the specialty. She paid particular attention to Chien and the strawberry birthmark on his forehead. A sudden shimmer permeated her entire body.

He was amazed at her beauty and certain that she was Vietnamese but was dressed casually in Western style clothing. Tran estimated her age in the early to mid-fifties. He was now thirty-five.

"The food's exceptional, ma'am," Torrie said while Chien just kept staring at her, mesmerized by her attractiveness. He seemed drawn to her in some unexplainable manner.

"Is this your first time here?" she inquired.

Chien told her he'd been at The House of Saigon several times but had never seen her working in the restaurant. He wondered if she was the owner based on her demeanor and the expensive jewelry she was wearing.

"Do you live in the neighborhood?" Sno Moreau asked him while continuing to thoroughly check him out.

Have I seen him before? His face looks familiar to me. He has that unusual birthmark on his forehead. Is this my son?

"No, not really but I like it around here; been to Wrigley Field several times. I have a condo in the Millennium Park area downtown."

She was shaking and groped for words and then said, "I've got to move on and chat with some of the other guests. Enjoy your dinner." She couldn't get away fast enough.

"Wow, impressive isn't she, Torrie?" She nodded in the affirmative and then continued to dip the last spring roll into the rapidly disappearing dish of soy sauce.

I wonder if she's married; I didn't see a wedding ring amidst those gold pieces on her slim but gorgeous hand. I really prefer older women. Torrie is young, cute and probably has some of those stupid girl hang-ups like Veronica. I'm going to shift gears here and see if I can latch on to her. Torrie hasn't responded to any of my feigned advances. This fine specimen of womanhood stared at me as though I really attracted her. I'll come back soon, alone and see what I can do. She and I; we've got a lot in common!

They finished their meal and went outside to their car. "A damn ticket," Chien exclaimed. "Don't those bastards have anything better to do?" He ripped it off the windshield, tore it into little pieces without reading the citation and then flipped the shredded paper remains into the wind.

"Let's get back to work, I have a ton of things to get completed this afternoon and paying a fine is not one of them."

He didn't say much to her on the ride back to the office. He was still thinking about the owner of the restaurant. There had to be a connection; he needed to get to know her better.

"Watch out!" Torrie screamed. Their Mercedes had veered off to the middle of the street and a Fed Ex truck was bearing down at them. Chien swerved just in time to avoid a head-on collision.

"Wake up and watch where you're driving or you're going to get us both killed."

"Sorry about that, too many things on my mind."

When they arrived back to their office building, Chien parked in the rear of the structure in the slot with his name posted on a black and yellow sign. They got out and walked around to the front not saying a word to each other. As they turned the corner of the building they saw two men standing by the main entrance.

"Are you Chien Tran?" the taller man asked bluntly.

"Who wants to know?" Tran replied with a sullen look on his face. He had a hunch that they were undercover cops but would play along anyway.

"We're police officers and I suggest you answer my colleague's question right away."

"I'm Chien Tran. What can I do for you today?"

"We have a warrant for your arrest issued by a federal judge. Please place your hands behind you."

"What the fuck are you talking about?" His face was getting redder by the minute and the veins on the side of his neck swelled. Torrie couldn't believe what was happening. She slid back to an alcove near the entrance of the brick building.

[164]

"I haven't done anything wrong, gentlemen. Excuse me but I have to get back to work. I'm already late for an important meeting."

Chien took one step toward the door and they grabbed him, swung him around and slapped a pair of handcuffs on his wrists. The shorter officer read him his rights.

"You're coming with us downtown. Resisting arrest is not a good idea, Mr. Tran."

As they led him away, he turned his head back to her.

"Torrie, don't worry. Call my attorney and tell him what's happening to me. Make sure he gets over to the Federal Court House as soon as possible."

Chapter 30

"LI CHONG, you've got to come over here right away. I need to talk to you and it's urgent."

"What's going on that's so important, Sno, that you can't wait until morning to call me?"

Li was able to put her off until the following morning. They agreed to meet for an early lunch at Bo Tan's in Little Saigon because she had a noon showing in the neighborhood. She was as anxious as Sno to get together. She thought that perhaps Sno found a condo building she was interested in buying!

Bo came out of the kitchen and greeted them. Sno had a few dates with him after she first moved into the nearby apartment but nothing serious developed. He was polite, considerate and entertaining but not interested in having sex with her. She figured the guy was gay. When she bought her condo and moved away she stopped seeing him on a consistent basis.

"You can't believe what happened yesterday, Li."

"So tell me, okay."

"I was in the restaurant doing some paperwork and decided to take a leisurely stroll around the tables to see how our customers were getting along. We just printed a new menu which by the way cost me a fortune. I may develop an electronic hand-held menu which would allow me to make numerous entre changes and price updates in a matter of seconds."

"So what happened?" Her friend was getting impatient waiting for the punch line.

These older Vietnamese woman talk, talk and talk before they get to the main point of the discussion. I don't think she intends to buy one of my properties.

Bo had taken a break and sat down with them. The restaurant wasn't busy yet, it was only eleven. He held off asking them what they wanted to order because he noted Sno's exuberance wanting to brief them on something apparently important.

"I think I saw him yesterday. He came in with a young girl on his arm. He constantly stared at me and after the meal paid the bill in cash. I was so stunned that I didn't ask his name. He is so handsome!"

"Um…who is the mysterious 'he' person?" Li asked with indifference.

Bo had a hunch who she was talking about. That was one of the things that annoyed him about her. She was always talking about finding a long lost son whenever they were dating.

She seemed to pay little attention to me most of the time, he recollected. I really enjoyed her company though. I wonder if she was ever interested in having sex with me…probably not.

Sno shot up straight in her chair and said, "My son, I think I saw my son. He was there yesterday, right in front of me. I could feel it. I wanted to touch him so badly, take him in my arms and explain everything to him."

Bo was the first to reply. "Good Lord, you haven't seen him since he was a baby years ago. What made you think it was him?"

Li picked up a menu and started to go over it. She really wasn't interested in Sno's wild-ass dreams.

How in the hell could this old lady know this guy was her son? I think that her apartment manager may have gotten her on dope. I told her to watch out for him but she obviously ignored my warning. The dear lady was worrying herself half to death wondering if she'd ever see the little bastard again.

"I absolutely know it; he is my son."

Bo replied, "How could you be sure?"

"I saw what appeared to be a birthmark on his forehead. I remember now that it was a tiny pinkish spot when he was a baby. I tried to wash it

[167]

off when I fed him but realized it wasn't going to come clean. It was a sign, a sign of distinction and it was my beacon of hope."

"So what's your plan of attack? Are you sure that he's the one and only?" Li asked now that she had settled on her food order.

"I'm just so excited that I had to share it with my two friends. That's the reason we came together here at Bo's. I need you two to give me some advice. I'm not sure of the next step. What should I do?"

Bo looked at Li. She looked for the waitress; she was starving and had that important showing in an hour.

"I think you need to cool it for awhile," Bo suggested softly. "There are many half breeds living around here and you need to be certain before you make a complete fool out of yourself."

"Bo Tan, that's an ugly remark you just made to me and I don't appreciate it one bit. His father was black and a proud, responsible soldier when we dated."

Yeah, really responsible, thought Li. He had his fun with her and took off running when he knocked her up...morally accountable? I'm afraid not, just the typical American GI!

"I'm sorry I hurt your feelings, Sno, I didn't mean it in a negative way. I should find better words to express myself at times like this." He knew he stepped out of line but wanted to be realistic.

"What are your thoughts on this, Li? You've been pretty quiet and I'd like your opinion."

"I agree with Bo, I think you should just sit back for awhile and develop a plan."

"No, I can't wait!" Sno was emphatic. "I just feel I have to make a move on this right now...but I'm frightened."

"You've been here over a year and a half," Li exclaimed. "You can wait a little longer and be sure that you are doing the right thing. You certainly don't want to embarrass yourself. Can we order now? I really have to go soon."

[168]

Bo left the table and went back into the kitchen. It was starting to get busy and he had to get to work. He wasn't comfortable yet with the new cook who proclaimed to be an expert on Asian foods. Sno and Li ate quickly and bid their farewells. Sno decided to go over and visit her old apartment manager. He might offer her some valuable insight.

"Come on in, Sno. I haven't seen you around for some time. Are you still dating Bo?"

"No, we haven't been going out for some time now. I've been tied up in my new business and I think he found another friend."

"So, you are available now?"

She wasn't about to open this door for him.

"I've missed you since you traded one of my spacious apartments for one of those new-age condos in the wealthier part of town. I thought we may've had something worthwhile going on."

Sno passed quickly over his remarks. She had very few friends in town but never had any feelings for this sloppy guy. In fact, he turned her completely off. He was helpful in the beginning but certainly not her type. Putting all that aside, he was intelligent and it wouldn't hurt to get another man's opinion how to proceed on her hunt.

"I'm involved with another guy right now," she fibbed. "I came over here to ask your opinion on a delicate matter that concerns me."

He pulled up his pants and adjusted his belt and his demeanor got more serious. He invited her to come into his living room and they sat across from each other in comfortable leather chairs.

"Can I offer you some tea before we delve into the problem that's bothering you?"

"Yes, thanks, that would be nice of you."

They talked for several hours. He told her he had a ton of influential friends and that he would use his network to locate Chien Tran. He also regretted that he hadn't followed up earlier on her mission of locating the son.

"I have to leave now. Please see what you can do for me."

"Hey, duty calls. I'll start making those calls right away."

Sno headed over to The House of Saigon with a renewed spirit. She would approach her quest in two separate directions. First she would spend more time in her restaurant knowing he would come back sooner than later. Secondly, she would let the apartment manager do his thing but hoped she would find him first. She didn't want to owe him a thing.

He is a lecherous sort and I want to keep as much distance from him as possible. I've seen the kind of bimbos that paraded by his apartment door. I have nothing to offer him in return for his help.

Several months later Sno was shocked when she saw Chien Tran's picture jump out at her from the Tribune. She followed the trial religiously and sunk into a mild depression about the entire episode.

No, I can't believe it, this just can't be him. Would my son lower himself to be involved in such a terrible scheme of cheating people? They got the wrong man!

Soon reality set in, it was her son, and there was no denying the fact. She had to devise some way of helping him.

Chapter 31

THE U.S. FEDERAL PRISON in downstate Illinois was constructed to operate as a medium security prison housing all male prisoners. The structure was almost an exact replica of the infamous Alcatraz in San Francisco Bay. The average sentence for the 800-plus incarcerated inmates was approximately twenty years. There had never been a successful prison breakout in its ten years of operation. Two prison riots over the years were put down successfully but did result in several changes in prison administration, all to the inmates' benefit.

"Welcome to God's Little Acre, roommate," his new cellmate said when Chien was led by the armed guard into his future home.

"Thanks, cheap rent for such luxury."

His roommate stared hard at him.

"I own the top bunk in this five star hotel room so make yourself comfortable down below. I always have to be on top, that's the kind of guy I am."

Chien thought this was unusual because he figured most people preferred the lower bunk in lieu of climbing on some type of contraption to get up on top. He preferred the lower level so this arrangement was getting off on the right foot as far as he was concerned.

"Fine, I'll take it although I prefer the top bunk," he said with a grin.

"Oh yeah!"

He wanted to see what type of reaction the big Indian would put forth. He needed to test him early on. There was a short silence, and then his roommate laughed loudly.

"Go to hell buddy! I have seniority here so be happy with being down below, okay? It seems to me you have little choice in the matter."

"In that case I guess I'll have to make the adjustment," Chien responded, tongue in cheek. He sized up his roommate and hoped the top bunk was heavily reinforced in some fail-proof manner. The guy was a load!

Spencer Littlewolf was an American Indian from the Oneida Tribe of Upper Wisconsin. Originally the Oneidas combined with several other tribes to form the Iroquois Confederacy in central New York. Many of the Oneidas later relocated to Canada and Wisconsin in the early eighteen hundreds. He was every bit five pounds on either side of three hundred that draped rigidly on a six-foot muscular frame.

He had massive tattoos on the bulging biceps of each arm depicting black buffalos with two bright red arrows penetrating their thick necks in a criss-cross manner. The arrows looked like a big "X" stamped on their furry necks. Spencer's head was tightly shaven and he spoke with a noticeable lisp. Chien was sure that nobody in the prison made fun of his speech defect for fear of being dispatched to the infirmary.

He saw Chien looking at his arms.

"You like? Some of the prisoners here make little tattoo guns from small motors stolen from different areas of the prison."

"Um…I prefer those cute little tongue studs instead, especially on big men like you."

"What the….! Are you some kind of queer?"

"Absolutely not, I was just pulling your chain."

"Well you better scrap that line of shit talk around here, little man, or you'll become someone's love interest."

From all he could gather over the next several days his cellmate was reportedly a hard worker in the prison motor pool. He irritated Chien with his constant complaining and bickering at night about how he was framed by the law enforcement agencies in Illinois.

Naturally, nobody residing in prison was guilty of anything.

"Why are you in the joint, roomie?" Chien asked in a serious tone.

[172]

"I was convicted of assaulting my girlfriend's former husband, an FBI agent. The assault took place in a casino in Joliet where I worked as a security guard. One night this jerkoff made fun of me."

"For what…being a big Indian?"

"Who knows? Maybe I talk funny."

Yeah, lisping like Bugs Bunny, Chien laughed under his breath.

"I beat the living shit out of the agent with a metal tray I swiped from a passing cocktail waitress. Supposedly he suffered a permanent injury which caused an early medical retirement."

"Ouch, that's not good."

"My defense attorney argued self-defense. The jury concluded that my defensive actions were mitigated. They also ruled that the tray wasn't considered a deadly weapon. I ended up getting a lighter sentence of three years.

"How long you been in the joint?"

"Too many short days and many long nights. I dream every night for the day that this Indian will be history around here. We'll still have plenty of time to get, ahem; better acquainted."

"What brought you to the Ritz?" Littlewolf finally asked.

"What is this…some kind of show and tell?"

"You look to me like one of those dignified Asian banker types who sip fine wine and play cutesy with the tellers although you got a pretty quick tongue. Better clip it around here."

Tran wasn't about to make a grand confession to some ruffian he'd just met. He hated first dates.

"Well? I'm waiting in great anticipation to hear your story."

"I got nailed for stealing a large amount of money which was legitimately owed to me but the court disagreed."

"Oh, it's that simple. I couldn't see you hurting anyone; knew it had to be some fancy stuff that got you in here. Anyway, I'm not interested in hearing all the non-gory details."

Spencer Littlewolf really enjoyed his job in the prison motor pool. The entire crew seemed to get along and morale was always high. Initially, prison officials misconstrued his detailed work history chronology. They thought he was a heavy truck mechanic when in fact he only had a commercial truck driver's license. They quickly found out that the only mechanical work he could accomplish with trucks was to change the engine oil.

The motor pool supervisor took an immediate liking to Littlewolf. During his first week on the job he broke up a fight between the head mechanic and one of the inmates clerking at the petroleum station. The mechanic was getting thumped over the head with a tire iron when Littlewolf saw the action and jumped to his rescue. The petro worker had to be carried out of the service area on a stretcher.

Luck would have it that the head mechanic was able to escape the fray with only major bruises to his hands and arms which he used successfully to fend off the head blows. The supervisor successfully lobbied to keep Spencer assigned as the dining hall truck driver.

Chien disliked everything about the facility to include the food, the mandated exercise programs and initially, his roommate. He had been living "high on the hog" before the jury returned their guilty verdict.

His mind drifted back to earlier times and he recalled some of the events surrounding the trial. His defense attorney Paul Keller almost orchestrated a hung jury based on a little-known legal technicality. Through several astute manipulations, Keller was able to reduce the felony counts from nine to seven. The expected appeal was filed, heard in record time and his seven year sentence was reduced to five.

"So, how do you like working in the kitchen?" Spencer asked him one day after Chien had been transferred to work there.

"Prefer that work to the menial and boring job that I had before."

The prison kitchen was a reasonable place to work. The hours were long but the work didn't require a lot of physical exertion on his part. He tried to get the assistant librarian's position but a convicted lawyer serving the maximum persuaded the prison administration to set up a legal section in the library and he was awarded the slot, much to the chagrin of Tran Chien. He lobbied for a separate financial section to be set up in the main library but the powers-to-be perceived that it would be a waste of time and resources. On an annual survey conducted by the prison, the majority of inmates were interested in legal subjects and the vast array of the legal ramifications that pertained to their own imprisonment.

"I heard they're finally going to let you teach an investment course."

"Sure enough; going to enroll?"

"Not my cup of tea. I prefer basket weaving."

Over the course of time Chien became more comfortable with his cellmate and they were becoming good friends. They did have several things in common. Both were of an ancestry which not everyone welcomed whole-heartily in their midst. Neither of them knew their fathers and both were raised in a non-traditional family environment.

"Chien, did you like the movie tonight?"

"No, why do you ask?"

"I never visited many theaters in my working days. If you ask me, the casino environment was one gigantic stage where performers acted in curious ways. You remember the saying that 'whatever happens in Vegas stays in Vegas'. Well that was my workplace in Joliet, pal."

Much later in Chien's prison stay Littlewolf shared with him his plans for the future. He was soon to be released from his confinement. Chien wasn't anxious to see the big guy leave. In a way, he was like the brother he'd never had and they developed an unusual bond in the stark prison. More importantly in terms of his survival mode, Littlewolf was well-known throughout the prison and always available to provide "big brother" services to his more delicate cellmate. Nobody messed with Spencer.

"I'm heading back to Wisconsin, Chien."

"What are you going to do there?"

"One thing for sure; no more casino jobs for this guy. I'm going to a remote location where I won't be bothered. I can hunt and fish like my father taught me on the reservation when I was a youngster."

"And where in Wisconsin will you find such a place?" He was curious. He wondered who'd want to live in total isolation.

"It's called Washington Island."

"I was not aware that Wisconsin had any islands."

"You don't know much geography, banker man, do you?"

"Not about the frozen wilderness."

"How 'bout a short lesson?"

"Only if you insist."

"The thirty-five square miles of Washington Island is connected to the northern part of the State's Door County by a five mile ferry ride over crystal blue waters. We are somewhat isolated and there aren't many year-round inhabitants because of the severe winter weather. I love it there; hunting and fishing at my door step whenever I need more food. Just to get out in the fresh unpolluted air is invigorating for this Oneida Indian."

"Whoa, big guy, that's way too far out of civilization for me. How did you find out about the area?"

"After I left the Oneida reservation I worked as a tour guide up there and fell in love with the place. I have a buddy there who lives on several acres. He told me any time I wanted to make the island my permanent home he would let me build or put one of those mobile homes on the rear of his property. That, my friend is exactly what I intend to do. I got a letter from him last week and he's already started to stake out the parcel for my homestead."

"I'm happy for you, Littlewolf."

"Thanks."

[176]

"When I get out of this joint I promise to come up there and visit you, that is, if you want to share your little island with this fellow ex-con friend of yours."

"Believe me; you are most welcomed at any time of the day, night or year! We could hunt and fish together. You'd love the people and the simplicity of our living styles."

I don't mind stretching the truth. I don't really care that much for this Asian, he's been no problem for me but I've had more than enough time co-existing with him in this "closet" of ours.

"Who knows for sure what will happen. I don't think they'd welcome me back in Chicago with opened arms," Chien laughed.

This Indian has got to be dreaming. I'm a big city guy, not one of those Daniel Boone outdoorsman types! San Francisco had been a location where I always wanted to live...almost like going home!

Chapter 32

BUSINESS was at an all-time high for Sno. The House of Saigon attracted customers as far away as the outlying suburbs. Most of the city guide books handed to hungry tourists listed her fare as unbeatable when desiring Asian foods. She even integrated some of Henri's old recipes adding several unique French-Asian plates.

Li Chong and Bo Tan were seated in a booth waiting for Sno to join them. Li hadn't been around the restaurant for several months. Sno was spending fewer hours in the kitchen and more time visiting her customers, especially the loyal ones. They were all anxious to see what she was wearing on any particular day. She was always smartly dressed in sleek, even revealing silk dresses accentuating her physical assets.

"So Sno, have you seen the man you insist is your son eating in here lately?" asked an inquisitive Li. She knew there was a certain Chien Tran in prison serving hard time for cheating clients out of large sums of money and was curious to know if he was Sno's son.

"No I haven't. He must be on some kind of long term assignment out of town, maybe even overseas."

Sno took the position that the mysterious man Li was referring to was actually her son. She was convinced that he was in fact her own flesh and blood. She'd read about Chien Tran's trial in the Trib and backed further off on her search. The newspaper pictures of Chien spread across the front pages showed his strawberry birthmark. She knew.

I refuse to share my personal thoughts and feelings with either Li or Bo. It hurts me so much to know that I've probably lost him but there is still hope. I have a plan to carry out. I'm not done yet!

Bo Tan was listening and watching intently at the body language displayed by Sno. He wasn't sure if Li was a true friend or a jealous bitch envying her success and her outright stunning beauty.

"Let's change the subject, okay?" he suggested softly. "Who's the new guy in the kitchen? I've noticed that he is sort of in charge back there. He's a nice looking older man, seems to fit in well here."

"Just call him Petri."

"Where'd he come from?"

"I brought him over from Bangkok after his wife passed away. My husband practically raised him. Petri cooked for us in one of our restaurants. When I heard he ran into some bad times I sent for him."

"Are you two…?"

"No, Bo, we're not, thank you."

"Will you introduce him to me after we eat? I'd like to get to know him."

"Why?" Li asked in a condescending manner. "Do you want to date him or steal him from her to work in your own restaurant?"

Bo didn't respond. He didn't like the Chinese lady.

Sno defused the squabble that erupted between the two of them and assured him that she'd bring Petri over to their table later. She excused herself and moved from table to table asking customers how they enjoyed their meal and if they had tried the new French-oriented seafood on the menu. She stopped at Bradley Simmons' table. He was finishing a meal with his friend, Paul Keller.

"Good afternoon, gentleman. I hope you like my new entrées."

"Yes ma'am," Bradley answered. I had a fish dish prepared in much that same way at a fine restaurant in Saigon. I happened to be passing through the city on my way to Bien Hoa during the war."

Keller nodded in agreement.

"I'm so glad you liked it. I've seen you in here several times but apologize for not meeting you earlier. I'm Sno Moreau and you are…?"

"Bradley Simmons."

Sno looked at the other well-dressed man. Bradley picked up a bad vibe and had a hunch what caused it.

"And this gent sitting across from me is Paul Keller. I'm sure you've never heard of me but surely you recognize one of the most famous defense lawyers in town."

"Stop it! I'm sure Mrs. Moreau couldn't care less what I do for a living."

Bradley looked at Sno and shrugged his shoulders.

She knew damn well who he was.

This poor excuse of a man was the lead attorney who defended my innocent son in that terrible, terrible trial that was spread all over the media for weeks on end. He could have done a much better job and got him off. Now my poor Chien is locked away!

Petri came out of the kitchen to ask her a question. He spotted her at Bradley's table and walked quickly over to them.

"Excuse me for interrupting folks, but I have a problem in the kitchen and need to ask the boss an important question. Please, I hope you don't mind."

She bid a hasty goodbye to them and guided Petri over to a small pantry enclosure. She resolved his problem and decided that now would be a good time to introduce him to Bo.

"Pleased to meet you," Bo said with a big grin.

Li Chong was more interested in gulping down the last piece of her dessert, dropping a chunk of the coconut meringue cookie on her lap. She quickly flipped it on the floor.

"Sno told me how fortunate she was that you agreed to help her out in this fine eating establishment, Petri. She told me she didn't know what she'd do without you."

"Thank you." Petri blushed.

Petri stared at Sno, wondering what kind of story she told the man. He also wondered why she decided to introduce him to this particular customer. He could never figure out her ulterior motives on most issues.

Both he and Sno sat down with them in the booth and continued their conversation. She let the two men talk as she glanced over to Bradley's table. He was in an animated discussion with that hated lawyer.

"Why didn't you tell me that Shamus Fenerty was brought into that Navy Pier murder investigation, Paul? For some unknown reason his sister Irene Finerty has given me the cold shoulder lately. You know her of course. I've been eased out of the police info loop until I heard recently that Shamus hired you."

"Who told you that?"

"Angie Ward called the other day for Rod but he was out of town so we chatted for some time on many different issues."

"What did you tell her?"

"Hey, hold up a minute; am I on trial or what?"

"Sorry about that, Bradley, please go on."

"Angie wanted to know if he was engaged. She must have been high on pot or something. I don't think Rod's the marrying kind. He's in a relationship with a young woman as we speak but I don't know how serious it is. He told me he broke it off with Angie long ago."

"And what else?" Keller pressed harder.

"Angie knew you were involved with the Shamus Fenerty investigation. She didn't tell me how she knew about all of this confidential stuff. You must have shared it with her, Paul. She said that you visited her last week. Something going on that I should know about?"

"Bullshit with your inference! I was back home to receive an honorary alumni award from my old school and gave a short address to the students in the auditorium. I never saw Angie. When I asked the school principal about Angie the guy told me she was on sick leave."

"So, now that the cat's out of the bag, what's the status of Shamus Fenerty these days?"

"All I can share with you at this point is that the FBI thinks they've identified Tom Scott's killer. An anonymous person fingered the 'hit man' who was traced to a certain lobby group in Washington. The FBI is convinced that the order came down from Washington because the hit man was on the books as a full-time employee of the International Brotherhood of Truckers and Transporters. He also had a criminal past history. However, they are a long way off from bringing anybody to trial. That's all we know for now. It appears that Fenerty is off the hook as far as the local enforcement people are concerned."

"Let me backtrack for a minute. Could this anonymous person have also committed the murder? You said that they 'think' they got Scott's killer. Were there other suspects?"

"Yes, a group of teenagers reported that they saw a hulking white-haired man lurking in the area near where Scott was murdered. They told the cops he reminded them of Frankenstein from the old-time movies. The investigators were unable to run that lead down so dismissed it. The anonymous person who came across the scene shortly after the slaying was sure of the killer. He was an associate of Tom Scott and allegedly came to town with Tom.

"Hmm, interesting," Bradley mused. "Why the terminology 'anonymous' when they knew he was with Scott. You'd think they would have known his name. Maybe the union powerbase wanted to frame their hit man. He probably knew way too much about the organization for his own good."

"Shut up, Simmons, you're reading way too much into this."

"Okay, Paul. Do you have any idea why Scott was back in Chicago? Has anyone determined the motive for the cold-blooded murder?"

[182]

"I don't know for sure why he returned to Chicago: probably putting the muscle to some goon attending an anti-labor group meeting in the Loop. Reportedly Scott was a reservoir of privileged and confidential information about the inner workings of the IBOTT. In addition, he was their 'go to guy' when they needed to stiff somebody who wouldn't play ball with them. Finally, Mr. Simmons, the union big wigs were reportedly upset that Scott was unable to convince Shamus to come aboard."

"Thanks for the clarifications. I think I'll give Irene a call and reopen the clogged channels of communication that developed between us. She hasn't referred a case to us in the last six months. I could use the business."

"Sounds like a winner Bradley, go for it."

Simmons sat back and smiled. He learned another important bit of information about Angie Ward.

Keller continued, "Do me a favor. Have Rod call Angie and at least say hello to her. She hasn't forgotten him and believes that he's still in love with her; that is, if he ever was in love with her to begin with."

"I will."

They finally got the check, paid their bill and left The House of Saigon. Sno watched them leave; hoping that one or the other of them would continue to dine with her.

I might have to rethink my hatred for the lawyer. In fact I might need both of their help if my plan to get Chien Tran out of prison was going to work. They are reportedly big shots around town and they can be useful. I've been in this country long enough to learn how people use each other to gain things they want for themselves. I'm no different!

Chapter 33

"HEY, SPENCE, how's it going?" asked Chien Tran.

"Just one more day closer to blowing this place; how about you?"

"Another day, another dollar," he laughed.

It was mid-morning when Littlewolf entered the dining hall to pick up the garbage vats. The Indian was whistling a happy tune Tran heard several times before but could never put the recorded words to it.

"Not much going on, roommate, just a few more days to go and I'll finally and gladly get on my hands and knees and kiss this place goodbye."

Chien had just returned from dumping a container of cooking grease into one of the vats labeled…Grease Waste. The vats stood four feet tall and had a circumference of two feet. They were heavy. A lid was secured to all of the grease vats by a spring-release mechanism to insure a tight seal. The vat contents were protected from the feisty little prison roaches that somehow survived the numerous insect repellent attacks by the preventive maintenance team.

He accompanied Littlewolf back through the huge dining hall past the storage room and into the solid waste room. For security purposes the rear ramp door to the outside could only be opened from inside the dining hall bank of switches. An electronic buzzer could be activated from the outside with a special key fob to get someone inside to unlock the door. Littlewolf disliked the inconvenience of waiting outside, especially in the cold weather for someone to respond to the call.

"I have a few questions for you, Spence."

"Shoot."

"Tell me exactly how long it takes you to drive to the county waste disposal activity main gate which I presume is monitored? Does anybody physically accompany you through the gate which I'm sure is locked and travel with you to the actual site where you dump the stuff?"

"It takes me about fifteen minutes from the east gate. I do have another inmate who comes with me on the trip. He's one of the prison trustees. Why do you want to know?" asked Spence. "Are you going to put in for my job when I get out of the joint?"

"No way, I enjoy the kitchen too much."

"Then why do you ask?"

"I'm curious. You seem to enjoy your duties more than most of the other stiffs around here. I get a kick out of these trustees, Spence."

"How's that?"

"They do everything possible to earn the trust of the warden and are given special privileges like going on off-site missions. I want to be one of those inmates helping the warden when he needs additional bodies to do chores around the prison that require my unique talent. That being said, I'm not going to kiss ass to get it."

"Why aren't you one of the anointed ones, Littlewolf?"

"I had been recommended for trustee status some months ago because of my excellent work and exemplary behavior during my time here," he said with tongue-in-cheek, and then laughed.

"Really?" exclaimed Chien with a surprised look because he was aware of the nasty stories about his roommate circulating around the prison.

"Yes sir, but it wasn't approved for some reason. They inferred that I was too close to the end of my sentence. I just drive; the trustee rides shotgun...so to speak. They put ankle monitors on both of us before we leave the East gate...that's how much they trust us!"

"When you stop at the gate waiting to exit does a prison guard climb up into the rear of the truck to inspect the cargo being hauled out of the prison? I'd think this security precaution was a routine matter."

[185]

"Actually, most of them do a pretty thorough job of checking us out."

"What do they do?"

"I have to jump out of the cab and go back around the truck to unlock and drop the truck gate for them. They climb in and do a quick visual inspection of the contents, and then count and record the number of vats. It's a routine task and takes about two minutes before they open the gates and wave us out of the prison."

Chien checked his watch. It was exactly ten o'clock. He made a quick entry in his trusty pocket notebook when Littlewolf went off to get the dolly.

Ten big vats, three with spent cooking oils and grease and the other seven with a pot-pouri of food scraps were due to be hauled out this morning. Twice a week runs were made outside the prison, usually on Mondays and Thursdays. All clean paper products were tossed into two recycling bins and were picked up at the front gate by a contract recycling company every other day. Dirty paper refuse was collected in large cardboard boxes that were incinerated by prison personnel every night.

"See you tonight," said Spencer.

"Okay, have a good rest of the day."

Spencer closed the back door. It locked automatically when shut. A bell resembling a church clock tower announcer rang automatically whenever the door was opened or closed.

Chien returned to the main kitchen area, went to one of the many large walk-in freezers and then took out ten boxes of frozen hamburgers. Another cook had already brought out the French fries to begin thawing. All the prisoners enjoyed the Thursday noon meal because of the popular menu.

"Hey, Cookie, what's happening?" one of the inmates shouted to him while working his way down the crowded serving line queue. It was Striker Stein, the big redheaded German. He was given the nickname Striker by his close friends. Nobody really knew his first name nor dared to ask unless they wanted to get cuffed alongside the head.

"How come you want to know?"

"You look so cute in that lily white apron of yours. How 'bout a date tonight, honey?"

He usually ignored such ridiculous comments. It took some time for him to adjust to the whistles and catcalls directed his way. Spencer told him it would happen often and taught him how best to react to them.

"No thanks, I got too much going on."

"Cookie, do you want me to beg for the date?"

"Forget it Striker!"

The inmate gave him a lecherous stare that turned quickly to a snarl of anger.

"Shut the fuck up, ain't no queers going to call me that name. To you it's Mr. Sir! Got it?"

"Yes, of course. Look, I'm just trying to do my job here by serving all you hungry guys this wonderful nutritious meal as fast as possible."

"You're doing a piss poor job of it!"

He turned a deaf ear to Striker's comment.

When he got back to his cell that evening, Littlewolf seemed upset with something. He sat cross-legged on the floor as if he was meditating or chanting to a long lost relative like many Indians often practice.

"What's wrong, Spence? You don't seem like your usual friendly self tonight. Something has to be really bothering you."

"I got a letter from my friend back on Washington Island." Littlewolf hesitated to elaborate, tears about to escape from the corner of his eyes.

"What did he have to say?"

"There was a ferocious tornado last week that caused considerable damage to my part of the property and the manufactured home he bought for me. A bank repossessed it from some dumb fool and my friend put it on my parcel of land. It needed major resuscitation before any human being could live in it and he started working on the needed repairs. When

[187]

the storm hit Washington Island he secured the property and told me the rest of the damage caused by the tornado could wait to be repaired until I got released. The storm even wrecked some of the pier placements where the car ferry operates and they suspended all trips across for two days."

"Well, at least you still have a place to go back to."

"Yeah, right, I can't wait."

"You and I both know," Chien assured him, "Anything worthwhile can be satisfactorily restored some way, maybe not to its original physical condition but certainly made livable again."

"Oh, that's well and good but I don't have any money set aside for major repairs up there. I still have to pay my friend for buying the mobile home. I hardly had enough saved before I got thrown in this joint. The casino was a fine place to work, offered me good benefits but the pay was just a notch above minimum wage. The majority of my savings went to that overpriced lawyer who defended me."

"How much money do you think you need?"

"My friend figured it would run as much as twenty thousand dollars including the price he paid for the trailer." The tears in his eyes finally gave up their hold and jumped down his cheeks.

"Look here, Spencer, I've got some money set aside that I'd be willing to advance you to cover your expenditures. I won't charge you interest and you can repay me when you're back on your feet again. I certainly can't spend the dough locked up in this godforsaken rat hole."

"I thought they froze all your banks accounts."

"Aha, I have two accounts in out of town banks under an assumed name. Hopefully they haven't found them."

"You are a true friend, Chien Tran."

"That's what friends are for."

Spencer began wiping the tears from his cheeks with the back of his hand. "I wasn't sure about you when you first got in here but you've earned my trust over time. I would be forever thankful to you if you back me financially. Once I get a job I'll set up some kind of repayment schedule. You can trust me to pay back every cent."

"Don't fret about it, Spence."

Look who's talking, thought Tran. This big Indian saved my ass on several occasions here. One time he put a loud-mouthed Polish sex maniac in the prison infirmary with a broken jaw for trying to force me to masturbate him in the shower my first week in the joint. He wasn't even reprimanded for assaulting the Polack because it happened twice before with two other new inmates. I sure hope there'll be no repercussions for me after Spence blows this place!

The saddest day in Tran's prison stay finally arrived. Spencer Littlewolf jettisoned his prison clothing and was smartly dressed in J.C. Penney's finest threads. Chien had advised him to open a new bank account when he got back home, preferably in the bigger city of Sturgeon Bay.

The plan would allow him to wire money to Spencer's bank account through an intermediary listed on the account with the bogus name. Tran knew that the rest of his monetary assets were frozen by the feds until he could complete the financial restitution process mandated by the court.

"Goodbye my good friend."

Well, maybe he's not a good friend but he's certainly become a better one with the offer of financial help. Who am I to turn it down?

"I will miss you, Spence."

"I'll let you know when I get settled up there and set up my bank account. After you begin wiring me money I can finish the repairs on my home. Meanwhile, try to avoid any occasion or physical confrontation that would pit you against some of those assholes we've dealt with in the past. I guarantee they'll try to lure you into a dangerous corner. I've introduced you to two of my other friends who vowed they'd do their absolute best to look out for you."

"Yes, and I'll be sure to hang with them."

[189]

"One last thing I need to tell you, Chien. There is a group of 'long-termers' here who can get you anything you want…drugs, cigarettes, liquor just to mention a few items. First you must find a way to gain their trust. They have inside assistance so be careful how you approach them if you want any prohibited items."

With those closing words, Littlewolf accompanied the prison guard down the long hallway and soon disappeared out of sight. Chien could hear the proclamations of several inmates wishing him well on his exhilarating journey to freedom.

He went to sleep that night in the empty cell wondering how long before they'd shove another inmate in with him. It didn't really matter to him. He didn't intend to stick around that much longer!

Chapter 34

"**DAD**, where in the hell have you been lately? I left several messages on your cell but you haven't called me back. What am I, for crying out loud, chopped liver or minced meat?"

"I'm so sorry, John," said Rod. "I lost my cell phone about a week ago and haven't informed everyone of my new number yet; been too busy I guess." He couldn't think of a better excuse.

"You've been frantically running around Chicago with all of your P.I. business and it's time for another visit up here. Jamie will be home from Afghanistan in a week to ten days and I'm sure you'd like to see your grandson before he heads off to his new assignment at Ft. Hood, Texas."

"I certainly do, John, I miss him."

He had been close to Jamie ever since he was a little tyke. John brought him to San Francisco one summer when he was a kid and Jamie almost got run over by a cable car. He was now an Army Airborne Ranger and tougher than nails. Rod hadn't seen Jamie since he graduated from St. Norbert College but they kept in touch through emails.

"Gosh, John, I'd love to come up there for a few days. Let me check with Bradley and see if I can get away and then I'll give you a ring back."

"Let me throw in one more carrot to entice you. The Packers are in town and playing the Bears at Lambeau the last Sunday of Jamie's leave; he heads to Texas the following Thursday. He has to report there on Thanksgiving Day if you can believe that!"

John was on the staff of the Green Bay Packers and tickets were not a problem. The organization had treated him well over the years. He raised Jamie as a single parent and was able to balance his demanding work schedule with Jamie's school requirements and the other important parenting responsibilities.

"I'll call you tomorrow, John. I'll find a way to make this happen."

"You better, and bring Torrie!"

Bradley had scheduled Rod to help Saul, one of the other P.I.s on an assignment in downstate Illinois. A teenage girl had run away from home and for reasons unknown the parents preferred not to contact any of the public agencies to help find her. The principal of the high school she attended had recommended Bradley's company to help the parents find the girl. He was in the Army with Bradley at El Paso and had a minor role in helping him corral human traffickers who penetrated the Army base.

"Can one of the other guys handle this assignment, Bradley? I've been invited to Green Bay for a special occasion with my son, John."

"Go for it, Saul can handle the case. I've heard many fine things about John and his soldier son. Of course I think you might be reliving part of your life through Jamie. I'm sure the Army is different now than when we served."

"Thanks, I owe you one."

"There is one proviso, though, Mr. Richards."

"And what might that be, Mr. Simmons?"

"Ya gotta root for da Bears!"

He had an early dinner with Torrie over at Dino's Praetoria near the U.S. Railroad Retirement Board Building on Rush Street. They were sitting at their favorite table by the front window. A few light sprinkles of snow dusted the sidewalk out front but soon dissipated. It was too early for snowfall to appear on the scene but he was now acclimated to the crazy Midwest weather and the unpredictable lake effect.

Rod was pleased with how their relationship was developing. He was taking it slowly with her and she was in no rush to the altar. Although they made love like newlyweds the stress of Chien Tran being in prison was wearing on her. She had been working 24/7 to salvage his business.

"How would you like to go up to Green Bay with me next weekend? John invited me to attend the big Packer-Bear game. It could well decide the conference winner."

"I've never been up there to a football game and who knows, it might be snowing."

"They don't cancel football games because it's snowing. Furthermore, this little moisture we're seeing now is an oddity. The weatherman predicts a sunny but windy game day with weather in the sixties."

"Did John invite me?"

"He knows about us and suggested that I should bring you along. He has plenty of room and you'll get to meet Jamie."

"Who's Jamie?"

"He's my grandson, silly. I've told you about him before."

"Oh yeah, he's one of the elite child killers our government sends out worldwide whenever they want to reduce the male population of a given country," she laughed. "I thought he was over in Iraq fighting the Taliban."

"Nope, he's being redeployed from Afghanistan and heading to Texas. He plans on one more enlistment and then is getting out of the service."

"Is he anything like you?"

"Yep, the spitting image; tall, blond and good-looking, mean as they come and...a first class woman killer!"

"Count me in. I need to meet this grandson guy of yours but I want to drive my own car. I don't trust that little shitty Honda that you should have hauled to the junkyard the first day you arrived here!"

"Super, I'll call John tonight and let him know."

Their meal finally arrived. They had planned to split an order of chicken cacciatore but he was extra hungry so had Dino toss in a big Caesar salad with a few of his famous garlic bread sticks.

He dropped Torrie off without going upstairs with her. He had to finish a detailed report Bradley wanted in the morning. They were in the process of bidding on a big contract with one of the local internet providers. He questioned his boss why they were going after it. Bradley was convinced that internet security was the next lucrative echelon for private investigation companies to ascend to.

He parked his Honda in the contracted parking garage a block away from his apartment. It was expensive but they gave him a good rate because he could squeeze the car into a space too small for most cars and had some minor water pipe leakage overhead. In reality, nobody else wanted the tight slot and he didn't care about his beat-up car's appearance. Last week Bradley told him that on the rare occasions he drove the beat-up Japanese car to work he shouldn't park it next to his Jag!

It was time to get back to John. He was surprised his son picked up the phone on the first ring.

"Hi, John, we're in for the visit to Green Bay."

"Super, I can't wait."

"Torrie is anxious to meet you and especially Jamie. She's close to his age you know."

"No, but somehow I suspected that. Believe me; we're all anxious to meet her. If I might ask, isn't she a little too young for you?"

"Go straight to hell! No pretty woman is off-limits to this guy. She's smart, rattles on a little too much occasionally, loves red wine and she's pulling in the big bucks. You knew she worked as stock broker, didn't you?"

"How would I know? You never share those secrets with your oldest and smartest son. Nope, but that's okay with me if she makes you happy. By the way, Jamie wants to run up to Door County right after the game. I'm giving him a two night stay at a B&B in Baileys Harbor; you know, one of those neat bed and breakfast places."

"Why'd you select Baileys Harbor?"

"Long story but I'll make it short. I met this neat lady at Lambeau Field. She is the niece of our defensive coordinator and he introduced us after one of our games. We've been dating ever since. She owns the B&B that Jamie is going to stay at."

"That sounds fantastic. I've never been to Door County. In fact, I've never been north of Lake Geneva. What's it like?"

"Why don't you and Torrie go up there with Jamie and find out for yourself. It'll give you more 'one on one' time with your grandson. The B&B has a couple of three bedroom suites. All of them have an amazing view of Lake Michigan; certainly plenty room for the three of you."

"Are you able to go?"

"No, I'm headed out to Georgia on a recruiting trip Monday morning after the game."

"It sounds intriguing. I've heard so much about Door County now that you mention it. They say it's a lot like Martha's Vineyard with all the shops, restaurants, lighthouses and ready access to water. Do you think Jamie would mind if Torrie and I can swing it?"

"Not at all; it's my treat and not his."

"I think I can squeeze a few more days out of Bradley and Torrie is basically self-employed now. I'm sure she would go along with it. Let's plan on it; thanks so much for you thinking about us."

"I'll let Jamie know, Dad, he'll be excited."

"By the way, who's your new squeeze?"

"Her name is Veronica Brown. She relocated from Chicago not too long ago. You'll really like her."

"Sounds good to me, I'm happy for you."

Rod hung up and went to the refrigerator and pulled out a cold beer. He then sat at his desk and pulled out the portfolio entitled *INTERNET SECURITY PROJECT* and went right to work.

Chapter 35

Green Bay, Wisconsin

"LAMBEAU FIELD is where the Packers play, right Rod?" "Yes indeed and we're finally going up there to see a game. John has been after me for years to visit him but it seems that I've always been too involved to get together with him. He came down to San Antonio several times when I worked there but I haven't reciprocated until now."

"And to top it off, we're going to meet your grandson Jamie. I can't wait. I'm so excited, I absolutely love family homecomings."

They were sitting in a booth in The House of Saigon enjoying a spicy dish of shrimp, bean thread noodles and too much *nuc mam*. The restaurant was crowded today and several big groups were being served in the larger dining rooms in the rear.

"How'd you ever find this neat place, Rod?"

I'm not about to share with him that I'd been here once before with my boss, Chien Tran. I know Rod wouldn't like the guy even though he never met him. He based his silly conclusion on things I shared with him about work. I've witnessed several signs that he might be a jealous lover and defensive about our age differences.

"Bradley has eaten here before."

"Did he like it?"

"Apparently, his wife saw the write-up in the Trib one Sunday and decided to check it out. She was in town on an overnighter and suggested they go there. He immediately fell in love with the place. Bradley said that he talked in great length with the owner. She is Vietnamese and came over here via Bangkok where she owned two famous restaurants."

"Torrie, I wasn't sure you'd be able to get away with me this weekend."

"I bet you were concerned about Rambo? Ever since the vet finally removed that stupid cone he's been a different dog," she sighed.

"How's that; he doesn't sniff the rear ends of big French hounds anymore?"

"Shame on you, Rod!"

"I've noticed that he tends to stay away from most dogs. He's mellower now. I guess you'll stow him away in one of those dog kennels for a few days."

"No, I don't use so-called dog hotels, honey. I hired a responsible dog sitter to come in. She's a student over at DePaul University studying law."

"I knew you'd find a way to keep Rambo under tow for a few days. Look, I was really referring to your work when I questioned whether or not you'd be able to get away with me this weekend. I'm sure you have a ton of things keeping you busy now that you are running the office."

"I feel so sorry for him. He was so successful and admired by everyone before his world fell apart. They were interrupted in mid-conversation.

"Are you enjoying your dinners, my friends? I see you ordered the special of the day. Several customers prefer rice instead of my egg noodles but I like to change up the menu periodically…keeps people guessing and they always come back."

Rod stared at this dazzling lady wearing the customary "Ao Dai". She had a perfect round face with huge bright eyes and not a blemish on her entire body that he could see. She had on "Guoc Mocs", a traditional Vietnamese sandal. He had seen some pretty Vietnamese girls dancing and singing in the NCO clubs during his tour over there but none as striking as her.

"I loved every bite of it," Torrie said with a warm smile. "It's our first time here together and we will definitely be back again."

"Good, I hope so. I'll look for you when you return."

Rod couldn't take his eyes off her.

She shook his hand with a firm grip and held on a little longer than he expected. Her penetrating stare zapped through his eyeballs; he was not too sure what was going on. Tiny ripples of sweat formed on his receding brow. Torrie picked it up immediately.

"I see you enjoyed the conversation with the owner," she hissed after Sno left there table.

"Yes, I thought she was nice."

"I'm not sure I want to come back here with you. I think she was a little too friendly. Were all the women over there like that, trying to latch on to you Americans?"

He didn't answer her as his mind drifted back to his days fighting the useless Vietnam War.

All the GI's fell in love with these pretty Asian girls after being in their country for a few months. Loneliness affects a man in many different ways and their culture knew how to take advantage of it. I was certainly no different from the rest of them back then, shacking up with some real sweethearts.

Torrie drove her car to Green Bay because she didn't trust his beat up excuse for an automobile. They motored through Milwaukee and soon admired the change of scenery once passing the City of Sheboygan. Red barns and tall silos were strategically placed on farm land for mile after mile. They were able to get a quick glance over at Lake Michigan through the leafless trees.

Neither of them spoke much. Torrie was thinking about Chien and his situation which she still couldn't figure out.

How could someone so financially successful be in trouble? What would happen to Windy City Partners if he goes to jail permanently which is likely? Who was the other partner in Windy City Partners? Chien never mentioned anybody nor have I witnessed a partner in the office. I certainly hope it's not that Veronica misfit who divorced him out of being jealous with his success.

"Have you ever spent much time in Wisconsin, Torrie?"

"Only in Lake Geneva."

"Hey, I remember the cottage where we enjoyed that exceptional weekend with several of your friends shortly after we met."

"Yes it was great. Every summer when I was young we always planned on two weeks taking advantage of the lake and all of its activities. I've never visited the northern part of the state though so I'm really looking forward to this visit."

There was a stream of cars with Illinois license plates all heading north for the big game. It was snowing slightly but melting as soon as the flakes made contact with the highway. The Packers were heavy favorites and rightly so because they seldom lost at Lambeau Field. John had recently moved to a condo overlooking the Fox River not too far from Lambeau Field so he could be closer to work.

"We're almost there," Rod said as he finished reading the Trib Sports page predicting a Bear's upset. His son "Googled" map directions to him. He was surprised how good a driver she was maneuvering through the heavy traffic.

"Great, I'm as anxious as you are to see them."

John and Jamie were standing on the porch in front of the condo complex drinking beer when they pulled up. After a few hugs and introductions they went inside and had a few more "bruskies". John took out some brats which he had grilled earlier and warmed them up.

"So Torrie, who're you pulling for?" Jamie anxiously asked. "Dad told me you were a true blue Chicagoan and I know they live and die for their Bears. Is that a fact?"

She didn't answer right away; visually assessing the tall, moderately built young man. He resembled Rod more so than his own father. He wasn't as big and powerful looking as John who was a football star at Stanford University. Jamie could be a recruiter's poster boy for an Army Airborne Ranger which he actually was in real life.

"Oh, sorry, Jamie, my mind was drifting off in another direction wondering why there were so many paper mills dotted along the river. Where are all the trees coming from?"

"Simple. Most of them are hauled in on trucks from Upper Michigan. They crank out all kinds of paper products that supplies most of the nation and even some parts of the world. Logging was the leading industry up here in the old days but they had no idea what to do with all the trees they cut down."

"Really," she said seriously. "That's weird."

He then laughed at his own stupid comment.

She picked up the gist and laughed with him. "They manufacture paper products, you goofball!"

"Now I will answer your comment about being a Bear fan. If you lived in Chicago your heart would bleed for both the Bears and the Cubs whenever they lose a game. I hope you don't see any blood on my jacket after this afternoon's brawl. Does that answer your question?"

"Yes, it certainly does. Let's everybody eat now, I'm starving!"

After dinner and several rounds of talking on a host of subjects, John showed them their sleeping quarters and they all retired.

Lambeau was packed to the "rafters" but they didn't care. They were comfortably located in the upper level sky box owned by a good friend of the Packer organization and well-stocked with food and booze. John was down on the sidelines with the team. Even though he headed up the scouting department, he didn't feel right being isolated from the grunts and groans heard on the field of battle. He liked to see the sweat and blood drippings from the interior linemen; reminded him of his playing days.

"So Jamie, your granddad tells me you're getting out of the Army after one more enlistment. What are you going to do then?"

He either didn't hear a word she said to him or ignored her.

The Bears kicked a field goal that put them ahead by three points with three minutes left in the fourth quarter. The mood in the sky box wasn't one of fun and joy but rather pain and sorrow. It drastically changed when the Packer rookie kick returner fielded the kickoff and lugged it all the way back for a touchdown. The Packers then recovered a Bear fumble on the next series and methodically ran out the clock.

"Why do they call themselves the Packers, Jamie? What's the history?"

"Please hold off on the questions."

Again she was snubbed by Jamie and getting a little miffed for being ignored for most of the game. The fans in the sky box were ecstatic. Beer glasses were clicking like huge grandfather clocks and high-fives were passed around the box like exploding firecrackers. Several of the occupants were drunk.

John came up after the game and joined them in their celebration.

"What a fantastic game!" Jamie howled in delight. They were driving back to John's condo to pick up their suitcases for the Door County run.

"I couldn't have scripted it better," Rod exclaimed.

Jamie took a quick look over at Torrie.

"I'm sure you didn't like the outcome but the Bears played well. Is that blood I see splattered on your coat pocket?"

"No, I couldn't find a big enough knife up there to thrust into my sorrowful heart. The drunken goon sitting next to me spilled some ketchup on my coat when he was jumping up and down on that miracle kickoff return; stupid cheese-caker!"

"Cheese head," Jamie laughed, "Get with it girl!"

"Whatever," she snarled back at him.

"You need to get the lingo down pat if you're going to spend any time up here."

"Don't count on it!"

They dropped John off at his condo, secured their luggage and then headed up to Door County. It was already dark and the snow was coming down harder. For some unknown reason it had taken a break during most of the game. Highway 57 heading north was crowded with Packer fans honking their horns all the way up past Sturgeon Bay to the point where Highway 42 split off. The B&B in Baileys Harbor, their destination, was located on the Michigan side of Door County.

"Dad is happy," Jamie said breaking the prolonged silence in the car. "He was the one who scouted that kick returner and insisted that he be selected in the early rounds of the draft last year."

"I suppose that makes all you cheese heads happy," Torrie responded with the correct terminology.

She was at the wheel and Rod was parked comfortably in the back seat. Jamie was riding shotgun trying to get the post-game interviews on her car radio.

"Please turn that off, it distracts me."

He shrugged, deferred to her and then punched the "off" button.

Torrie didn't want to hear anything more about the game. She had mixed feelings about the outcome. Rod and Jamie were happy and she understood their excitement. She was looking forward to spending two days with two handsome men. She was curious to observe how her boyfriend would socialize with Jamie after not seeing him for years and more importantly, how his grandson might react to her joining them.

"How soon are we going to be there?" she turned her head quickly and queried Rod. He was taking a nap in the back seat.

"Why do they call it Door County, Jamie?" She needed conversation; she was getting sleepy at the wheel.

"You sure do ask a lot of questions." He wasn't comfortable with the opposite sex being glued to his hips. He dated periodically but had little time to develop serious relationships because of his demanding military duties.

"Yes, and nobody seems to answer them!"

"Sorry about that. Okay, hang on. Here we go. Back in the early days there were numerous shipwrecks in the narrow passage between the peninsula and Washington Island."

"Where's Washington Island?"

"I'll show you on a map later, bear with me. The natural hazards of the strait combined with the waters of Green Bay meeting the open body of Lake Michigan sunk many a ship."

"Wow, *Porte des Morts Passage,*" she exclaimed.

"You're correct...death's door." He was amazed she knew French. "I took several French classes at St. Norbert's. I guess you also learned the words in college or somewhere else along the way."

"Oh, you took a foreign language. I thought that all you did in college was play hockey, drink beer and chase the cute co-eds."

"That's really funny, Torrie. Where'd you learn French?"

"It was really just a wild guess. So that's why they call the area Door County; how amusing." She was bored but had to keep awake.

Jamie picked up the vibes and started to tell her some jokes and she laughed heartily with him. She told him a few but he didn't find them funny but laughed anyway.

Rod woke up with all the chatter getting progressively louder. "Are we there yet?"

[203]

Chapter 36

Door County Wisconsin

BAILEYS HARBOR was captivating at this time of the year. The lighthouses guarding the shoreline stood like giant guardians of old. Veronica's B&B was nestled in behind several huge evergreen trees west of town. There were three other cottages on the same street but only the one across the street from her was occupied.

"Welcome folks, I'm Veronica Brown the owner."

"My son told me about you. I'm impressed."

She smiled in appreciation and turned a shade of blush rose.

He introduced Torrie and Jamie.

"I'm glad you were able to make it. I had a cancellation earlier today so you will be my only guests for two days. Let me show you to your rooms and you can unpack and get comfortable. Have you had dinner yet?"

"No, not yet," Jamie said. He immediately liked the owner.

"We came directly here from the Packer game," Rod offered. "Do you have any suggestions where we should go to eat?"

"As a matter of fact I do; it's John's favorite hangout when he's up here. The neat pub in town serves our popular perch dinners. I trust you've heard of tasty fish fries although I prefer mine pan-fried. I have a strip map for you to use while you are in these parts. I even circled my favorite pub on the map for you. You can't miss it if you go back out to Highway 57 and drive two miles back to town."

"Sounds good to me," Torrie chimed in. "We can unpack later. Let's get going."

All three of them were starved. The brats, chips and pop corn munchies they consumed in the Packer sky box at the game were long depleted from their system. They found the tavern without any problem but didn't like the waiting time. It was packed with a rousing group of Packer-backers and two older gentlemen wearing stained Bear sweatshirts.

"This is my kind of world," Jamie said. "I feel isolated from all of the world troubles and our country's involvement in a war that we probably can't win. I hope it ends soon, lost two good friends there."

"But you are a soldier, Jamie," Torrie prodded. "You were awarded two Bronze Star medals with a 'V' for valor. It's your duty to fight the enemy. Your granddad here did the same thing in that disastrous mistake forty some years ago in Vietnam. Am I right, honey?"

Rod didn't answer her.

He was on his second Bombay Sapphire martini and his mind was far adrift on other matters.

I wonder how Angie is doing. I think of her often which is not good because I have this fiercely loyal and wonderful young lady with me now. What more could an older man ask for? Yet, I feel for Angie. She wasn't dealt a fair hand to play out the rest of her life. I regret our little spat at Buckingham Fountain the last time I saw her. I should call her when we get back home.

"Grandpa, wake up," Jamie ordered as he nudged him squarely in his ribs. "Torrie's talking to you."

"Oh, sorry about that, I was trying to visualize what we were going to do for the next two days. John was kind enough to give us the coupons to the B&B but never told me what fun activities are available to us in or around Baileys Harbor; looks pretty remote to me."

"I'm sure Veronica will brief us," Jamie assured him.

They ate a plate of pan-fried perch with fries and slaw, commenting repeatedly on the delicious meal. The two Bear fans were locked in a heated discussion with several locals and the conversation got louder by the minute. Jamie thought there was going to be a fight but the bar manager separated the men before a punch could be thrown. The Bear fans left in disgust, swearing they'd never again set foot again in Packerland.

"Good riddance," Torrie said. "I can't believe they're from my home town! What poor losers!"

When they got back to the B&B they found the owner reading a murder mystery in the living room by the stairwell that led upstairs. After a short exchange of greetings they followed her on a tour of the facilities and then hauled their suitcases upstairs.

"Great place you got here, Veronica."

"I appreciate that Jamie, all of my customers seem to love it."

Rod bid everyone a good night and went up alone. He was tired. It was a long day and a longer night for an old soldier. At her invitation, Torrie and Jamie joined Veronica for an after dinner drink.

"You sure have a wonderful home and obviously a successful business here," Torrie remarked, not having heard Jamie make the same comment earlier. "It's clean and seems to be well-maintained. How long have you owned the place?"

"Thanks for the kind words. The B&B was passed down to me from my parents when they died. My older sister got the original homestead. I grew up in Fish Creek which is located on the Green Bay side of Door County. They bought here as an investment and ultimately moved over full time. When they passed on I hired one of my cousins to operate it for me. After a few years she got tired of being tied down and contacted me to tell me she wanted out. By coincidence, my divorce became final and I decided to move back here and take over the B&B full time."

"Where were you living before the divorce?"

"In downtown Chicago, Jamie."

"What kind of work were you involved in?" Torrie asked with considerable interest.

"I was employed by an investment firm."

"What a coincidence," Torrie jumped in. "I am sort of running one right now in Chicago. The owner went to prison a few years ago on mail fraud, money laundering and running a Ponzi scheme. I'm co-operating with the authorities trying to unravel everything. It's taken a long time to set things straight for the deceived investors."

Jamie was no longer a part of the conversation. He couldn't add any substance to their conversation and really wasn't in tune with the world of finances. But he couldn't keep his eyes off of Torrie. Her mannerisms and passion for the subject they were talking about excited him.

Grandpa roped in a good one here. How in the world could an older guy like him keep up with this young lady? I give him a ton of credit!

"That's interesting," Veronica interjected. "Which of the many firms are you associated with?"

"I work for Windy City Partners on Clark Street. We were successful until he…"

There was an immediate break in the conversation as Veronica gasped, smothered her chest with both arms and then shot back in her chair spilling the contents of her peppermint schnapps on her sweater. She stared at Torrie in disbelief.

Torrie and Jamie were blindsided, not knowing what to say or do until Veronica finally broke the silence.

"That son of a bitch Chien Tran owned that firm. I read where they hauled his skinny Asian ass off to prison in Illinois. I hope he rots in hell!"

Both visitors were shocked at her outrage and complete reversal from her earlier appealing personality.

"What's wrong; why the outburst of anger?" Jamie asked quickly trying to put a damper on the rage and get her settled down. He'd faced enemies in battle before but this was a new challenge for him.

"I was married to the monster."

Torrie lurched back and stared at her in shock.

[207]

"He's the reason I'm back here. I couldn't get far enough away from the crook. The longer I lived with him the more I saw a negative change going on in his life. He was selfish and protective of everything he owned except me. I'm sure his bad heart will conk out in prison before the other inmates try to kill him."

Torrie gulped hard, turned several shades of red and then swung around to grab Jamie's arm.

I hope she doesn't know that I've been visiting Chien in prison ever since he was put in there. I'm still loyal to him regardless of his situation. He's been a great boss; maybe the problem is his rapid ascension from being born a bastard baby in a foreign land and then adopted by a man of power and influence in our great country. Rod would probably get jealous if he found out that I had been visiting Chien Tran.

Jamie sensed Torrie's shock and placed his own arm around her shoulder and tried to pull her tightly to him. This was an awkward task since both of them were still seated facing Veronica.

"Let's change the topic, okay?" he suggested.

"Fully agree," Torrie pitched in.

Veronica sat numbly, not saying anything more.

Jamie was stymied. He didn't know what else to do. He'd rather take a punch to the gut then be a peacemaker in a losing fight.

Why the hell isn't grandpa down here when I need him?

"I apologize for my outburst," Veronica said with a sudden relaxed look. "I had no right to go off like that, especially since I don't really know you both personally."

"Apology accepted." Torrie's blotchy red face returned back to its natural flesh color.

"So what's the schedule for tomorrow?" Jamie inquired.

Veronica told them what time breakfast would be served and outlined several tourist attractions in the area. She suggested a leisurely drive around the entire county stopping for lunch at an unusual Swedish restaurant where goats could be seen grazing on a roof layered with sod.

"Great idea," Torrie said.

Shortly after midnight the lights were turned off and they all went to bed. Sleeping in different parts of the house, both Torrie and Veronica tossed in bed all night. The morning couldn't come soon enough for both of them.

"Good morning, dear."

Torrie had finally fallen asleep at dawn.

He nudged her a second time and she woke up.

"Sorry, Rod, I had a terrible dream."

She decided to fill him in on the strange night she and Jamie had with Veronica before they went downstairs to breakfast.

"Wow, I heard of awkward coincidences before but this one takes the cake. I wonder if John is aware of her background."

"Does it really matter?"

"Probably not, I should skirt around the issue with John and not even allude to knowing about her failed marriage. He likes her a ton."

"Suit yourself, Rod, that's for you to decide."

"Let's have a super good day and play the tourist role. Jamie said that he'd hang around and check into the local fishing scene. According to your son, Jamie was constantly out fishing in his younger days while growing up in Wisconsin. He also built a deer stand somewhere north of Green Bay before he entered the Army; an avid sportsman I'd say!"

"Yeah, anything involving knives and guns."

After breakfast they all went their separate ways and agreed to meet at the same pub downtown for a six o'clock happy hour. Veronica was going into Sturgeon Bay to shop for more food. She volunteered to furnish the steaks if Jamie would get behind the grill.

Sitting together at happy hour Jamie asked, "Grandpa, tell me about the intrigue and dangers of being a P.I. in Chicago. Dad never tells me much about your activities other than you seem to be enjoying the work. I sort of envy you."

Torrie interrupted. "He's always so busy that he hardly finds time to be with me. Every time he comes over my dog barks at him like he's just another stranger rapping on my door."

"She's partially right, Jamie, it's challenging."

Torrie smiled at both of them and ordered another pitcher of beer for their table. She loved how Jamie admired his grandfather and wondered what kind of father John was and how he managed to raise Jamie successfully as a single parent.

Rod poured each of them a beer and they clicked their glasses together.

"Becoming an investigator is something you might want to consider after you get out of the Army. Your experience and training would fit in well with our work. Bradley's company is growing and we should hear soon if we are awarded a big contract involving internet security."

"How does that interface with your field of private investigations?" Torrie asked him. She didn't know about the potential contract and was upset with him for not sharing the information.

Rod hesitated for a few seconds before he responded. There was no longer a confidentiality issue on their part because the cutoff date for bid submissions had elapsed and it was now relegated to a matter of public information. He could offer some general comments about the project.

"C'mon Grandpa, spill it out."

"Alright, if you insist. Traditionally P.I. professionals are well-versed in every type of surveillance technique known to man. There is a growing need to protect a company's proprietary information that travels in space via internet linkage. Lurking out in cyberspace is another kind of criminal that will do anything to gain privileged information to sell to the highest bidder. The federal government has already taken steps to protect their information. Private industry is just getting started and we want to be on the leading edge of this movement."

"Wow." Torrie looked intently at him.

"Sounds exciting to me," Jamie laughed as he hoisted another full cold mug of beer to his awaiting mouth. "Perhaps I should take as many computer courses as possible when I get down to Fort Hood, Texas to become more proficient in the new age of fighting crime."

"Not a bad idea." Rod felt that his grandson would enjoy that line of work.

After consuming three pitchers of beer they went back to Veronica's place and Jamie grilled four huge T-bone steaks. Rod and Veronica stayed inside the house and visited after dinner. Torrie and Jamie took a walk out in the moonlight. They were on the beach front looking out on to the lake. The cottages with their huge outdoor fire pits circled the harbor and lit up the shoreline giving off a flickering, eerie glow. She reached for his right hand but it wasn't available. He had both hands stuffed in his pant pockets.

"This is such a breathtaking area, Jamie. I'd like to spend more time up here. It's so nice meeting you and spending precious hours with you in nature's wonderland. I feel a certain charge racing through my body."

"I love it up here." He did not pick up her words and body language.

"Do you have a steady girlfriend?"

"Are you kidding me," Jamie laughed heartily, "Unless you consider those nanny goats over in Afghanistan a viable option? I spent the majority of my time detailed to a Navy Seal team hunting down selected al-Qaeda highly-placed operatives."

"Oh my God, that's so dangerous! You could've gotten yourself killed! No wonder the Army awarded those medals."

"On top of that, why do you think they pay me top dollar?"

She gently nudged his hand out of his pocket and placed hers firmly in his grip. "I'm cold, Jamie, do you mind?"

[211]

He didn't answer, he was perplexed.

What's going on here? This lady is coming on to me. She's a neat chick and grandpa really knows how to pick 'em. I wouldn't dare make a move on his girl. I wonder if he knows that she is such a big flirt.

"I think we'd better get back to the B&B or they'll be sending out a search party for us," he said with a nervous laugh.

Veronica had a glowing fire in the hearth slapping waves of hot air at them when they came through the front door. She was sitting alone in the living room leafing through a Woman's Day magazine.

"Where's Rod?" Torrie asked.

Jamie looked around and also didn't see him.

"He's upstairs packing."

"Why? We have another full day here," Torrie noted, not ready yet to say goodbye to Jamie.

"What's all this about, Veronica?" Jamie was confused.

"Ten minutes ago he got a phone call from his partner. He wouldn't tell me what it was all about, only that he had to leave right away. Obviously something important was happening in their business."

Jamie raced up the stairs to confront his grandfather. Torrie followed a few steps behind him.

"What the hell is going on, Grandpa? It looks like you came face to face with a ghost, please fill me in."

"We have to head back to Green Bay; we'll drop you off at home. I've got to return to Chicago right away."

"So what on earth's the rush? We just got here, can't it wait?"

"No, one of our important clients just committed suicide."

Torrie was at the door and heard Rod.

She asked him, "Is it someone I know?"

"Yes, I think you do. You knew vaguely what surveillance work I was committed to back home. I got a call from Bradley a few minutes ago and…"

"And what, Rod?"

"Shamus Fenerty is dead. His wife discovered him sprawled out in the front seat of his car parked inside the garage."

Chapter 37

THUNDER raked the skies all over southern Illinois. Chien Tran had been in prison for almost two years and still had a difficult time sleeping. He kept reflecting back to when his good friend Spencer Littlewolf was released from prison. At his suggestion, Chien had tried to buddy up with some of Spencer's former friends but never really hooked on with any of them. In prison the unwritten rule among inmates was based simply on a…"what can you do for me" attitude. They could and would protect him but he had nothing to offer them in return. He envisioned a terrible scene that he was on an isolated island surrounded by hungry sharks.

"What's up, Chien?" asked the head cook in the dining hall.

"Nothing doing, why do you ask?"

"No reason, just being friendly. It's this stupid weather around here, makes everything glum. I hate it. My arthritis is killing me. Does it ever bother you?"

"Not really," Chien said. "I have other issues."

"Well, get over them buddy, you got several more years to make the adjustment here."

"Yeah, right."

The morning meal was finished and Chien went back into the storage rooms and checked all of the garbage vats. He guessed they'd be full by Thursday, two more days to wait. He had much more planning to do and he would finalize those plans tonight after his class.

"Senor Professor, what ya going to teach us tonight?" asked a burley Mexican man serving twenty years. He wore a faded black patch over his left eye. The man constantly interrupted him in class.

He couldn't figure why this dumb inmate wanted to learn how to invest his meager savings in turbulent market times. But then again, most of his students wanted to get rich quick, just like him. He'd answer him.

"The value of long-term investing, that's what. This strategy has been proven effective over the long haul. Investors buying quality dividend-paying equities should be rewarded."

Inmates everywhere in the prison didn't know this man's real name and were afraid to ask him for fear of being kidney-chopped. Somehow he earned the reputation as being a mean man and should be avoided at all costs. He was a loner.

"It ain't gonna help me none, Senor Professor. I'll be too old when the governor commutes my sentence."

Ignorant jerk, the governor has no control over a federal prison. This crazy dope dealer put two border guards in the hospital down in Laredo, Texas. One is still on life support. This guy scrambled all the way up to Joliet before he was finally captured in a blazing shootout.

"Maybe you ought to drop my class and take up bird watching. I hear that's an exciting course and it's all conducted outside."

"Ain't no way, Jose. Just for fun I want to see how you high and mighty money changers get whacked off by screwing innocent folks out of their life savings. Isn't that what happened to you?"

"Not quite."

Chien ignored the comments and finished the roll call. The inmates earned college credits for his course and most of them were reasonably serious about the class. One student already earned enough credits to get an associate degree in business from a participating college in the community.

When class was dismissed he headed back to his cell but forgot that he had some paperwork to do in the kitchen. He'd been tasked with reconciling the quarterly financial accounts for the dining operation. At first he objected but then figured out he might be able to earn more privileges. His goal was to become a trustee but knew he had a long way to go to reach that pinnacle.

"I got to go back in the dining hall to finish a report," he told the guard captain.

"It's late; can't it wait till tomorrow?"

"No sir, the warden wants it on his desk first thing in the morning."

"Fine, I'll have somebody escort you."

"Thanks."

When he went into the dining hall the guard told him he'd be waiting in the little alcove outside the main entry to the dining room. He had a Playboy magazine curled under his arm.

"Come get me when you're finished in there. The boss man said don't be down in the kitchen area more than an hour so get your work done right away."

"I shouldn't be more than a half hour."

The entire area was dimly light. He walked through the dining hall to the far back, past the storage room and into the little office. He clicked on the light.

"Good evening, Cookie."

Chien swung around to see Striker sitting in the corner of the kitchen office. He froze.

"Ah, er, what are you doing here? How'd you get past security? Shouldn't you be back in your cell?" He was frightened, worried and knew what was coming next.

"I thought we had a date tonight. Me and the security guard out there; we're big buddies, told him you had requested an urgent meeting with me."

"No...no, you got it all wrong."

"Come closer to me. I'd like to suck on that pretty red fruitcake thing on your forehead." Striker took off his striped shirt and flung it in the

[216]

corner. A huge picture of Adolph Hitler was tattooed across his belly and a red swastika enveloped each nipple of his barrel chest.

Chien stared at the grossness in front of him and wondered if he should yell and scream but nobody was nearby. The guard wasn't anywhere within hearing range. It wouldn't do any good anyway. He had to think hard, think fast. He was in deep shit and he knew it.

Now I know how this hoodlum got back here after dark? I'd been told that some of the inmates bribe their guard team with drugs and money. Striker was allegedly a dealer in Chicago when an undercover SWAT team flushed him out. I got to come up with something quickly or...

Striker took two steps toward him. He gleamed in excitement, even began to drool. Strings of saliva were dripping on his filthy chest.

"It's time now, Cookie, I won't beg for it."

Chien lurched backward and hit the door hard, slamming it shut.

"Drop those pants, turn around and bend over you sweet thing," Striker ordered as he was untying the strings on his own prison pants.

Chien hesitated, his mind spinning out of control.

"Hurry it up, Daddy's about to come home!"

Chien slowly turned around facing the closed door. He spotted a clip board on the desk to his right but just out of reach. He began to drop his pants in a slow and measured manner. Striker was closing in. He could feel the monster's hot breath bathe his moist neck.

Striker's pants hit the floor. He was huge!

He was breathing so heavily that Chien thought the animal might be having a problem. His own heart muscles were screaming for a time out. Then all of a sudden he experienced it again and he knew.

"Agh, oh my God I'm having a heart attack," he screamed, falling hard on the concrete floor grabbing at his chest. He rolled over several times, fully snarling his pants around his ankles. It hurt like hell.

"Get up you sick bastard or I'll flop on the floor next to you and we'll finish it right then and there."

"No, wait…please; let me take these pants off."

He tried to stall him off.

I got to do something right now; anything to stop this pig. Think, think hard! God this hurts! My heart feels like a gigantic balloon ready to burst. Am I going to die right here in this fucking hell hole?

Striker saw him clawing at his chest with one hand and fumbling at his pants with the other, wondering what the hell was going on.

Oh, good, the Asian must be really aroused, he's ready for me!

Chien spotted a sharp pencil on the floor underneath the desk. He reached over and grabbed it while Striker was readying himself for his initial thrust.

"Fuck you," he screamed while spinning around and then planted the pencil deep into the naked German's left eye.

"Oh no, agh…" Striker screamed in severe pain.

The punched eyeball spit out blood and oozed fluids down his face. He lay writhing in agony trying to pull the embedded pencil out of his eye. It wouldn't come out. It was sunk in so deep that he could hardly grip the one inch eraser housing that was left behind.

Chien got up, tidied his prison garb and then raced out of the kitchen office, his chest pounding like a jackhammer. He'd never felt this intense pain before. It was like his heart was separating the rib cage to catapult out of the chest cavity. He tripped and fell on the floor, hardly able to upright himself, the searing pain immobilizing both his arms and legs.

"Hey, what's your hurry," shouted the guard at the hallway entrance of the dining hall. The Playboy magazine flew out of his hands.

Chien was gasping for air which was in short supply at this juncture.

"I'm having a goddamn heart attack. Get me to the infirmary right away, please, I'm dying!"

"Hold on buddy, I'll radio it in."

Meanwhile, Striker lay unconscious out back in the kitchen office.

Help finally arrived and Chien was placed on a gurney and wheeled quickly to the infirmary where a doctor was waiting to examine him.

"This man is having cardiac arrest, get me that ampoule of epinephrine," the doctor ordered his associate.

"Is he going to live?" the guard asked, concerned that he might be in trouble for not preventing the catastrophe.

"Oh yeah, he'll survive again. I've been treating him for this condition ever since he came in here, any other poor bastard would have been dead by now."

"Should I alert the warden?"

"No, not necessary, this is pretty routine stuff around here. You should know that by now."

The doctor then took the ampoule from the associate, inserted a syringe into it and drew out enough of the contents to fill it. He then quickly jabbed the loaded device into the rib cage and plunged it directly into Chien's heart.

"Agh, oh my God," he shouted in obvious pain, half passed out by now. Visions of wingless angels chasing after headless dragons were racing through his mind. He was the lead dragon carrying two screaming kids under each arm.

"Hang in there, Tran," the doctor said matter-of-factly.

They decided to keep him in the infirmary overnight for observation. It was late Wednesday evening. The medical orderly would monitor him through the night.

Chien was given a mild sedative to help him sleep. He was deep in thought now, his mind having rebounded.

I can't go to sleep. Tomorrow is the scheduled garbage run to the outside grease dumps. My plan won't work now, that fucking no good

Striker might be dead. How am I going to explain what happened back there?

The medical orderly came over to check his pulse. He appeared to be fast asleep. The orderly dimmed all the lights and walked into the adjoining treatment room. He didn't hear his patient get up and walk over to the treatment table and open up the top metal cabinet drawer next to the table. He pulled out about three feet of hollow plastic transparent tubing and bit it off with his sharp incisors. The tube opening was about three-fourths of an inch wide. He then grabbed a surgical mask from the drawer below.

I think I just might need these precious items real soon, he muttered to himself. I don't believe they'll fully search a sick man when they escort me back to my cell.

He shoved the items in his prison pants, climbed back on the flat, hard infirmary bed and drifted off to sleep.

Chapter 38

"THANKS SO MUCH, Veronica, sorry we couldn't stay longer. Your place is great and you're a fine host. We appreciate it, don't we, guys?"

Jamie and Torrie nodded aggressively.

"Yes, I fully understand why you have to cut your stay short. You have a rain check; come back anytime."

Rod asked Torrie for the car keys. He planned to drive but Jamie quickly vetoed it. He knew that his grandfather had way too much on his mind. It was dark and the roads might still be slippery. All they needed was an accident to delay things.

"Did Bradley give you any details on Fenerty's death?" Torrie asked from the back seat. She was perplexed.

"Yeah, Grandpa Rod, fill us in so we know what's going on."

"Sure, but he was pretty sketchy on the preliminary details."

"Did someone murder him?" Torrie was edgy, she suspected Rod knew more than what he was willing to share.

"We don't know yet. The car was parked in the garage and the engine was still running when they found him."

"Had anyone reported him missing?" Jamie asked as he became more interested.

"According to his wife, Shamus had called earlier in the day from work that something came up and he'd be home late. When he hadn't gotten home, she went out to the garage to check and see if he took the family car to work that morning or if Max drove him in the limo. That's when she found him slumped over the steering wheel and she called 911."

"Wow!" Jamie said. He always liked who-done-it mysteries.

"Ditto that," Torrie chimed in.

"Could someone have been waiting for him behind the garage to kill him?" Jamie was reaching for an answer before one could be provided.

"Apparently there were no signs of a struggle but that's all we know right now. The cops are searching for any shred of evidence like a footprint, a strand of fiber, even a fingerprint. He had several enemies according to Lois."

They passed a fender-bender at the Highway 42/57 junction.

"Probably too many brewskis," Jamie laughed. "They love to throw them down around these parts. I should know, I was one of them!"

John was waiting for them when they got back to Green Bay. Jamie had called ahead to advise him of their change of plans.

"Please take care of yourself, Jamie," Torrie wished sincerely as she hugged him goodbye. She hated to leave him. A chill raced up her spine.

"Roger that, will do."

Rod briefed his son on all the details and told him that he'd be back sometime in the future to finish out the stay at Veronica Brown's B&B. He also told John that he liked her and was glad his son was dating her.

"She's a first-class lady, Dad, and who knows where all of this will lead. She did tell me that she had an unhappy marriage in the past but I didn't probe her for details; must have been a messy one."

It was well past midnight when they got back to Chicago. Torrie suggested that he sleep at her apartment but he wanted to get back to his own. There were too many crazy thoughts bouncing around in his mind and he needed to pop in some sleeping pills that he had in his bathroom cabinet.

Early the next morning he took a taxi over to Simmons & Simmons Investigations. It was still gray outside and the traffic was heavy.

"Who goes there?" Graybeard shrilled, "Friend or foe?"

Bradley had moved the big cage out from his office and into the entrance foyer. The bird had been squawking too much lately for no apparent reason and he was fed up with it.

Rod ignored the stupid bird and went directly into Bradley's office. He was on the telephone engaged in a serious conversation. The other investigators hadn't arrived yet. He collapsed in a chair across from him. He had a hangover from the sleeping pills and was still tired. The pills had helped but couldn't contain has rambling thoughts. Five minutes later Bradley eased the telephone back on to the receiver.

"Morning boss, what's new?"

"Sorry to spoil your big reunion in Wisconsin."

"I understand and accept. What's the latest on Shamus Fenerty?"

"That was Irene Finerty on the phone. Everything I tell you must be held in strict confidence. She was beside herself and initially hesitated telling me the latest news."

"Why's that?"

"The police are in the process of sorting out some of the clues that have been collected in the case. I wouldn't have believed it in a hundred years."

"Believed what, for God's sake? Get on with it."

"They just arrested Angie Ward. She is a 'person of interest' in the death case. It is now being investigated as a homicide."

"Jumping Jesus, Angie Ward, Irene's cousin? I can't believe it! I thought Shamus committed suicide." He hunkered down in the chair and rubbed his eyes repeatedly. He couldn't cope with what he'd just heard.

"Nobody knows for sure what went down at this point. They found a suicide note stuffed in Fenerty's coat pocket."

"What'd it say?"

[223]

"It was in Fenerty's handwriting. It was a goodbye note to Lois. Shamus confessed to her that he'd been having an affair with Angie Ward ever since her husband was killed in the car accident. He said he couldn't live with the deception anymore. He apologized to his sons and asked them to forgive him."

"Get the fuck out of here, Bradley!"

"Hold on a minute and hear me out."

"Get to the point, will you." Rod was angry about the whole scenario but didn't know why. "How did Angie become a prime suspect in the alleged murder?"

Bradley hesitated, collecting his thoughts. Irene had told him so many disjointed things on the phone he should've taken notes. She was in a state of shock herself. He was fully aware that she probably felt responsible for not looking after her cousin enough.

"The police found something belonging to Angie's on the back seat floor of the car parked in the garage. They found her fingerprints on the dashboard and steering wheel. They also found traces of marijuana in the back seat. Irene knew she was hooked on weed."

"So how does that implicate her?"

"The police theorized that she rode home with Shamus and waited in the garage until he went in and confessed their relationship to Lois. They presumed she was then planning to go into the house to offer her own apologies to Lois for her part in the affair. She always liked Lois."

"I don't get it yet, Bradley. Do they think Angie actually killed him?"

"At this point they're grasping for straws. Paul Keller is at her side and won't let her say anything to the cops."

"What does Sister Irene think about all of this?"

"She's extremely upset with us that we didn't complete our surveillance mission of Shamus. She said that if we'd done our job properly we would've picked up the obvious…the fact he was having an affair with her cousin. That's why I called you back here."

[224]

"She may have a point here. We may have closed the books on him much too soon."

"Perhaps."

"Way too soon…way too soon," echoed a voice in the hallway. They both hustled out of the office to see who overhead their conversation. Nobody was there, and then they saw Graybeard jumping up and down in the cage whistling a "way too soon mates, way too soon" verse.

The front door opened and the other two investigators walked in wondering what was going on in the front vestibule.

"Good morning, mates," Saul said to his cohorts.

"And to you," responded Graybeard, waving one of her clawed feet.

"Shut the fuck up, both of you," Rod snapped. "Can't you see we're in deep *kimchee*?"

"What's going on?" Jorge asked as he joined his associate by the bird cage. "Aren't you overjoyed in seeing both of our smiling faces this fine morning?"

Rod went back to his office and pulled some old files out of the cabinet. He wanted to review the entire detailed surveillance report that they sent to Irene Finerty to see if something was overlooked. He felt bad for Angie and was happy that Paul Keller was advising her.

Bradley took the other two investigators back to the library and briefed them on the situation. They knew nothing about the involvement of Simmons & Simmons in the past surveillance of Shamus Fenerty. He swore them to silence because of the possible explosiveness of the case. He was sure that Irene Finerty briefed the police investigators of their past surveillance of Fenerty.

"How does Rod fit into all this?" Jorge asked. He wasn't wearing his do-rag today but donned a white baseball cap with the stiff bill turned backwards.

"At this point we don't know for sure but I doubt he'll be implicated."

"Is there anything you want us to do?" Saul pitched in. He also was concerned. The entire episode had "explosiveness" written all over it...in indelible ink!

"Not at this point, guys but I'll dial you in at a moment's notice if need be. Thanks."

Rod continued reviewing his surveillance files to see if he missed anything that would've tied Angie Ward to Shamus Fenerty. He found nothing. He was highly perplexed.

I can't seem to get that she-devil woman out of my life. I must be suffering from some kind of extreme sensual addiction to the woman. Her and Shamus...who would've believed? Angie, a school teacher of all things and she thought I'd be a good teacher instead of a sneaky private investigator. No way could I put up with a bunch of snotty-nosed 'spoiled to the flesh' kids, especially teenagers. Ugh, the thought of it!

Chapter 39

STRIKER was found early the next morning by the head cook scurrying after some paperwork in the kitchen office. Apparently his cell mate propped up a dummy-like figure in Striker's bed the night before that passed the guard head count. The German was lying in the far corner of the room naked and in a coma. The medics were called in from the infirmary and loaded him on to a gurney. He was barely alive. The guard accompanying the medics told the head cook he didn't know any of the details about the bloody assault until now.

"What the hell happened to him?" asked the first cook when his boss came out front to the serving line.

"Don't know for sure. Word on the street is that Striker had a 'big time case' for Chien Tran. I wouldn't doubt for a minute that he tried to seduce him in our back office."

"Where's Tran right now?" asked a second cook who overheard the conversation.

"He should be here any minute. I was alerted earlier that he spent the night in the infirmary with some kind of heart problem."

"Oh boy, Striker finally got what was coming to him," added a third cook who was slicing more tomatoes for the salad bar.

"Yeah, but if he survives, Tran is a goner if in fact he was the culprit," chipped in the head cook. The other two nodded in agreement.

Later that morning the guard on duty the previous night with Chien Tran came forward and told his boss about the inmate's race out of the kitchen in great pain. Circumstantial evidence implicated Tran as the perpetrator.

Chien finally showed up for work during the lunch serving period. All eyes in the dining hall were glued to him. Word of the fight spread like wildfire up and down the hollow corridors. He was the newest prison hero; that is, to everyone except Striker's inner circle.

His investment class was cancelled for the evening. He was glad. The Mexican would probably have cornered him for all of the bloody details. Chien knew the guy hated Striker because of an earlier confrontation with the German, reportedly with no clear-cut winner.

The next day Chien was called to the warden's office.

"I'm reviewing the incident that occurred last night. We're trying to figure out what the hell to do with your sorry ass. I might stuff you in confinement for a month. You're a fucking danger to everyone around here. Poor Striker, of all people, for God's sake!"

"Is he dead?"

"No. The doctor told me he'd survive. You're lucky, mister."

"He tried to rape me! Doesn't that mean anything to you?"

"That's not the story I heard."

"What the hell!" Chien cried in total amazement; he couldn't believe what he'd just heard.

"I got a sworn statement from the shaken Striker that you lured him into the kitchen office on a promise to 'lay down' for him. He said that you'd offered sex to him on several occasions in the past."

"He obviously was in no condition to say that, warden. You can't believe him. He's a liar and everybody around here knows that."

"It's a moot point at this time. We're evacuating him to another federal prison that is medically equipped and staffed to treat his eye injury. You probably blinded him for life."

"Warden, what if I get a witness that heard Striker proposition me?"

"You dumbbell; anyone in the joint would perjure themselves for a price. I wasn't born yesterday."

Chien was escorted back to his cell. He was relieved of duty for that day. The warden told him to write out a detailed report of what happened last night. There would be an internal investigation and maybe he would be exonerated if he stayed out of trouble for the remainder of his prison sentence.

"Please get this to the warden," Chien asked the cell wing guard after he signed off on the statement.

"Sure will, tough guy."

The warden was happy to get rid of Striker. The big German was nothing but trouble for him and finally got what was coming to him. At the same time he knew there'd be an investigation. He'd take his chances on that because his supervisors knew he ran a "tight ship" with limited resources. He was also a little confused about the whole incident.

How could this slim Asian guy whip Striker in a fight? He must have some mysterious power bestowed upon him. I take my hat off to him but he needs to be watched more closely. I can't afford a repeat or my ass is grass.

Chien was back at work in the dining room the next morning.

"I heard you lucked out with the warden," the head cook said. "Not many of us in the joint are as lucky as you. We expected the hammer to drop on you, hard…very hard."

"What can I say?"

He was feeling real good now. Everyone he came in contact with applauded him for his victory over Striker. However, none of them knew his days were numbered if he didn't get his heart repaired soon. It certainly wasn't in the cards while he was in federal custody. He was getting worse every day.

He was busy serving the infamous soup of the day. The inmates constantly gripped about the "watery" concoctions with the mysterious ingredients. He was stirring the soup with a huge ladle when one of the inmates slipped him a note. He turned around to see if anyone was looking and then stuffed it in his back pocket. He would read it later.

"I hear you're a big hero now, Senor Tran." Class was over for the evening and his Mexican student seemed elated. "I couldn't a done a

[229]

better job myself on that useless piece of garbage. He wasn't that tough, either."

"Forget it. It's done."

"Nobody around the joint will forget it. You'd better watch your ass around here; your days on this planet might be numbered."

"Thanks for the heads up."

He went back to his cell to relax and do some reading. Torrie had sent him a letter bringing him up to date with her activities. Her visits were becoming less frequent. She told him that most of the restitution has been made to the deceived investors and that the feds were following that process closely. She had to sell most of the properties to come up with enough assets to pay them off.

Just before lights out he remembered the note in his back pocket. He ripped it out and read it.

He knew it was coming but not this quickly. It read...

You are a dead man you Asian prick. You will be history by this weekend!

Chien tore it up and checked the calendar on the wall. He'd lost track of time ever since the assault took place. Tomorrow was Monday. They'd be picking up the grease and food scrap vats to haul off to the outside civilian dump. If he valued his life, now was the time to execute his plan!

He was allowed to go down to the kitchen earlier than normal Monday morning. After all, he was now famous so pushed for more and more privileges based on his notoriety. He went into the waste room containing the grease and food scrap vats and paper products containers. All of the vats were full except one food scrap vat. He replaced the spring-latch lock on the partially filled vat with a homemade mechanism he'd been working on for months. It would spring in place when shut but not lock.

He tested the spring lock several times to insure that it seated properly without locking. He was comfortable with his innovation.

"Good morning." The chief cook seemed much friendlier when he came into the kitchen area.

"Hey, how's it going?" Chien responded with a relaxed smile.

"Pretty good, thanks. I got a note from the captain of the guard unit that you can leave at nine-thirty for a doctor's appointment. How's the old ticker doing these days anyway?"

"I'm still here."

Chien purposely traded assignments with another cook who wasn't working the receiving line this morning. He did not want to receive any more messages or hear any comments that he was a goner. At nine-thirty he alerted the chief cook that he'd be checking out for the infirmary. He walked out the front entrance of the dining hall, did a ninety degree turn and immediately slipped through a door leading to the back of the kitchen. He opened another door and slid into the solid waste room.

It was dark in the stinky room. There were no windows to the outside. He walked over to the food scrap vat, the one with the top latch he modified. He then opened it and climbed in. It was a tight struggle to get down far enough in the smelly vat so that his head could comfortably clear the top cover. He closed it but not tightly. Now the wait came. When he finally heard the voices he tightened the latch.

"Hey, partner, hurry up and get this shit outta here so we can finish up early today. I got big plans for the rest of the day."

"Good idea."

So far...so good for me. I got to release the lid on this vat soon to get some air. I'm dying in here!

Chien could feel his vat being wheeled out and loaded into the back of the truck. The rear ramp truck door was slammed shut. He quickly removed the surgical mask he had donned, opened the lid slightly and shoved one end of the plastic tubing out of the vat and the other into his dry mouth. He had to estimate the time of the run from the rear of the dining hall ramp to the East gate so he could get enough air into his lungs.

Soon the truck came to a halt at the entrance gate.

"Drop that ramp so we can jump in and inspect," ordered the guard.

"Yes sir," responded the trustee riding shotgun in the truck.

When Chien heard the gate guard give the order he quickly pulled the plastic hose back in, closed the lid cover and put the surgical mask back on. He was soaking wet from sweat and almost threw up again. The first time he let loose was when he was being hoisted up the ramp to the back of the truck. A chunk of the vomited food stuck to his mask and made him retch once again.

"How come you only got eight vats this time?" the guard asked the trustee as he made a note in his log.

"Don't know, buddy; don't fill 'em, just haul 'em."

"What do you mean by that? Did you forget the other two or weren't they ready to be carried off?"

"They only gave us eight of 'em."

"Okay, get your sweet asses the hell out of here."

Chien was relieved. Two of the three crisis points were behind him now. He went through the same drill again to get more air into his starved lungs. He experienced a fainting spell coming on and hoped that he wouldn't pass out. His heart was galloping faster than usual and he didn't have the pill to pop in his mouth and slow his heart rate down. He forgot the little magic box under his bed when he left for the kitchen this morning.

Fifteen minutes had passed and the prison truck came to a stop. He presumed they had reached the county dump.

"Swing it in here, boys," said one of the county employees. "You can drop those dirty vats off over there on those two large pallets. The steam-cleaned empty vats are over on the next set of pallets. Make sure you pick them up before you leave."

Chien quickly pulled his air vent back in, shut the lid cover and readied himself to be wheeled off of the truck. He wasn't sure he would make it. He drifted in and out of a coma-like trance on the short run to the county

[232]

facility. His heart was pounding so loud he was afraid that the trustee and other inmate would hear it.

"That's it, partner, we're out of here."

"See you guys on the next run and be sure to have a nice day," the county employee said as he locked the gate after them.

Chien couldn't wait a second longer. He'd blacked out but came out of it. He tried to pop the cover open but it didn't budge. He garnered up all of his remaining strength and karate chopped the lid. It sprung open and the vat fell over. He slowly crawled out of the stinking container, drew in several deep breaths of fresh air and then turned his head around slowly.

There, standing twenty feet away from him and staring directly into his face was the county employee.

Chapter 40

BO TAN was perched on a bar stool in The House of Saigon waiting for Petri to come out of the kitchen. It was still early afternoon between the lunch and dinner rush crowds. The bar area was immediately to the left of the entrance to the restaurant and separated from the dining area by multi-colored wall murals with no particular design.

"Hey, Petri, what's going on?"

"Not much, good to see you."

"When will Sno be back from her bank run?"

"She just walked in the front door."

Sno walked over and put her arms around both of them. She reached into a shopping bag and pulled out two wrapped packages, giving the larger one to Petri and the other one to Bo.

"What's this all about?" Petri asked. He immediately became suspicious.

"Open it, stupid and see for yourself," Bo laughed.

The package contained an oak humidor passed down through the ages with half inch sterling silver initials depicting the letters HLM for Henri Louie Moreau. Petri opened the humidor lid and found a pair of solid gold cuff links and a gold stickpin.

"What a nice surprise, Sno, you shouldn't have done this."

"You have been a wonderful friend over the years and I wanted to reward you with something dear to my heart. You knew my Henri well and I know he'd appreciate you having this."

"How could one forget such a wonderful, giving man like Henri? You were so fortunate to have spent a good share of your life with him. Thank you so much."

"I've heard so much about him," Bo said as he opened his package. It contained a Rolex watch.

"You shouldn't have, Sno, I…"

"Hush up. You've helped me out tremendously in my stay here. I'm not sure what I would have done without your guidance and fellowship, not to mention your off-beat humor."

"Nor I," Bo laughed at the "humor" connection.

Paul Keller entered the restaurant with a pretty Eurasian girl hanging on his arm and saw Sno in deep conversation with her two male friends.

"I have great news for you, Sno; can we talk alone?"

"Of course, let's go back in my office."

Keller looked at Petri and then at Bo. "Can I leave this angelic lady with you two gentlemen while I talk with the owner? It won't take more than ten or fifteen minutes. My friend's absolutely dying for a glass of merlot."

"Well, if we have to," Bo lamented.

Keller took that as a yes. "I'll be back soon, honey."

Paul followed Sno back to her office. She stopped briefly at two tables to acknowledge and thank her customers for dining at The House of Saigon. Each of the men got out of the booth and gave her a big hug while their female counterparts let out big sighs.

"Please tell me what I want to hear," Sno said after they sat down in her office behind the closed door. She had let bygones be bygones and hired the renowned Keller to see if he could find a way to get her son released from prison.

"We did it Sno, we absolutely did it! I got the call an hour ago."

She got up and gave him a tight squeeze, kissed his cheeks repeatedly and thanked him.

"We need to celebrate, Paul. We need to start right this minute."

"Hold on. We really should have Torrie here because she was so instrumental in getting it done."

"True, without her it wouldn't have happened. Tell you what, we'll have yet a bigger celebration when my Chien gets back here and Torrie will be the co-featured guest."

"Let's go out and tell Bo and Petri," she said. "They will be thrilled to hear the news."

They were engaged in a spirited conversation when Sno and Paul wandered over to them. Petri was apparently trying to make a major point judging by the way his hand was circling wildly in the air. He told Bo that a blind golfer just won a big PGA tournament. Bo wasn't sharp enough to immediately grasp the fact that the contest was played at night. Paul's date showed no interest in the conversation whatsoever and chug-a-lugged her glass of wine.

"I do not agree with that ridiculous statement," Bo said finally pointing at his friend. "Show me proof and I'll kiss your wide behind!"

"Hey, everyone," Sno shouted, "I've got great, great news to share with you. My son will be getting out of prison right away. His sentence has been commuted after having served two of his five year incarceration."

"Why are they releasing him early?" Bo asked.

"You tell them, Paul."

He nodded at Sno but had a hard time simplifying the details.

"When Sno first contacted me almost a year ago, I brought in a well-known attorney from Los Angeles to help me with another strategy. He was a former Member of Congress and knew the ins-and-outs of Article II, Section Two of the Constitution which gives the President the power to grant pardons for offenses committed against the United States."

"Was this the same hot shot lawyer in the OJ murder case years ago?" Bo asked intently.

"No it wasn't, please allow me to continue."

"The Supreme Court had interpreted this Article to also extend the authority to commute sentences. My associate successfully maneuvered our request all the way up to the top of the legal ladder. It was referred to and reviewed by the Department of Justice and then forwarded to the President for action."

"Um...you lost me," said Petri.

"Jesus, honey," Paul's girlfriend finally entered the conversation. "You're not teaching a bunch of third year law students about constitutional law for God sakes; give them a break!"

"Yeah," Bo chipped in. "You're talking to a couple of true-blue foreigners here. Why would the 'Prez' cut him loose?"

"Hear me out, everyone."

Sno nodded, and then put her fingers to her lips indicating they should shut up and listen.

"Not only was Torrie able to complete the entire restitution amount but she also found a way to add lost interest earnings on everybody's investment."

"How'd she come up with all that money?" the girlfriend asked. She now became interested in the conversation. She was also a trial lawyer.

"Windy City Partners had millions invested in commercial property both in the U.S. and in emerging countries. The assets appreciated considerably over the short time of the investment."

"Did the President pardon him then?" Petri asked, now understanding more of the details.

"No, a pardon would in essence state that no crime was committed which is not the case here. By commuting the sentence he acknowledged the crime but basically gave him a lesser time to serve."

"I don't get it," Bo countered.

"I'll explain it another way. Chien was initially sentenced to seven years but we successfully appealed it down to five years shortly after the initial trial. By commuting the sentence, the President agreed to reduce the remaining sentence to the time he had already served in federal prison."

"Why don't you tell these two guys the rest of the story, Paul?" suggested his girlfriend. "They should know all of the facts in the case."

"Now you sound like a hot-shot lawyer, but you're right."

Petri and Bo stared at both of them. Sno just smiled.

Paul continued, "Our Los Angeles attorney suggested I get Sno involved in the process from the beginning. Even though he was well-known in Washington, another heavy-hitter would certainly help our cause."

"So...?" Bo droned. Petri waved his hand in a "come on" gesture.

"Sno contacted her priest friend at the New Age Buddhist Church of Mahayana to see if there was any way he could assist her. Priest Quan had been on a brief religious mission back in Bangkok during the trial of her son so wasn't fully aware of the situation."

Petri chimed in, "How could he help Sno?"

"Good things happen to good people," Paul assured him. "Quan grew up in Thailand with the current Thai Ambassador to the United States who happened to be an occasional golfing partner of our own President."

"Ah...so, I get it," Bo exclaimed. "The President is nearing the end of his second full term and had nothing to lose by commuting her son's prison sentence."

"Something like that," Paul laughed, "The precedent had already been established by former presidents not worried about possible repercussions in getting reelected. On a side note, the amount of time Chien spent in house arrest and the long trial that ensued was deemed a part of his prison sentence already served."

"You mean he's free to come home right now, this minute?" Petri asked pointedly.

Paul smiled and then looked at Sno. "Yes, as quickly as someone can run down there with decent clothes and pick him up. She just found out. We've already contacted the warden advising him we'd be at the prison day after tomorrow to get him. A stretch limo has already been reserved. She asked the warden not to inform Chien. She wants him to be surprised when she shows up."

"Do you want me or Bo to go with you two guys?"

"Thanks, but its best if just Paul and I go. I've been planning this for so many years I'm not sure how I'll react when my son climbs into the limousine but Paul will be there to support me."

She fell silent for a moment.

I'm not sure what my little boy will do when he sees me. I trust he won't reject my love and hope for reconciliation after these many years. Maybe he'll spurn me and even disown me for giving him up to the orphanage. So many possible outcomes but I'll gladly take my chances!

Chapter 41

Somewhere in Illinois

CHIEN TRAN was twenty feet away from the county dump custodian as he crawled slowly out of the upended vat. The custodian was staring in awe, not believing what was happening before his own eyes. A few minutes earlier he'd heard some coughing and puking noises coming from one of the vats and decided to walk over to investigate.

"What's going on here?" asked the shocked custodian with a sheepish voice. He knew damn well what was happening but couldn't put the obvious words together.

"What are you up to?"

Chien didn't respond. He measured up his opponent. The custodian was an older man, sickly looking and probably not weighing a hundred pounds hanging from a skinny bent-over frame. He knew he could overpower the guy without any problem. However, he failed to notice the crowbar clamped tightly in the custodian's right hand, partially hidden behind his back.

He ignored the custodian's question and asked one of his own.

"Where's your sanitation station located? You know what I'm talking about, the place you people use to recycle the prison vats?" Chien demanded in an authoritative voice.

"It's back there behind that large garage building." The custodian pointed in a direction behind the escaped inmate. He continued to walk closer to Chien.

It was a big mistake.

"Tell me what you intend to do with that crow bar, old man?" He spotted the weapon as an immediate threat. The man waddled closer to him lifting up the crowbar to a strike position.

"If you want to live to see you grandkids graduate from college, you'd better drop that thing right now, old-timer."

"Oh, I see what you mean; don't be alarmed." The custodian started to noticeably shake and quiver. "I use it to open up these stinking vats." He stopped in his tracks and flipped the crow bar off to the side. He didn't like the penetrating eyes that were dissecting his every movement.

"Are you going to hurt me?"

"Depends."

The old man started to cower. "If you get out of the dump right away I won't blow the whistle on you."

"I'll kill you with my bare hands if you reach for your cell phone or even try to alert those other guys by the garage. Do you understand me?"

"Yes sir, I do."

The custodian started to weep. He didn't trust the inmate and knew his life was in danger. He fell to his knees and started to pray.

Chien laughed at him.

"Please don't harm me. Take the keys to my car and you can get the hell out of here. It's parked over by the main entrance where your truck came through a short time ago."

"Give me the fucking keys, right now!"

The custodian got up and started to reach in his pockets when Chien kicked the old man's hands with his raised foot.

"Stop, I'll do it, stand still. I want to make sure you don't have one of those police whistles in there to blow for help."

Tran came forward and roughly spun him around. He reached into the man's front trouser pockets and took his car keys and cell phone. He then quickly lifted the custodian's wallet out of his rear pocket.

"Now take your clothes off."

"What the…."

[241]

"You heard me. Do it now old man or you die!"

The custodian hesitated but finally obeyed the order and quickly shed his coveralls. Chien was getting nervous. He kept peering over at the garage to insure that nobody was watching him. He picked up the crowbar and bounced it hard over the custodian's head and then stuffed him in the vat.

"But I'll die in here," the custodian yelled as he quickly came to. Tran ignored him and slammed the cover shut. "Go to hell!"

He then circled back and picked up the crowbar and forced it through a pair of U-bolts extending upward from each side of the lid so that the cover could no longer be opened from the inside.

Chien shed his stinking prison clothes and struggled into the older man's clothing. He ran over to one of the parked cars inside the front gate. There were three of them. He got in, shoved the key into the ignition and cranked the engine to make sure it was the custodian's vehicle. The engine turned over. He jumped out of the car and went into the little guard shed and flipped the switch that opened the county dump main gate. He climbed back into the custodian's car and sped off.

I got to find a car wash and hose myself off, he said to himself. I'll locate a thrift store or Salvation Army outlet to get some decent clothes. The old man's clothes don't fit and I'm about to be strangled.

Chien drove for an hour on the back roads and came to a small town about fifty miles from the federal prison. He knew he had to act fast and dump the car. He was sure that an "all points" bulletin would soon flood every conceivable communication channel and alert law enforcement agencies state-wide. He reasoned they'd find him missing at the noon roll call. He glanced at the watch he swiped from the old man. It was straight up twelve.

"That will be exactly twenty dollars, sir."

The cashier at the Mid-County Thrift Shop was courteous to a point. She was repelled by his odor and anxious to get him out of the store wondering what he was going to do with all the odds and ends he bought. "I hope your kids will have fun with the costumes come Halloween."

[242]

"Here's ten bucks more if you throw in that walker over there. I broke my left leg years ago and its several inches shorter than the other. This rig will help me ambulate properly."

My damn legs still give me fits. I think I damaged some nerves when my body was twisted in every direction in that prison vat.

"Sure will, sir; you have a good day."

He found a car wash about three blocks down the street. Nobody was there so he quickly hosed himself down. He went behind the last stall and changed into his new clothes, aware that he looked ridiculous but didn't care. He wasn't going to the country club for lunch with his banker cronies. The gray, long-haired wig fit a little too tightly on his head but that was alright, he'd get used to it. The wool tweed sport coat and plaid pants fit perfectly. The thick black bi-focal glasses were appropriate.

About five miles out of town he pulled off into the thick woods. A gravel road lead back seventy-five yards to a pair of partially demolished out buildings. He pulled the custodian's car around the back of the second building and parked. He ripped opened a bag containing a Big Mac and fries that he'd picked up on his way out of town. He was famished. After he chomped down the fast food, he got out of the car and tossed the car keys into the creek flowing between the two buildings.

Chien walked back out to the main road. He hadn't hitch-hiked since he was in college and remembered one time when he was picked up by a queer who groped at him while speeding down the highway. That was the last time he stuck his thumb out for a free ride.

A pickup truck soon appeared around the bend. It stopped for him.

"Where ya heading, buddy? I don't normally stop for hitchhikers but today is your lucky day."

"I'm on my way to Chicago."

"I love that outfit, granddad. Where'd you steal it from?"

Chien ignored the insult. He looked hard at the driver. He was probably in his mid-thirties and more hillbilly than city-slicker. His CD player was blasting out the latest Faith Hill release.

"Ain't she just great? Not only does she have a fantastic set of lungs but a million dollar face."

"She's okay, but my guy is Willy Nelson."

"You got to be kidding me, right?"

"Nope, love the gravel voice."

"What 'ya going to do in the Windy City? They got an AARP convention going on there?"

Chien hesitated. He hadn't thought that far ahead.

"Ah, er, I'm going there and then up to Wisconsin to visit my grandkids. One of 'em is getting baptized next week. The little tyke has no idea what it's all about but I am a great believer in God's work and his daddy wants me near him."

"Want a snort?" asked the young driver as he pulled a flask from underneath the front seat.

"Nope, I never touch the stuff."

"Fine, suit yourself. I'm going as far as Joliet. I got a big time head-turner stashed up there that's dying to see me. I've been out of town for a week and she keeps calling me...can't live without me!"

Should I kill this clown or just swipe his truck? Maybe I'll just have him drop me off at a Greyhound station. I'll grab a bus up to Green Bay. I wouldn't dare head up to Washington Island to hook up with Spencer Littlewolf. I'm sure that's the first place the feds would look for me knowing that we were cellmates.

"Bring me over to the nearest Greyhound station we go by, young man. I'll catch a bus for the rest of the way."

"Will do; there's one on the way to my girl's apartment."

Chien got off at the bus station and bid thanks to the young man. He went inside and bought a one-way ticket to Green Bay knowing that multiple stops in-between would take lots of hours. He didn't care; he was now on his time, not the fucking prison watch.

He was in luck; a bus was leaving in an hour. After he purchased his ticket he went into the main waiting area and sat down to watch television. The six o'clock news broadcast was interrupted. He was sure they'd flash a picture of him across the screen.

Tran was relieved when the newscaster reported that a five car pileup on Interstate 57 created a horrible traffic tie-up.

"Yikes," said an older lady sitting across from him. "That's a bad one, probably some stupid ass teenager texting his girlfriend."

"I suppose so." He got to his feet and shoved the walker out in front of him. It was time to get more familiar the contraption. He needed to pee and excused himself.

When he returned, the old lady was gone. He looked out the window. Her bus had come in and she was in the process of boarding it. Good, he wanted to be alone. He needed time to think.

What the hell am I going to do in Green Bay when I really want to get up to Washington Island? Wait a minute. Spencer Littlewolf told me he has family there. Maybe I can hook up with them until things die down. Surely the feds will slack off if they can't find me. I need to call Littlewolf and see if he can help me. I'm sure he will; the Indian owes me big time! The last note I got from my secret banker is that my ten thousand account balance would soon be overdrawn.

It was dark when he finally got on his bus. He pulled out the cell phone he lifted from the county custodian. It read nine o'clock.

Chapter 42

Enroute to Wisconsin

IT WAS A LONG, boring ride up to Green Bay. The bus stopped at most of the smaller towns along the way. He was too fidgety to get any sleep on the overnight journey. On top of everything else, he was running low on cash. The money he stole from the dump custodian was almost gone. He needed sleep, his nerve endings were frayed. When he got off the bus at his final destination he found a pay phone to call Littlewolf. He hoped that the number the Indian gave him was still a good number. It was.

"Hey, Spence, this is your old buddy Chien. Do you have time to talk?"

"Jesus Christ, Tran, where the hell are you?"

"I can't tell you, my good friend, the cops may have your phone line tapped."

"So, why would they do that? I haven't done anything wrong."

"It's because of me. Just be careful what you say, okay?"

"What the fuck! Did you get a hold of some weed in the joint? You're not making any sense to me, little man."

"Think hard. Do you remember what we talked about before you got out of prison?"

"Yeah, kinda but we talked about many things. Hey, I've been sending money back to your bank if that's what you're all concerned about. Offhand I think I returned over 'five thou' of what you loaned me."

I don't mind telling this guy a lie. I have no intention of repaying any part of his loan. He was stupid in the first place to lend it to me. If he wants it, he can come and try to get it.

"No, I trust you. It's all about family...we talked about your family."

"Oh yeah, sure, I recall." He had no clue what Chien was referring to.

"Take care of yourself, little man. Call me when they finally let you out of there."

"Don't hang up on me, don't..." It was too late.

"Damn it," he shouted out to nobody in particular.

The Indian says he's been repaying the loan. My banker told me the account has been drawn down drastically. What's going on here?

He was getting tired and knew he was on edge. Finally he remembered the name he wanted to get from Littlewolf. He contacted the long distance operator for information on families living on the Oneida Indian Reservation outside of Green Bay.

"Please repeat that name."

"Littlewolf," Chien said.

"I got twenty of them. Do you know the first name?"

"Havner, I think. Look for a Havner Littlewolf."

"I don't have a Havner Littlewolf, sir, but I have a Havner Hawk."

"Good, what's the number?"

The operator located the number and gave it to him.

He jotted it down on a scrap of paper. It was getting late. He would call Havner first thing in the morning and hope for the best.

Chien was totally exhausted and needed to locate a place to stay for the night. He found a discarded map of the city at the Greyhound station and studied it.

"Where to, mister?" the female taxi driver asked in a hoarse voice.

"Take me over to Bay Beach and the Wildlife Sanctuary."

"It's dark outside, buddy. What are you going to do, camp out with the geese for the night?"

"Nah, just gonna commune with nature, young lady."

She dropped him off at the main entrance to the sanctuary. The map he studied indicated that it wasn't a fenced property with a controlled entry gate. He got out and walked about five yards from the cab when he heard her shrilling yell.

"Hey, old man; you owe me twenty bucks for the ride."

"Chalk it up to charity, honey, I ain't got any money. And by the way, take care of that cold!"

She got out of the taxi and came after him with the walker he deliberately left in the back seat.

"You old mother f.....! Take this cheap contraption with you and shove it up your smelly ass!"

The taxicab sped away almost hitting a speeding pickup truck when she did a quick U-turn and left the park.

Chien walked around the sanctuary and found a good spot to camp out for the remainder of the night. He pulled the woolen blanket from the knapsack he bought from the thrift shop and carefully spread it on the ground. He had an extra quilt in there also in case it snowed during the night. He noted an excessive amount of geese shit all over the area.

Why haven't they flown south? It's already December. I guess they're Canadian geese and love the freezing cold. At least somebody's getting enough food, he laughed. Ah...my second night as a free man, he said softly falling off to sleep wondering what the next day would bring.

Chapter 43

ANGIE WARD was in trouble, deep trouble. She was a person of interest in the death of Shamus Fenerty. Assisted suicide is what the FBI tagged it. The school district placed her on administrative leave pending the outcome of the investigation. Her former student and friend Paul Keller was with her initially but soon made himself conveniently unavailable but did arrange for an associate to provide legal support.

"Your late," Bradley said. "I'm sorry to cut short your vacation up in Door County but felt you should be here. There are a ton of things going on and our entire crew is working overtime."

"Sorry about that. Torrie dropped a bomb on me that took time to defuse. I don't believe it!"

"Believe what?"

"She told me that we were getting way too serious in our relationship. She said we should stop seeing each other for awhile, let things settle down. She implied we needed to focus more on our own individual lives than trying to match up with each other."

"Like trying to measure the fallout, huh."

"Something along those lines."

"I get the feeling that I'm too old for her. I also think she got it on real good with Jamie the last few days. Lastly, I'm convinced she has some strong feelings for that no good criminal inmate she worked for. I know that something was going on between them. She runs down there to visit him every chance she has available."

"Was she aware of your suspicions?"

"No, never did let on. Do they allow conjugal visits in federal prison?"

"Jesus, Rod, get off it, man. Maybe it's good that you two are in a so-called cooling off period. You're acting like a spurned lover."

"Screw you, Simmons," he shouted and stomped back to his office.

"Screw, screw, screw...the world's all blue," Graybeard whistled from the front of the office complex.

Several days had passed when Bradley decided to call Irene Finerty. They hadn't talked to each other since she first informed him of her brother's death. He was curious to see where the investigation was heading. Rod had finally cooled off and was working on the new cyber security contract they were awarded.

"Hey, Irene, it's Bradley. How're things going?"

"As expected, dimwit, I'm still pissed at you."

"Why?"

"You weren't at my brother's funeral."

"I wasn't invited."

"It was a funeral, not a damn wedding reception, Simmons."

"Ah, er…, please forgive me. I know how you feel."

"Do you?"

"No."

"I didn't think so."

"Will you talk to me now or do I have to make an appointment?"

"What do you want to know, I'm awfully busy?"

"Irene, please take a few minutes and brief me on the status of the Shamus investigation. Did someone actually kill him? Is Angie Ward still a suspect?"

"Why do you want to know?"

"I felt a certain closeness to your brother, especially after we proved he wasn't cheating on his wife. Also, I think my partner is going to contact Angie and try to rekindle their relationship."

"Okay Bradley, sorry for my gross ugliness. I'll bring you up to date."

"You're excused."

"First things first, Mr. Investigator. Shamus apparently was not murdered. The law enforcement guys, collaborating with the county ME determined that he probably committed suicide by carbon monoxide poisoning. All suppositions have been put on hold awaiting the final results of an autopsy."

"What about Angie Ward? I heard they found her fingerprints all over the car and placed her on house arrest pending the outcome of the investigation. How did they ever match her to the prints? Did she already have a criminal record on file?"

"Hold on there, let me talk."

"My mind is running on overdrive, Irene."

"Shamus was in fact guilty of infidelity, not with Candi, that porno actress but with Angie Ward. He knew her husband, in fact, played football against him years ago. He read about the terrible accident that killed the guy and put Angie in the hospital and decided to attend the funeral. Angie found some solace in his being there to honor her late husband. She had called him several times asking him to come over and help her out with some problems she was experiencing. His limo driver drove him over to Libertyville several times and an affair soon blossomed."

"Holy shit! I would have never suspected those two."

"My cousin is really one messed up lady."

"But her fingerprints were…"

"I know, I know," she cut him off. "I think I told you most of these facts when we spoke earlier so bare with me if I'm repeating anything."

"Sure thing, I know this whole thing has a major impact on you personally."

"Yeah, but I'm adjusting. Here's what we think happened. Angie was riding in his personal car that night. Max, the limo driver was given the day off. Apparently the guilt had placed such a heavy burden on Shamus that he became suicidal. The investigators had the notion that Angie may have helped him commit the suicidal act because her prints were all over the car."

"I'm with you so far but I ask you again; how were they able to trace the prints to Angie?"

"They didn't have a previous file on her. They found a copy of her last pay stub from the school district. The investigators concluded that Angie's purse somehow fell on the car floor and spilled some of the contents. Perhaps she was trying to pull out her cell phone to call someone for help or maybe just reaching in there for Kleenex. Maybe there was a tussle between them; her trying hard to convince him not to kill himself. We'll probably never know."

"So far so good but how did they rule her out?"

"Angie confirmed that she was with him and was in the parked car when Shamus told her he couldn't face his wife with the truth. When he told her he was going to take his own life she lapsed into a state of shock. According to the police they were smoking tons of pot."

"But, but…"

"Hang on; I'm almost there."

"Okay Irene."

"When Angie finally realized what was happening she hopped out of the car, panicked and took off. She ran down the street until she could hail a cab and got out of there."

"How did the ME come to the conclusion that Shamus himself was responsible for the fatal act?"

"I'll discuss this in two parts. First, he was driving an old 1959 Ford station wagon he restored several years ago. It was his pride and joy. Nobody else was allowed to drive it. Older cars of that vintage were not equipped with electronically controlled combustion and catalytic converters so running a hose from the exhaust pipe into a sealed space can cause death from carbon monoxide poisoning fairly rapidly."

"Ouch, I was not aware of that and I thought all us private investigators knew everything!"

"Are you ready for the second part?"

"Yes, go ahead but slowly please."

"Several elements got Angie off the hook. They couldn't find her fingerprints on the hose that was wedged in the driver side window. Secondly, the ME placed the official time of death at ten-fifteen that night. The police were able to corroborate her story with the taxi driver that took her home that night."

"How'd they do that?"

"She remembered the name of the taxi company. When the police ran it down they got the exact meter reading that was recorded listing both the time of the pickup and the fare generated."

"I don't believe this is a standard practice, Irene."

"You're correct, it isn't. But in this case the dispatcher had it recorded because of the amount the driver charged her. The trip from Highland Park to Libertyville cost her $125.00."

"What was the third element, so to speak?"

"It's actually related to the second one," she said after a slight pause. "The exact time that the taxi driver flipped on his meter arm the evening in question registered an eight-ten p.m. reading."

"How come Lois didn't hear the garage door open or the old Ford chugging up the driveway?"

"They live in a mansion. She was probably in the back of the complex. The boys were away at a basketball camp in Madison."

"So, what's with Angie? Is she a free woman?"

"Technically, yes, at least up to this point. The police are waiting for the final results of the autopsy. That should take some time because of all the toxicology studies the ME ordered."

"Certainly, those tests take forever."

Irene continued. "We feel comfortable though. The district attorney reviewed the complete files of the investigation and feels there was insufficient evidence to pin a murder rap on Angie right now. He is concerned that most prosecuting attorneys wouldn't win the verdict of an assisted suicide case based on the facts of this case; so why bring charges against her?"

"Now Bradley, when are we going out to lunch again? I believe it's your turn to pop for the bill." She then hung up.

He was relieved and believed the barbed wire fences were mended by letting her talk out the unfortunate incident. Maybe they'll start to see more investigation work come their way from her again. He also wondered how much he should tell his partner.

There was a rap on his closed door.

"Come on in please." It was Rod.

"I've got a Sno Moreau on the other line. I'm sure you remember her; she owns The House of Saigon. She wants to talk to you."

"About what?"

"I have no clue, maybe she wants to take you to a movie, you idiot; answer the damn phone!"

Chapter 44

"BRADLEY SIMMONS here, ma'am, how may I help you?"

"This is Sno Moreau calling. You may remember me from eating at my restaurant. Paul Keller recommended I call you."

"Yes, I remember, what can I do for you, Mrs. Moreau?"

"Please call me Sno. I need your help right away. My son is missing and I need you to find him."

"If at all possible, can you come to my office so we can talk in more detail? Do you know where we're located?"

"Yes, I'll see you in an hour."

Rod swung by his office with two cups of steaming hot coffee.

"Care to brief me on your long conversation with our friend Irene Finerty?"

"How'd you know I was talking to her?"

"Just a wild ass hunch, boss."

"I'll brief you later. Right now we got something brewing with the owner of The House of Saigon."

"What does that neat lady want from us?"

"Hang tight, she'll be here soon. I think I'll have a big and exciting job for you."

"What about the cyber space contract?"

"It can wait for now."

"But…"

"She seemed disturbed when I spoke with her a few minutes ago. Let's hear her out."

There was a sudden and loud interruption in the front hallway.

"Santa Claus is coming to town, he…"

Bradley went out to the front of the office suites and threw a blanket over the bird's cage.

Maybe he or she is not so dumb, he thought. Maybe the idiot bird confuses the words 'sent a' with Santa and 'clause' with Claus; words we use around here all the time. Yet, Christmas is right around the corner!

An hour or so later Sno Moreau rapped on the front door. Bradley greeted her as she came in. He led her down the hallway to his office.

"Please meet Rod Richards, my associate."

She nodded and shook his hand softly.

"So, how can we be of service?"

She took off her heavy fur overcoat and tossed it over a chair. She wore a tightly knit green sweater with matching skirt and a silver chain link belt wrapped firmly around her tiny waist. He noticed the high leather boots she wore. They were still caked in ice from the outside sidewalk.

"As I told you over the phone, I need you to find my son."

Keller had told him in passing the other day at lunch about the commuted prison sentence, a real rarity for the type of offense committed. He couldn't imagine why her son would be considered "missing" from the federal prison after he had been given a free pass to leave for good.

"Where is your son now?"

"I have no idea, that's why I'm here talking to you."

She gave them her version of her son's imprisonment and subsequent commuted sentence. It was a little different from Keller's. She concluded that the whole Ponzi scheme was a big hoax aimed at getting rid of her son because of his well-publicized success. In any event, it was big news in Chicago. Both he and Rod read Keller's follow-up article in the Trib.

Bradley wanted her to be more specific with the details about the missing person status.

She said with a deep sigh, "I called the prison warden and he told me he'd have my son ready for me by the time I arrived. I hired a limo and planned to go down there right away to pick him up."

"So, was he waiting for you?" Rod finally weighed in.

"Hear me out, please. As a further act of kindness Mr. Keller had planned to go to the prison with me to pick him up but had an emergency come up and had to back out. Bo Tan, one of my good friends went with me. When we got to the prison I was in shock. My son was nowhere to be found. The warden told me that earlier in the day they conducted an all-out search of the prison and prison grounds but couldn't find him anywhere. He disappeared in thin air!"

"Did the warden offer any opinions?" Bradley probed further.

"Like what?"

"Please don't get upset with us, Sno. We're just trying to develop some facts about his missing status."

"Have you heard from him at all?" It was Rod's turn to dig.

"Hold on, let's backtrack here a minute," Bradley suggested. "Did the warden have any idea why he was missing? Could he have been killed by one of the inmates? Were there any signs of escape? Did he overpower the guards and climb the perimeter fence? Did he steal a truck and crash through the front gate?"

"Yes and no." She began to sob.

Bradley offered her a handkerchief.

"He told me that after the roll call that found Chien missing, they got the formal notification that his sentence was commuted. The warden implied but didn't really come out with it that he ordered the guards to abort the search for my son. I guess he reasoned that however my son got out of there didn't really matter to him. They weren't going to commit any more resources to find him. In his terms, Chien Tran was a free man."

[257]

"That's interesting."

"How's that, Mr. Richards?"

"I know that an investigation will be ordered by higher authorities to determine how he escaped. I'm sure the warden has been put on notice. Even though it's a medium security prison, inmates just don't happen to disappear from that environment without leaving tell-tale signs."

"I'm afraid my son is going to get killed or he's going to kill someone in the process. He's probably in hiding somewhere. I'm sure he doesn't have any money or clothing to protect him from this harsh weather. You've got to find him right away."

Bradley looked at Rod, then back to her.

"Please," she cried aloud, not able to control her emotions any longer.

Rod got up and went over to console her.

"Can I get you some tea?" asked Bradley. "It might make you feel a little bit better."

Rod concurred as he held her hand.

"I'd like that. Sorry for being so emotional."

"Have you gone to the police?" Bradley continued to delve.

"Yes I have. They told me there was no crime committed and even if one did take place later it was completely out of their jurisdiction. It was at that point that I turned to Paul Keller for advice. He apologized for not being with me at the prison and then suggested I contact your company."

Rod served the tea and offered her some scones to go along with it. She quickly grabbed the cup of tea but left the scones on the plate. Both he and Bradley ate the scones while finishing their tea.

"Mrs. Moreau," Bradley stated with a more officious note in his voice, "We would be glad to help you. Let's go over the terms of our missing person's contract. It'll just take a few minutes."

They spent several minutes with her clarifying some of the conditions she deemed needed more discussion. She didn't even hesitate at the high fee Bradley quoted or the projected costs that would involve travel expenses and sundry items to get the job done.

"As you can see, gentlemen, I don't care what your services will cost me. Just get my son back!"

Bradley explained that his associate would be working with him on the case and suggested the two of them retire to his office for further discussions. They excused themselves and left Bradley's office.

"I just have a few more questions to ask you before you leave," Rod said after several minutes mulling over his plan of action.

"Go right on, whatever it takes."

"I need you to get me a list of all his known friends and any other contacts he had with their addresses and telephone numbers."

"I'm sorry, I afraid I don't really know any of them. I've never communicated with Chien."

"Why is that?"

"He doesn't even know that I exist. We've never talked or written to each other. I have no idea what people he became acquainted with over the years. That's why I'm hiring you. Mr. Keller said that you folks were the best in the business and I intend to find out how good you really are."

"I see." He really didn't; they'd have to start from scratch.

Sno Moreau left Simmons & Simmons imbued with the hope that they would find her son and bring him back to her. Rod briefed his boss on the specifics of his conversation with their new client.

"Better get going, Rod, you know what you have to do…times a wasting."

"Roger that. What did Irene Finerty have to say?"

Bradley took the time to fill him in on all of the details he'd been privy to thus far in the investigation. He commiserated with Rod knowing that his associate was once in love with her.

"Wow, that's some story! I'm glad for Angie. She's really a special person but at the same time never should have hooked up with a guy like Shamus. I never suspected her of having an affair with another man, even while yours truly was dating her."

"So, the story ends here, my friend?"

"Maybe, maybe not," Rod smiled.

"What are you implying?" Bradley was almost afraid to go there.

"Didn't Irene tell you that Angie Ward invested heavily in All-State Trucking Enterprises with the proceeds paid out by her deceased husband's insurance company long before the company went public?"

"What the f...!" bellowed Simmons. "No, Irene never said a thing. How did you know about this?"

"Frankly, I forgot all about mentioning it until now. One day while we were still dating she made an off-hand comment about investing in a large, privately owned trucking operation. Angie said she knew the owner through a mutual friend. I didn't put 'two and two' together until the other night that it was Shamus Fenerty's company.

"Good Lord, Richards that could impact heavily on the investigation! She had a motive to kill him. I better call Irene back right away."

"Why don't you simply let the investigators do their own homework, boss and get the hell out of the three ring circus you're mired in?"

Chapter 45

Green Bay, Wisconsin

"WAKE UP BUDDY, we don't allow overnight camping on the bird sanctuary grounds. Get up and get on your way or I'll haul your sorry ass to jail."

"Hey, hold on there a minute," Chien said as he collected his thoughts.

The officer stared a hole through the shaggy trespasser's wide-opened eyes. Chien decided he'd better comply without creating a scene.

"Okay, okay, I'm on my way. Officer, would you be so kind to give me a lift to the Greyhound station?"

"Bundle up your gear and hop in. Be sure to shake all that snow and geese shit off those blankets. I don't want to get the inside of my cruiser all wet and smelly."

The officer dropped him off at the station and he went inside to make his telephone call. He turned back to make sure the squad car had departed. He didn't want any trouble with the law. He was sure that the APB was still active in the law enforcement communication channels.

"Havner Hawk here; how may I help you?"

"It's Chien Tran, your nephew's former cellmate back in the Illinois prison. Did he tell you anything about me and that I might be calling?"

There was an extended silence on the other end of the line.

"Er...no, I don't believe he did. Maybe he talked to my son; just a minute please, I'll get him for you."

"Who is this?" asked a much younger voice.

"Chien Tran. I'm a friend of your cousin Spencer Littlewolf. He told me to call you if I ever got up this way."

"Spencer is not here, sir. He lives on Washington Island up in Door County."

"I'm well aware of that. I gave him a lot of money to restoring his home when it was destroyed in that big tornado that hit his little island about a year ago."

There was another long silence on the line.

"What big storm are you talking about, mister? We haven't had a tornado hit anywhere in the state for years. In fact all the cherry growers up in Door County are crying for rain. It's been dry up there for several years now. Tornado you say? No way, one never happened on Washington Island."

Chien was shocked. He wouldn't believe that Littlewolf would stiff him like this. He advanced him a considerable amount of money to fix up his property. He had to get up there and find out for himself but it was way too hot for him now. The feds were probably still searching that little island for him.

"Look here, are you sure you don't know who I am?"

"I do vaguely, sir. I think I remember Spencer mentioning your name while he was staying here a few days after he got out of prison. He needed to settle up some debts before he went up there. My cousin was a terrible gambler, lost his shirt every time he wandered over to the casino here."

"Please let me talk to your father again."

"Sure, hold on for a minute."

The older Indian got back on the line. Chien talked to him for at least ten minutes and the man agreed to come over to the Greyhound station and pick him up; it wouldn't be soon enough!

Chien went into the washroom and tried to clean up. He looked like a bum. He let the warm water run as long as possible, splashing it all over the exposed parts of his skin and then exchanged his wet clothes for another set of damp ones. He then shed all of the props that turned him into an old man and returned to the bench housing his other gear.

"What are you, a Houdini-type or an underpaid change artist?" He stared down the young female inquirer sitting on the bench behind him.

"What do you think?" Tran snarled. "Take your choice!"

The lady got up and went to the far end of the terminal and found another bench.

He spotted an Indian-looking older gent with long braids climbing down both shoulders enter the bus station. He was looking around for someone. He wasn't sure if this was Littlewolf's uncle. He continued to read.

Havner Hawk walked into the bus station like a person with a mission. He was tall and gangly, sporting a clump of thick black hair protruding from both his ears and his craggy nose. He was smoking a corn cob pipe. He found Chien Tran paging through a tourist guide.

It had to be him, thought the Indian. Tourists don't hang around this place. Nobody else in here fits the guy's description.

"Hello there, sir. Are you looking for me?"

"Who are you?" The Indian asked him to be sure.

"Chien Tran, I talked to you on the phone."

"Yeah, alright, I know. Let's sit down and chat for a few moments."

They found an empty bench near the coke machine. The Indian ran his eyes up, down and around Chien. His mind didn't compute what he saw.

"You don't look like no ex-con to me. What were you in there for, stealing the collection basket at St. Patrick's Cathedral?" He blurted out laughing. Several bus patrons turned around to look at the older man.

Before Chien could respond, the old man continued, "Are you carrying?"

"No."

The Indian look relieved.

"Look, please, I'm no trouble to you. Spencer assured me that you'd help me out."

"He did, did he?"

"We were close friends in prison, lending a hand to each other whenever necessary. We even roomed together like I told you before."

"What do you mean roomed together? Were you in some kind of all boys' dormitory?" The Indian was a real comedian.

Chien threw up his hands in disgust.

I'm wasting my time here! Indians are really weird!

"You don't look like any Indian to me. I thought my nephew told me his cellmate was an Apache Indian from Oklahoma. That's why I told him the guy was welcomed up here any time. We Indians have to stick together. The white man took everything from us, our land, our natural resources, our women, you name it."

"Look, I'm sorry I bothered you." Chien got up, grabbed his gear and then headed for the front door.

"Hold on a minute, young man," the Indian screamed at the top of his lungs. "Nobody walks away from me when I'm talking to 'em."

Just then a young man came through the front door and almost knocked Tran over.

"Father," he said walking toward the older Indian, "Have you found the man yet?"

"You betcha, he's standing next to you. Bring him back here so we can continue our little pow-wow."

Chien and the lad walked back over to the bench near where Havner was standing.

"Because you speak highly of my nephew, Spencer Littlewolf and he knows you, I've decided to bring you back to the reservation for a few days under two conditions.

"And they are…?"

"First, you leave my home when I tell you. Secondly, I don't want you mixing with any of my neighbors. Having an ex-con in the neighborhood could dirty our reputation among the tribe. Do you understand me?"

"Yes I do, that's kind of you."

"No problems?"

"No problems," Chien Tran assured him.

They left the terminal on Cedar Street near Whitney Park where snow banks lined the outer perimeter. It was still snowing and Chien thought the Indian was driving too fast for the road conditions. They crossed the Fox River heading over to the west side of the city and drove along the railroad tracks turning on to Lombardi Avenue.

"What's that huge stadium on the left?"

"That, Mr. Tran is the Temple of God," answered Havner.

"What temple you say?"

Havner's young son piped in, "The Green Bay Packers play there. They are the greatest team on earth according to my friends. I've never been to a game because my father doesn't believe in the sanctity of professional football."

"What do you mean by the big word 'sanctity' when referring to a ridiculous physical contest?"

"The whole city and the entire state live and die the Packer fortunes. My father believes there are more important things in life than games. He thinks it's ridiculous that grown men get paid enormous amounts of money to satisfy their male egos."

Havner shook his head in agreement.

Chien knew exactly what the young lad was talking about. He read periodically about the Chicago Bear team but was more interested in baseball even though he didn't follow the home team Cubs.

They continued driving to the Oneida reservation, passing the local airport and a gigantic casino on the right side of the highway. Chien couldn't believe such a huge gambling operation was located in the small town of Green Bay.

"How well does that casino do?"

"Why do you want to know?" The young son was curious.

"You are so far north and have such a small population to draw from. Look at the size of the complex. Every available parking space is occupied. Four buses are lined up out front."

"My father will answer your question."

Havner took a few long drags on the pipe before he spoke. Smoke bellowed up from the hot bowl. He looked professorial and said with a stern voice, "Partner, that's what we call revenge. It's one of the few ways we can recapture what rightly belongs to us. You see, gambling is an inherent disease of our white brethren. We have always tried to find a way to get the edge on them and we finally found a way. We suck millions of dollars from their pockets in there."

"Do you work in the casino?"

"Yes I do. I work as the pit boss for the two craps tables."

Chien mused for a moment and said, "I like the game, played it all the time in Joliet before I went to prison."

"Are you ahead of the game...moneywise?"

"Probably not."

"I rest my case. I suppose you consider it an entertainment expense," Havner retorted with a sneer. "You white people are paying for the privilege to be entertained. Sometimes you win, most of the time you lose."

"I stopped keeping track of the money aspect. I simply enjoy gambling on the rare occasions that I find the time to indulge myself."

"We love your kind, white guy. You help us more than you think."

Havner finally slowed the vehicle down to an acceptable and legal speed limit. Moments before he almost slid into the back of a breaking taxi cab before down-shifting his pickup truck.

"We're almost home. My wife is expecting us and has prepared a large meal. I hope you like our food."

"I'm grateful, sir."

When they pulled up to the house Chien was surprised to see a neat brick ranch-style home sitting on at least an acre of land and beautifully landscaped. He expected something more primitive.

"Here we are. Let's go in and get comfortable."

Tran really enjoyed the friendship and comradeship of the close knit family. He had several long conversations with Havner's son who was interested in the world of finances. He conducted several tutorials for the lad. Tran loved the intimacies displayed by the Indian people within their community.

"Thanks so much for giving me a cultural lesson about your people, Havner."

"I hope you appreciate us more now."

"Sure do. You people sure have an interesting history."

One strange thing occurred to him while living with the Indian. Not much was brought up about his nephew. Havner had a short fuse when it came to most ex-cons. He hated that Littlewolf served a term in prison. It was a family disgrace. Chien felt the vibes.

It was time to go. He was refreshed and extremely satisfied with the wonderful friendship he developed with Havner's family and sensed they accepted him even though he served time in prison. He also felt close to the Oneida Indians and would love to live among them at some point in his life. However, he had definite plans for the present. Chien wanted to go to Washington Island and hook up with his now questionable friend, Spencer Littlewolf. Something fishy was going on up there and he needed to find out what bothered him.

"Where do you want me to drop you off?" The old Indian was playing race car driver again.

"Just take me back to the bus terminal and I'll head out from there."

"Where do you intend to go from Green Bay?" Havner pushed for the obvious answer.

"I'm going up to see Littlewolf on Washington Island. He's expecting me. I'll be sure to tell him how grateful I am to you and your family."

"Good luck, Chien Tran. My wife, son and I enjoyed your time with us. It is our wish that the many spirits living among us lead you to your ultimate goal."

"Thank you," he said sincerely.

"I have one last word of advice to you."

"And what would that be?"

"I've noticed that you seem to be impatient. There is an old saying that goes something like this: 'be patient, you can't see the bright stars in the sky until darkness arrives'...how 'bout that, Mister Chien?"

"Thanks for the advice, there might be something to that."

Havner Hawk stoked up his corn cob pipe and laid rubber as he pulled away from the bus terminal. Chien went inside and plunked down on a bench but had no intention of grabbing another bus. The terminal was empty.

His plan was to hi-jack a car at one of the nearby malls. He was convinced that the people up here were so trustworthy they'd leave the keys in the ignition of their car when going in to shop.

He moved to another bench near an older vending machine and pried open the rusty coin box with a screw driver he swiped from Havner's garage. He emptied the contents into a paper bag and left the terminal.

I wonder if they've stopped looking for me, he questioned himself. I hope they found that old man in the stinking vat back there. If he's dead I'm in big time trouble; they'll never give up looking for me!

Chapter 46

CHRISTMAS in downtown Chicago was always an exciting time of the year. The department stores along Michigan Avenue were busily satisfying the gift needs of frenzied shoppers. The popular Water Tower stood out like a snow-capped zenith emerging from a frozen earth.

Rod was lonely. He needed to take a break from his pursuit of Chien Tran. He had been working day and night following up on leads and non-leads. He found himself going around in circles. Exhaustion and frustration had set in.

He called his son to see what he was doing for Christmas. John told him he was going down to Texas to spend some time with his younger brother and that Veronica was going with him.

As a last resort Rod decided to call Torrie Strait.

"Hi, Rod, how's it going with you?"

"Fairly well but I need to take a break from hunting down your former boss. He's disappeared in thin air."

"Did you ever get over to see Michael Howzer like I told you?"

"Yes, Michael was of no help to me. He's retired now and living up in the Milwaukee area. He said that he'd given up on Chien once the 'crook' left his firm. He'd even lost track of Chien's ex as he tried to contact her several times. Seems he stole several of the major accounts Howzer had built up over the years. Several of his good friends were caught up in the Ponzi scheme. Weren't you aware of that?"

"Um…I really can discuss the details of the case at this point," she replied.

"Okay, so what are you doing for Christmas?"

"I'm going down to Texas and meet Jamie at Ft. Hood. He's taking a few days of leave and wants to show me around. We're going to spend Christmas Day in Dallas. You knew I was dating your grandson, didn't you?"

"No I didn't! It's hard to date a guy who's hundreds of miles away unless you call swapping e-mails a date. You dropped me like a hot potato after our foray up in Door County. I suspected something might be brewing between you and my grandson but then my intuitions were obviously working overtime. I figured he'd be man enough to tell me if he had the 'hots' for you."

"I'm sorry, Rod; it is what it is!"

"Well, have fun in Texas. Give Jamie my regards."

That little bastard! How could he do this to me? He stole my girl right from under me. I had no fucking clue! Torrie was hot, too hot for me apparently. They both can go straight to hell as far as I'm concerned!

He decided to call Angie Ward. His left brain urged him to stay far away from this woman. The right side argued that they once were lovers and that maybe something…anything, even a tiny hope that an attraction might still be there. He rationalized away her affair with Shamus Fenerty.

They were cousins for Pete's sake; what kind of sexual creativities could come from that kind of family relationship? I bet she was stoned the whole time they were doing it!

He got a recording. Her number was disconnected. He decided to call Irene Finerty. She was a cop and should know Angie's whereabouts.

"Merry Christmas, Irene, this is Rod Richards."

"And the same to you. I heard from Bradley you were hired to track down Chien Tran. Any luck?"

"Nah, going around in circles but I'll find him."

"I'm sure you will. He's no longer an item for us in the police business or for the feds; that is, so long as he keeps his nose clean. Off the record though, I might be able to help you."

"Thanks for the offer but I'm running solo on this, at least for now. How can I reach Angie? Her telephone number has been dropped from the system."

"Why do you want to call my cousin? She had nothing to do with Chien Tran as far as I know but stranger things have happened to my family members."

"Don't be such a prig, Irene. I want to check on her; see how she's doing after all the drama surrounding the death of Shamus."

"She's not interested in you, Richards!"

"What? Let me be the one who decides that, Finerty! Give me her number."

There was a long pause on the line. Rod thought he heard a click, then a thud with the handset.

Maybe she hung up on me, the bitch; wouldn't doubt it...those Finerty's or Fenerty's are a weird Goddamn bunch!

"I'll give you her number under one condition." She had softened up.

"And what might that condition be?"

"Here's her number," she said reading off the digits. "Jot it down. Go ahead and call her to see how she's doing. Angie is fragile and could use some moral support from someone she knows. Do not, however, try and see her. I repeat, do not go to her."

"Don't you worry about your cousin; she's a big girl now and can make her own decisions."

"You heard me loud and clear, Richards...stay away from her." She hung up without waiting for a reply from him.

He wondered what that was all about. He concluded that Angie may still be a suspect in the death although both the Tribune and Times reported she was no longer suspected of the crime.

Irene must be on weed. It seems to run in the family; too few highs and way too many lows!

[271]

"Hi, Angie, it's Rod Richards. How the heck are you doing?"

"What do you want?"

"I, er…want to wish you a Merry Christmas."

"Okay. So what else do you want?"

"I was wondering if you had any plans for Christmas Day. I thought it might be nice if we could sort of get together like old times. Remember our Christmas in Libertyville? We had such a wonderful time together."

"That was ages ago. What have you been up to lately? Did that hot tramp of a broker finally drop you?"

"Hold the sarcasm, Angie, it's not becoming of you. To answer your main question, I'm not really doing anything in the social arena. I've been too busy working an interesting missing person's case as we speak. My mind, body and soul told me I needed to take a break."

"I have no plans for Christmas Day. I'm kind of on a little island here all to myself. Nobody out there seems to care about me anymore. Everybody still thinks I was responsible for the death of Shamus. You know about all this, don't you?"

"Um-oh…just what I read in the papers. You're innocent, let's leave it at that."

"Do you want to get together with me? That would be nice if you do. I'd like that."

"Why did you drop your phone number?"

"I moved, bought a neat penthouse on the north branch of the Chicago River near Wacker Drive."

"Did you have to resign from your teaching position?"

"Yes and no. They put me on paid administrative leave while the investigation was going on. Scuttlebutt amongst the teachers and administrators strongly implied that I killed him. I didn't miss them but sure missed the kids while they put me in limbo. When they finally were assured of my complete innocence they asked me back to teach. I told them to go straight to hell and decided to move away."

"But a penthouse downtown…"

"Enough, Rod, come on over and see me tomorrow. We can make plans for Christmas and I can fill you in on everything that's happened to me after Shamus killed himself. I feel relieved, like a new person having put all that behind me. In fact, I do miss you. Write down my new address."

He was excited. Maybe there was an ounce of a chance that he and Angie could rekindle their relationship. He remembered how passionate she was on their Caribbean cruise and during their courtship period.

I don't care about your past with Fenerty, Angie Ward. Let sleeping dogs lie. That was then…this is now! Let's make the best of it.

He needed to call and make an appointment with the warden of the federal prison where Chien Tran was incarcerated. In his earlier run through Illinois he didn't visit the facility and he knew now that was a huge mistake. He needed to talk to various individuals in the prison to see if Chien had any close friends there. He was hoping that one of them would offer a clue where he may be living.

After numerous phone calls and typical run-arounds he was unable to hook up with the warden because he had been transferred to another federal prison. He wasn't given the name of the prison; only that it was on the east coast. The present warden was initially no help. He did however, suggest he come down and talk with their prison chaplain who might be able to help him.

It was raining out. The snow had reluctantly surrendered to the warmer weather and he was worried they wouldn't have a white Christmas. He drove down south and located the prison. After some initial resistance, he was ushered in to see the chaplain.

"No, I didn't have much to do with Tran while he was in here," the chaplain said meekly. He was dressed in sweaty workout attire, like he'd just returned from a rigorous tennis match.

"Did you have any contact at all with him, sir?"

"He never went to any of the prison services as far as I know. I think he was an avowed atheist like most of them here."

"Chaplain, please think hard on this. Were there any occasions where he visited you or you went to him?"

"Yes, now that I think about it."

"What brought you two together?" Rod had to push hard for any bit of information he could garner from this closed-mouthed man of the cloth.

"I was called down to the infirmary one day when he was having a heart attack. He maimed one of the other inmates and fell into some kind of cardiac arrest after their struggle. He almost died on us."

"What did you talk about in the infirmary?"

"Not much really. They had him on meds."

"Think harder, it's important. Did he want you to notify any family members about his condition?"

Rod was getting impatient. This guy was not helpful.

"Wait a minute, he was either hallucinating or in a trance from the drugs the doctor gave him. I did remember something he said like 'don't tell Littlewolf'. He mumbled it several times."

"Who's Littlewolf?"

"Spencer Littlewolf was his old cellmate. He was released several months before Tran's prison sentence was thrown out. From what I could gather, they apparently looked after each other."

"Do you know where he lives?" Rod asked with renewed enthusiasm. He was now on to something.

"No I don't. Even if I did I couldn't release that information to you."

"So, who else around this place can tell me?"

"I'm not sure."

Rod observed that his body language suggested otherwise.

[274]

"Why don't you amble downstairs and ask the legal office. They have an attorney on call, maybe they can help you."

He thanked the chaplain for his assistance, and then was escorted down to the legal office by one of the burley guards.

"I hear you're looking for Chien Tran's cellmate."

"How'd you know that?"

"Nothing happening in this joint gets past me."

Rod stopped him in the hallway and offered him a cigarette. He didn't smoke anymore but bought a pack of Marlboro's in the prison sundry shop on his way to the warden's office. He thought it might come in handy.

"We all liked your main man, never gave us any trouble. He put the hurt on some German bad guy who tried to rape him and became somewhat of a hero around here. Tran plucked the guy's eye out with a pencil of all things. His former cellmate was an Indian from Wisconsin; Oneida Tribe I think."

They arrived at the legal office.

"Thanks for your help. Here, take the whole package of smokes. See you."

He visited with the legal clerk, a perky Chinese lady. Like the rest of the staff members, she couldn't offer any specific information, begging the party line on confidentiality.

"He was some guy, that Chien Tran."

He was beginning to think his man was some kind of God around here. Maybe he'd see a statue of him in the hallway on the way out.

"Chien Tran is a lucky stiff," the clerk giggled. "He lived on the edge; believe me, not many like him around here anymore."

"What do you mean by that?"

"Well, sir I can tell you this much which doesn't violate confidentiality because it's public information."

"Go on, please."

"His sentence was commuted but the poor soul didn't know a thing about it. He successfully escaped from this prison; first man to have ever accomplished that feat. He hid in a dirty kitchen waste vat which was taken out of the prison walls to a local dump."

"How thrilling," he laughed to himself. He wished he had a bag of fortune cookies to offer her but conjured up the thought that maybe the Chinese people also hate them as much as he did.

"He almost killed one of the county workers who discovered him."

"I hadn't heard about that, what happened?"

"Yeah, bopped him over the head with a crow bar and stuffed him in the dirty vat he used to escape prison. Fortunately for Chien Tran, one of the other workers was on his way over to sterilize the vats and heard some moaning coming from one of the dirty ones. He noted a crow bar affixed to it and opened the lid and presto, out popped the old geezer."

"Close shave, huh?"

This lady was a real standup Jay Leno-type. No, on second thought, more like Letterman.

"Right on; Tran could well be back in prison for life if the old fart had died in the vat of all places." She snickered at her word "fart".

"Thanks anyway for your help. Please call the guard and have him escort me out of the prison."

"Sure will. Sorry I couldn't offer you much help."

"I fully understand what confidentiality means around this place. It'd be a shame if word got out that some inmate was painted a rotten egg! Think of how that could be misconstrued and taint your reputation."

Rod drove the hundred or so miles back home to Chicago, elated that he at least had a starting point to find his man. Now it was time to do some research about the Oneida Indian Tribe in Wisconsin.

He was in deep thought when he pulled the Honda into the rental garage. Wait a minute, now that I think of it, Mike Howzer rambled on and on that Chien's ex-wife might be living somewhere in Wisconsin.

[276]

Maybe he's headed up that way to bum some money from her. Perhaps he thinks he can lay low there until things cooled off. I better call John and give him a heads up there's a remote possibility that Chien Tran might be in the Green Bay area or even Door County for all we know. Veronica Brown owns the B&B we stayed at in Baileys Harbor. Maybe John should at least warn her to be on the alert.

When he got home he called his son and got the answering machine. John was with the Packer football team in California for a game against the San Diego Chargers. His mind shifted back to the conversation he had with Angie Ward. He decided to call her.

"Hi, Angie, it's Rod, can I come over?"

Chapter 47

THE SUN TIMES BUILDING was aglow with multi-colored lights streaming rays of hope and joy to all who viewed it. It was Christmas day and the sun shoved aside the few lazy clouds stretching out in front of it. There wasn't any snow left around to make it a worthwhile white event but he wasn't discouraged; he would be with Angie again!

"Come on in, Rod. I asked the doorman to escort you up here...afraid you'd get lost trying to find me."

"No problem, everybody around here seems to know you."

"Oh, don't be silly."

He couldn't believe the opulence of the place. White-carpeted rugs led to an unbelievable view of the Chicago River and the majestic Tribune Tower. The furniture was Scandinavian throughout. Light colors were the preferred design around here, even Angie's original dark hair was dyed a light shade of blond. She wore a tanning booth beachside tone. The sweet smell of marijuana permeated the heavenly scented perfume that she was wearing. He remembered it from the cruise; it drove him absolutely crazy then as it was doing right now.

Wow, she must've paid a mint for this place, he theorized. She looks even better than when I visited her long ago by the Buckingham Fountain. Shamus was sure a lucky man to make love to this irresistible creature. I wonder what his wife was like; had she given up being intimate with the Irishman?

"Rod...Rod, what in the world are you dreaming about? Come over here and give me a big kiss for old time's sake."

He readily complied.

"Would you like some champagne or are you still a Bombay Sapphire gin disciple?"

"I'll have whatever you are pouring. This place is almost as beautiful as you. I would've expected your recent ordeal would have put a major strain on you."

"Thanks for the compliment. You look pretty good to me although I think you lost some weight."

"Not really, just working out more than before. Bradley tossed in a membership to one of the most expensive and up-to-date fitness centers in Chicago. He still lifts weights almost every day."

She poured them both a glass of gin and remembered to add a twist of lemon in his. They sat down on a love seat by the bay window. He saw the gold-plated bamboo bong perched on one of the end tables opposite from them.

"I remember how happy we were when we first met on that wonderful cruise," she began. "You were seeking divine intervention for your next adventure and I was just looking for a small taste of it. School teachers are conservative and I needed something more. You gave me that, Rod."

"That's nice of you to say that. Do we want to remember those times as a bump on life's twisted road or as the gateway to a more meaningful experience?"

"It's your call. I suppose you're wondering why I have such a nice place here in downtown Chicago."

"The thought occurred to me."

"How well did you know Shamus Fenerty?"

He hesitated answering her.

I'm curious if she knows that her cousin Irene Finerty once hired me to scope out Fenerty's activities and determine if he was being faithful to his wife. I'm fully read in on the details about her involvement with Shamus. Is she aware that I knew all about her own affair with him? What a convoluted mess and now here I am trying to bed the gorgeous infidel!

"Um...not well; mostly what I read in the Trib."

"Just exactly...how well?"

He suppressed a grin. "Look, Angie, I'm not here to play games with you. If there's something you want to say to me, come out and say it. I don't really like playing these kinds of cat and mouse competitions."

She burst out crying and then went over to the end table, grabbed her bong and fired up.

He didn't know what to do or say. He hated the sweet aroma of pot.

"Maybe I should leave."

"No, please stay. I really need to clear some things up with you."

"Like what?"

She began to pout.

"Alright, let's have another drink and you can begin telling me what went on between you and Fenerty."

He got up and poured them each a healthy serving of gin and then strolled over to the curved bay window and looked down at the Chicago River. Two sightseeing boats were passing each other near the Wacker-Wabash junction turn of the river. He could barely make out the tourists crammed on the roof platforms.

Angie took a few more tokes and put the bong back on the end table. She seemed much more relaxed now. He handed her the drink and stared directly into her eyes. They were large and glassy but gave off a slight sparkle. She loosened up and began to talk freely.

"Shamus Fenerty and I had an affair right up to the time he committed suicide. I met him at my husband's funeral and he became my support structure that got me over the hump. He also helped me invest money. We began seeing each other periodically. Shamus claimed that his wife Lois was more concerned with her own professional growth than with the intimacies of their marriage. They even slept in separate bedrooms, took separate vacations."

"Were you intimate with him right up to the time we were making mad passionate love on the Caribbean cruise?"

"Yes."

"How could you, for Christ's sake!"

"How could I do what?"

"Be screwing both of us at virtually the same time. What kind of a pervert are you that would bend so low to satisfy your sexual appetite?"

She started to cry again. He didn't care. She changed the subject.

"Shamus had me invest heavily in his trucking company. He told me that some day in the near future he was going to go public with it. I mean, have an investment company bring it to Wall Street and have stock issued. He said I would be filthy rich if I hung with him."

Rod remembered back to the time he was tailing Shamus and the meetings with that porno star and the now deceased Tom Scott.

"Who else was going to get rich on the initial public offering?"

"I, er...hesitate to tell you."

"Why? It's public information now."

"I suppose so. I got a quarter of the shares, Max Schnel, his limousine driver got a quarter of the shares and Shamus got the rest."

"What? You're kidding me, right? What about Lois?"

"He left her out; convinced that she was already independently wealthy from a family inheritance coupled with her successful professional practice. She had her own banking account and he wasn't privy to it."

Rod was in shock; he couldn't believe what she was telling him. He did know earlier when they began dating that she had a financial interest in his company.

"I cashed in most of my shares after the mandated Wall Street 'lockout period' would allow me. I paid a mil-three in cash for this place. I love it!"

[281]

Angie was now reeling with the soothing effects of the marijuana coupled with a second glass of gin, straight up. He contemplated asking her for some grass. He needed something, anything to help him sort out all of this because his rational mind was nowhere to be found. He settled for another glass of gin.

"I'm not going to sleep with you today."

He didn't hear her. He was still asking his brain to shake out some clues for her complex behavior. She would tax a well-respected shrink.

"I said I'm not going to have sex with you today," she repeated again, this time with more emphasis on the "sex with you" phrase.

His cell phone rang; he picked it up. She gave him a "better remember what I just said buddy"...stare.

"What's going on, boss?"

"Where are you right now?"

"I'm over at Angie Ward's new penthouse having a drink."

The cell went quiet for a few moments. Angie looked over at him wondering what was going on. She noticed a serious look on his face. She excused herself to the bathroom.

"Get the hell out of there right now."

"What did you say?"

"Stay clear of that lady, you dunderhead. Irene just called me. There is a new slant on Fenerty's suicidal act. The forensic studies are in. They found traces of arsenic in his bones and hair follicles. One of the new investigators didn't fall for the suicide presumption. They're now approaching it as a homicide case."

"How's that? Did I hear you correctly?"

"The whole death episode appeared to the investigator as being too presumptuous...too neat of a package to tie up so rapidly. The investigator studied Fenerty's entire history and family background and concluded that he was too strong of an individual to force such a cowardly act of suicide upon himself."

"My thoughts entirely."

"The super sharp detective pressed the ME to conduct further testing using gas chromatography and infrared spectroscopy to find a chemical fingerprint for possible poisoning molecules. The ME pursued the request and they finally found the arsenic and slight hemorrhaging in his body cavity. There was also evidence of a blunt instrument blow to the back of his head which they missed earlier. Someone had been spiking his food and possibly drink. The ME thought that if it weren't for the so-called suicide, old Shamus would probably be dead by poisoning within the month."

"Holy shit, that's some serious business!"

"I told you most emphatically to get your ass out of there right away. Angie Ward has resurfaced as a murder suspect."

He clicked off his cell. Angie returned and came over to his side on the love seat. She put her long arms around his shoulders and pulled him closer. He almost succumbed to her "passion flower" aroma.

Maybe she changed her mind about having sex with me.

Silence permeated the still air as they sat motionless.

Why in the world would she kill him? She's a rich woman, thanks to him. I can't believe what the hell is going on here. This whole situation is way out of my league!

"What was all that about, Rodney?"

He noticed that she had warmed up considerably, purring when she talked. She even remembered his hated official first name.

"That was Bradley. He's out of control. Something came up and he needs me back at the office right away. Why don't you call me when you're ready to have sex with me again!" he said with a forced laugh, grabbed his coat and then walked out on her.

Chapter 48

SNO MOREAU was getting impatient. She hadn't heard from Simmons & Simmons regarding the status of her son. They should have found him by now. Maybe she made a mistake hiring them but Paul Keller was specific, that is…they were by far the best agency in town to locate missing persons.

"How's business going?" asked Li Chong. Bo Tan was with her and led her to a table where Sno had been talking with Petri. The four of them ordered an aperitif. Chong hadn't seen her for several weeks and heard through the realtor grapevine that she might be looking for another restaurant location.

"Hi Li, I'm fine. Where've you been lately? Tired of my food?"

"I've been busy. The real estate business is picking up. I found a neat location for your Cordon Bleu restaurant."

"What? How did you know about my restaurant in Bangkok?"

"Research, honey; when we first met you mentioned having two restaurants in Bangkok and expressed hope in opening another one at some point in time to honor your late husband. Your place here is always packed. It's time to expand and I have the ideal location for you."

"You do, huh?"

"Of course, I'm a hot shot realtor."

Bo Tan looked at Petri and shrugged. They were both bored and didn't like Li Chong. She was too aggressive for them. Sno Moreau was more than capable of determining her restaurant future. Petri was wondering why Bo Tan was with Li. Maybe something was going on between them. She reminded him of a gigantic jellyfish encircling an unsuspecting swimmer with those poisonous tentacles reaching out everywhere.

"Is it true?" Petri asked her. "You're expanding?"

She ignored him, staring tersely at Li Chong.

Sno was ready to expand her operations. Business had been outstanding and she was ready to introduce a new French restaurant in honor of her husband. The Tribune repeatedly featured the House of Saigon as one of the best finds in the Chicago dining world. She had been a guest on two of the local major television talk shows and her reputation grew. She certainly wasn't interested in having the Chinese lady taking charge about finding her a new restaurant site.

"Changing the subject here," Bo Tan inserted himself. "How's the search for your son going? I'll never forget the ugly prison scene down there when we went to pick him up and he was no longer there."

"Nothing new, thanks though for asking." She didn't want to get into a discussion about her son, her heart still ached.

There was a disturbance in front of the restaurant at the hostess desk. The restaurant was full, even overbooked with reservations. The young hostess was overwhelmed. Sno left her friends and went to the front entrance to investigate.

"Excuse me, ma'am, how can I assist you?"

"This impolite girl said we had an hour wait to be seated. I don't believe her. I see an empty booth over there and I insist that we be seated immediately."

Sno looked intently at the well-dressed lady and her tall albino accomplice. She had defused many situations like this in the past. The Chicago elite expected immediate recognition and of course, rapid service without question.

"Please give me your name and I'll see that you get seated as soon as possible." A long wait for a table was a routine happening here. She would find a way to accommodate them. The young hostess was embarrassed but Sno was an expert at defusing confrontations.

"Lois Fenerty and my dear friend Whitey. Write that down. I'll just take a seat here until you call us. I trust it won't be too long. Actually, we have some important business to discuss so find us a secluded spot in the back of the dining room."

"I'll see if I can arrange that for you, ma'am. In the meantime, will you have a glass of wine on the house? We're serving an excellent Bordeaux this evening."

"That would be fine for me but Whitey here will have a coke."

"I'm sure we'll have you seated in a few minutes. Thanks for your patience." Sno issued some instructions to the restaurant manager and left.

Bo Tan and Petri witnessed the disturbance at the front hostess station. They were impressed by the graciousness which Sno exhibited handling the altercation. Li Chong was bored with the entire episode. She was ready to leave without eating. Bo gave her a stern look and she sat back in the booth without saying anything, totally ignoring the two men.

"Do you know who that is?"

"No, should I?" Petri responded with a "who cares" attitude.

"Don't you read the Trib?"

"Of course I do; I follow the Cubs and the Bears."

"You idiot Petri, get with the program."

Li Chong suddenly came to life. "That lady is accused of murdering her husband, a successful trucking executive and a Democratic big wig. Everybody in Chicago knows that she's innocent. The big goof was balling a school teacher over in Libertyville. All of a sudden he was overcome with guilt…committed suicide."

"Oh yeah," Petri said, now engrossed in the conversation. "I read somewhere that he was going to run for governor."

"Who's the albino?" Bo asked nobody in particular.

"He's probably her new lover," Li exclaimed. "I'd like a chunk of that vanilla ice cream in my bowl anytime!"

"Stop this nonsense," Sno ordered as she sat back down with them. "Give the poor lady some space. She's still mourning her husband's death. The albino is probably a relative or close family friend."

They ordered another round of aperitifs. Sno had the waiter bring some spring rolls with a small bowl of nuc mam. Li Chong refused to eat them, insisting that lowly peasant food made her violently ill. Petri and Bo devoured the food much to Sno's delight.

Lois Fenerty and Whitey got seated diagonally across the room from their table and were seated in the last booth in the rear of the dining area. Sno signaled a…"I told you so" sign to Lois as she saw them being led to the back by the hostess.

"What do you think?" Lois asked him after they finished their appetizer.

"The food is real good. That pretty lady who helped us must own the joint; at least she acts the role."

"Not the food you idiot, I mean the investigation. Has your buddy on the police force told you anything new?"

"Nope; he said they're about to wrap it up."

"Any mention of the poisoning?"

"No, he's just a beat cop, Lois, doesn't have the chief's ear."

"Then I suggest you stop paying the deadbeat if he can't deliver what we need to know. In fact, don't ask me to dole out any more money, Whitey. See if you can find somebody else higher up the food chain. That shouldn't be a problem; they all seem to know you!"

Lois hated the bodyguard. However, his mere physical presence assured her of some sense of security. He was mean-looking and ugly and resembled a bleached-out Frankenstein character. He wore oversized black combat boots that had a sharp knife embedded in the toe of the right boot that released whenever he pounded the boot heel on the floor or concrete. She knew everything about him. Shamus had paid his bail bond on numerous occasions. Why he wasn't in prison was a mystery to her. Being a practicing behavioral psychiatrist wasn't enough to figure this bastard out.

"Did you get the insurance money yet?" Whitey asked her.

"Why are you so anxious to know?"

"I want my split, that's why. Shamus paid me a good chunk of change to watch his back but now he's gone and so is my financial lifeline."

"Be patient you fool. The will is being probated as we speak. We're in for a lot more money than his life insurance policy is going to pay me."

"How's that?"

"Fortunately that suicide exemption in the policy terminated last year so I should get the proceeds pretty soon. I'm more anxious to get my hands on the twenty-five million shares of preferred stock he owned that is in the process of being transferred over to me."

"Why did he give that ignoramus harlot so much stock?"

"You can't figure it out?"

"Of course I can," he laughed too loudly. "He was bedding her big time when the company went public. Oh, sorry, I imagine you're still sensitive about that issue but get real, Doctor Bloodless; she had him by the balls. She was scamming him, knowing that she could blow the whistle any time and bring him down."

Lois tried to finish her entree which was now a challenge because it was cold. She had promised Whitey a big payoff if he'd help her dispose of Shamus. Several months before his demise she had started a regimen of lacing her husband's food with an arsenic compound. She reminisced.

I'm so darn happy with Whitey. The way he set up the carbon monoxide poisoning was a stroke of genius. It was our good fortune that he happened to be outside near the back of the garage smoking a joint when Shamus drove inside with the bimbo and parked.

Whitey stared across the dining room at the other table. He didn't like the owner and her chums staring over at Lois and him. The two Asian

[288]

goons were falling all over the good-looking owner and ignoring the other bitch at their table.

I wouldn't mind that owner falling all over me. She'd come up begging for mercy, believe me! Get rid of those two other slant-eyed goofballs and hop aboard with me!

Bo and Li got up, bid their farewells and left the restaurant. Sno and Petri headed back to the kitchen. It was crowded now in the House of Saigon and the noise level was high.

"Why do you think your husband provided so much stock for Max?"

"That one throws me, Whitey. Maybe Shamus was so appreciative how Max looked after the boys, a guilt trip some would say. He played with them, took them to ball games and movies. My guess is that he furnished the love and attention that my husband never seemed to have the time or inclination to give them."

"Max was an asshole," shouted Whitey.

"Not so loud! There had to be some strong male bonding between the two of them. Shamus never had a brother and Max seemed to fit that bill. I don't bemoan the fact that he gave him a large amount of stock; it's that whore Angie Ward that's going to haunt me the rest of my life."

"I'm with you there. We were lucky how things went down that night. When the bitch raced frantically out of the garage I went in there to check on Shamus. He was in a big time stupor and waved the suicide note back and forth in front of my eyes. I doubted he had the guts to do the job so I found a tire iron and clunked him in the back of the noggin."

"Yeah, my big white hero and you set up the gadgets for him to breathe in the 'fumes of death' and we got away with it. They'll pin it on his slut."

"The arsenic was just not working fast enough so... Let's get out of here, Lois. I got some work to do back at the mansion."

"Like what?"

"My fair lady, it is much better that you not know."

Chapter 49

WHITEY dropped Lois off at the office of a clinical psychologist in downtown Evanston. She told him that she was brought in as a consultant by a close friend to visit with a middle-aged couple undergoing marriage counseling.

My, my, he thought to himself as she got out of the car. How unique; her with the ultimate in marriage indiscretions offering advice and assistance to another husband and wife in need of supportive guidance! What's next? I give up!

"Don't bother to pick me up. My good friend asked me to stay overnight because he has also scheduled an evening group session he wants me to sit in on. I'll take a cab home in the morning from the motel."

"Your choice, see you later," he bid her farewell and sped away.

Group session my ass, he surmised with a lecherous grin on his big face, probably a pokie...pokie threesome session! Oh well, nothing new with this lady. I should have exposed the shrew long ago but Shamus had to know she was sleeping around, something I guess the shrinks all call group therapy!

Whitey had lived with Max Schnel in a two story guest house in the rear of the Fenerty mansion property. He and Max weren't friends and barely co-existed, keeping their distances from each other as often as possible. Whitey seriously injured one of Max's close acquaintances in a bar brawl before Fenerty hired him to become his personal bodyguard. Max never forgave him. He was presently visiting relatives in Germany and would be gone for a month.

The roads were wet and slippery as Whitey drove home. Christmas decorations were in evidence everywhere. Every street light in Highland

Park was strung with flickering red and green bulbs. The local weatherman predicted a heavy snow.

His twisted mind was racing in overdrive.

I hate this fucking season, everyone trying to outdo each other with gifts and kindness. I wish this investigation was over. I don't regret what I did, the bastard deserved it! Fenerty had every reason to plant his cheating wife in the dirt but she got to me first. The big payoff will set me up for the rest of my wonderful life.

"Hello, Mr. Whitey," the maid greeted cheerfully when he walked into the mansion. She was preparing to go home and was carrying a bundle of wrapped gifts. She was always friendly with him so he didn't mind chatting with her on occasion because she kept her distance and never inquired about his services with the Fenerty clan.

"Going to a Christmas party are you?"

"No, Mr. Whitey, I wrapped these items here and they are for members of my family. We will exchange gifts tonight. I hope you have a Merry Christmas and Happy New Year."

"Whatever…see you next week."

When she was gone Whitey went into his house in the back, climbed the stairs and sat down on his bed. He decided it was time to take a "trip". He went to a locked cabinet and pulled out a bottle of the colorless and odorless acid, a thick eight inch expansion rubberized band, a needle and a syringe. He decided to inject the stuff intravenously because he would get higher much quicker than using the sugar cube.

He stretched out on his bed for several minutes and contemplated his next step in the aftermath of Fenerty's death. After about an hour of pure relaxation he started to feel the wonderful effects of the acid.

Lois had left a message on his cell phone to get rid of the bottle of poison as soon as he got home after dropping her off. She panicked the night of the murder and decided to hide the bottle of poison content in a flower box attached to the rear kitchen window.

Before the murder investigation began Whitey decided to remove the bottle labeled *Granules of Arsenious Acid* from the flower box but wasn't sure how to dispose of it. He found a secret place to stow it in the four car garage. There were multiple storage areas including an attic with closets where Fenerty stored his hunting rifles and fishing gear. He was sure that nobody would ever find it in the safe where he stashed it in the upper rafters.

Whitey got out of bed and floated miraculously down the stairwell and went outside to the garage. He searched all over for it but he couldn't find it. He totally forgot where he had hidden the incriminating evidence.

Did they discover the stuff when they were here during the investigation? I would have been told by my cop buddy if they found it. The prick, he's useless; we're cutting him off anyway. Where is the shit hiding from me?

"Hello there, neighbor," signaled an elderly man as he was walking up the driveway. He was scared of the strange-looking monster standing in front of him. Several neighbors told the old man that a freak of nature was living in the back of the mansion and to stay clear of the place at all costs.

Whitey knew the old coot lived several houses down the block and was annoyed that his critical mission was being interrupted by him.

"I got a Christmas gift for the lady of the house," the old man stammered, then stuttered as he began to shake and back away from Whitey. "Er…ah…would you be so kind to give it to Mrs. Fenerty when she gets home?"

"Of course I'll do that for you." Whitey snatched the gift from the trembling visitor nearly snapping the major bones of his wrist into small fragments.

"Be careful you don't hurt yourself on the slippery ice."

Whitey watched the little man in absolute awe. He couldn't believe what he witnessed unfolding in front of him. He was experiencing the ultimate sensations of his acid trip.

The old man skipped down the slippery surface on a pair of black racer ice skates. He was dressed in a Chicago Black Hawk uniform and started to swing his hockey stick in several directions and then stabbed it at the ice. Whitey thought he saw a solid black rubber object fly off the ice and bounce off a parked car across the street. The car rose three feet off the concrete from a launching pad, turned into a rotary position around and sped toward the hockey player. As it was about to crash into the man, it changed its shape and turned into a big silken parachute. It quickly enveloped the hockey player, and then rose rapidly to the sky. The hockey stick fell out of the sky and was honing in directly at Whitey. He ducked, then spun around and ran toward the garage.

He hung around in the garage until darkness set in challenging his warped brain and still couldn't remember where the arsenic was hiding from him. A shrill voice from the floor of the garage shouted at him that it was time to act! He marched out of the garage and located the twenty-five gallon tank of gasoline Shamus kept outside for all of his power equipment. He then filled several containers of the volatile flammable liquid and charged back into the garage.

It's time for the grand finale...ha, ha, ha! Oh boy, what fun!

He poured the gasoline over the walls, floors, and cabinets and then climbed up into the attic and repeated the soakings.

Satisfied with the first stage of his work, Whitey then ran a gasoline-drenched cord from a stack of wrinkled up newspapers on the floor in the center of the garage leading to the rear back door and extending ten feet out. He lit the tip of the cord and scrambled through the thick hedge separating the property from an easement in the rear of the mansion. He took a minute to stare back proudly at his act of arson.

Oh, oh, it looks like the fires of hell! I love it! Those geometric patterns of black fiery clouds excite me. Oh...ah, I'm getting hard all over. Agh...I'm turning into a slab of stone! I can't move. I'm buried in concrete. Help! Someone get me out of here. Help me, please!

He continued to be mesmerized by the racing flames reaching skywards and blackening the entire neighborhood.

[293]

Did I see the remnants of the plastic tubing and duct tape that I used to kill that cheating prick fly out of there? Yeah, oh yeah...burn in hell baby! It's so hot the concrete is melting away under me. I feel like Satan wired tightly to a flaming cross. Aha, I can move again, yeah!

When he was sure that the destruction of evidence was complete, he calmly walked over to the next street to his parked car. He stopped abruptly in his tracks as he spotted Tom Scott sitting on the hood of his car smoking a cigarette.

No, it can't be, I wiped that fucker off the face of the earth on that carnival mockery Navy Pier. Fenerty had a real hard on for the guy messing with his actress squeeze in the hotel room. Had he been reincarnated as the devil's hired assassin to hunt me down and kill me?

Instantly, and without warning, Tom Scott slowly dissolved into a silver hood ornament on his car. Whitey stood in awe at the transformation throwing off numerous multi-colored sparks. He looked up and down the street to see if anybody witnessed the aberration and then climbed into his car and took off. One kid riding a bicycle on the street smiled, waved at him and then continued pedaling down the street. The bike-rider spun his bike around when he heard the "steel on steel" thud of Whitey's car bouncing off a parked minivan.

Whitey took one last look back at the raging ruins behind him and then sped around the street corner.

What a trip! Oh my God; what a marvelous, fucking trip! I am damn good at what I do. Soon, everyone in these parts will be calling me a hero!

Chapter 50

CHRISTMAS had passed and Rod Richards was lonely. He spent the several Holiday days alone, holed up in his apartment, periodically glancing out the window at the snow banks in front of his place. They were now turning a dirty gray as the thaw and heavy traffic reduced the iced mounds to an ugly mess. He finished his research and laid out his revised plan to find Chien Tran. The prison trip was extremely helpful.

He learned that the majority of the Wisconsin Oneida Indian tribe was located near Green Bay. He concluded that Tran would seek safety with his old prison cellmate, not knowing that his prison sentence was commuted and that he was a free man. Tomorrow he would drive up there but first he wanted to alert Veronica Brown that Tran might be seeking her out in case John wasn't able to contact her. He'd hoped she was back from her Texas trip with him.

"Hello, Veronica, Rod Richards calling."

"Hi Rod, hope you had a great Christmas."

"I did," he said not wanting to tell her the truth. "How was yours?"

"Oh, my, I just fell in love with San Antonio and was so glad to meet your other son. John and I spent a lot of time on that lovely River Walk they have down there. He showed me the old hospital where you worked and now his brother is employed there."

"Glad to hear that all went well. I need to alert you about some possible trouble heading your way; not sure if John mentioned anything to you."

"What do you mean?"

"I can't confirm this but I have reason to believe that your former husband might be trying to find you."

"Oh my God! I thought he was in prison."

"He escaped from that federal prison in Illinois not knowing that his sentence had been commuted. He is technically a free man now, but a dangerous one at that. Conceivably he has no means of support and is foraging for money, food, even clothing and a place to hide out. Law enforcement is probably hunting him down as we speak."

He heard a gasp on the other end of the line.

"But…but, why me and why Door County?"

"Your old boss Mike Howzer might have told Chien Tran at some point after the divorce that you settled down in Baileys Harbor. We're not sure of that because when I visited him he seemed to have the early stages of dementia. We have to assume the worst possible scenario."

"I have to agree with you about Mike. He called me one time shortly after the divorce but I never heard from him again."

"Moot point at this stage. I've learned that Chien Tran's former prison cellmate was an Oneida Indian and has family in the Green Bay area. The man may even be living there or somewhere in Door County for all we know."

"Why are you involved in this mess?"

"His birth mother hired Simmons & Simmons to find him. It's a long story and someday I'll share all of the details. She's afraid that he might get hurt or even get killed. The interesting fact is that he apparently doesn't even know his mother exists. She gave him up for adoption at a young age when Saigon was being overrun by the hordes from North Vietnam.

"That's interesting. I only knew of the kind and generous older couple in Evanston who raised him. He never shared any other information with me. We weren't married very long.

"Bradley told me to run point on this mission of mercy for his mother."

"Thanks for the heads up. I'll be sure to lock up everything which is a rarity in these parts. We don't have much crime around here."

"Please call me and the local sheriff's office right away if he contacts you. Enter both of our cell numbers in your phone for quick access."

"I'll do that. Incidentally, if you get up this way in your search you can stay here with me. Door County is isolated after the Christmas Season and I wouldn't mind the company."

"Sounds like a winner. I'll coordinate with John. Maybe he can get up there also."

"Good luck getting him to come here with you. The Packers are heading for the playoffs. I don't plan to see him any time soon."

"Thanks for the offer Veronica; I might just take you up on it."

He hung up and decided to call Bradley. He hadn't seen him for several days now. He didn't enjoy the Christmas party Bradley had thrown. Most of the attendees were boring and there were no pretty maidens to be seen anywhere. He missed Angie and wondered what she did over Christmas. He needed to brief Bradley on his plans to head north.

"Good morning boss. I'm on my way up to Wisconsin to find Chien Tran and bring him safely back home to his mother."

"Sounds like progress. Have you recovered yet from the holidays?"

"Well sort of…out every night partying takes a toll on an older man. You married honkies wouldn't know that side of life anymore my friend."

"Did you see Angie after my phone call to you about her situation?"

"Nope, I sure haven't. I'm laying low on that front for awhile. I'll contact her when I get back. Why do you ask?"

"I'm just curious, that's all. I had lunch with Irene yesterday and she asked about you. You should be aware that police investigators are tapping your close friend's telephone lines and bugging her condo. They initiated steps to conduct their own surveillance of her. She's not off the hook yet. I would prefer you continue to stay clear from her. Let's allow the talented investigative authorities prove her innocence."

"Whatever you say, boss. I'll keep you posted on the Chien Tran case. I suggest you call Sno Moreau and give her some sort of encouragement that we are moving forward on this. Tell her we should have some information for her within the week."

"Rod, you never disappoint me...your optimism is overwhelming. I'll call her but not promise anything. Keep me posted, I don't like surprises."

Just for the hell of it, he called Angie.

Screw all the precautions! Bradley is overprotective. It's my personal business and I'll do what I damn well please.

She picked up the phone on the first ring.

"How's it going, Angie? It's Rod here. I'm sorry I didn't contact you over Christmas but I was out of pocket."

She needs to think I'm in no big rush to get back with her. I'd rather she not beg, though.

"Can you come over and see me right now?"

"What do you have in mind?"

"I'm depressed. I'm getting threatening telephone calls accusing me of killing a popular man and the future governor of the State of Illinois. I'm going to stop answering the phone. You are the only one I can rely on. I want to put my head on your shoulder to feel comfort and secure again."

He wanted to go see her badly. They were two of a kind; isolated individuals without any support systems in place to secure them. Nobody really cared for either of them any longer. He contemplated seeing her on his way out of town but had second thoughts. He was on an important mission and needed to steer clear of any roadblocks, especially roadblocks of this nature.

"Look, Angie, I can't come over now. I'm heading out of town on an important assignment. I'll call you when I get back in town."

"I may not be here when you return to the city. I'm thinking of leaving Chicago."

"Hold on, don't do anything drastic. Why don't you get in touch with Paul Keller and seek his guidance? He can be trusted."

"Thanks, I'll do that. Be careful out there and please call me when you get back. I want to be with you so badly I could cry and cry."

He hung up without adding anything further or acknowledging her plea. He'd go to her as soon as he returned from his mission. They'd pick up where they left off on that scintillating cruise aboard the Port Caller.

He packed a suitcase, tossed in his .38 caliber police snub nose pistol, some surveillance equipment and then secured his little Honda from the garage. He got on the Tri-State and drove to Wisconsin. The roads were no longer slippery since a warm spell of weather attacked the remaining snow banks and reduced them to a series of collapsed deflated balloon-like images. He pulled off in Milwaukee to get a brat and a beer.

He planned to stay in John's condo on the Fox River but felt uncomfortable. His son was still out of town so he arranged to stay at the casino hotel by the airport. He presumed that this was a good starting point for his pursuit of Chien Tran because the casino was operated by the Oneida Tribe.

When he got to his room he unpacked and then found a telephone directory. He looked for the name of Littlewolf in the listings but was unsuccessful. He dialed the operator and was told that there were several Littlewolf numbers listed but all with recently restricted listings.

He decided to go downstairs and see if the craps tables were hot. He hadn't tossed the dice since his Caribbean adventure. Edging his way into an opening at the second table he flipped a hundred dollar bill on the green felt surface. Chips were slid over to him and he began with a "come" bet.

"Are you doing any good?" he asked a short stocky man next to him.

"Nah, the table got cold and I'm out of here."

Rod continued playing and noticed a tall, gawky older-looking Indian dressed in a casino uniform talking to the stickman at the other table.

Just for the heck of it when he comes over here I'm going to ask him if he knows of a Spencer Littlewolf or even heard of Chien Tran's old cellmate. Oh, oh, he's moving this way.

[299]

"Excuse me sir, sorry to bother you but do you know if there are any Indian workers at the casino by the name of Littlewolf?"

"Why do you want to know?"

"I've been asked to deliver an important message to him."

"Sorry, friend can't say that I know anyone around here by that name." The tall Indian then walked back to the other table where the action had picked up.

It was getting late. Rod was tired and ready for bed. He returned to his room and poured a drink from the room liquor cabinet. He flipped on the television set and channel-surfed until he found a local news broadcast. The ten o'clock news was in progress and he was shocked by the images reflected on the screen.

The female newscaster reported that someone in the parking lot of a crowded mall had taken cell phone pictures of a pregnant lady being savagely attacked. She stated that an Asian-looking man assaulted a pregnant lady, knocked her to the ground and then viciously kicked at her. He stole her purse, car and then sped out of the mall area. The newsperson further reported that the stolen car was seen heading north on Highway 57 toward Door County. The police gave chase but lost contact with him.

Son-of-a-bitch, he theorized, I'll bet that's him. It's a long shot but if it's him I think I know where he's heading...Baileys Harbor and to his ex-wife.

He grabbed the telephone on his bedside stand and called Veronica. She didn't answer at first so he hung up and tried again. This time she picked the phone up on the first ring. She was already in bed. A quick introduction fully awakened her. He demanded that she leave her B&B immediately.

"Go to one of your friends! Let me know where you're staying. Veronica, listen to me, this is urgent...he damn near killed a lady in Green Bay and swiped her car. He's heading your way."

It was too late! He heard a loud thud as her telephone dropped to the floor.

[300]

Chapter 51

SHARDS OF GLASS flew at her as she jumped away from the shattered front bay window. It was too late. One piece slashed her on the upper right arm and blood started to escape from the wound.

It was him; the monster coming at her with a startled look of fear and desperation in his penetrating eyes. A small piece of glass was embedded in his forehead next to the strawberry birthmark and it started to bleed. Another gash was bleeding from a puncture wound over his right eyelid. Blood was also squirting from his elbow which got slashed when he smashed the brick through the thick double-paned glass window and crawled through it. The brick fell from his hands. He was a mess

"Hi, Veronica; you were sure difficult to locate but I don't give up easily; you know that, don't you?"

"It's you!" she screamed in desperation. "Why are you here? What do you want from me? I know they're looking for you."

Chien Tran walked straight over to her and slammed a vicious closed fist at her head. Blood spit at him from her shattered nose and she fell immediately to the floor. He picked up a large shard of glass from the floor, knelt down next to her and held it against her throat. She was able to edge away from him and kicked him as hard as she could in his crotch.

"Ouch, oh…you son-of-a-bitch, I'm going to kill you!"

He quickly found the piece of glass he dropped when she kicked him in the balls and slowly crawled back over to her.

"Beg for mercy you no good rotten pussy!"

A car horn sounded outside. He froze, got up and then snuck over to one of the other windows facing the street. A pickup truck without backup lights pulled into the driveway across the street. Veronica crawled her way to the hallway leading to the kitchen, rolled over and then struggled to get up. He walked over to her and kicked her in the head. She slid back down to the floor, unconscious.

"I hope you die, you slut," he screamed and then went back to the living room window again to double check whether or not the truck across the street pulled into the garage. It did, he was safe, at least for now. He turned off the living room lights. He was having a hard time focusing clearly out of his right eye because of the blood streaming down from the cuts on his head.

He walked past her prone body and went into the kitchen. A small area light above the stove was still on. He stared back at her still sprawled out on the hallway floor. He couldn't make out her pretty face because it was smeared with blood. Her nose was disfigured, slanting off to the left and her right arm was covered with blood.

He opened all of the kitchen drawers and found a flashlight, then turned the kitchen light off. He worked his way to the bathroom and located a first aid kit in a cabinet above the toilet. He needed to stop the bleeding on his arm and face and maneuvered over to the sink. He turned on the faucet and splashed cold water all over his face, grabbed a towel and dabbed it dry. He repeated the process with his damaged arm. Returning to the cabinet he pulled out a small bottle of hydrogen peroxide, a box of bandages and then finished dressing his wounds.

He flashed his way back to the kitchen area. All of a sudden he heard a scratching noise behind him and a weak tug on his pants.

"Help me, please," she said softly passing in and out of consciousness. "Call...a...ambulance, I can't breathe. I'm going to die."

He almost puked went he shone the flashlight on her face.

"Go to hell!" he screamed at her.

She passed out again at his feet.

With the flashlight flickering dangerously low due to failing batteries he hurried throughout the rest of the house collecting whatever he could find that would help him. He found a shotgun in one of the bedroom closets and breathed a sigh of relief that it was fully loaded. Next to the shotgun was a hunting knife and he took that also. He knew that Veronica hunted with her old man when she was young and knew how to handle weapons.

What else can I gather up to help me survive in this barren wilderness? Maybe I should grab some food from the pantry. I'll certainly need sustenance and maybe she has some bottled water stashed somewhere around the place.

He continued to forage and found an old police radio stowed on a shelf in an upstairs utility room. Flashing his way back to the living room he found her purse on a chair and grabbed it…the flashlight gave out. He then disappeared through the front door and jumped back into his stolen car.

Chien swung south on Highway 57 satisfied that he had enough provisions to support him until he could get over to Washington Island the next day. A loaded shotgun and a miniature Bowie knife gave him a funny feeling inside and he laughed aloud.

Be careful everybody, I am now categorized as armed and dangerous! Ha ha…ha ha; I'm going to get you, better not get in my way!

Leaving Baileys Harbor heading toward Jacksonport he squinted at the rear view mirror through his swollen right eye. It hurt like hell. His head was pounding, his bad heart thudding. He pulled out the embedded shard of glass then cleansed and bandaged the wound on his forehead.

"Son of a bitch!" he shouted at the top of his lungs. A trailing vehicle with flashing lights was closing in rapidly on him.

Chapter 52

HIGHWAY 57 north out of Green Bay was devoid of traffic. All of the snow had melted and the roads were quick. Rod sped up the four lane highway at eighty miles an hour which is all that he could get out of the worn out Honda engine. Suddenly he saw the red flashing light easing up behind him. He pulled over immediately.

"Stay in your car and put your hands on the steering wheel," a voice reported over a loud speaker.

Rod complied in disgust. He was pissed at the poor timing.

The officer came up to the driver's side and motioned him to roll down the window. He quickly flashed a bright light inside the car and then at Rod's face.

"What's your hurry, bud? You ain't no A.J. Foyt at the Indy 500!"

"I'll tell you if you take that damn light off me."

The officer told him to put the inside car lights on which he did.

"Let me see your driver's license and evidence of insurance."

Rod fumbled through the glove compartment and gave him the requested items. He was pleased with himself that he shoved the insurance form in the glove compartment at the last minute. He'd lost the old one and this replacement came in the mail a few days ago.

"Look, sir, there is a murder taking place up in Baileys Harbor; I got to get there right away."

The officer laughed as he was checking out the insurance papers.

"I've thought I've heard 'em all, buddy, but this one takes the cake. We haven't had a murder up there in years. Tell me who is getting murdered and I'll tell you whether or not you can race up there in time to stop it?"

"Call the Brown County Sheriff's office and they will confirm it," Rod shouted in anger. He was rapidly becoming unglued.

"Look, friend, I'm with their office and we don't handle police matters up in Door County."

"Please listen to me. A female friend called me an hour ago and said that she was being attacked. I'm a private investigator on my way up there."

"Oh yeah, and I'm the sitting Pope in Rome. Get the fuck out of the car."

As he was getting out, Rod dug into his back pocket to show him his P.I. license. The action startled the officer. He grabbed him, spun him around and told him to put his hands on the front fender where he could see them. Rod complied but still got frisked.

"Okay, let's see the license."

The officer took the document and scanned it.

"Alright, if something bad was coming down in Baileys Harbor tell me why you didn't call the cops up there?"

"I did just that before I left my hotel and they said they'd check into it. Why don't you call them for yourself and check out my story?"

He told Rod to get back into his car and then radioed back to the dispatcher and talked to him for several long minutes.

"You're correct, mister, there was a break-in and subsequent assault on a lady up there. Some teens were driving by her house and saw the smashed in front window and called the police. They are at the site investigating the case as we speak. I'll let you go this time but drive within the speed limits, there is nothing you can do to help her right now."

"Is she dead?"

"No, our dispatcher said she was beaten up pretty badly. Fortunately the local cops called an ambulance shortly after they arrived. The lady is being treated in the emergency room at a nearby hospital and might even be home by the time you get there."

Rod took off and drove the speed limit up to Baileys Harbor. He went right to her B&B not knowing exactly where the hospital was located. The front bay window had a sheet of plywood affixed to it. He figured that there would still be some uniforms completing the investigation. He was wrong. The front door was partially ajar and he went in cautiously. His pistol was drawn and ready just in case.

Before he could search the house he heard a vehicle pull up to the driveway. He peered back out through the opened door and was surprised to see Veronica getting out the passenger side of a police car. He holstered the pistol. The cruiser took off. She walked up to him, a huge bandage affixed across her nose. Her face was swollen, both eyes blackened and she looked like she was at death's door. Her right arm was bandaged and in a sling.

She didn't say a word as they walked into her house. He wanted to squeeze her in his arms but backed off.

"Did he do this to you?" he asked with compassion as he sat down on the couch.

"It was him, Rod. The bastard almost killed me. While I was transitioning in and out of consciousness I saw him go into the kitchen and fill a sack up with food, then he walked by me with my father's old Remington pump-action shotgun that he used for hunting rabbits. Dad warned me that single females were vulnerable and should always be prepared. A gun was supposed to serve that purpose but it sure didn't help me.

"Good God, was the shotgun loaded?"

"Unfortunately…yes."

"Was that all that he took from you?"

[306]

"I don't know for sure. My purse is missing and dad had an old hunting knife stored with the shotgun that he probably took with him. Anyway, he's prepared to kill any human being that gets in his way. I never saw such vicious looking eyes and beastly demeanor. I thought I knew him well; he's a changed man and he's insane!"

"How come the badges left so soon after dropping you off?"

"The cops that just brought me home said they were leaving right away to assist the others in hunting for him. They told me they were minimally staffed at this time of the year and didn't have a body on board to sit home with me. They were assured by the ER doctor that I would be okay on my own."

"I think you should be in the hospital. Well anyway, I'm here and I'll find him. He can't get away with this!"

She saw the pistol strapped to the back of his belt as he shifted positions.

"Rod, he's crazy. You can't go after him, you're no vigilante and he'll kill you for sure. Please let our local police forces do the job."

"No, I can't do that, I'm way beyond committed!"

Chapter 53

IT WAS PAST midnight and they were both exhausted. He decided that Chien Tran wouldn't a have a logical reason to circle back here unless he decided to kill her. He already had everything he needed to sustain his escape. She went to bed after taking the pain killers the hospital ER gave her. He stretched out on the couch, refusing to go upstairs to bed. He chambered a round in his pistol and set it next to him. He wasn't about to take any chances, implementing the necessary precautions he learned in the Army when operating in known enemy territory.

At seven o'clock the next morning Rod heard a pounding on the front door. He grabbed his pistol and circled around to a side window and peered out. He saw a uniformed police officer and let him in.

"How's she doing this morning?"

"I'm not sure, officer, she's still sleeping. Do you have any news for us? Did you get the low-life bastard?"

"Are you her uncle?"

"No sir, just a close friend. Did you find him?"

"No such luck. We alerted all of the law enforcement agencies in the area to include Brown County. Our supervisor is almost sure the thug is headed back to Green Bay to mix in with the local populace. He would stick out like a swollen sore thumb up here."

Rod didn't buy it. He felt strongly that Tran would head up to Washington Island to reunite with his old Indian cellmate. The local cops would have no basis to figure that out. He considered telling them his theory but he wanted to be the person to find Chien Tran and bring him back alive.

"Did you catch him?" a sleepy-eyed Veronica asked the cop as she descended the stairway.

"Sorry, ma'am, we lost him. Chief says that he's probably hunkered down in Green Bay. The boss thinks you're safe now. Here's my personal card, call me anytime if something comes up, okay?"

Rod wasn't impressed with how things were being handled. He suspected that it would be futile to paint the picture that he himself had implanted in his head. He knew where the desperado was going and he'd get him without their help.

"Veronica, I'm leaving right away to go after him. I know where he's heading and it's not back to Green Bay."

"What did you say? Where would he be hiding out?"

He filled her in on his assumption and then took time to explain the relationships that existed between former cellmates. In most cases they become blood brothers, attached to the hip and sworn to protect each other forever.

"Please go to a friend's house and stay there until I get back. You can't stay here, much too dangerous. I'll keep in touch with you and you call me if you see or hear anything out of the ordinary. Are you going to contact John?"

"What do you suggest? He's really tied-up now with the football team. I'm afraid he'll drop everything just to be near my side."

"It's your call, but if I know my son, he'll be here before dusk!"

He gave her a hug and headed for the door.

"Please, please be careful, Rod."

"I'll do the best I can. Take care."

He drove out of her driveway and went into town for breakfast. His time in the Army taught him to never pass on a major meal without a clue where the next one would be waiting to be served. He found a little diner and filled his empty gut with a hearty helping of pancakes and sausage.

"More coffee, sir?"

"Yeah, fill 'er up and please fix me one to go."

While he was finishing his coffee he decided to call Bradley and bring him up to date.

"Good God, Rod, how's she doing?"

"She'll survive but it appears we have a deranged marauder on our hands here. He now has weapons at his disposal and is dangerous."

"Be careful, we're not in the police business to apprehend gangsters. Let the cops do their job! Better yet, haul your ass back here to Chicago right away. You're too old to be playing Lone Ranger."

"Screw you, Simmons! You know me better than that. I'm here for the end game. I'm afraid if the cops are involved there'll be a dramatic stand-off and he'll get shot, even killed. I promised his mother I'd bring him home to her and I intend to do just that."

"You frickin asshole, you always thought you were bigger and better than the competition…do what the hell you want to…I don't care!"

"You got that right, boss."

There was a long hesitation on the other end. Rod thought he'd hung up.

"By the way, while I got you on the horn there has been an interesting development in the Shamus Fenerty case. Do you have the time to hear me out or will it delay your pursuit of the bad guy?"

"They pinned a murder rap on Angie, didn't they?"

"Nope, somebody else surfaced. The albino they call Whitey was apprehended for a possible DWI while driving erratically through the main streets of Highland Park. His right bumper was missing and the right side of his car was severely caved in.

"That guy is a maniac," Rod exhorted.

"The fool bragged that he'd torched the Fenerty garage trying to get rid of the orange-clad devils he found hiding in there. The police called in

[310]

the FBI and they discovered an unlocked but still sealed fire-proof safe amidst the smoldering ashes. Inside the container they found the incriminating evidence: arsenic, leftover tubing more than likely used in the alleged suicide, duct tape and several pairs of gloves."

Rod gasped and took a deep breath. "So Whitey's the culprit?"

"Everything seems to point to him. He kept alluding to the fact that he was the only human being capable of 'punishing the big-shot' for his indiscretions. He's undergoing psychiatric evaluation as we speak. Lois has been pegged as an accomplice; so has Angie. They'll probably have it all unraveled by the time you bring Chien Tran back here."

"Jesus H. Christ, I don't believe it. I must be dreaming!"

"Nope partner, facts are facts…you better get moving now."

Rod clicked his cell off and studied a map of the entire Door County peninsula. He tried to determine the best way to Washington Island and soon discovered the only way to get there was by ferry.

He paid his bill and hustled outside to his car. The damned thing wouldn't start. "Ah, shit the battery is dead," he shouted out to a passerby.

"There's a garage just down the street. Call them and they'll come and give you a jump start. I'd do that but I left the jumper cables in the garage."

"You need a new battery," reported the bearded garage owner. "I can give you a good deal and get you back on the road right away."

He had them replace his old one and took off in disgust.

When I get back to Chicago I'm going to run this piece of decayed shit off Navy Pier and get me a new Toyota Avalon or maybe even a Lincoln Town Car.

Chapter 54

PLUM BOTTOM ROAD off Highway 42 was void of all traffic. It certainly wasn't unusual for this time of the evening because of the late hour. The weather was unusually warm for this time of the year but he could feel a cold spell on its way in.

After his foray with Veronica and the escape from the local cops, Chien was famished. He was sure that he'd lost them. He wondered if they could've picked up the license plate of the stolen car when they rode past Veronica's place earlier on routine patrol. He should have ditched it but he still needed wheels up here in this godforsaken land. It was now several hours after the incident. He found a small eating place that was miraculously still open, pulled around the back and then parked by the dumpster.

"What'll it be, stranger? We're about to close for the evening but I can whip you up something quickly."

"Coffee and please bring it right away. I'll also want ham and eggs over easy with an English muffin or even wheat toast if you have some."

"Coming up," she said and went back to fire up the grill.

She brought his coffee over as directed, poured him a cup and then stared at him. He glared back at her figuring she might be suspicious that something was wrong.

Did they broadcast my break-in at Veronica's place? I don't hear a radio blaring or see a television set anywhere in this greasy spoon. I had her old man's police radio on all the time and nothing of any importance came over it. This lady might be trouble.

"What's wrong with your arm? I see blood soaked all the way through that makeshift bandage you have. Your eye looks terrible, mister. I got a medicine kit in the back and I'd be glad to do some first or second aid on you; maybe clean you up a bit."

"Um...no, I'll be alright. That's kind of you to ask though. You wouldn't believe how I cut the arm so I'm not even going to bore you with all the gory details."

"But your eye..."

"I said I'm fine, lady," he said defensively, "Now please hustle up the food."

"Okay, suit yourself."

She headed quickly back to the grill. "I don't recognize you, sir, are you from these parts?"

Chien worried further. He didn't like the probing.

This old bag wouldn't shut up...must've been a slow day. I wonder if they're all like this up here.

"Nope, I'm from Green Bay visiting my sister. Are the eggs ready yet? I'm starving, hadn't had a thing to eat all day."

She completed his order and delivered it to his table. She then started to stack dining room chairs on the tables after which she picked up a broom and started to sweep up the dirty diner.

Tran scarfed down the food, slapped a twenty dollar bill on the table and went out the door. He looked back at the woman and saw her shaking her head as she snatched the twenty dollar bill off the table and stuffed it in her blouse.

After he got back in the car he searched a Door County map conveniently found in the glove compartment. The police radio was reporting a car accident on the bridge in Sturgeon Bay. He listened longer; no mention of him or the assault.

I'm relieved, good news; the locals didn't blab about me!

He decided to camp out for the night at Lost Lake; according to his map, the smallest and the least inhabited of the three lakes in Door County. He reasoned it was too late to catch the car ferry at Northport Pier to get over to Washington Island. That would have to wait until the next morning. A motel or a B&B wouldn't work as he was trying to avoid contact with anyone who might be on the lookout for him.

He recalled the incident back in Green Bay when he overpowered that young woman in the mall parking lot. He remembered that several witnesses were nearby but apparently too shocked to try and stop him.

I wonder if that pregnant bitch delivered on the spot. She flailed away at me but was too weak to stop me. Veronica is another story. She put up a good fight, kicked me square in the nuts. I should have killed her right then and there. Now every cop within a hundred miles is hunting me down. Thank goodness I got that special police radio from her and it will keep me informed. Screw it, I'm a survivor, I'll live! I'm armed and dangerous!

Chien swung north on County Highway T at Bley's Corner and watched closely for a side road that would lead him into the little lake. At a white church building to his right, he turned left on Wendt Road which he was sure would take him to the water. About two hundred yards down the gravel road he saw smoke coming from the chimney of a small log cabin house. It house was dilapidated and most of the small front porch gave way to the hard ground below. He immediately cut off the headlights and slowed to a crawl for fear of arousing any occupants inside.

As he approached the house he noted that the gravel road reverted to a grass-covered by-way near the end. He slowly made a turn away from the broken down structure. Soon he saw the lake and decided to stop there and sleep in the stolen car. He was beyond fatigued. His wounded arm was throbbing, almost loud enough as if to scream, "fix me, please; someone fix me!"

He was awakened by a loud pounding on the hood of his car. It was morning. He was feeling nauseous. His mind was crammed full of cob webs; he couldn't remember where he was or how he got there. His eye was now completely swollen shut. On top of that, his bad arm was numb now and the makeshift congealed bloody bandage was lying next to him.

"What the hell are you doing here, mister? Can't you see the no trespassing signs posted everywhere around the property?"

Tran looked at the guy; reminded him of a gnarled old mountain man he once saw in the movies. He was carrying a rifle and Chien sensed that he could be trouble. He tried to get out of the back door of the car but his arm wouldn't move until he latched on to it with his other hand and then sprung out of the car.

"What's that shotgun doing in the back seat? You plan on poaching here on my land, mister?"

"Um, no, I got lost last night and was so tired of driving I pulled in here to rest but fell asleep. I'll get out of here right now."

"Where ya headed?"

"Washington Island."

"You're nowhere near there. Looks to me like you better get over to an emergency room and get that arm and shut eye looked at first."

"Thanks, I'll do that right away."

"I'd get rid of that shotgun, at least shove it in the trunk. There are several county sheriff dudes running around here, more than usual at this time of the year. I heard over the radio that someone beat up a lady over there in Baileys Harbor; bastard almost killed her."

I wonder if this old goat is suspicious. Maybe I should kill him; nobody else seems to be around this desolate back strip of woods. Someone might hear the boom of my shotgun, though. I better just get the hell out of here.

Chien hopped into the driver's seat and cranked up the transmission, backed out and waved a hurried goodbye to the old man. He flipped on the police radio and all he heard was some sporadic chatter about the Green Bay Packers and their march to a possible Super Bowl game.

That's all these backwoods dimwits around here talk about; hunting, football and the stupid Packers, he mused. A major crime was committed in their back yard and they seem to care less. I got to get over to

Washington Island right away. My luck is about to run out. I'll give Spencer a call when I get to the car ferry.

The old man watched Tran's car until it disappeared out of sight. He started to trudge back to his lake cabin in deep thought and then all of a sudden stopped dead in his tracks.

Son-of-a-bitch! That low life must be the culprit from Baileys Harbor. I should've nabbed the bastard on the spot!

He quickly reached into his bib overalls, yanked out a cell phone and then dialed a number.

"Junior, it's your uncle at Lost Lake. That woman beater you're looking for just pulled away from here and is headed for Washington Island. It looked to me like someone already caught up with him…I think he's been shot. Be mighty careful, he's got a shotgun. Tell your deputies to proceed with extreme caution. He's 'armed and dangerous' as we like to say around these parts."

Chapter 55

BO TAN and Petri were returning from a shopping errand they ran for Sno. She was running short of vegetables in The House of Saigon and expected a big rush for the noon meal. They lugged the groceries in through the back door of the restaurant. She was in the kitchen preparing batches of her now famous egg rolls.

"Thanks, fellas, I do appreciate it."

"Have you found another location yet for your new restaurant?"

"Yes Bo, but I'm not at liberty to tell you the location. I've been sworn to secrecy by my new realtor. He is a little weary of going around Li Chong who works in the same office. The man is aware of how possessive Li is and would have a stroke if she knew about our arrangement."

"I haven't seen her around here, lately."

"She's probably mad at me anyway for avoiding her."

"By the way, Bo, I'm really concerned about you," she said in a voice barely audible.

"Why is that?"

Petri perked up and was waiting for the explanation. He knew that Sno had no love interest in the guy. Anyway, Bo preferred other men.

Sno went on to explain her concern. "You should be spending more time at your own restaurant. You of all people know that customers appreciate the presence of an owner when they eat at their establishment. We have all learned in this business that without adequate supervision, a ton of food disappears out the back door."

"I closed her up. Business fell off considerably and the competition in the area was overwhelming. I'm too old to chase after customers. I got enough cash stashed away, I'm not hurting."

They were stunned. Petri couldn't believe it. She wrestled with Bo's reasons for getting out.

He had a great operation going when I first moved into Little Saigon. Everyone, including myself must be aware that demographics do change over time. One must recreate their withering competitive advantage from time to time to keep up with the changes. Maybe I need to examine my own business before competition also swallows me up!

"There's a telephone call for you up front, Sno," said a pretty young waitress. A Mr. Simmons said that it was urgent."

"Hello, Bradley, please tell me you've found my son."

"Well, yes and no. I just got off the phone from Rod. He's located him up in Door County, Wisconsin."

Sno shouted wildly with joy. Bo and Petri heard her and came running up front to see what was going on.

"What do you mean by the 'yes and no' inference?"

"Rod told me there was some trouble up there. Your son apparently doesn't know that he's a free man and is doing everything possible to avoid law enforcement officials at all costs."

"What do you mean by 'all costs'? Is he in danger?" she pleaded to know, her heart began to skip a few beats.

"I'm sorry to tell you that he's in trouble. Chien assaulted several people including his ex-wife. Rod promised me he'd find him before he got into any more trouble and bring him back to Chicago as soon as possible. I have the utmost confidence he'll do that."

There was total silence on the other end of Bradley's phone. She had sunk slowly to the floor, her eyes rolled up. Bo tried to catch her but he wasn't quick enough. Petri froze.

"Hello, hello, is anybody there?" Bradley cried.

[318]

Petri finally took the phone out of her hand. "Who the hell is this? This better not be some kind of joke. Whatever you told her shocked her so much she passed out."

Bradley regretted making the call but sensed that he had to at least cushion her for a possible negative outcome. She had placed her complete trust in Simmons & Simmons so he was compelled to deliver.

"So you think that you can corral him before the cops get to him," Petri asked tersely.

"We're doing the best we can. I have complete faith in my man up there. He's an experienced operative. He was a war hero in Vietnam and hasn't an ounce of fear in his body. He'll bring him home."

"He'd better be that good, Mr. Bradley. She'd fall completely apart if anything bad happened to him. Her goal in coming to this country was to find her son; you fully understand that, don't you?"

"Absolutely, please put her back on the line."

"No, I think she's had enough bad information from you for one day. I'll assure her that you're confident about the situation now that your man is on top of it, right?"

Bradley heard the phone hang up on the other end. He was not happy with the way things were progressing but really couldn't blame Rod for anything. The situation was out of his control but he was sure his associate would find a way to bring about a favorable outcome.

Sno regained her sense of urgency and had a look of despair. She regretted hiring Bradley for what had become an overwhelming task. Maybe she should have been content to let the police agencies find him but up until this point, they had no legal reason to apprehend him.

"Here's some water, Sno, drink it slowly."

Bo was gentle with her. "Bradley's man will get your son. I know that you want this thing resolved, but you've got to back off and relax. You can't solve anything that you have no control over."

"Thank you. I lay awake every night waiting for the call telling me he's safe."

"Do you have any sleeping pills?" Petri asked. "They might help relieve some of that stress and fatigue you're experiencing. You need rest."

"Bo, please take me home now. Petri will run things around here. I can't think straight and I'm a burden here to both my staff and my customers."

He escorted her out of the restaurant and drove her home. She didn't say one word to him on the thirty minute drive to her condo. He parked the car and walked her up to the doorman.

"Everything is going to work out just fine, believe me. Your long journey is not over yet, but a happy ending is right around the corner. You'll see for yourself soon enough."

She didn't respond. He hugged her tightly and handed her off to the doorman, returned to his car and then drove away.

My poor Sno, he pondered. What in the hell is going on? Her son is running around like a wounded animal in the wild woods of the north, not knowing that he is a free man. If he gets killed there is no way I want to be around Sno Moreau. She'll not survive the deplorable news!

Chapter 56

THE CAR FERRY to Washington Island was running late because of the choppy waters in the estuary between the Northport Pier and the Island. Tran had stopped at Mink's Bar in Gill's Rock for a couple of "shooters" before completing the final stretch home. He had rewrapped his wounded arm and hoped that it wasn't infected. His closed eye didn't hurt as much but was starting to leak a sticky substance that he periodically wiped off. He was drenched in sweat.

"Hey buddy, slow down. I think you've had enough to drink," cautioned the gray-bearded but baldish bartender wearing tight-fitting denim shorts. "I certainly don't want you to fall overboard when you hop that ferry. It's happened once or twice before and I don't want to be sued for pumping too much alcohol. Get it!"

Chien was depressed; he hardly heard the bartender speaking to him. He tried calling Spencer Littlewolf earlier in the afternoon but a voice recording told him that the number had been disconnected. It didn't matter; he was going over there anyway.

"I'll stay inside the passenger cabin for the entire trip over; promise you."

"That's what they all say, mister. Yet, some goofballs find a way to slip over the guard rail. Pretty hard to do when you stay in the protected cabin, hey? By the way, what's with the eye?"

Tran ignored the inquiry. He was getting sick and tired of people asking about his condition and telling him what to do. He became belligerent. He stood up straight and got up in the bald man's face.

"Look, Curley, Moe or whatever jerky name they call you around here; what I do is my own fucking business, okay?"

"But…but I…suit yourself; what the hell do I care!"

It was late afternoon and the shallow sun was quickly disappearing from the cloudy horizon. He no longer had the stolen car; he'd dumped it deep in the woods south of Gill's Rock. Unfortunately he had to leave the shotgun and the police radio behind but he kept the knife.

He hitched a ride over to Northport with a farmer driving a beat-up pickup truck with a load of baled hay. Ugly dark black clouds were playing tag with each other trying to shake some rain from their swollen bowels.

The strong winds arrived mid-afternoon and the rowdy group of tourists up from Chicago was worried that the next car ferry over to the Island might be delayed or canceled. It was an oddity to have so many tourists visiting Door County this time of the year.

"Hello there, young lady," he said to the pretty associate inside the Welcome Center at the pier. Her lapel badge read "Christy" in big black letters.

"Hi there to you, sir," she said with a big smile and pointed to the men's restroom. She had witnessed this scene many times. Water closets were few and far between on the north end of the peninsula.

He wanted to kill some time before boarding the car ferry over to Washington Island. He knew that the inclement weather very seldom altered the sturdy vessel's schedule. His kidneys were damned near floating to his throat and he needed to pee.

"How can I help you?" Christy offered when he came back from the john. "I just made some fresh coffee and you're welcome to be the first to try my new formula."

"Thanks a lot."

She was good-looking and perky. Chien liked what he saw. He hadn't been with a woman lately and immediately felt warm and fuzzy.

"You just missed all the excitement. The sheriff's boys were here a few minutes ago looking for a bad guy. Why they'd ever come up to Northport searching for him is way beyond me."

"Really? I hope they catch him."

"I hope you'll like the coffee. The powers to be had cut back on the standing Starbucks' order and went to a less expensive brand. In the late afternoon I like to lace the coffee with some chicory."

"Why thank you, I might just try some of your elixir," he forced a laugh through his pained body.

He was bored, impatient and didn't give a shit about the coffee; he needed a quick fix and slugged it down anyway.

"What's the matter with your arm; it's bleeding, and that ugly bulging eye? What heavyweight around here did you go ten rounds with?"

He glared down at his arm and saw blood sneaking out from behind the makeshift bandage he crafted from a pair of cotton shorts. He should've taken up that the old hag's offer at the cafe last night to repair the gouge. He was unable to move the arm; it was glued to his hip and it hurt like hell.

"I'll get some stitches in the arm when I get over to the other side. I caught the damn thing on some barbwire back at a friend's farm while we were repairing the fences around his cherry orchard."

"Don't wait too long. You've heard of gangrene, right?"

She was too inquisitive to suit him so he decided to take a short walk. It was stuffy inside and he needed to get some fresh air. He didn't like the fact that two men were sitting on one of the benches reading the newspaper. One of them had watched with interest his interchange with Christy.

& & & & &

Rod's endorphins were racing rampantly throughout his entire body, just like when he parachuted out of airplanes. His palms were sweaty gripping the steering wheel. He loved the drive through the beautiful countryside but he was on a mission. His jaws were tight, his eyes alert.

He was back in 'Nam again running point for his squad. They were chasing a band of Cong through the thick underbrush of the humid jungle. They were close, he could sense their nearness, smell them, feel them and all of a sudden...

Rod thought he spotted him as he swung around the curve leading up to the Welcome Center. He immediately pulled his car off to the side of the road and quickly yanked the binoculars to his eyes. It was him! He knew it was Chien Tran from the pictures he'd been given by his mother. Chien didn't seem to notice the parked car as he began to rumble further down a short pathway behind the Welcome Center into the wooded area.

How should I approach this guy? He's got Veronica's shotgun somewhere but I don't see him carrying it. Where's the knife? Maybe he even has a stolen pistol on his person. He looks like he's about to fall over. What the hell's wrong with his dangling arm? His eye looks like it's about to pop out of his head. I better take it slow and easy. I've hunted wounded animals before and they're dangerous and unpredictable.

Chien finally spotted the parked car on the side of the road. He was dizzy, clutching at his bad arm. He thought he was about to pass out when he saw the tall man open the car door and begin walking straight at him.

Something is definitely not right here, he reasoned. I don't like this picture! This guy's got to be a fed. Something tells me that I got to lose him somehow before he catches up to me. I might even have to kill him!

Tran started to run back into the woods as fast as he could but tripped on a partially rotted tree stump and stumbled into a clump of brush.

Rod was rapidly catching up to him when he saw the man fall. He automatically reached around for his pistol but it wasn't there. He remembered leaving it locked in the glove compartment of the Honda.

Son-of-a-bitch! You big dummy! So be it. I've been taught to kill with my bare hands if necessary...and I will surely do it!

"Chien Tran, Chien Tran," Rod shouted out. "I'm not going to hurt you, I promise. I have some good news to tell you. Please wait; stay where you are until I catch up with you!"

It happened again, that unforgiving moment he experienced all too often. He never forgot the excruciating pain that rammed his chest walls like a giant iron wedge breaking up a cement sidewalk. He'd experienced it several times in the past two weeks but not this severe. He was having a major heart attack and he knew it.

It has finally come down to this...I'm going to die right here in these miserable woods. There ain't a soul around here who gives a shit about me and is willing to help.

Through his half-opened good eye and wrenching from his pain-filled body he saw the law coming after him. He kept stabbing at his chest with his one good arm like he was trying to pull out some object embedded deep in his ribs. Rod feared he was going for a pistol and rushed him.

"No, no, you're not going to take me! I won't go back to that stinking prison, I'll die here first!" He grabbed a low hanging tree branch and lifted himself off the ground just as Rod met him at the edge of the pavement.

Rod didn't see the hunting knife in the hand of his good arm until it was too late. Chien thrust it at his chest. He saw the steel blade coming at him and at the last possible second spun away from the knife as it buried itself deep in his left arm high above the elbow.

"Agh...you bastard!" Rod shouted in pain. In a split second he laid three sharp karate chops across Chien's throat with his right hand sending him sprawling backward five yards and to the hard pavement.

"Fuck you lawman," Chien screamed as he grabbed for his damaged throat.

"Get up or I'll finish you off on the ground!"

While contemplating his next move Tran reached around behind him for a shiny object he noticed lying next to him. It was a long piece of galvanized pipe. He ignored the unbearable pain that now encompassed his entire body, stumbled back to his feet and started again toward Rod.

"Stop, stop right now or I'll kill you with my bare hands."

Chien hesitated for a split second.

The hunting knife was still stuck in Rod's arm and was dangling like a wet noodle. He didn't think it penetrated his humerus. He jerked it out of the thick muscular part of the arm below the shoulder and hurled it at as hard as he could at Tran's chest. It flew tumbling several times over and over through the air and the steel butt of the knife struck him in the chin. The blunt end smashed his lips and shattered several of his front teeth.

"Take that, Chien Tran, you no good, rotten son-of a-bitch," Rod shouted incoherently. He was in for the fight of his life!

Chien lost consciousness and fell at Rod's feet. He stepped back from the injured man and ripped off his own entire right shirt sleeve and then wrapped it around the arm wound, tightening it into a tourniquet. He then bent over and checked Tran's neck for a pulse. He found one but it was weak.

Holy Christ, please don't let this man die on me! I need him alive. I lost control...I was going to kill him on the spot...he deserves to die! I have an important mission to complete. This pursuit can't end here!

Chapter 57

SEVERAL of the bystanders waiting for the ferry had gotten out of their cars and were joking with each other. When they heard the commotion behind them, two men and an elderly lady ran slowly over toward the two combatants.

"Leave the poor guy alone, you big jerk, can't you see he's hurt," shouted one of the men.

"Someone, anybody administer CPR to him," cried the lady, her hands cupped under her chin.

Rod stepped back as the other man knelt down and started CPR on the unconscious Tran. He almost puked when he saw Tran's face. Greenish-white pus ran from below the severely infected eye and co-mingled with several exposed pieces of the fractured teeth in his half-opened mouth.

Another bystander who had remained by his parked car ran back to the Welcome Center to call 911. The EMS unit arrived in record time and tended to Tran. One medic took over the CPR function while the other one injected something into Tran's chest.

"Is he dead?" Rod was extremely worried.

"Not yet, but if we don't get him to the hospital right away, he will be. By the way, who are you, mister?"

Rod hesitated for a moment and then said, "I'm an undercover cop."

A sheriff's car arrived at the scene and quickly surveyed the situation. When the uniforms were assured that nobody was in danger, they began to question the witnesses and get their names. The folks awaiting the car ferry heard the loud whistle which announced its arrival at the pier. They hurriedly returned to their parked cars and watched the ferry empty out so they could drive aboard and forget the gross scene they'd just witnessed.

"I wonder what's going on there," commented the driver of the first vehicle coming off the ferry as he slowly crept along. The car approached the EMS medics and a tall weather-beaten man standing over a prone body.

"Looks to me like some poor tourist had a heart attack," said the young lady sitting next to him. "Those EMS types are working pretty hard on him."

"Tough shit," the driver responded with a wide grin on his big face. "Those rich Illinois turds think they own our little place in paradise." The car then negotiated the curved road away from the Welcome Center and disappeared.

Spencer Littlewolf was the driver of the second vehicle off-loaded from the ferry. He shot a quick glance over at the commotion taking place by a downed man and then accelerated past the scene in a big hurry. The Oneida Indian was concerned that he might be late for work, his fourth day of employment in the maintenance department at a nearby hospital.

"You better come along with us and have that arm looked at by a doctor," one of the medical technicians suggested to Rod. He decided to loosen the tourniquet and inspect the wound. "The bleeding seems to be under control but you'll need stitches to close that gap."

"I'm okay; just get him the hell out of here before he conks out for good. I'll follow you to the hospital."

It seemed like an eternity to the worried Rod before the caravan reached the hospital. Chien was quickly off-loaded onto a waiting gurney and wheeled into the emergency room.

He walked behind the medics into the ER but was told to wait in an adjacent treatment room for one of the other staff doctors to check him out. The uniformed highway patrolmen from the earlier site of the struggle arrived. They shuffled over to the hospital entrance and went in.

Rod watched them through the partially opened door talking to one of the nurses. All three of them were in deep whispered conversation. Rod had an idea what was going on. He was sure they were informing her that the injured person was being sought by every law enforcement agency in Door County. His arm was throbbing in pain so he loosened the tourniquet. He heard a frantic announcement over the hospital intercom.

"Maintenance, bring another manual external defibrillator to the ER, stat; I repeat…stat!"

Rod decided to call Bradley while he was waiting for a doctor to come in and treat him.

"Holy Jesus, is he going to live?" Bradley yelled into the cell phone. He was out of breath having run from the back of the office suites to get to his cell phone which he'd left on his desk.

"I don't know yet, they're working frantically on him."

"I sent you up there to bring him home to his mother, not to skewer the bastard, Richards."

"Hold on, boss, let me explain…"

"He damn well better live or our client will probably sue our collective asses off."

"For what?"

"Who knows…she has Paul Keller in tow. Remember him?"

"Sure. He's your best friend so…no problem."

He was getting perturbed with Bradley.

"Do you want to hear about my own combat wounds?"

"You got hurt too?" Bradley questioned in a sarcastic tone of voice. "You, the decorated combat veteran going up against a banker kinda guy; get real, Richards. Come off it."

He laughed it off. Bradley could be a complete asshole at times.

"He nicked me pretty damn good with a rusty old hunting knife, boss, but I'll probably live. I might have to collect huge amounts of dough from your employee disability insurance when I get back to Chicago. Gotta go, a doctor is on his way to treat me. I'll call you back when I get a status report on Chien. Ta...ta, good buddy."

He heard a commotion outside the treatment room door and looked out in the hallway. A doctor dressed in green scrubs heading his way almost got knocked over by a burly Indian racing up the hallway wheeling a piece of medical equipment to the ER.

"What the hell was that all about?" he asked a doctor coming into the treatment room.

"I'm not sure; the team in the ER is working frantically on that guy they just brought in. Apparently there was an equipment failure but the situation should be rectified pretty soon. Let's have a look at you."

Spencer Littlewolf walked slowly back down the hallway, a big smile gracing his face.

What a stroke of luck! I'm living the good life. That Asian ex-con stretched out in there more than likely won't be coming after me for his money. He was foolish to trust me, a hardened criminal for Christ's sake! If by some miracle he ever survives and makes it over to my piece of paradise I'll bury him alive.

The doctor examined Rod's wound and told him that he was a lucky man. The blade could have penetrated his chest, punctured his heart, lungs or even severed the major artery in his upper arm.

"I'll clean it up, put a few stitches in, give you a tetanus shot, an antibiotic and then send you on your way."

"I wonder how that beat-up guy is doing in the other room, doc."

"When I'm done patching you up go talk to the head nurse out there, she'll brief you. Meanwhile, those two law enforcement officers are eager to interview you."

"Thanks a lot doctor."

When he was finished treating Rod the doctor started to leave the room but hesitated and then turned back to his patient.

"That should take care of you. In parting, I have some words of advice for you. You're way too old to be playing cops and robbers! Now go home and get some rest, okay?"

The two lawmen were anxiously awaiting him when he walked out of the treatment room. The nurse had already left the area.

"Mister, you're in a world of hurt…deep, deep trouble!"

"What do mean by that?" Rod ventured to ask. He had an idea what was coming next. He looked over his shoulder and saw an orderly wheeling a body from the ER back to the hospital morgue.

"The bastard we've been hectically looking for just died. We're taking you in and booking you for murder!"

Epilogue

ROD RICHARDS spent three days in the county jail before he was released on his own recognizance. Bradley had flown Paul Keller up to Door County and he successfully negotiated Rod's release with the authorities. Witnesses to the fight at the Welcome Center were located and corroborated his that he acted in self-defense.

An autopsy confirmed that the cause of death was a massive heart attack related to a congenital heart defect. Keller got a forensic cardiologist to provide a sworn statement attesting to the fact that the condition had been surgically correctible but apparently totally ignored by the decedent.

When Sno Moreau was briefed on the unfortunate death of her long lost son she was so distraught that she had to be sedated and subsequently hospitalized. Bo Tan and Petri ultimately nursed her back to reality, but that wasn't enough. She sold her business to them and went back to Thailand with Chien Tran's urn. She vowed to return to Ho Chi Minh City and spread his ashes in the Saigon River. She was never heard from again.

The court ruled that Shamus Fenerty was murdered by Whitey, his non-trusty albino bodyguard. Lois Fenerty was found to be a willing accomplice by methodically lacing his meals with arsenic. Both of them are pending sentencing after the "trial of the decade" in downtown Chicago. Angie Ward was cleared of any wrongdoing after being lectured severely by the judge presiding over the trial for her minimal role in his demise.

John Richards finally found his true soul mate. He and Veronica Brown got married. His son Jamie served as the best man in a huge wedding staged on the fifty yard line in Lambeau Field. The entire Green Bay Packer roster served as honorary groomsmen.

Torrie Strait decided that Jamie Richards was too wild and not responsible enough for her to continue a more serious relationship. When she visited him at Ft. Hood, Texas over Christmas she learned more than she needed to know about the significant role he played in "black operations" conducted in far-away Somalia. He was way too scary for her.

Rambo had to be put to sleep by the vet. He had developed a severe and advanced case of canine distemper and the virus infected his entire bodily system. Torrie buried him in a pet cemetery and left Chicago for parts unknown.

Bradley Simmons and Rod Richards severed their three year relationship in a heated exchange over the Chien Tran foray. Bradley tried to connect with Sno Moreau before she left the country but she wouldn't see or talk to him. The local news media crucified his agency for the handling of the case. He sold the firm to Jorge and Saul; his other trusted associates and became a part-time lecturer in Criminal Justice at a local community college.

Rod Richards reconnected with the rich and famous Angie Ward. They decided to take another Caribbean cruise and get married in the Cayman Islands. He went back to college to earn enough education credits to become an elementary school teacher. Angie sold her condo and all of the stock she had in Fenerty's old trucking company and donated it to charity.

He and Angie moved back to the sleepy Chicago suburb of Libertyville. The nearby school district that employed Angie welcomed her back with opened arms. They both taught school there until their mandatory retirement ages.

www.ingramcontent.com/pod-product-compliance
Lightning Source LLC
Chambersburg PA
CBHW071527260626

47170CB00002B/545